Praise for th[...]

'A brilliant settin[...]
Napoleon's Wars.'
Manchester Evening News

'There is both power and fascination in the army detail,
the brutality, the harsh organisation and the barracks
conditions. It is as compulsive as the sailing data in the
Hornblower books. I can hardly wait for his next book.'
Daily Mirror

'Vitality by the bucketload.'
Daily Mail

SARA FRASER
writing as R. CLEWS

The King's Bounty

Futura

A **Futura** Book

ISBN 0 7088 4327 1

Printed and bound in Great Britain by
Mackays of Chatham PLC, Chatham, Kent

Futura Publications
A Division of
Little, Brown and Company (UK)
Brettenham House
Lancaster Place
London WC2E 7EW

THE KING'S BOUNTY

CHAPTER ONE

Shropshire, November 1812

The early morning sky was patterned only with wisps of grey cloud and the pale sun had not yet tempered the cold winds that blew across the wild bleak countryside. High above the moorland, a solitary kestrel hovered, its wings beating rapidly as its keen tawny eyes searched the thick carpet of dark mauve-green heather below. Then, using the wind's power, it soared to find fresh ground, hoping to sight quarry beneath the clumps of bright green gorse, whose yellow petals glowed like honey in the sombre landscape.

A brown ribbon of earth wound over the low hills and across the moorland. Its surface of hard-packed soil and rock was deeply rutted and strewn with potholes, but for travellers across this desolate waste, it served as a roadway. Even now, with the dawn barely broken, there was movement of man and beast upon it.

A small trap drawn by a plump well-groomed pony came lurching from the south. The pony's reins were handled by an elderly man clad richly and warmly in a high fur-collared greatcoat and stout topboots and breeches with a low-crowned hat on his grey head. On the seat beside him the sole passenger, a small tassel-capped boy clung tightly to the brightly burnished brass guardrail and peered eagerly about him.

He sighted the hovering kestrel and shouted aloud in his excitement.

'See, Grandpapa! See above us! There's an eagle!'

The elderly man chuckled fondly. 'Bless you, boy! That isn't an eagle, it's a hawk.' Then, seeing the shadow of disappointment darken the young face, added quickly ... 'But dammee for an old fool with weak eyes! You're quite right. I see it clearly now ... It is most certainly an eagle.'

The boy beamed in happiness and, as the trap passed beneath and away from the flurrying wings of the bird, he twisted his head, reluctant to lose sight of the beautiful creature.

Abruptly, from a hidden dip in the road, a horseman appeared cantering towards them.

'Look boy, there's a fine soldier for you to see,' the old man said.

The solitary horseman was muffled in a long black riding cloak which streamed out along the glossy black flanks of his mount, imparting to him an aura of dark menace which not even the gaiety of the long red and white plume waving above his shako could dispel.

The elderly gentleman brought the pony to a halt and the small boy asked anxiously, 'Why do we stop, Grandpapa? Is that man going to hurt us?'

His grandfather smiled reassuringly. 'Of course not, boy.'

His grandson became silent. The soldier reined in beside them and the elderly gentleman raised his hat.

'Good morning to you, sir,' he greeted politely. 'Can I be of assistance?'

The tall soldier's pale grey eyes set in a lean cruel face were cold, and his voice was clipped and arrogant.

'Captain William Seymour, Ninth Light Dragoons ... Your servant, sir.' He nodded curtly in salute, then went on. 'Have you by any chance passed a convict convoy on the road?'

'A what, sir?' the old man questioned.

The dragoon's thin lips tightened. 'A convict convoy, sir.' Each word was enunciated so slowly and carefully as to be insulting.

The old man flushed in offence. He shook his head. 'No, I've not,' he snapped.

'Goddam the scum! They should have been on the march long since, the pox-ridden bastards!' the soldier cursed viciously.

The elderly gentleman flicked his reins. 'Giddup, old lazybones! I bid you good day, sir.'

The trap lurched forward, and the small boy, who had been still and apprehensive during the brief exchange, turned round in his seat to gaze at the tall dark figure, who sat on the motionless black horse, ignoring the farewell.

The kestrel was still hovering above the track, but low now, as if it had sighted prey. Even as the small boy gazed, the soldier's hand went to the saddle holster on the horse's neck, and then swung aloft grasping the butt of a long-barrelled pistol.

'Look Grandpapa, what's that man going to do?' the child

8

demanded anxiously.

The old man glanced back and the aimed pistol jerked, the sharp crack of its report echoing across the moor. The hovering bird was flung savagely upwards then, wings fluttering weakly, it plummeted to the ground and sprawled dying across the heather.

'He's killed my eagle!' the child's voice shrilled in horror. 'That man has killed my eagle!'

He flung himself against his grandfather, tugging at the man's lapels with frantic fingers. 'Why, Grandpapa? Why did he do that? Why did he kill it?' he demanded, the sobs already choking in his throat.

The old man held the boy, stroking his cheeks and throat, to comfort him, and his face was grim as he watched the dark figure canter away. He shook his head.

'I don't know why, boy ... Some men seem born only to destroy life ...' he said sadly.

Many miles to the south, a long column of men and animals was moving slowly across the moors. A hundred ragged, barefoot men were chained together in five separate files, each numbering a score. The files were distanced from each other by gaps of up to forty yards and in each gap rode two or three blue-tunicked dragoons, their shakoed heads bent against the biting edge of the wind, the harnesses jingling on their glossy-coated horses. Other men in civilian dress walked on foot at the side of the files. They carried long thick canes in their hands and their voices were hoarse from constant bawling of threats and curses.

In addition to the chain threaded through the iron bands clamped to their right ankles, the shaven-headed convicts also wore long-fettered wrist manacles. When the men moved, the rust-streaked metal rubbed pitilessly against their skin until it broke through to the raw flesh, causing it to tear and bleed. The fetter sores of the men who had travelled the most miles had ulcerated until they were pus-filled, poisonous yellow-green craters, and those afflicted bit their lips and moaned many times during the purgatory of the long marches.

The heavy iron ankle chains dragged over the surface of the rough track, snagging sometimes upon a jutting point of rock, causing the files of shuffling men to stumble as their leg-irons were abruptly halted by the trapped links. In the last file, a convict trod with his bare foot on a jagged stone. He cried out in shock and pain and knelt to examine his injury, forcing his companions to stop in confusion.

'Move along! ... Gerron you barstards! Move! Move!' The turnkey, Abe Dalton, ran to the kneeling man and, lifting his bamboo pole, brought it slashing down across the man's shaven head. The stubbled pallid skin burst and a thin line of blood welled across the scabbed scalp.

'I'll swing for yer! Yer pox-rotten pig!' the convict screamed, and hurled himself at his tormentor.

The long chain threaded through his ankle-iron tightened and the band of metal jerked to a halt, bringing the leaping body thumping to the ground. Dalton's thick lips, which had slackened in fright at the man's assault, firmed up, then curled back in a grin compounded equally of shock and relief.

'Master Dalton? Goddam you, Master Dalton! What's the delay?'

Josiah Lees, officer of the Government Transport Board, and civilian head of the convoy, reined in his horse by the fallen man.

'A prisoner tried to attack me, your honour.' Dalton tugged at his lank forelock.

'Blast your soul, Dalton! Cannot you deal wi' that sort of nonsense yet? Are you bloody gormless still?' Lee's well-fleshed jaw quivered in his rage. 'The whole bloody convoy's being held up by your section ... Take that soddin' animal's name. When we halt tonight, you shall have the privilege of flogging the bugger. Now get that sod up and moving!' he roared. 'D'ye hear me man, move!'

Terrified at his superior's anger, Abe Dalton kicked with his iron-shod boots at the man sprawled helplessly before him.

'Gerrup, you scum! Gerrup!'

The men on each side of the fallen convict hauled him to his feet and, supporting him as best as they were able, shuffled on. Satisfied, Lees spurred his mount to gallop back to the head of the column. A tall convict was leading the last file and, using the thud of the officer's hooves as a cover, he whispered to the man behind him.

'Tell Johnno not to fret, he'll not be flogged this night. Wait for my signal then do what we planned.'

A tap on his lean rump showed him that his message was understood.

Hour after hour, the convict convoy struggled across the

moor. The sun grew stronger and the men began to sweat from the effort of dragging their heavy chains. The heat and moistness of their unwashed bodies released in turn a thick stench from the caked filth on their skins and the escorts moved farther away to escape the vile odours of the convicts. Josiah Lees rode at the head of the line, silently cursing the absent military commander of the convoy, Captain William Seymour.

'It ain't fair, God rot me! Why should I have to take sole charge o' the bloody convoy. That poxy whoreson! Spending his time swillin' drink and rogerin' the wenches in Shrewsbury instead of bein wheer he's supposed to be ... 'ere wi' me! It's his place to command the bloody convoy, not me ... 'E's the army orficer.'

His bitter musings were interrupted by one of the civilian guards touching his thigh.

'Well? What ails you, man?' Lees snarled.

The guard knuckled his forehead. 'The cap'ns up ahead, Marster Lees.' He pointed to a horse and rider topping a distant rise of the track.

Lees squinted, straining his eyes but could only discern a shapeless moving blob.

'Damn your eyes iffen you'm mistaken, Turner. I'll cut your bollocks off,' he threatened.

The man scowled up at his superior's lowering face. 'It's that mad bugger all right, Marster Lees.' His voice was surly and aggrieved. 'T'se got the sharpest sight in all Wiltshire, I 'as.'

'We'll see, Turner ... We'll see,' Lees growled, and touching spurs to his horse, he went forward to meet the oncoming rider.

They met a good mile ahead of the convoy. Lees forced himself to smile.

'Good morning, Captin. I hope you had a pleasant night of it in Shrewsbury.' His voice strained to sound jocular as he pointed back at the dust-kicking files. 'My bloody oath, Captin! You did yourself a good turn all right. Makin' sure you warn't riding all morn in the middle o' that bunch o' gallows' meat. They stinks worse than a bloody midden.'

William Seymour's expression was contemptuous, and his nostrils widened visibly as he caught a whiff of his companion's own stale body. He nodded curtly, causing the plume of his shako to sway to and fro.

'As military commander of this convoy, neither my actions

nor my motives are answerable to you, Lees,' he snapped. 'I'll thank you to tend to your own affairs in future ... And try to remember that you are my inferior, both in rank of government and in your station in life.'

Lees' face hardened. 'Be damned to you for a stuck up barstard, William Seymour,' he thought, and turned away.

The road ahead snaked through a series of sharp bends, and on each side thickets of brush and woodland pressed upon its verges. The column shuffled on, and each section in turn disappeared from the other's view as it entered the bends. In the rear section, the tall convict leading the file watched narrowly until the blue backs of the dragoons directly in front of him went from his sight round a curve in the road. He turned his head and glanced first to his right rear, then to his left. The turnkey, Abe Dalton, was eight paces distant at his left and behind the section two dragoons slouched in their saddles, lost in their own thoughts. The tall convict slapped his right thigh sharply, then halted, clasped his throat with both hands and, giving vent to a strangled cry, dropped heavily to the ground. The section came to a stumbling halt and the second and third convicts on the chain started to yell out.

'Hey turnkey, this bleeder's gawn down wiv the fever!'

'Turnkey, come quick. This cove's dropped dead 'ere.'

Dalton swore loudly. 'God blast his bloody eyes! He's got no right ...' and ran to the twitching body.

The convict lay curled on his side. The turnkey grasped the wiry shoulder and tugged to turn the man over on to his back. The man's bright blue eyes opened and his lips twisted in a savage grin. His hands shot upwards, one to grasp Dalton's shaggy hair, the other to hold a wicked-bladed knife to the exposed jugular vein.

'Now, cully!' the convict hissed. 'Shout and tell them bleedin' sodgers to stay wheer they be ... Tell um everything's all right.'

Dalton gulped hard, his protuberant Adam's apple jumping beneath the stubbled skin of his dirty throat. The knife blade pricked sharply and drew a tiny spout of blood. He shouted, 'Stop theer you two. Everythin's all right.'

The dragoons at the rear of the section were supremely uninterested in the delay. They reined in their horses and grumbled to each other. The tall convict, shielded from the soldiers by his fellows crowding forward, jerked with his head at the great rusty padlock which clamped the end of the long chain to his ankle iron.

'Get that unlocked, cully! Quick! Or you'm dead meat,' he hissed.

Dalton's hands trembled violently as he snatched the ring of keys from his belt and inserted one into the lock. Stealthily yet rapidly, the convicts began in turn to thread the chain through the holding rings on their irons. Nine were free before the dragoons became suspicious. The youngest one kneed his mount towards the knot of men.

'What's holding us up so long?' he queried, then noticed the end of long-chain lying free on the ground.

'You bastards!' he shouted, and turned to snatch his carbine from its holster at the rear of his saddle. Even as his hands felt the smoothness of the polished wooden butt, the tall convict's knife ripped into his stomach. The soldier screamed and fell forward off his horse. A flung rock caught the remaining dragoon on his temple, knocking him stunned from the saddle. The rest of the convicts slipped free from the chain and then, at a wave of the hand from the tall man, scattered in all directions.

For some seconds, the turnkey lay shivering in terror, his hands scrabbling at the dirt of the track. Then, realizing that he was unscathed and no convicts were near, he clambered to his feet and ran shrieking fearfully to alert the rest of the column.

It was late afternoon and Captain William Seymour's hard thin lips were tight as he scanned the hillsides that stretched above him. From its round case hanging upon the saddlehorn, he took a small telescope and wrenched it to its fullest extent. His horse blew noisily through mucoused nostrils and moved restlessly beneath him, pawing at the soft marshy ground with its polished hooves.

'Be still, blast you!' Seymour hissed and, putting the glass to his eye, he studied the thick windswept vegetation. He was alone, his squad of troopers had one by one been sent back to the regiment's camp at Ludlow with the convicts that they had recaptured. Now, of the twenty men who had escaped earlier that day, only two or three remained at liberty, and Seymour was certain that at least one of them was hiding on the hillside before him.

He replaced the glass and urged his mount forward, intending to circle the face of the hill and thus force his quarry to alter position. As he circled, Seymour checked the long-barrelled horse pistols, taking them from the holsters at each side of the horse's shoulders and seeing that the flints were well fixed and the pans contained powder. Next he loosened his curved sabre in its scabbard.

Seymour was in his late twenties and had been a soldier from his fifteenth birthday, except for one period when he had been forced to leave the army for what his superiors considered to be excessive brutality to soldiers under his command. He himself had seen it only as the maintenance of good discipline. The long-drawn-out wars with the French had been a blessing to Seymour. The British army had become desperately short of officers, so many of them being killed, mutilated, or dying of disease all over the world. The officials at the Horse Guards had been reduced to giving commissions to totally unsuitable applicants to fill the gaping ranks. His sadistic tendencies apart, Seymour was a magnificent combat officer, without fear, and already a veteran of four campaigns. When he re-applied to purchase a captaincy in the cavalry, the overwhelming need for soldiers of his calibre ensured that his previous misconduct was overlooked. It was not of his choosing that he was now acting as an escort to convict convoys, but his regiment had been decimated in Spain and had been brought back to England to recruit and gather strength afresh. Seymour had been forced to return with it, and lived only for the day when he could once more go to war.

He was half-way up the hill when thirty yards to his left a bird burst out of the heather. Seymour smiled his satisfaction.

'You're there, are you?' he muttered, and wheeled his horse. Even as he did so, a man leapt up from cover and began to run down the hillside, bounding over the heather and battering straight through the thick clumps of gorse bushes. Almost immediately a second man jumped to his feet in the same spot and, shaking his fist, hurled imprecations at his companion's retreating back. Seymour heard the words as his mount neared the man.

'You yellow-gutted barstard, Smith! You poxy coward!' Nearly sobbing with rage the shouting man turned to face the dragoon. 'You'd a never sin us if that bugger 'adn't lorst his nerve,' he bawled. 'You'd a never sin us.'

Raging wildly, he came at Seymour whirling his fetter

14

chains about his head. The captain didn't even bother to check his mount's easy canter. He drew one pistol from its holster, cocked it and fired. A small black hole appeared in the top of the convict's head and he toppled face downwards into the heather, his chains wrapping their links around his neck and shoulders as he fell.

At the sharp crack of the pistol shot, the running man dropped to his knees, holding his hands high above him. 'Doon't shoot, yer honour! Please doon't shoot!' The man's face was a torment of terror and the sweat of fear lathered his head and neck. Seymour halted in front of the fugitive, he raised the empty pistol, cocked it again and aimed. The convict's eyes widened in horror, his mouth gaped in a silent scream and across the front of his ragged breeches a dark flush of urine spread itself. Seymour clicked the trigger, then threw back his head and roared with laughter. Moaning incoherently, the convict rocked his body backwards and forwards while tears streamed from his bloodshot eyes.

Seymour dismounted and, grabbing the man by the scruff of his thin neck, he hauled him bodily to his feet.

'Stop snivelling like a snot-nosed brat, you scum.' He shook the convict, who was a small man, fiercely. 'I'm not going to kill you ... Not yet anyway ... There's a few questions I want the answers to ...' His voice became almost jocular. 'Who knows? If you give the right answers you might even live long enough to be hung from a gallows tree ... Now! What's your name?' The small man drew a great hiccuping breath. 'It's Smith, yer honour ... Jackie Smith,' he answered.

Seymour released him and stepped back so that he might see his man more clearly. Before he could put another question, the convict began to babble out a torrent of pleas. The captain cuffed him across the side of his head.

'Slow down your words, you dirty little animal, I cannot understand you when you splutter so.'

Smith's mind raced, he caught his breath and his furtive eyes intent upon the other's face, said, 'I can tell you who it was led the escape, yer honour, and who stuck the trooper and what's more, yer honour, I can tell yer how to get yer 'ands on a pile o' rhino ... God strike me if I lie, sir ... I knows about Turpin Wright's rhino, I swears it!'

'Who is Turpin Wright?' Seymour demanded.

'The cove that led the escape, yer honour; and give the

sodger the blade in 'is guts.' Smith had caught the reaction in Seymour's eyes at the mention of money. Quickly he pressed on. 'Turpin Wright's got a load o' rhino and jewels and suchlike hid away, sir ... On me mother's grave! I could 'elp yer to get hold on it.'

A small muscle at the side of Seymour's left eye began to twitch. 'You are trying to bribe me!' he spat the words. 'I am an officer of the King's army, and you, you gutter filth, dare to try and bribe me.'

He stepped forward and kicked Smith viciously in the stomach, using the flat of his boot. The convict's breath was smashed from his body. He doubled over and rolled in whooping agony upon the soggy ground, crushing the heather flat beneath him.

'I should kill you for that insult!' Seymour hissed.

Jackie Smith pressed his face into the fragrance of the broken heather tufts and despite his pain felt utter relief.

'You'll not kill me now, you barstard!' he exulted silently. 'You'm too interested in that bloody rhino o' Turpin Wright's. I saw it in yer bleedin' eyes ...'

CHAPTER TWO

It was almost dusk when Jethro Stanton walked up to the
door of the lonely alehouse, and the air was becoming cold as
the pale November sun sank rapidly from view. He came to a
halt, shuffling his feet in the white dust of the road and lifted
his slung blanket-roll from one aching shoulder to the other.
His parched tongue flicked across his dry cracked lips and
after a moment's hesitation, he went through the low open
doorway of the inn.

A woman was lighting an oil lamp as he entered, but she
ignored him, busying herself in trimming the lamp wick until
she was satisfied with the result, before she looked directly at
the young man. He came farther into the room so that the soft
light shone fully upon him. He was tall and strongly built,
wearing the rough, brown moleskin suiting and heavy boots
of a labouring man. Taking off his wide-brimmed felt hat he
smiled at the woman, his white teeth gleaming in his weather-
darkened face.

'Good evening, mistress, I'm wanting ale and a bite to eat,
if that is possible.' His voice was soft and cultured, contrast-
ing oddly with his clothing.

The landlady's hard, middle-aged exterior hid an impres-
sionable heart. She thought the young man was very handsome
and his smile charmed her.

'Set ye down,' she said. 'I've good fresh-brewed ale and
some bread and cheese ... unless you wouldn't mind waiting
for a while. I've got a rabbit aroastin' for my man's supper ...
There'll be enough for both on you, I reckon, it's a fine big
buck.'

Jethro nodded gratefully. 'That'll stick to me ribs, mistress,'
he told her. 'Is there a pump that I may wash under? I've
been walking all day and I'd like to clean myself.'

'Goo out and round to the back theer, young man,' the
woman instructed and bustled away into the rear regions of

17

the inn. From a vantage point behind a tiny unglazed window, she watched the muscles of Jethro's lithe hard body writhe and bunch like coiled snakes beneath his smooth tanned skin, as he clanked the pumphandle up and down and laved the dust of travel from his head and body, gasping under the gouts of cold clear water. After drying himself on a strip of rough towelling he had taken from his blanket-roll, Jethro dressed once more and made his way back to the taproom. Smoothing his thick black hair with his fingers, he seated himself on one of the crude benches that flanked the long scrubbed wooden table.

The landlady placed a pewter tankard full of foaming ale in front of him. Lifting it, he tilted back his head and drank deeply until it was all gone. Sighing with satisfaction, he put the empty tankard on the table.

'You spoke truly, mistress ... It is indeed good ale that you brew.'

The woman smiled her gratification at the compliment and going to a row of barrels standing on trestles at the rear of the room, she refilled the tankard. She stood across the table from Jethro and eyed him speculatively as he sipped from the fresh pot.

'You'm not from these parts, young man?'

Jethro shook his head. 'No, mistress, I'm what you would call a travelling man. Is there work to be found in this district?'

The woman shook her head. 'Not now, I shouldn't think. Though mind you there was work aplenty when the harvest was got in, there's so many o' the young lads away at the wars from these parts ... Ahh! and a lot of older 'uns too, come to that.' She shook her head sadly. 'The silly buggers sees a redcoat and lets the recruiters fill their bellies full o' drink and their empty yeds full o' tales o' glory; and then nuthin' matters to 'um, but to take the shillin' and leave the plough ... Orf they goes and follows the drum. Ahh!' She shook her head once more. 'Theer's a good many poor mothers aggrievin' for their sons in these parts, and young girls aweepin' for their 'usbands and sweethearts ...'

Jethro nodded but remained silent. The silence lengthened and the woman, sensing that he wished to be alone, left him at the table.

The darkness deepened across the heavily wooded heath and later the moon rose. Under its cool light, a man came

18

stumbling over the tussocks of grass and brush, his hands straining against the shackles that fettered his wrists in an effort to stop the chain clinking as he ran. The runner sighted the white-washed walls of the inn and halted, cocking his head to listen for sounds of his pursuers. But all he could hear was his own rasping breath and the soft wind rustling the grasses. He grinned to himself and went cautiously towards the building.

'Pssst! Master!'

Jethro was startled out of his reverie by the sharp sound.

'Pssst! Master!'

He looked at the door, but could see no one. The sound came yet again.

'Pssst! Master!'

Jethro got to his feet and went outside the door. The moon was well risen by now and Jethro could see clearly that the ground around the inn was empty. There was a hoarse whisper.

'Over here, master!'

Jethro looked to his left, and saw in the shadow cast by the overhanging eaves a darker shadow which moved towards him and became a man.

'What do you want with me?' Jethro demanded.

'Shhh! Not so loud, master. For the love of God! Not so loud,' the man begged, lifting his hands in supplication. As he did so, there came a jingle of metal and Jethro stepped back, feeling for the knife he carried in his coat pocket. The man quickly lowered his hands.

'Take no alarm, master,' he begged. 'I mean you no harm, I swear it! I'm looking for your help that's all.'

Jethro let the knife fall back into his pocket and said quietly, 'Step into the light, so that I can see who I'm talking with. I don't fancy conversing with shadows.'

The man did as he was bidden. He was middle-aged and shaven-headed. As tall as Jethro, but gaunt and ragged, his wrists were fettered by chain-joined manacles. His bare feet and calves had been torn in his flight across the heath and trickles of blood, black in the moonlight, oozed down into the dust. From inside the inn came the landlady's voice.

'Are you theer outside, young man? Is anything the matter?'

Jethro opened his mouth to answer, but before he could do so the man ducked back into the shadows, slumped on to

19

his knees in the dirt and shook his head pleadingly, holding his fingers to his lips. Jethro stared hard at him, then made his decision.

'I'm just enjoying the night air, mistress, I'll be in in a moment.'

He went to the other and lifted him to his feet.

'Now listen carefully,' he whispered. 'Go and hide in the scrub over there, later I'll see what's to be done to help you.'

Surprisingly the man grinned at him. 'Can I trust you?' he questioned.

After a moment Jethro grinned back. 'Do you have any choice? Now go! Quickly!'

He watched the stranger scuffle away, then re-entered the inn. On the table was an earthenware bowl filled with smoking meat and also a fresh loaf of bread. The landlady smiled at him.

''Ere young man, theer's your vittles, all nice and hot. If theer's anythin' more you' needin', just call.'

Jethro nodded. 'My thanks to you, mistress.' He waited until the sounds of voices and eating from the back rooms of the inn told him that the woman and her husband were busy at their supper, then taking his kerchief from his neck he wrapped half of the bread and meat in it. He stole out of the door and went to where the fettered man was hidden.

'Here's some food.' He pushed the small bundle into the man's hands and, not waiting for a reply, ran back to the inn. The man tore open the kerchief and grabbed the food, using both hands to cram bread and meat into his mouth. A small spring near by served to quench his thirst. With his ravenous hunger appeased, he lay back on the grass and belched contentedly.

'Well, young Jethro Stanton,' he murmured, 'I doon't know what you'm dooin' here, but thanks be to God, I run into you. You'm a true son o' Peter Stanton's, that's for sure; and youse made a friend for life in Turpin Wright; and that's as sure as Turpin Wright is the name I was born wi'.'

He closed his eyes and rested as easily and peacefully as if he were a king on his royal bed.

No sooner had Jethro finished his meal than from outside the alehouse came the thudding hooves of hard-ridden horses and the jingling of metal. Commands were shouted and through the still open doorway Jethro saw a troop of cavalry galloping past. Even as they passed he saw two or three men rein in their horses directly opposite the door and dismount in a flurry of dust.

One of the horsemen stamped and jangled into the ale-house. He was short and wiry, smartly uniformed in the crimson and dark blue tunic, white crossbelt and white chevrons of a corporal of Light Dragoons. He rested his left hand on his low-slung sabre and his eyes were hard beneath the stiff peak of his cockaded shako.

Disturbed by the commotion, the landlady and her husband came out from their quarters.

'Yes, soldier? What can we do for you?' The landlady's tone was hostile.

The dragoon didn't answer. Instead he called over his shoulder, 'Timpkins, is Macarthy at the rear?'

The other, a big trooper, came to the door carrying a cocked carbine in his hands. 'Aye,' he grunted in reply.

The corporal nodded. 'I'll thank you to stand aside,' he said to the landlady, and drew his sabre. Steel glinted in the lamplight and the landlady's husband whimpered in fear and pressed back against the wall. The woman was unafraid, her face flushed and she retorted, 'You're not chasing rebels in Ireland now, soldier, nor in the bloody Peninsula neither. I'm a freeborn subject of His Majesty, God bless him! And I'll not be ordered around by gutter-sweepings in my own home.'

The dragoon extended his sword arm until the point of the sabre was only a fraction of an inch away from the plump throat of the woman.

'Now you listen to me, you fat cow!' he warned. 'This morning a convoy o' prisoners was going along on their way to Shrewsbury, and most of 'um were gallows-bait ... Well, they turned on their escort and a score o' the scum got away. One of our lads is lying at death's door this minute, because one o' the bastards stuck him wi' a blade. Now we've recaptured all on 'um but one, and he's the bloody ringleader, and a worser son of an whore never breathed ... Our orders are to search every inch o' these parts until we get him ... So out o' my way! Or you'll find yourself on the road to the gallows for helping the bastard.'

The landlady stood her ground. 'I don't blame the poor buggers for escaping!' she blurted angrily. 'I reckon that most of 'um were in gaol for next to nothing anyway.'

The corporal sighed heavily and lowered his sword.

'That may well be, woman,' he said wearily, 'but it's not my place to question my orders. I've no wish to go to the halberds to meet the Drummer's Daughter, and have the skin stripped from my back wi' her kisses.'

He pushed her to one side and went into the rear of the house. They heard his boots clumping across the floor over their heads and then down the stairs. Joined now by a man who had been at the back of the building, the corporal came into the taproom once more.

'Timpkins!' he shouted. 'Come in here.' He turned to the landlady. 'Draw three pots of ale. And give us a quartern o' rum.'

Her temper rose again. 'Have you money?' she snapped. 'There's no free drink for the likes o' you.'

The dragoon took coins from his belt pouch and threw them contemptuously on the floor, where they bounced and rolled across the dark stone slabs.

'I don't doubt but there's enough there to pay for the piss you serve in this dunghouse,' he sneered.

The woman made no movement, but her husband, a stoop-shouldered wreck of a man, scrabbled for the money and ran to fetch the drink. The dragoons took off their shakos, and settling their carbines and sabres on the benches, sat down at Jethro's table. When he had taken the edge from his thirst, the corporal turned his attention to Jethro.

'I don't suppose you've seen anythin' of our runaway, have you?'

Jethro shook his head. 'No, I've not. What was he wanted for?'

The soldiers looked at each other and laughed.

'What was he wanted for? What wasn't he being hung for, more likely,' Macarthy, an Irishman, answered. 'He calls himself by a dozen names and he's the one and only first-born son o' Satan. He comes straight from the pit of hell, does that one. Murder, highway robbery, sham coinin', burglary, forgery, false enlistment, desertion ... Be God! T'would fill the Newgate Calendar for a year just to list what he's done. They say he was even a pirate once, not to mention a mutineer...'

The corporal broke into the recital. 'Paddy's exaggeratin', but he's right when he says that the bugger should ha' been hung years ago. They say he was one o' the Nore mutineers, a big mate o' Richard Parker's. But he managed to get away before they could get a rope round his neck. The bastard gar-

22

rotted a marine sentry wi' his own ramrod and swam about five miles through a bloody gale that even men o' war could hardly ride out. They thought for years that he'd bin drowned, but the bugger showed up again in a militia regiment. I'd like to get my hands on him. He'll not live to see the hangman if I do, I can promise you that.'

Timpkins, the silent one, nudged Macarthy with his elbow and they both laughed aloud.

'Oi'll tell you why the corporal's so bitter against the man, shall I?' the Irishman choked out between gusts of laughter. 'You see our noble corporal won't be a corporal much longer. He was one o' the escort this morning, under the lovely Captain Seymour, who's the purest bad bastard that ever walked. Every man jack on the escort stands to have the balls tore offa him if we don't catch the bugger.'

The two troopers rolled in their seats with laughter, while the corporal cursed and swore at them to no avail. Suddenly Macarthy's laughter stilled and he held up his hand.

'Quiet a minute!' He dug his elbow deep into the side of the guffawing Timpkins. 'Listen, damn ye!'

From outside the horses could be heard moving restlessly and one gave a high-pitched whinny of alarm. The three dragoons got to their feet, careful to make no noise. The corporal and Timpkins each took up a carbine and the Irishman drew his sabre. They crept towards the door and at a signal from the corporal charged outside.

'There he is!' the Irishman shouted, and Jethro also jumped to his feet and ran to the door. He saw in the moonlight a scene which seemed frozen into stillness.

The fettered man had been mounting one of the horses and now he hung poised, his eyes like black holes in the moon-silvered shaven head. The soldiers' mouths were open and their cries blended into one excited peal. The tableau shimmered then blurred into fluid motion. The fugitive flung his leg across the saddle, his heel gouging desperately at the horse's sweat-streaked flank.

The Irish trooper leapt at him, his sabre whistling towards the man's neck. Wright swayed under the crescent of steel and in the same instant brought his hands together and whirled the long fetter chain over his head. The heavy links wrapped themselves around the trooper's sword arm and Wright jerked savagely, bringing the man stumbling towards the horse. The trooper collided with the beast and began to fall back, as he

23

did so the chain slipped from his arm and the convict lifted his foot and pistoned the heel against the other's jaw. The Irishman was spun round by the force of the blow, his eyes rolled up in his head and he tumbled senseless to the ground. The fettered man drove his mount in a wild snorting, rearing circle, forcing the remaining dragoons to jump to safety from the menace of the flailing hooves, then galloped away from the inn.

The corporal kept his head as the escaper rapidly widened the distance.

'Shoot the horse, Timpkins!' he ordered curtly.

Timpkins aimed the carbine and fired. The horse staggered, galloped a few yards more, then dropped, pitching its rider over its head. The man's flying body cartwheeled and thumped into the dirt, causing the dust to spurt, then remained still. The corporal slapped Timpkins' shoulder.

'Good shot, lad. Now mount up and go and see if the bugger's dead.'

The fallen horse and man were less than fifty yards from the inn and Timpkins trotted his mount towards the prostrate heaps. As he did so, the fettered man stirred and forced himself up on to his hands and knees.

The corporal lifted his carbine. 'I'll make sure of the bugger this time,' he grunted, and took careful aim.

The moonlight was so bright that the target was as clear as if it had been high noon. Bang! The gunbarrel flew up into the air and the lead ball keened harmlessly skywards. The corporal swung to confront Jethro, his face suffused with incredulous anger.

'God rot your bloody eyes!' he roared. 'What in hell's name did you do that for?'

Jethro faced him steadily. 'I knocked the gun up to stop you murdering a helpless man,' he answered, his own anger rising.

There was a shout from Timpkins, causing both men to look round. The fugitive had picked himself up and was making off into the scrubland, leaping the clumps of furze like a cat.

'There's your bloody helpless man for you,' the corporal raged, and cupping his hands to his mouth he screamed, 'Get after him, you damned fool!'

The trooper drew his sabre and spurred his horse over the scrub in pursuit; the corporal also drew his sabre and jabbed the point against Jethro's stomach, forcing him back to the wall of the inn.

'You and me will wait right here, my fine friend. You'll hang for what you've done this night.'

He raised his voice and shouted for the landlady and her husband. When they came from the corner where they had been cowering ever since the first shot was fired, the corporal indicated the still unconscious Irishman.

'Take him inside and see what you can do for the useless bugger,' he snarled. His expression brooked no argument and the couple meekly obeyed his orders.

The fettered man and Timpkins were by this time out of both sight and hearing and the minutes lengthened. Jethro moved once and immediately the sabre point was twisted dangerously into his taut stomach muscles, ripping the skin so that he felt a white hot pain and a trickle of warm blood fall down his belly. The corporal began alternately to taunt and abuse him, and as the tirade went on and on, Jethro closed his eyes to block out the hate-filled face.

'You fancy-spoken bugger, you! You'll swing and be throttled in place o' that gaol rat whose life you saved ... And I've news for you, you whoreson, I'll make it my business to see that you're a long time adying, you bastard! And another thing, you ain't saved his life at all, because if Timpkins don't settle him, then I'll save the hangman a job and slit the bugger's throat meself. We'll see if you can stand the sight of a bit o' blood when Timpkins brings that—AGGGGHH!'

The rabid voice was abruptly choked off and the sabre clattered to the ground.

Jethro opened his eyes to see the corporal's eyes bulging from his head and his tongue protruding from his gaping mouth, while his hands scrabbled uselessly at the iron chain buried in his throat. In seconds the dragoon's body arched, limbs jerking frantically and went suddenly slack. His garrotter lowered him gently to loll across the fallen sabre.

The attacker grinned at Jethro's stupefied expression and winked.

'Turpin Wright is not the sort o' man to leave a good friend to face trouble alone,' he chuckled.

Before Jethro could recover himself sufficiently to answer, the sound of hooves was borne on the gentle wind, and far down the road they could see the small black silhouette of a fast-approaching rider.

'Come on, cully, that's the fool that was chasing me. I give him the slip as soon as I started running then come back here to see what there was to see. I 'eard this pig,' Wright stirred the corporal's inert body with a kick, 'a-promising you all the torments of hell, so I thought I'd better get you out on it. Come now, let's be away afore that trooper gets here.'

Jethro needed no urging, and the two men ran into the scrubland and were lost in its shadows before Timpkins reined in his lathered mount at the alehouse door.

CHAPTER THREE

'You damned fools!' Captain William Seymour's tall elegant body shook with the intensity of his anger as he faced the three soldiers standing rigidly to attention before him in his tent later that night. 'You had Turpin Wright in your power and then by your own crass stupidity let him escape you.'

'No, sir, begging your pardon,' Corporal Ryder's leather neck-stock had saved him from death by garrotting, but the croaking of his voice demonstrated the terrible pain and effort it cost him to force speech from his damaged throat. 'It warn't our fault sir, it were the other one who 'elped him to ...'

'Keep silent, blast you!' Seymour's arm rose and he whipped his hard hand backwards and forwards across the corporal's face until the man broke ranks and cowered against the canvas tent-wall. The captain's lean cruel features were drained of colour and the outer side of his left eye twitched erratically. 'I'll see to it that the three of you get the flesh dragged from your bodies by the lash, for this night's work ...' His eyes were merciless as they switched from one to the other of the men, then his anger erupted uncontrollably and he drove his fists at the heads and chests of the two troopers, until they also fell back to crouch at the side of the corporal, their arms shielding their bleeding faces.

'Get out of my sight!' Seymour screamed. 'Or by God above, I'll kill the three of you.'

He launched himself at them with renewed fury, using his spurred riding boots to kick them from the tent. Once alone he remained standing until his anger had abated, then sat on his camp bed and tried to plan what action he could take to save himself from his superior's wrath at the escape of Wright.

'Captain Seymour, sir?' a man called from outside.

Seymour rose and lifted the tent flap. A sergeant holding a flaming torch which spluttered and flared in the gusts of wind, stiffened and saluted.

'Yes, sergeant, what is it?'

'If you please, sir, Major Hickey wishes to see you immediately. He sent me to light you to his quarters.'

'Very well.' Seymour took his black riding cloak from the bed and fastened its folds across his shoulders, covering the splendour of his blue regimentals with their crimson facings and silver lace. Then he fitted his shako at a rakish angle on his blond hair and followed the sergeant through the lines of bell-tents.

There were four troops of the regiment quartered in this large field on the outskirts of Ludlow town, and as William Seymour's Hessian boots crushed down the downtrodden grass, he mentally cursed yet again the orders which had brought him here two weeks previously to act as escort to convicts.

Major Henry Hickey, the second-in-command of the regiment, had made his headquarters in a tumbledown hut in one corner of the field. He was seated at his desk, his grey head bent studying the documents before him, when Seymour entered the room. He looked up and in the fitful gutterings of the two candles on his camp table his face showed deep-etched lines of worry.

'Thank you for coming so promptly, Will,' he said quietly. 'Be kind enough to close the door. I have that to say which I do not enjoy saying, and do not want others to hear.' Seymour did as he was bid, then stood stiffly in front of the desk, his face impassive.

The other man sighed gustily. 'I fear that this affair may cost you your commission, Will,' he said sadly. 'These men, the escaped convict and his accomplice, have made a laughing stock of both you and the regiment. I shudder to think of what the colonel's reaction will be, when he hears of this day's happenings. He will demand that you be court-martialled.' The side of Seymour's eye began to twitch erratically.

'Be damned to the colonel!' he spat out. 'He's nothing but an old woman. And be damned to you also, Hickey, for not turning out every man we have here to hunt those bastards down!'

The other's expression was shocked. 'That is unjust of you, Will,' he protested. 'I turned out a full troop ... You know full well that I have had the "route" come today. We must

28

march north tomorrow. I could not order the men out.'

Seymour bent and placed his two hands on the desk top.

'Then let me have a small party, and detach me to hunt the pair of them down ... By God, Major Hickey! You owe me that much,' he urged, adding silently, 'you weak, snivelling turd!'

The older man seemed undecided, his fingers twisting and turning around his quill pen.

'You were my father's oldest and dearest friend,' Seymour pressed him. 'When he purchased this captaincy for me before his death, he begged me to regard you as my second father. He said to me that since he had once saved you from disgrace, you would always remember him kindly, and act so towards me, his only son.'

The major nibbled his lips and, in a flare of petulance, he burst out, 'Indeed I have always served you with kindness, Will! You seem to forget that when you applied to join this regiment you had already been made to resign from the army once for ill-treating the men under your command. It was only my insistence that finally decided the colonel to accept you, and then he did so with reluctance because you had also gained a well-deserved reputation as a duellist.'

The tiny muscle at the side of Seymour's eye began to throb once more as he struggled to control the almost overwhelming lust to tear and batter the man before him. He straightened his body and kept his hands tight-clenched to his side. When he spoke, his voice was thick with rage.

'I was but a boy then, Major Hickey. But I believe in discipline and the only way to discipline the scum that come to the army is by instilling fear into their very souls. By showing no mercy to those who would challenge the lawful commands of their betters. As for the other, the duelling ... Well, I tell you, Major Hickey, that if the Devil himself were to offend my honour, then I would call him out.'

The major felt fear course through his body, and realized that if he was not careful, he might well be facing Seymour with a pistol in his hand at dawn. Hastily he tried to mollify the man. 'No, no, Will. Do not misunderstand me. I think that you are right in what you say ... Indeed it is a most noble trait in a man that he should be ready at all times to defend his honour. Why, I myself have on occasion ...'

'We are wasting valuable time, sir!' Seymour contemptuously cut short the protestations. 'While we talk the convict and his friend are escaping from us. Let me take some men and go after them. Give me just a little time.' Seymour's mind had been working and now he saw a possible way out of his predicament. 'There, I'll strike a bargain with you. Give me a month only. If I have not caught them by a month from today, I'll save you from the Colonel's rage by sending in my papers and leaving the regiment. That way we shall both avoid a court martial for failing in our duty. For make no mistake, in the code of military justice you, as my command-ing officer will be held equally responsible with me for what has happened.'

Major Hickey snatched at this chance to wriggle out of a dangerous situation.

'Very well, Will. It's a bargain. But mind! I can only spare you a handful of men.'

Seymour grinned savagely. 'Three will be sufficient, Major, I have the very ones. I'll warrant they'll be like true hounds of hell in the chase. Success in it is the only thing that can save them from the lash ... and from me.' He left the major's quarters and, deep in thought, made his way back to his tent. When he reached it, his soldier servant was inside cleaning accoutrements.

'Leave that now,' Seymour ordered. 'Who is the sergeant of the main guard?'

'Sarn't Wilkes, sir,' the man told him.

'Good! Go to him and tell him that Captain Seymour wishes the convict, Jackie Smith, to be brought to his tent for questioning.'

The man saluted and left the tent.

Seymour sat on his camp bed and waited. 'Like all good generals,' he thought, 'I must make sure that I have a line of retreat open to me in case of need.'

Dawn was greying the night sky before Jethro Stanton and Turpin Wright dared to halt for a rest. Jethro sank to his knees and rested on his hands, his head and body parallel to the ground while he drew in great gasps of frosty air. His companion remained standing, his head and shoulders moving constantly as he peered about him.

'Phew!' Jethro lifted his head. 'You drive a hard pace, master.'

Turpin Wright grinned down at him, showing brown snags

of broken teeth. 'Theer's naught to make the feet feel lighter than remembering the stink o' the hangman's armpits when he puts that bloody rope around your neck, my friend.'

Jethro nodded. 'I believe you. There were times last night I thought you were flying above the ground.' He pushed himself erect and clambered to his feet. 'Where are we, do you think?'

Wright scratched his shaven head, causing his fetters to clank softly.

'Well, it's hard to know exactly, but I reckon we'm on the south-west side o' the Long Mynd, about seven mile from Craven Arms crossroad.'

'That means we've been travelling towards Ludlow,' Jethro pointed out anxiously. 'There's nigh on a regiment of cavalry there. I saw them when I passed through. We should have headed the other way and widened the distance, not shortened it.'

'Hold hard, friend,' Wright chuckled. 'That's the mistake the other fools made, who broke away wi' me. I'm willin' to lay you odds that they'se all bin took be now ... No, the best thing is allus to head wheer they'll not expect you. Straight towards um. We'em safe enough 'ere and once I get rid o' these,' he shook the chain joining his wrists, 'then we'll show 'um a clean pair o' heels, all right.'

'Oh no!' Jethro lifted his hand in a gesture of negation. 'Not we! Only you.'

Turpin Wright's bright blue eyes twinkled happily. 'Think agen, Jethro Stanton. Think agen.'

The young man's jaw dropped in sheer surprise.

'Ahr!' Turpin Wright nodded and chuckled. 'That shook you, me aknowing your name like that, didn't it, Jethro? And I knows a lot more besides.' He laid his forefinger upon the side of his twisted nose. 'I never forgets a face, nor a name. I knew you the minute I clapped me peepers on you larst night at the alehouse.'

Giving Jethro no time to recover from his shock, he went on, 'Now, the way I sees it, Jethro, the sodgers 'ull be arter you as strong as they'm arter me, and if you was to leave me now ... Now I needs your help to get these bloody bracelets off ... Well, if they was to take me, they'd force me to give your name to 'um, 'udden't they? They'd not let me rest easy until I did, 'ud they?'

For a moment, quick anger rose to Jethro's head, but some-

31

thing about the other man's twinkling eyes and infectious chuckle disarmed him, and in spite of himself he laughed.

'You're a bloody rogue, Turpin Wright,' he said, then admitted, 'But I take your point, the soldiers are also after me now ... It seems we are to be fellow travellers for a while longer, so we'd best shake hands on it and be friends. But tell me, how is it you know me?'

'I'll gladly take your hand, young 'un,' Wright said, and followed words by action. 'But as for the other, well, it's a long story and there's no time to tell it now. Have you money?'

'A few pence only,' Jethro told him. 'I had some more stowed in my blanket-roll back at the alehouse. No doubt the lobsters have drunk it away by now.'

'Don't fret about it, I'm the man to find more,' Wright said. 'If our luck holds we'll ha' plenty and to spare shortly. Come, let's get on, we've a lot o' ground to cover.'

'Which way do we go?' Jethro questioned. Wright winked at him. 'Towards the land o' sheep, rain, and pregnant women, wild Wales. But the next stop is a place called Bishops Castle. I know a blacksmith there, who's got a close mouth and a greedy heart. Just to make it hard for 'um, we'll circle and come up to the Castle from the south.'

Avoiding the lanes and beaten tracks, they pushed on through the thick woodlands and over the gently rolling hills, until, through a gap in the luxuriant golden, russet, and green mantle of leaves, they sighted on a hillside the long rising street of houses that was their destination.

Thomas Marston, the fat town crier and constable of Bishops Castle, Shropshire, felt greatly honoured by the confidence entrusted in him by the elegant cavalry officer who was sitting on the opposite side of a table in the bar parlour of the Three Tuns, a small inn near to the centre of the town.

'Your very good health, sir.' He lifted yet another glass of claret to his lips and sipped noisily, savouring the rich fruitiness of the expensive wine.

Captain William Seymour's pale eyes were scornful as they watched the ruby contents of the glass being sucked into the bloated rolls of red flesh, but his lips moved and courteously returned the compliment.

'Ahhh!' the crier breathed his delight. 'A most excellent wine, sir, a most excellent vintage.'

'Please! Allow me!' Seymour lifted the bottle in front of him and, waving away the weak protests of the fat man, he refilled the empty glass.

The crier leant forward and whispered hoarsely, 'But, Captain Seymour, sir, I do not understand why you do not wish for a hue and cry to be raised in this parish for these desperate men.'

Seymour's thin nose wrinkled in distaste and he moved his head to escape the fumes of stale, wine-laden breath. Fighting down the impulse to smash his fist into the stupid self-satisfied face before him, he smiled and put a finger to his lips.

'There are certain highly placed personages who wish this matter to be dealt with as discreetly as possible, my good sir. I regret that I have my orders and can say no more on the subject, except to tell you in strict confidence that your own part in it is being watched very closely by those who have your best interests at heart. I know that they share my trust in you to carry out my instructions in this matter to the letter. You will not find me, or them, ungrateful.'

He winked at the other and pulling a purse from inside his tunic he tipped several gold coins on to the table between them...

In the low-ceilinged, black-beamed taproom of the same inn, two of the three soldiers accompanying Captain Seymour were equally puzzled at his intentions.

'Jase! I don't understand the captain's ways. Why the hell don't he raise a hue and cry here? And what the hell are we doin' here, anyways? We're bloody miles from nowhere and anywhere they're likely to be. It stands to reason they'll head for Liverpool and try to find a ship,' Trooper Macarthy shook his sandy head in hopeless mystification.

His friend, Trooper Timpkins, eased his large frame upon the wooden, high-backed fireside seat and looked glumly at his empty drinking jug.

'I couldn't arf do wiv anuvver jug of ale ...' he muttered. 'Or small-beer come to that.'

'Shut yer mouths, the pair on yer,' Corporal Ryder's throat pained him greatly and he could still only croak. 'You may rest easy that that barstard in theer knows what he's about. If you warn't so bloody bone-'eaded, you'd ha' cottoned on to what he means to do already.'

'Oh, should we now? I suppose you're in our noble captin's confidence, are you, Corporal dear?' the Irishman jeered. 'Well, if that's the case, perhaps you'll be kind enough to tell us two stupids what it is the bloody madman means to do.'

The corporal held up a hand warningly and jerked his head towards the fourth member of their party who was squatting on his haunches by the door; a short, weather-beaten man with the shaven head and ragged clothes of a convict whose wrists bore the chafed sores made by manacles.

'Wait a minute,' he croaked, then turned and beckoned to the man. ' 'Ere, Smith, get over 'ere.'

The short man started nervously and bared uneven yellow teeth in a grimace intended to be an ingratiating smile. He shuffled to the table.

'Yus, Corporal? What is it, Corporal?' His lips drew back in the momentary rictus once more.

'Gerrout round to the stables and check the 'orses,' Ryder croaked at him. 'Give 'um a rub down while you'm theer.'

The man nodded and knuckled his forehead in salute.

'I will, Corporal, I will.'

Head down, he shuffled from the room.

Once satisfied they were alone, Ryder spoke rapidly to the others. 'Seymour had that little gutter-rat in his tent wi' him for an hour afore we left the camp larst night ... His name's Jackie Smith, him and Turpin Wright was gooin' to be hung together in Shrewsbury.' The corporal tapped his head with his grimy fingertips. 'I know me old throat's bin buggered up, but me bleedin' headpiece is still workin' all right. It's as clear as bloody daylight what the captain means to do.'

'Well, gerron and tell us, for the love o' Christ!' Macarthy burst out impatiently.

'I'm agoing to, ain't I, if you'd gi' me half a chance,' Ryder croaked indignantly. 'Turpin Wright's got a load o' stolen rhino and suchlike hid away somewheer about these parts, and he's got some old cronies from his thievin' days 'ere abouts as well ... Seymour means to 'ave his cake and eat it. He knows bloody well that he faces a court martial, even if he manages to catch Wright and the other bastard, because the colonel hates his guts, so he means to get hold o' the rhino and slit the gizzards o' Wright and his mate. Then he'll be off to Ameriky or some such place and live like a bloody lord.'

Timpkins' heavy brow furrowed with the unaccustomed

34

strain of thought. 'What happens to us then, Corporal?' he growled.

Ryder hawked and spat on to the brick floor in disgust. 'What allus happens to poor silly buggers like us?' he croaked bitterly. 'We'll goo to the halberds, whatever he does, and mark my words, the Drummer's Daughter 'ull drag the life from the three of us. Then we might get lucky at that,' he added as an afterthought, 'we might only be strung up like that bleedin' informer we got wi' us,' he finished gloomily.

'Wait now ... hold on a minute. How the bloody hell do youse come to know so much?' the Irishman questioned doubtfully, and suddenly sat back slapping his hands upon the table top. 'Did the captin tell youse his plans then?' he jeered.

'No, you thick Paddy bastard!' The corporal lunged across the table and grabbed Macarthy by his tunic collar then jerked him forward until their eyes were only inches apart. 'While you and that bloody wooden-yed there was sat pissin' your britches aworritin' what was going to happen to you, I was outside Seymour's tent listening to what passed between him and that bloody gallows-rat, Smith. Do you doubt me, cully?' he finished threateningly.

The Irishman shook his head and placated the corporal, patting his arms. 'No, Corporal dear, no. I believe youse, honest I believe you.'

'Good!' Ryder spat out, and pushed the trooper back into his seat. 'Now,' he went on, 'there's summat I wants to know from you two. I got a few ideas of my own about that rhino ... and about Captin Bloody Seymour. What I needs to know is if you'm awillin' to join me?'

Macarthy pondered for several seconds, then grinned.

'I'm wit you,' he said.

'And you?' Ryder turned to Timpkins.

'Ahr, I be,' the big man rumbled.

'Good!' The corporal's hard face showed his satisfaction. 'You just wait for me to gi' the word. I'm sick to death o' taking orders and being kicked from pillar to post. I wants me a bit o' soft living for a change.'

'Jasus Christ!' the Irishman exclaimed delightedly. 'We'll all be able to go to Ameriky and live like bloody lords.'

'That might well be so, Paddy,' the corporal hawked and spat on the floor once more. 'But I'll get more joy in settling wi' Seymour when the time comes ...'

35

CHAPTER FOUR

Once a week there was a market in the town and it was being held this day. Jethro and Turpin Wright lay high up in a densely bushed coppice of young elms and for more than an hour watched the steady stream of country folk passing along the road beneath them: ploughboys and farm labourers in elaborately embroidered white smocks, breeches and high-low boots, their unkempt hair and ruddy faces half-hidden by floppy, broad-brimmed bullycock hats. They laughed and joked in their soft rustic burrs, as they eagerly anticipated the flagons of rich brown ales and porters awaiting them in the town. Then a trio of haughty journeymen-gardeners with short jackets, feathered cocked hats, and blue aprons about their waists, keeping their own company, for they were men of exotic skills when it came to the growing of rare plants and flowers. Rough-looking drovers, numbered leather badges strapped to their arms, thrashed their recalcitrant cattle along a straight path and cursed horribly in a dozen different dialects when the beasts baulked and slithered, trying to escape the sight and smell of a gang of slaughtermen, whose high legshields were thick with the blood of dead animals and whose red-striped waistcoats and scarlet fisher caps made a glaring advertisement of their trade.

There were milkmaids, yoked across their sturdy shoulders like oxen, their overskirts rumped above their knees to display green gowns. Their pink faces flushed and sweating beneath flat be-ribboned hats from the weight of burnished copper cans full of cream and milk. Old women and young girls carried huge wickerwork baskets laden with vegetables, eggs, herbs, cheeses, and butter. Hucksters, cheapjacks, and packmen, canvas tuck-packs bulging with gew-gaws and fripperies, hurled insults when wagoners driving their team of bullocks and shirehorses, straining to haul the heavy carts over the deep ruts, forced pedestrians into the roadside ditches. Not even the proud yeomen farmers on their thoroughbred hunters, clad in costly broadcloth, high-crowned beaver hats, and polished leather gaiters, could make the lordly wagoners give way. It took the gentler persuasions of the bevies of pretty, giggling, calling girls in their bright fresh aprons and saucy poke-bonnets to do that.

Occasionally a carriage full of the wives and daughters of the richest farmers would lurch by, the effect of fine horse-flesh, shining paint and harness, fashionable gowns and feathers nearly always ruined by the spectacle of a yokel coachman, pressed into service from the farmyard for the day and still bearing the dried dung of pigs, sheep, and cattle thick upon his boots and clothes.

Turpin Wright nudged Jethro. 'We'em in luck,' he whispered. 'It's market day. You'll not be noticed in this mob. When you gets into the town, turn right at the church and make your way to the top o' the hill to the town hall. You can't miss it, it's got a clock tower. You'll hear the blacksmith afore you'se got half-way up the hill. He'll be shoutin' and ravin' fit to bust.'

'Why?' Jethro questioned innocently. 'Is he a man of anger?'

'You could say that,' Turpin told him. 'He's one o' them ranters ... a bloody ranting preacher ... But don't let that fool you, boy. He's a regular Newgate Knocker, a real up and downer that one, and as wide as the ocean. He wears a beard and calls hisself George Jenkins. If you'm in any doubt, ask for Hellfire George, they all knows him around these parts. Get him on his own and tell him that Turpin wants to do a bit o' business wi' him ... But mind! Goo careful! Say nothing about what bloody state I'm in or wheer I'm hid. I'll lie low here 'till you comes back. If it's dark, whistle three shorts and a long.'

Jethro nodded his understanding and without any more words he slipped through the coppice away from the road. He moved around its flank and stepped into the procession behind a small flock of sheep, baaing and bleating plaintively as the crook-wielding shepherd and his pair of wiry black collies chivvied them along.

Turpin Wright had spoken truthfully. Jethro heard the ranter before he was half-way up the town's hilly main street, pushing his way through the market-day crowds.

'Hearken, sinners! Hearken to one who knows. Does not the

37

psalmist tell us that HE shall come down like rain upon the mown grass ... That HIS enemies shall lick the dust!' The deep bass voice thundered above the heads of people and animals, but they ignored it, being too busy haggling, chaffing, laughing, and greeting each other, to notice the threats of eternal damnation that the tiny dark-clothed preacher, his minute face hidden by a bushy crop of fierce black bristles, hurled at them.

Hellfire George stamped one small buckled shoe upon the wooden box he stood on, until the thin wood cracked and began to give way.

'Consider the Book of Jeremiah, you spawn of godless heathens!' Again the sonorous tones burst from the crop of whiskers. 'Does not the blessed Jeremiah tell us ... Amend your ways and your doings!'

'AMEN!' 'AMEN!' 'HALLELUJAH, BROTHER!'

Around the wooden box were grouped a party of converts clad in sombre clothing. The men with heads bared and their meek women wearing plain white scarves to hide the vanity of clean, brushed hair from the sight of their grim God.

'Can the Ethiopian change his skin, or the leopard his spots? Jeremiah asks us that ... I also, George Jenkins, ask that ... and I tell you, *No! No! They cannot change except through the will of the Lord God most high!*'

A man in the forefront of the crowd lifted both arms heavenwards and with eyes screwed tight-shut and head jerking uncontrollably began to croon unintelligible gibberish.

The little preacher's red-rimmed eyes widened in ecstasy.

'LORD BE PRAISED! BLESSED BE YOUR NAME. AMEN. AMEN.'

He pointed at the man. 'Look there, brethren. The Holy Ghost has entered our brother and he speaks with the tongues of angels!'

The man's gibbering became a torrent of high-pitched screams. His distorted face empurpled, his mouth frothed while his entire body shook. Two women began to weep loudly and flopped to the ground to lie face downwards, arms stretched sideways like human crucifixes.

'HALLELUJAH! HALLELUJAH! HALLELUJAH! PRAISE GOD! PRAISE GOD!' The ranters lifted their heads and bawled out their joy, tears streaming down cheeks, sobs choking throats.

'OH LOVELY JESUS, I THANK YOU. OH LOVELY JESUS I THANK YOU FOR THIS DAY'S TENDER MERCY.' Hellfire George's thunder drowned all other exultations. 'I THANK THEE JESUS FOR BRINGING THESE WEAK, SINFUL, UNCLEAN WOMEN TO THE FOOT OF THY THRONE ... FOR WASHING THEM IN THY BLESSED BLOOD, AND FOR LETTING THEM JOIN WITH US, YOUR NOBLE ARMY OF MARTYRS.' 'AMEN BROTHER! AMEN TO THAT', a man bellowed, and sank to his knees and hammered his forehead against the cobbles.

'Theer surry, it's as good as a bloody play, bain't it?' a ruddy-faced ploughman laughed at Jethro's side. 'Them silly buggers does this every week. It's as good as a play to watch the bloody loonies.' He leered lasciviously and jerked his head at the female ranters. 'Mind you, surry, theer's one o' they wenches I 'uddent mind sharing my bed wi'. I'd gi' her summat as 'ud make her pray to the Lord all right.'

Jethro looked across at the woman the ploughman had indicated. Taller than her companions, she wore a bright yellow kerchief on her head instead of the white of the others, and its glowing colour framed her dark handsome face and thick coils of chestnut hair. Unlike those about her, she was not praying and shouting exultations, but instead appeared sullen and ill at ease, and her full lips were pouting in disgust as she stared at the spectacle of the women lying on the ground.

Jethro nodded. 'Aye, she's a rare pretty one, master,' he said and not wishing to continue the talk, moved nearer to the ranters. He halted to stand behind two farmers bargaining over a young calf which one of them led on a rope.

'Thee shanna!' the one with the calf stated vehemently. 'Thee shanna gi' me that.'

His companion's heavy face was red and greasy with good living.

'That I shall.' He was equally vehement.

'Thee shanna!'

'Then theer's no more to be said, surry.'

'Tek it then! And may you roast in your own fat, you old sod!' The calf's owner cursed good-humouredly, well content with his bargain.

The greasy-faced one laughed uproariously and spat on his horny palm. The other did the same and they brought their palms together with a resounding crack.

''Ull thee gi' me some luck wi' it?' the buyer asked.

The seller grinned and nodded. ''Ere, you bloody robber! 'Ere's a shillun'.' He tossed the coin in the air for the other to catch.

'Ahr, it's a good 'un!' Greasy Face bit the coin. 'Come on, I'll wet thee throat wi' this.'

The pair moved away, dragging the sad-eyed, squealing-frightened calf behind them.

There was now a clear space between Jethro and the wailing group of worshippers. He stared at the tiny-bodied preacher who, sensing Jethro's gaze, looked over his disciples' heads and met the young man's eyes. Hellfire George's eyebrows lifted in silent question, and he nodded as if to ask whether Jethro was a worshipper.

Jethro gave a slight shake of his head, and with his lips mouthed silently, 'Turpin Wright.'

The preacher's eyes became wary, and flicked about quickly to see if anyone had noticed the interchange. He winked at Jethro and then started to whip up the flagging emotions of his flock once more.

'Fear the Lord God! Honour the King of Heaven!' he roared.

'AMEN! AMEN! AMEN!' they rejoined.

'BE VIGILANT, BRETHREN! BECAUSE YOUR ADVERSARY ... THE DEVIL! YES, SATAN HISSELF! THE DENIZEN O' THE PITS OF HELLFIRE AND TORMENT! LIKE A ROARING LION WALKETH ABOUT, SEEKIN' WHO HE MAY DEVOUR.'

The worshippers groaned loudly and yet more women threw themselves to the ground as human crosses, while their menfolk raised their arms on high and babbled wildly in senseless tongues.

'I come among you to lay hands on you in the name of Him who is the mightiest of all kings.'

Suiting the action to his words, Hellfire George stepped down from his box and was immediately lost to view. Jethro glanced about him to see if anyone was paying attention and, satisfied that the passing crowds gave him no heed, he moved forward. Almost instantly, the tiny preacher came to him.

'Come brother, come and receive the blessed laying on of hands from the Lord's humble servant.' He placed his hands on Jethro's shoulders and pressed him downwards so that he could whisper, 'Did you say Turpin Wright, cully?' His whiskers tickled roughly against Jethro's ear.

'Yes, he sent me. He wants to see you. It's urgent,' Jethro whispered back.

'Tell him to come to the smithy tonight,' the preacher instructed, then shouted aloud, 'Pray to the Lord God, you poor sinner. Only He can save you. Only He has the power to cleanse your black soul.'

To the chanted chorus of hallelujahs and amens, Jethro stepped back into the passers-by and was swallowed up by them. Unknown to either Jethro or the ranter there had been one interested viewer of their brief exchange; Jackie Smith, muffled in an old bottle-green watchcoat, with a battered straw hat hiding his shaven head. He also slipped into the passing crowds and followed the young man's tall figure. Jethro felt in his coat pocket for the few pence he had left. He passed a cooked meat stall and the rich, hot, spicy smells of frying sausages and black puddings, pigs' trotters, and sliced liver caused his stomach to lurch and his mouth to water. He had eaten nothing since the half-bowl of rabbit the previous evening and many hours and long hard miles of travel separated him from that meagre supper.

A motherly, plump-featured countrywoman had stopped to rest her basket of goods on a convenient window ledge. Jethro halted and brought out his remaining coins.

'What 'ull thee 'ave, my 'andsome?' The woman chuckled, but her small eyes were calculating.

'I'll take some cheese, good mother,' he told her. 'And you can sell me a couple of onions as well.'

'The wenches 'ull not like to kiss thee, if thee ates these old onions, I'll tell thee. They be powerful hot to the tongue I'll promise.'

He smiled at her. 'The only girl I've seen that I'd want to kiss this day is you,' he said, and winked at her.

She cackled delightedly and cut him a large chunk of moist golden cheese. 'Get on wi' thee. Th'art a young rip. I'll wager you'd far sooner kiss summat like that 'un over theer than an old 'ooman like me. Though, mind you, a few years back I was a lush armful for any man, I'll tell thee.' She cackled again and her shrewd eyes twinkled as the young man stared appreciatively at the passing woman.

It was the yellow-kerchiefed ranter, only now her face had lost its sullenness and her lips smiled and her cheek was flushed as she talked to the tall blond-haired and mustachioed

41

young man who walked beside her. Jethro felt a spasm of envy for the man's good fortune in knowing such an attractive creature, then turned back to the market woman.

'Ere! I'll gi' thee these onions for thy cheek,' she smiled ...

Jethro thanked her and walked on, pushing the cheese and onions into his coat pockets. With his last money, he bought two penny loaves from a bread-seller and headed away from the town. A small figure stealthily dogged his steps.

When Jethro reached the thicket where he had left Turpin Wright, there were only isolated travellers on the road. The young man looked about him, then, fumbling with his laced cod-piece at the front of his breeches, he went into the woodland as if to relieve himself.

Once under the shelter of the trees' still thick foliage of dying brown and yellow leaves, he made his way through the undergrowth. Jethro found the flattened bracken where he and Wright had lain, but the man had gone. He began to quarter the woodland, calling softly.

'Turpin? Turpin, it's me!'

He had been searching for some minutes when there came a faint outcry which was abruptly cut off before it could gather volume. He ran towards the sound, kicking aside the heaps of fallen leaves and tearing through the thorns and branches of clinging brambles. Out of the corner of his eye he glimpsed a flurry of movement. It was Turpin Wright and another man locked together in silent combat, rolling over and over on the soft layers of dead and rotting vegetation. Before Jethro could reach them, Turpin Wright had pinned his opponent beneath him and was holding a knife to his throat.

He looked up as Jethro pounded to him, and panted, 'I spotted this bleeder followin' you ... You wants to take more care, cully.'

'Who is it?' Jethro questioned. 'Do you know him?'

'Oh ahr.' The convict pulled away the broken straw hat from where it had jammed over his prisoner's face. 'I knows this little ferret only too well ... Doon't I, sweetheart?' He reached with black-nailed fingers and twisted the man's ear until it seemed it would tear from the shaven head. The man opened his mouth to scream and the blade of the knife slid in warning across his throat. He clamped his tongue between his yellow teeth and writhed in silent agony.

'It's little Jackie Smith!' Wright spat out. 'He's a stock-

42

buzzer by trade, that's all he's got the guts for, pinching bloody handkerchiefs and faking the Kinchin-lay. He tried fanning the pockets of a cove in Ludlow a few weeks since and the traps took him. Twenty-three times he's bin nabbed, to my knowledge. They was agoin' to top him along a me and a few others this time.' He twisted Smith's ear, wrenching his head from its pillow of earth. 'Warn't they, Jackie, lad,' he taunted through clenched teeth. 'They was agooin' to top you along o' the flash coves. The only time you'se ever bin in good company in your bleedin' life. What was the matter, Jackie? Warn't there nobody you could turn nark on this time, to save your scrawny neck?'

'No, Turpin! No!' The man gasped in torment.

'Leave him be!' Jethro spoke sharply. 'He's done us no harm, there's no need to torture him so.'

Wright snarled a curse and released the bleeding ear. Smith's head thumped back on to the dirt and he lay gasping for breath, his eyes shifting from one face to the other and his lips pulling back in their peculiar grimace.

Jethro bent over him. 'What are you doing here?'

Smith's eyes grew cunning. 'Nuthin', marster! I didn't know anybody was in the wood ... I'se bin runnin' since we got away from the convoy. I wus on Turpin's chain, he'll tell you ... We all got away together. I didn't know he wus here ... Honest, I didn't ... I swears it! On me mam's grave, I swears it!' The words spouted from him, flecks of spittle spraying from his slack mouth.

'You dirty lying little barstard,' Wright growled, and sat back, moving the knife to the man's genitals. 'I takes my oath, Jackie Smith, that if yo doon't give us the truth, I'll cut your balls off and ram 'um down your mouth ... And if you reckons I'm bluffing, then remember Ranny Powell ... Or 'as you forgotten 'im? Now tell us how you got rid o' your bracelets, and how you come by that coat and hat, and how you knew I was 'ere in Bishops Castle?'

Smith's weathered face blanched and through dry lips he croaked, 'Easy now, Turpin, easy. I'll tell you everythin'.'

'Good! Then tell, an' remember, one bloody lie and you'll not be a man no longer.'

'It was Seymour made me do it,' Smith burst out. 'I had to tell 'im, or he'd ha' killed me.'

'How much does he know?' Wright demanded.

'He knows you got rhino hid somewheers around 'ere. An'

43

he knows you got pals in this town. That's all he knows, I swear that's all he knows.'

'And you?' Wright shouted. 'What was you supposed to do?'

'I was told to find yer and join up wi' yer,' the man gabbled. 'Then when I'd found wheer the rhino was stowed, I was to tip the wink to Seymour.'

'Wheer's the bugger now?'

'In the town theer,' Smith said hurriedly. 'Waitin' for me to come back.'

'Shut your mouth!' Wright brutally cuffed the little man, who lapsed immediately into terrified silence. Turpin levered himself up from the trembling body beneath him and stood erect, shaking his head musingly. Then, to Jethro's surprise, he began to laugh.

'What's the matter?' Jethro asked. 'Have you gone mad?'

His companion sobered abruptly and rested his hand on Jethro's shoulder. 'Doon't worry, my friend. I've not gone Dolally Tap,' he answered quietly. 'It just struck me as funny, that prize bugger Seymour getting greedy for my rhino.'

'Is it true?' Jethro demanded. 'Have you got money hidden?'

Wright pursed his lips in warning. 'Allus remember, matey. Little pitchers has big ears,' he said, and suddenly whirled his wrist chain around his head and brought its doubled links whipping across Smith's temple. The man's head jerked horribly at the impact and Wright knelt by his side. He pushed open one closed lid, exposing the white, glistening eyeball.

'It'll be all right to talk and make some plans now,' he told Jethro coolly. 'This bugger 'ull be out cold for an hour or more.'

CHAPTER FIVE

Night fell and the market was over for another week. The country people went back to their villages and hamlets, their farms and isolated cottages. The wandering traders packed their pots, pans, bolts of cloth, flimsy wisps of silk, and assorted gew-gaws and headed for the next town, the next market. The lucky animals were driven along the lanes by their new masters who would let them breed and eat for a few more months, or even years. Others lay bloody and flayed under the slicing knives and chopping axes of the butchers, or snorted fearfully and rolled their eyes as they waited to be brought to the still busy slaughterers. The small town lapsed slowly into its customary torpor until the next market day should arrive; and soon only the flicker of light behind closed shutters, the solitary footsteps of a man returning from his work and the occasional burst of laughter or snatch of song coming faintly from the town's taverns showed any life in the dark streets.

George Jenkins' smithy was some distance from the town, a tumbledown huddle of sheds standing alone over the brow of a hill, on a lane leading off the road to Montgomery and to Wales. Sarah Jenkins, Hellfire George's only child, took the bright yellow cloth from her hair and shook out the thick loose coils until the rich chestnut fell in long rippling waves of colour about her neck and shoulders. She lit the rushlight which gave dim illumination to the interior of the living shed. Then she busied herself at the crude charcoal-burning iron stove on which a savoury-smelling mutton stew bubbled greasily. The shed's walls were part stone, part brick, part wood, the whole jumbled haphazardly as if the builder had taken the materials at random and carelessly flung them together. Its long sagging-roofed interior was partitioned at each end by unplaned warped planking to form sleeping cubicles, one for the man and, at the other end, one for his

45

daughter. The stove was placed across from the door and above it a small hole had been punched through the roof to let the fumes of fuel and food escape. When the wind blew, as it did tonight, from the west, the smoke was blown back into the room, forming a thick fug which left greasy deposits on the earthwashed walls and the broken boxes and chairs that furnished the living quarters. All around the walls were nailed garishly coloured tracts, taken at random from the Old and New Testaments. It was one of these that met the young woman's fine green eyes as she glanced up from the stove.

'CHARITY SHALL COVER THE MULTITUDE OF SINS ... BOOK OF PETER.'

Sarah Jenkins clucked her tongue against her white teeth and her handsome face twisted momentarily in scorn.

'It would take a deal of charity to cover that old hypocrite's sins,' she muttered, thinking of her father, then went from the room to stand outside in the rubbish-strewn yard. She lifted her arms above her head and stretched to ease the stiffness in shoulders and back.

'Why did I ever come back here?' she wondered discontentedly.

As her eyes adjusted to the darkness she could see the squat outline of the ramshackle forge, its open front a gaping black yawn across the yard, and next to it the low, windowless brick hovel which her father had mysteriously barred and locked three days before and forbidden her to enter. Her curiosity was roused afresh as she looked at the hovel and she sauntered across to it, her tall well-shaped body moving with a natural grace and her skirts held high on her long slender legs to prevent their red cloth trailing in the deep layers of mud and dung.

At the hovel she paused for a moment, listening carefully for any noise in the lane beyond the smithy that could denote her father's return. Once satisfied that she was in no danger of discovery, she bent, drawing the thick glossy coils of hair from her ear, and pressed it to the deep crack running diagonally across the rough, nail-studded door. The faint rasping gurgle of half-choked breathing sounded clearly through the crack. Sarah waited, hoping to gain some insight as to who, or what, was within. Twisting her head, she whispered through the crack.

'Who is it in there? Tell me who it is. Don't be afraid, I want to help you if I can.'

46

She listened for a reply, but none came. Only a faint moan and again the gurgles of breath.

'Be damned to it!' She turned from the door in irritation. 'I'll have it out with the old sod, this night,' she vowed to herself. 'I've a right to know what it is he's up to. He'll not find me so meek and frightened of him as my mother was, poor soul.'

Sarah had been in service as a housekeeper for a gentry family up in Cheshire for some years, and had only returned to keep house for her father, following her mother's death, a few months previously. Those months had been more than sufficient for her to confirm what she had always suspected. That beneath George Jenkins' pious, God-fearing façade, there flowed strange and evil currents. She was by no means an innocent herself, but she did not enjoy seeing wickedness hidden under a cloak of piety. The tramp of feet and the murmur of voices sounded from the lane. Quickly Sarah re-crossed the yard and when her father opened the door of the living hut, she was seated on a broken-backed chair gazing with chin resting on hands at the glowng heap of charcoal.

His tiny figure strutted into the centre of the room and his foot thumped down hard on the rammed-earth floor once, twice, three times.

'Now, father, there's no use you stamping your foot at me,' she told him calmly. 'I'm not my mother. You'll not frighten me with your tantrums.'

The ranter's eyes reddened in temper and his delicately shaped hands, calloused and hardened by his work, clenched and unclenched rhythmically. Strangers seeing the smallness of George Jenkins, laughed and doubted when told he was a blacksmith, comparing him mentally with the great muscled men in their fringed leather aprons who normally worked at the forge and anvil. Those who knew him quickly warned the strangers to hide their scoffing doubts. For Jenkins possessed within his minute frame an almost demoniac strength; and there was no man in the county who could swing the heavy sledgehammers as long and skilfully, or handle the beasts brought to be shod as easily, as could Hellfire George.

'Why did'st thee sneak off from the meeting, daughter?' His huge voice boomed the question as a threat.

'Because I didn't choose to stay!' she rejoined spiritedly. 'I'm sure there were quite enough hypocrites and Jack o' Bedlams there, as it was. It didn't need me also to make a

47

show of myself.'

He tugged at his black whiskers and his reddened eyes held murder.

'In the blessed Book o' Job, it says, "Who is this that darkeneth counsel by words wi'out knowledge?" That's what you'm adoin' now, you shameless strumpet! Speakin' wi'out the knowledge of what it is to worship the Lord most High wi' a pure heart.'

Before she could answer, a man's voice called from the doorway. 'Make haste, George! Let's do what we come 'ere to do.'

'I'll spake to thee later, you Jezebel,' Jenkins warned his daughter.

He rummaged in a wooden box that flanked the stove and took from its innards half a wax candle. Lighting it from the flickering rushlight, he left the room, shielding the flame with his hands.

In the forge, Jenkins took off his black coat and dirty white cravat. In his shirt-sleeves, he arranged a sledgehammer and cold chisels on the work bench. He pointed to the great anvil in the centre of the floor.

'Put thy leg on there, Turpin. I'll get rid on that ankle-iron first.'

Turpin Wright nudged Jethro and handed him the knife which he had been pressing against Jackie Smith's back.

''Ere, matey, tek this and if this bugger makes one move, then stick him.'

Smith's lips bared his yellow teeth. 'I'll not move, Turpin,' he tried to speak lightly. 'You con trust me. I'm your true friend.'

Wright nodded. 'I knows that well, Jackie. Specially when I'se got a blade at your throat,' he answered dryly.

Hellfire George hefted the sledgehammer and moved to the anvil. The candle flame threw grotesque wavering shadows across the tiny smith and he seemed to grow taller and broader.

'Now, cully. Keep still,' he ordered, and as easily as if it were made of twigs, he swung the huge iron sledge high, and brought it down on the ankle iron at the point where the ring of metal was joined. There was a sharp, clanging crack and the fetter split neatly into two halves.

Turpin Wright opened his tight-shut eyes and gaped at his leg in wonder.

'Rot me bleedin' balls!' he breathed. 'I never felt a thing.'

48

'No, my bucko! That's because I'm the finest ironworker you'm ever likely to meet up wi',' the ranter boasted.

Jethro was also impressed. 'I think that you're speaking the truth when you say that, Master Jenkins. I do indeed.'

So engrossed were the men with what they had witnessed, that none of them heard the faint rustle of petticoats brushing along the side of the forge wall. Sarah, unable to contain her curiosity as to who her father's mysterious visitors were, had crept across the yard and was listening at a spot in the wall where a brick had fallen, leaving a hole.

Hellfire George's red-rimmed eyes stared bleakly at Jethro. 'I bin wondering who you might be,' he said with hostility. 'Thee doon't have the stamp of a lag. I bin wonderin' how you come to be wi' Turpin 'ere. Be you one o' the flash boys who broke from the convoy?'

The young man shook his head. 'No, I wasn't in the convoy. I've never been a lag in my life.'

'Then who and what be thou?' the ranter demanded to know.

'That's not for you to worry about,' Jethro answered levelly. 'I mean you no offence, Master Jenkins, but I prefer to keep my own counsel.'

'What thee prefers to do, be neither 'ere nor there, young man.' Hellfire George's voice was menacing. 'When thee comes 'ere to my padding-ken and sees things that only the flash boys oughter see, then I wants to know all about thee. I've no fancy to be giving shelter to informers and the like.'

Jethro's temper, strained by lack of sleep, rose.

'The insults that come from your mouth are too bold for your tiny body,' he told the other angrily. 'I'll not be accused of informing by you or anyone else.'

In his excitement he stepped forward. The ranter, thinking he was in danger of attack, swung the sledgehammer in threat.

'I'll bust that pretty face o' thine,' he warned. 'I'll break thy bloody skull! Big as thee might be, I'll break it!'

'Give over, the pair on you!' Turpin Wright jumped in between them. 'Hellfire speaks fair, Jethro.' He put his hand against the younger man's brawny chest. 'He's a right to know what sort o' coves he's ashelterin'.'

He swung on the ranter. 'I'll tell you who this is,' he said forcefully. 'This is Jethro Stanton. He's from the town o' Redditch, back in Worcestershire, same as I be meself.'

49

He grinned at Jethro's surprised face. 'Oh yes, Jethro. I'm an old pointer lad, from the needle-mills just as your Dad was ... His Dad was a great man,' he told Jenkins, chopping the air with his hands to give emphasis to his words, 'he was a captin o' the Luddites, was Peter Stanton, and I knew him well. He was bloody well destroyed by the government's spies, murdered together wi' his mate, Batten the prizefighter. Peter Stanton 'elped me more nor one in different ways, and bad bugger though I may be, I don't forget friends nor favours. I'll swear for this lad 'ere, as a straight 'un. As straight as a die!'

After a momentary hesitation, Hellfire George lowered his hammer.

'That'll do for me, Turpin,' he boomed. 'Now get thy arms on to that anvil and I'll quit them bracelets for thee.'

The wrist fetters proved tougher to strike off than the ankle-iron and while the blacksmith struggled with cold chisels and hammer to the accompaniment of Turpin Wright's curses and groans, Jethro's thoughts dwelt on the chain of events that had brought him to this thieves' den in the company of rogues and convicts. The memory of his father burned across his mind, fanned into a flame by the words of Turpin Wright.

Peter Stanton, a man who all his life had fought for the oppressed masses of England's poor, who had finally been driven to join the Luddite movements which, in the north and midlands, dared to challenge the might of the ruling classes. Peter Stanton paid with his life for his beliefs. Government agents had murdered him six months before, and the grief that Jethro felt was still raw and all pervasive. He had loved his father deeply, for there had only been the two of them for many years. Jethro's mother and two baby sisters were buried together in a pauper's grave far away in distant Ely. Jethro shook his head, driving the bitter memories from his mind.

'Someday, when I have learnt enough, and experienced enough of this world and its ways, then I shall avenge all their deaths,' he promised himself. 'But at this moment I must think only of how to escape the noose that is dangling above my own head.'

Sarah had risked a peep through the hole during the altercation between Jethro and her father. She appreciated what she saw.

'My! But you're a pretty fellow!' she thought, staring admiringly at the young man's fine physique and handsome regular features.

She remained crouched by the wall until a triumphant exclamation from her father told her that the task of freeing Turpin Wright was completed. Then, gathering her skirts about her knees, she glided silently away.

Turpin stood up, rubbing his bleeding wrists and cursing softly at the pain of abrased and bruised flesh. The ranter looked at him speculatively.

'Thou'rt gooing to be needing clothes, Turpin,' he mused aloud.

'Ahr, and proper food and rest for a few days as well,' the convict retorted. 'And does you know summat, Hellfire? I reckon you'm willing to provide 'um all. At a bloody stiff price.'

The ranter chuckled richly. 'That I be ...' he answered. 'That I be.'

'How about this man?' Jethro pushed Jackie Smith to the anvil. 'What do we do with him in the meantime?'

The ranter lifted his red-rimmed eyes heavenwards.

'Blessed be the Lord for His infinite mercies,' he intoned sonorously. Then spoke directly to Jethro. 'I'se got a little place next door to here. It's built as strong as a dungeon, so it is. Well, what I suggests is that we fits the hound up wi' a collar and chain and we puts him in theer. He'll be snug in that kennel, I'll warrant ... Theer's already a guest in there in a manner o' speakin', but he'll not trouble our Jackie, I'll be bound.' The ranter's rich chuckle issued from his black whiskers again. 'No! I reckon they'll get on right well together.' He pointed at Smith's apprehensive face and with the other hand picked up a long thin piece of flattened metal. 'Get thee neck across that anvil, Smith. I'se got a nice cravat 'ere for thee.'

It took only a very few minutes to fashion the crude collar and chain around the small convict's neck.

'There! That'll hold him.' Hellfire George picked up the free end of the chain and pointing to the candle said, 'Bring that glim, Turpin.'

He dragged the whimpering, frightened Jackie Smith behind him and led the way to the small thick-walled hovel adjacent to the forge. The air inside was cold and damp. As the party ducked one by one under the low lintel of the doorway, Jethro heard the gurgling of straining congested lungs.

Turpin Wright held the candle aloft so that its dim glow showed what the hovel contained ... It was a man dressed in a blue uniform jacket and white breeches. He lay flat on his back, his legs and arms bound with ropes and around his neck an iron collar and chain fastened to a ring-bolt set into the side wall.

'My bleedin Christ!' Turpin Wright uttered.

'Now, Turpin,' the blacksmith reproved him gravely. 'Thee knows I doon't like blasphemy.'

'Who is he? What's he doing here?' Jethro demanded, and went to kneel by the man's head. He stared at the thin un-shaven grey face and the black cavities of deep-sunk eyes, then felt with his hands the clammy wetness of the skin of head, neck, and chest.

'This man is seriously ill!' he exclaimed angrily. 'He must be near to death ... Why are you keeping him here like this? It's bloody inhuman!' His searching fingers felt the hard crust of dried blood that matted the hairs on the side of the man's head.

Jethro got to his feet and faced Jenkins. 'Come on, let's hear the truth of it.' His voice was harsh.

The tiny ranter's red-rimmed eyes, focused on the candle flame, betrayed signs of insanity.

'It doon't consarn thee, who or what this cove is,' he answered.

Turpin Wright took a long breath. 'I reckon young Jethro's right to ask, Hellfire,' he intervened. 'That cove's a Frenchie, I can recognize the uniform. Now me and Jethro got troubles enough wi'out adding Frog officers to 'um. What's he doing 'ere?'

Instead of answering, the ranter dragged Jackie Smith, whose whimpers had redoubled on seeing the chained man, across to the wall opposite the door and busied himself in padlocking the chain to another ring-bolt set there. He snapped the lock and tugged hard on the chain.

'Theer, that'll hold you, you miserable sinner,' Jenkins said with satisfaction, and only then did he answer. Still crouch-ing, he looked back over his shoulder at his two questioners and told them. 'That Frenchie is going to meet his Maker. He's only awaiting to start on the journey, so to speak. He's lucky, so he is, for I'm agivin' him the chance to make his peace wi' our Blessed Lord afore he crosses over the river o' life.'

Jethro shook his head in amazement and exasperation.

'But what in God's Name is a French soldier doing here?' he repeated.

The tiny blacksmith came to his feet in temper. 'T'se told thy mate, and now I'm telling thee,' he shouted. 'I doon't hold wi' taking the Lord's Name in vain. If thee keeps on adoin' it, then thee and me am agoin' to fall out.'

'All right, George, all right,' Turpin Wright interposed impatiently. 'Never mind that now, just gi' us the answer.'

The ranter looked from one set face to the other, then suddenly relaxed and smiled easily. The tremors of madness disappeared from his eyes and he spoke in his normal tone.

'Well, it's easy explained, friends. Theer's some Frenchmen living here in Bishops Castle and at Montgomery. They'm officers who've bin made prisoners-o'-war and then paroled. Some on 'um got a fair bit o' rhino wi' 'um as well.' He paused and winked. 'A man's got to live, friends. I helps them all I can, and they pays well.'

'And him?' Jethro pointed to the sick man. 'Are you helping him also?'

The ranter shook his head in lugubrious sorrow.

'Ahr, that's a tragedy. The poor young man come to see me not three days since, and begged me to 'elp him escape back to France. Well, I told him that I couldn't do that, becos' I'm an Englishman and loyal to my King. I told him that by breaking his parole he was breaking his solemn given oath, and that was a mortal sin and terrible in the sight of the Lord our God. He went off his 'ead, so he did, tried to stab me wi' a pitchfork. I had to tap him on the head and chain him up for his own safety.' He smiled sadly. 'The poor boy's 'ad a brainstorm, he's gone dog mad. That's why he's still 'ere. If I was to let him go free, they'd send him to Bedlam, or worse still, the hulks. Not only that, but the traps 'ud be down on me like the wolves of Judaea, becos' they'd say I was helping a prisoner ... No, I prayed to the Lord most Merciful for guidance and He told me in one of my periods o' meditation that I should keep this poor sinner here, and care for him until he's recovered his senses.'

'You're a bloody madman, you damned liar!' Jethro's barely held temper burst out at this rigmarole, but before he could continue Turpin Wright grabbed him from behind and hustled him into the yard.

'Be you wanting to put the ropes round our necks, cully?'

The older man's vehement question was purely rhetorical. 'Becos' if that's what you wants, you'm going the right way to do it. It's no concern of ours what that bloody maniac in theer is doing wi' bloody Frenchies. We need his help for the next few days and if you keeps on like this we'll not get it.'

'But,' Jethro began. Wright's big calloused hand clamped over his mouth.

'Lissen, you young fool,' the convict whispered. 'I'm thinking the same as you. That the bugger is promising these Frogs he'll help 'um get away, then cheatin' 'um of their rhino. He arn't the only one in this country who's doing it, not be a long chalk he arn't ... But it's no concern of ours! If we'm not bloody careful we'll be feeling a rope round our own throats. So just keep your mouth shut, and your thoughts to yourself ... You'se got a lot to learn about life, my young cock, and you'd better learn it quick.' He pulled his hand from Jethro's mouth. 'Now?' he asked. 'Has you understood me?'

Jethro nodded and kept silent, but inwardly promised himself that he would do something to aid the sick, helpless Frenchman.

Turpin Wright regarded the young man's face narrowly, then nodded. 'Good! I see you'se got the makings of a flash cove. Cummon, we'll make our peace wi' that bleedin' loony ... Hark to him!'

From inside the hovel they heard Jenkins lecturing Jackie Smith.

''Ull you never see the Light o' the Saviour, Smith? 'Ull you allus be one o' the Gadarene swine? Th'art blind man! Blind and cursed! Does not the psalmist say, "The Heavens declare the Glory of God, and the Firmament sheweth His handiwork."?'

'God rot me!' Wright cursed. 'I reckon that bleeder 'ull drive us as mad as he is afore we gets out o' this place.'

Together they re-entered the hovel.

CHAPTER SIX

Captain Henry Chanteur of his Imperial Majesty's Third Chasseurs à Cheval stood outside his quarters in the half-timbered Porch House and glanced up at the clock on the town hall of Bishops Castle. The ornate hands pointed to the hour of ten. The young Frenchman stroked his long mustachios with his slender fingers and then in the same motion smoothed his hatless blond hair and the side-whiskers that stretched to an inch below his ears. Ruefully he glanced down at his uniform. The dark green jacket and pantaloons with their red piping and cuffs were stained and shabby and the silver shoulder epaulets blackened with tarnish, while his half-boots had cracked across both top leathers.

'Ah well!' he sighed resignedly. 'This isn't Paris, after all.'

He began to hum a gay tune and sauntered down the long high street towards the church of St John Baptist which, surrounded by low stone walls, squatted in the middle of lichen-covered gravestones, its grey walls made mellow by the unseasonably warm sunlight.

The few townspeople about their business in the street paid no attention to the tall enemy soldier passing by. French officers on parole had been billeted in the Porch House and other buildings in the town for some years and had become a commonplace to the phlegmatic inhabitants. Chanteur had been a prisoner-of-war for three years and in a way that was inexplicable to himself had found a certain happy contentment with his lot. His lips twitched in amusement, the reasons for some measure of his contentment were not entirely obscure. The local girls were fascinated by the romantic, dashing foreigners suddenly dropped into the dull tenor of their lives; and in spite of the resentment of the rustic beaux of the district, many liaisons and loving attachments had been formed, even some marriages made. Although in his twenty-sixth year, Henri Chanteur had felt no desire to enter into any permanent bond, until some months previously he had encountered the woman he was now on his way to meet.

He reached the churchyard that faced the bottom of the high street and turned left, taking the road towards the south-lying village of Clun. She was waiting for him a mile out of the town, standing by the white post which marked the limits of the parolees' freedom of movement. As he approached she came to meet him, her tall figure with its full hips and breasts moving gracefully.

They stopped a pace distant from each other, and Henri Chanteur felt his breathing begin to quicken. She wore a wide-brimmed straw hat tilted forward over her green eyes, its sides pulled down slightly by the broad ribbon that crossed its low crown and was tied in a bow under her faintly cleft chin. Her glossy, chestnut-hued ringlets were brushed back from her handsome face, and the soft skin of her neck was touched by the tints of the past summer's sun. As were the top halves of her proud breasts, displayed to his gaze by the long-sleeved, low-cut blue dress. A pale blue woollen shawl had slipped from her shoulders as she walked and now she pulled it back around her upper body.

'Sarah, you hide much of your beauty doing that,' Chanteur smiled at her. His English was nearly perfect, only the slightest intonation betraying his French origin.

She returned his smile. 'There's nothing there that you haven't seen too much of already,' she told him frankly.

'Come!' He held out his hand. She clasped it and they left the road and made their way across the fields to an old barn half-hidden by the outer fringes of the woodlands. When she entered its shadowed interior, Sarah Jenkins shivered. 'It's cold here,' she said.

The Frenchman folded her into his arms and pressed his lips to her soft throat. 'We shall soon be warm,' he whispered, and drew her farther inside to where the piled straw promised a comforting bed.

Five miles to the south of the barn, Constable Thomas Marston's horse cast a shoe as he and his companions were riding out of Clun village to begin the journey back to Bishops Castle.

'Goddam and blast it!' he cursed. 'Hold hard, gentlemen.

I've suffered a slight mishap.' Grunting heavily, he dismounted.

William Seymour held up his hand and the three dragoons behind him halted. Seymour used his knees to turn his horse and went back the twenty yards to where the fat man was puffing and blowing his distress.

'I must offer my profound apologies, Captain,' the crier began.

Seymour bit back the scathing rebuke that rose to his lips and merely nodded curtly.

'Corporal Ryder!' he shouted. The man rode up to him and saluted.

'Take Mister Marston's horse back to the smithy we came past, and get it attended to.'

'Very good, sir.' The corporal rode away trailing the crier's mount behind him.

Seymour ordered the two remaining troopers to dismount, then did so himself and allowed his horse to crop the thick coarse grass at the side of the roadway. Marston grunted his way to an old milestone and lowered his vast backside on to its flat top. Pulling a large spotted handkerchief from a pocket let into his many-caped overcoat, he took off his bicorn hat and mopped his sweaty, sparse-haired scalp.

'My solemn oath!' he puffed. 'But it's uncommon warm for this time o' the year, sir.'

The dragoon captain regarded him with distaste.

'Is it?' he said coldly, and began to walk away from his companions.

Ahead of him was the high, abrupt slope of Colstey Hill. Seymour gazed up at it and thought what a strong defensive position it would make. Then, unbidden, another train of thought thrust itself into his mind. The disappearance of Jackie Smith. Behind the mask of haughty indifference he showed to the world, William Seymour was desperately worried.

He and his party had left the cavalry camp at Ludlow in the early hours of the morning when Major Hickey was asleep. Without bothering to obtain the consent of his superior officer, Seymour had ordered the release of the convict into his own custody. Now the man had gone, only God knew where, and the responsibility for his escape lay squarely upon the shoulders of the captain.

'When I catch him, I'll flay the little gaol-rat alive,' Seymour promised himself, then thought bitterly, 'That's if I ever do catch him.'

It was because of the convict's disappearance that the party had ridden to Clun, to make inquiries and alert the constable there. Seymour started to retrace his footsteps and the cheerful glow of sunlight did nothing to dispel the gloom he felt at what was now certain to follow.

'They'll definitely court martial me after this,' he told himself. 'That damned old woman Hickey, and the blasted colonel will never allow me to send in my papers quietly. They'll insist on court martialling me as an example to others.' He tried to force the forebodings from his mind. 'But all's not lost yet ... I can still get my hands on Turpin Wright's hoard. He's got to be around this district somewhere, and must eventually show himself. When he does, I'll be waiting ... No, I'm not beaten yet!'

Thomas Marston was also a worried man. Bishops Castle was a borough, and in his joint positions as town crier and constable, he was answerable to the bailiff, the recorder, and the council of aldermen for his actions. He had failed in his duties by not proclaiming a hue and cry when he was first told that escaped convicts were believed to be in the parish; and to make matters worse, he had found out only that morning that a French officer had broken parole the previous week and had not been seen since.

'Oh God, life has become a burden,' Marston groaned miserably on his milestone.

It was part of his duties as constable to check every day that the Frenchmen were still in their billets. He was responsible through the council to the Government Transport Board and paid by them to carry out this supervision. It was a chore he had neglected frequently, preferring to spend his time drinking ale, and spirits when he could afford them, in the bar parlours of the Three Tuns or the Boar's Head, or with the rich farmers in the Castle Hotel. Marston's future looked bleak. At the very least the bailiff and council would strip him of his prestigious and lucrative offices when they discovered his neglect of duty and what amounted to acceptance of bribes from Seymour. At worst he might be sent to prison himself.

Marston was thankful when the corporal returned with the freshly shod horse and he could find release from his fears in the effort of remounting. In sullen silence the party continued their journey.

'Now! Now! Now! Ohhh God, now!!' The woman's naked hips arched in ecstasy and her fingernails dug deep into the lithe muscled back of the man thrusting into her body. They reached a climax together, moaning in exquisite pleasure, and then were suddenly still. Their only movements the rise and fall of ribs under which the lungs strained to draw air.

After long moments, Henri levered himself back and knelt between Sarah's sprawled thighs. He spent minutes gazing at the beauty of her body, collapsed in satiation beneath him, then bent his head and with his mouth covered each erect nipple in turn, biting delicately at their brown hardness. Afterwards with his lips he nuzzled the firm roundness of belly and thighs, tasting the salt sheen of perspiration and breathing in the rich, powerful scents of a woman who had enjoyed total fulfilment. He smiled and kissed her sun-tinted throat and cheeks and the red moistness of her mouth.

'Je t'adore,' he murmured. 'I adore you.'

She lay passively accepting his homage to her body, then in one swift movement she had slipped from under him and was standing upright, cupping her jutting breasts in her hands and squeezing them to ease their sweet ache. Henri stood and tried to take her in his arms again, but she pushed him away.

'No! It's finished now,' she told him.

'Very well, *ma petite,*' he smiled fondly. 'We will rest for a while and talk of our future.'

'Our future?' she echoed his words, her face mirroring her surprise.

Henri became solemn. *'Mais bien sûr,* our future. I want us to marry.'

Sarah's lips opened, showing the gleam of white teeth behind their love-swollen redness.

'Did you say marry?' she asked incredulously.

He threw back his head and laughed in delight, then came to her and took both her hands in his.

'That shocks you, does it, *ma petite fleur?*' he asked tenderly. 'Did you not ever hope that some day I should ask you to marry with me?'

She stared at him and her face wore an ambiguous expression. Slowly shaking her head, her voice devoid of inflection, she answered. 'In all truth, Henry, no. I never did hope that one day you'd ask me to marry you and be your wife.'

He lifted her hands to his lips and rained kisses upon her fingers.

59

'Then-you-may-cease-to-worry-about-it,' he told her, spacing each word with a kiss. 'We shall marry as quickly as possible. My mind is made up.'

'Oh no!' she said emphatically. 'We shall not wed as soon as possible ... In fact, we shall not wed at all.'

It was his turn to be shocked..

'*Mais que dis-tu?*' he burst out. 'What are you saying? Why not marry?'

Sarah tugged her hands free and began to dress rapidly. Unlike most women, she did not use stays and in a very short time she was fully clothed except for her long pink cotton stockings which, with her frilled garters, she rolled up and put in her round reticule. All the while she was dressing, Henri, still naked, stood before her hurling questions at her. She pulled on her leather pumps with the wooden pattens and crammed her hat on her loosened hair. While tying the broad ribbon under her chin, she started to answer him.

'I'll tell you why I don't want to marry you, Henry. To begin with, I don't love you. Oh you're good looking enough, with your blond whiskers and brown eyes to turn any girl's head ... But I'm not in love with you.'

His jaw dropped and he held out his hands, palms facing her.

'But you let me make love to you!' he ejaculated. 'And what is more, you enjoy it very much when I do so.'

She smiled ironically. 'Well, Henry, you're a fine lover. I'm bound to enjoy it, am I not?'

He sighed heavily and his lips curved petulantly. 'I do not understand you.'

There was a touch of asperity in her voice. 'No, Henry, I know well you do not ... But I don't wish to marry anyone yet, even though he may be the world's most potent lover. Least of all do I wish to wed a foreigner,' she added.

'A foreigner?' His voice rose in exasperation. 'I am not a foreigner. I am a Frenchman. An officer of the Empereur Napoleon's army, the finest army in the world ... It is an honour for any woman to become the wife of one of the Empereur's soldiers.'

Sarah sniffed indignantly. 'Any foreign woman, maybe ...' she retorted. 'But I am English. Goodbye, Henry.'

He moved to block her leaving. 'Please, Sarah, don't leave me. Don't go,' he begged quietly; and what to Sarah had been almost farcical became suddenly very sad. His soft brown eyes had lost their initial hurt pride and were now beseeching.

She reached out and touched his cheek. 'I must go, Henry,' she said softly. 'If only to avoid trouble with my father.'

'But I love you,' he persisted quietly. 'Marry me and I will protect you from your father.'

She shook her head. 'No. I mean what I say. I've no wish to wed you, or anyone else.'

'Then when will you come to meet me again?' he asked.

'It is better that we do not meet again. Feeling as you do, it would only bring you a greater pain,' she said. 'I'm very fond of you, my dear, and I will always stand as your friend. But if we ever kiss again, it must be as a brother and a sister would kiss ... no more.'

'Why are you saying these things?' he questioned excitably. 'Why have you suddenly decided to leave me? Is it something I have done to anger you?'

With an effort she controlled her growing impatience.

'You haven't angered me ... Listen, Henry. When I made love with you, I was not a starry-eyed young maid. You're not the first lover I have taken. And you will not be the last ...' She realized that she was making him jealously angry and that with his emotions in such a turmoil she could not hope to make him understand why she was rejecting him.

Seizing the moment while he was still distracted by her words, she sprang to his side, pushing him hard enough to unbalance him. Gathering her skirts above her knees, she ran for the road. Naked as he was, he ran shouting after her.

The horsemen were in sight of the barn when the young woman ran from its tumbledown walls with the naked man in pursuit. Macarthy, the Irish trooper, sighted the pair first.

'Jasus and all His saints!' he exclaimed, and spurred his horse to draw level with his officer. 'If you plase, sor. Can I spake wit you?'

'What is it?' Seymour growled.

'It's that, sor, over there.' The trooper pointed at the fleeing girl and her nude pursuer.

Seymour laughed brutally. 'Blood and wounds! I always knew that the rustics bedded down with the haste of rabbits, but this is beyond belief.'

At that moment the Frenchman stubbed his toe and came to a standstill. Turning, he limped back to the barn.

Seymour spoke to Thomas Marston. 'This is hardly a military matter, Marston,' he sneered. 'I would think that it behoves you to take some action, does it not, since you are the constable?'

The fat man's resentment at the other's tone spilled out. 'I do not need anyone to tell me where my duty lies, Captain,' he replied huffily.

Seymour's cold eyes held enjoyment. 'Then I suggest, sir, that you arrest that fellow running around without his britches, and hold the woman for questioning so as to ascertain what has occurred.'

'I intend to do just that, sir,' the constable puffed pompously, and then flushed with mortification as he realized the trap he had fallen into. If he went after the woman the man would be able to make his escape, and vice-versa. Even as he pondered his course of action the woman was lost to his view behind a coppice.

'Damn the female!' he cursed aloud. 'I'll take the man.'

'You are valiant, sir,' Seymour sneered. 'Have you considered that he may have a weapon inside that barn?'

From the capacious pocket of his greatcoat the fat man produced a small brass-bound pistol.

'Indeed he may, sir,' he spluttered angrily. 'But if he attempts violence against my person he'll bitterly regret it, that I swear.'

Without further words, Marston left the dragoons on the road and drove his mount across the fields to the barn. Inside the building, Henri finished dressing and, downcast and despondent, went slowly from it.

'Stand fast in the King's name, or I'll shoot!'

The young Frenchman looked up in surprise at the noisily breathing fat man on his spavined horse. The pistol in the podgy hand was aimed at his chest.

'*Merde alors!* What is happening here?' he exclaimed.

Marston's sombre forebodings of earlier lifted from his mind and he felt like shouting out in joy.

'What luck!' he thought. 'What wonderful luck!' Aloud he said, 'I'm the Constable of this borough and the King's law. Did you really think you would escape me, Frenchie?'

Henri immediately understood the import of the other's words. He shook his head.

'I am not the man who broke parole. My name is Henri Chanteur. I only left my billet at ten o'clock this morning. I can prove that I slept there last night.'

Marston stared hard at the man in front of him and was reluctantly forced to accept that he looked completely different from the description of the prisoner who had escaped.

'That don't matter,' the fat man blustered, determined to do something that would overlay his earlier inefficiency. 'You've still broke your parole by trying to attack that young woman ... That's a hanging matter, that is.'

'Nonsense!' Chanteur was scathing. 'That young lady is my fiancée, we are going to be married. All that happened was a lovers' quarrel, nothing more. If necessary I will give you her name and you may ask her yourself. *Non, m'sieur*, there has been no crime committed by me. If you try to bring these charges of attack, then you will be laughed from the court-room.'

For a moment Marston felt baffled, but then the sneering tones of Seymour sounded from behind him and acted as a goad to his thoughts.

'Goddam me, if this gentleman is not speaking the truth, Marston. I have the young lady here with me, and she has told me the very same as he has told you.'

The captain of dragoons had come up unnoticed by the two men, with Sarah Jenkins riding pillion behind him.

She stared defiantly at the constable. 'It's the truth. We had a quarrel, that is why he was chasing me.'

Marston glared at her. 'Do I know you, young woman?'

'My name is Sarah Jenkins,' she retorted, unafraid. 'I'm daughter to the blacksmith.'

The constable nodded. 'Oh yes. I heard tell that his wench had come back to keep house for him ... How will he, a preacher, enjoy hearing that you've been playing the trollop wi' bloody Frog prisoners, d'you think?'

'*Ferme ta gueule* ... shut your mouth!' Henri growled and started forward.

The fat man's eyes fixed on him. 'Just one step more, Frenchie, and I'll put a ball in your heart,' he warned.

'Keep calm, Henry.' The woman's tone was hard. 'Don't you see that the fat bugger would like to shoot you. It'll save him being the booby of the townsfolk when they hear how he's been running around arresting people for meeting in barns.'

Her words gave Marston his way out. It was so simple he had completely overlooked it before. He grinned in relief.

'Yes, that's right, young woman. That's just what I'm going to arrest him for, and more than that. I'm going to get him sent to the hulks for this day's work.'

'Don't talk silly, you fat ...' Sarah began, then bit her tongue and looked back over her shoulder at the road.

The constable laughed in satisfaction. 'Yes,' he panted. 'This barn lies a fair bit beyond the Frenchman's Mile, don't it ... nigh on two hundred yards, I should judge.'

Sarah realized the futility of further argument. The laws governing parolees were strictly adhered to. They were allowed freedom of movement within the Frenchman's Mile, that was up to the white posts set on the main roads a mile from the town's centre. One yard past those posts and a parolee could immediately be arrested, and sent without right to further appeal back to the hulks.

Henri had the sense to keep silent. He knew that his only hope now was the possibility of perhaps being able to bribe the fat man; and if he antagonized him any further, then even the largest bribe would not suffice.

'May I have some words with the lady?' he humbly requested.

The constable was about to refuse when Seymour intervened.

'Do you think that is wise, Mister Marston?' he queried. The supercilious expression of the tall officer inflamed Marston.

'It is my decision to make, Captain,' he snapped, then said, 'Come girl, you may speak with the prisoner for a few moments, but only that.'

Sarah slid from the horse's back and went to Henri. Her green eyes were troubled. 'Oh, Henry, I'm truly sorry,' she told him. 'It is my fault that this has happened.'

'*Non cherie, non.* Do not think that,' he said tenderly. 'But listen, there is still a chance that you may be able to help me.' Whispering rapidly, he instructed her to go to his fellow parolees and tell them of his plight. If between them they could raise sufficient money, it might be possible to buy his way out of his predicament.

She nodded. 'I will do all that I can, Henry. Trust me.' She let him kiss her mouth and then walked rapidly away, unhindered by Seymour or the constable.

'Move along,' Marston ordered. 'And remember there's a ball here itching to find your heart, Frenchie.'

Chanteur made no reply, and submissively walked in front of the horsemen back to the road and through Bishops Castle, uncaring and unheeding of the excited stares and comments of people in the streets.

Sarah went first to the Porch House but the other parolees billeted there were all absent. She left a message explaining what had happened with the old woman who cleaned the house and then hurried to her home.

When she reached it, she found Jethro and Turpin sitting by the charcoal stove in the living shed. They had slept on a pile of straw in one of the outhouses, so this was the first opportunity she had had of studying her father's guests by the light of day. In spite of her preoccupation and concern over Henri Chanteur, Sarah again felt a strong reaction to Jethro ... She was charmed when, upon her entering the room, he rose and bowed slightly in reply to her greeting. Turpin Wright was not so gallant, he merely nodded, then leaned forward and spat in the glowing charcoal.

'Your father is out, he has gone to Ludlow, Mistress Jenkins,' Jethro told her, and pointed to the bubbling iron pot suspended above the fire. 'I hope that you will not be offended by our making free with your pot, but my friend and I were so hungry we began to cook a mess of oatmeal for ourselves.'

She appraised him openly, admiring the sun-darkened features and the clean black hair that fell gently across his forehead.

'No, sir, indeed I feel ashamed that you should have been forced to prepare your own food in this manner. You'll think me a poor housekeeper, I'll be bound.'

He returned her smile, and for the first time in many days felt a surge of desire. 'I think only that you make a very beautiful housekeeper,' he said.

Pleased at his compliment, she took off her hat and busied herself in fetching herbs from the herb-box in her cubicle and adding their savoury fragrance to the oatmeal.

'You'll need more than this gruel to fill your stomachs,' she told the men. 'I've some barley cakes I baked only yesterday, if you would like them.'

'They would indeed be most welcome, and thank you,' Jethro answered.

'I've a firkin of fresh ale in the brew house as well,' she smiled. 'I'll draw some to wash down your food.'

She came close to Jethro and reached across him, her hands

65

seeking the earthenware jug that hung from a peg on the wall above the young man's head. The warm, clean scent of her body filled Jethro's nostrils and he felt the pressure of her breasts against his shoulder as she leant over him. He stood and lifted the jug down for her. Momentarily their bodies touched at thighs, hips, and chest and the blood surged in his head. He ached to crush her to him and explore the firm roundness of her full breasts with his hands and lips.

Despite Sarah's recent sexual satiation with Henri Chanteur, she also felt her body responding disturbingly to Jethro's nearness. She drew in her breath sharply and noted the trembling of her fingers as the young man's strong brown hands closed about them as he gave her the jug. A pulse throbbed beneath the soft skin of her throat. She forced herself to turn away from him and left the room. Jethro watched her go and it was some moments before he could compose himself sufficiently to say casually, 'She's a pleasant-mannered wench.'

His companion chuckled and slapped one hand on Jethro's knee.

'It warn't her pleasant manners that had you alickin' your lips, cully. It was her bilboes that you was alookin' at the most.'

Jethro grinned. 'To be honest with you, Turpin, I couldn't help but remark their sweet shape,' he admitted.

Turpin roared with laughter. 'No, nor me neither, old as I be. She'd mek a rare tasty bedmate, that 'un.'

Jethro sobered suddenly. 'That's as may be. But I can't help thinking that she must be a hard one beneath her pretty skin. She must know about that Frenchman lying in that hovel. How long do we stay here, Turpin? It's a dangerous quarter for us with the soldiers searching here.'

'Till next market day,' Wright told him. 'That 'ull be Friday.'

'What do we do about Jackie Smith and the Frenchie in the meantime?' Jethro wanted to know. 'And when shall we have the money to pay Jenkins? I don't think him to be a patient man when he's owed a debt.'

Turpin pondered the questions for some time, then spat in the charcoal again and admitted, 'I'm bloody stumped as to what to do about Smith and the Frog, cully; and I'm bloody uneasy in me mind about Jenkins.'

'Why? You've money hidden away to pay him with, haven't you?' Jethro asked.

'No, not money, matey ... plate! Silver plate, a bloody great pile on it. But we needs a buyer. That's why we 'as to stay here until Friday. The mountain Welsh comes up to the market then wi' ponies and cattle to sell. They camps close to 'ere in a meadow called Welshman's Leasow. It's among them bloody savages I'll find a buyer. They'se allus got rhino about 'um for stolen goods.'

'Cannot you just sell it to Jenkins?' Jethro questioned. 'I'll swear he's got enough money to pay the price.'

His friend shook his head emphatically. 'God rot my balls, no!' He almost shouted the words. 'That bleedin' madman can't be trusted as far as you could throw him. Why d'you reckon he's helpin' us now?'

'I thought he was an old friend of yours,' Jethro stated.

Turpin laughed bitterly. 'Friend? Him? That loony's a friend to no man, not even 'isself. Why, if he thought he could get a reward, he'd peach on hisself, so he would. I'll tell you why he's helpin' us, shall I, it's becos' he's hoping that he'll be able to trick us into leading him to the silver, then he'll do for the pair on us if he can, and cop for the lot.'

'Where is it hidden? This silver plate?' The young man's curiosity was by now overpowering.

'It's right under these buggers' noses,' Turpin said glee-fully, 'it's down in the graveyard theer. Buried in the old squire's grave along wi' him and his missus.' He crowed his delight. 'And so it should be, a part on it belonged to 'im in the first place.'

The rogue's twinkling eyes and irrepressible high spirits overcame Jethro's initial distaste at such a hiding-place and he too began to laugh.

Their laughter would have been stilled had they seen Sarah Jenkins standing just outside the shed door with the full jug in her hand. She had been on the point of re-entering the room when Turpin Wright's last words, uttered loud in his excitement, had carried clearly to her sharp ears.

'Now I wonder what it is that's buried in the old squire's grave,' she puzzled, and a tiny voice began to whisper in her mind, 'perhaps it's something that could save Henry from the hulks, and get me away from my father with sufficient means to live like a lady ... live like a lady.'

CHAPTER SEVEN

Cling cling cling ... cling cling cling ... cling cling cling cling cling ... clingggg ... As the last echoes of the handbell died the stentorian shouts of Thomas Marston, resplendent in his full regalia of black three-cornered hat and silver-laced green coat, carried through the cobbled streets and bounced off the jumbled walls and crooked roofs of the town.

'Oyezzzzz, oyezzzzz, oyezzzz ... by order of the high bailiff of this borough ... Let it be known that a French prisoner-of-war, by name Marcel de Lengues, has broken his parole. A reward will be paid by the council of aldermen of this borough for his capture. He is of height, five and a half feet ... of bulk, thin ... of hair, black ... of mustachios, black ... of dress, a blue coat with red epaulets and facings, white breeches and riding boots, in the manner of the French heavy cavalry. Any citizen who sees this man must by the law of this realm raise the hue and cry ... This proclamation is given in the name of His Most Gracious Majesty, King George the Third ... upon this day of the tenth of November, eighteen hundred and twelve ... God save the King!'

Marston sucked in breath and jangled the bell, then began once more. 'Oyezzzz, oyezzzzz, oyezzzz ... by order of the high bailiff ...'

Doors and windows opened and people came running from shops and houses to gather about the crier. It was two days since Marston had arrested Henri Chanteur but that action had not saved him from the wrath of the high bailiff and council of aldermen. He had been summoned before a full meeting of the council and warned that any further instance of neglect of his duties would mean his dismissal both as town crier and as constable. The council had ordered him to raise the hue and cry for the Frenchman, but fortunately they had not yet found out that Turpin Wright and his unknown helper were reputed to be in the neighbourhood. His own fears of dismissal and a combination of bribes and threats from Captain Seymour had ensured that Marston did not inform the council himself about the fugitives.

George Jenkins, returning from a two-day visit to Ludlow, heard the bell and stood to listen to the proclamation. Behind his whiskers his lips smiled happily. Waiting until the crier had finished his third and final call and was waddling down the street, Jenkins fell into step with him.

'I bid you good afternoon, Marster Marston.'

The fat man grunted a reply.

'About that runaway Frog,' Jenkins went on, determinedly pleasant. 'What amount 'ud the reward be?'

'Twenty-five guineas,' the crier told him sullenly.

'And what if the man was dead?' Jenkins persisted.

The crier grunted a halt, and his small eyes in the vast red fatness of his sweating face, squinted suspiciously at the tiny blacksmith.

'Does you know summat about him, George Jenkins?' he wheezed.

The ranter held up both his delicately formed hands in mock horror.

'My word, Marster Marston! What ever possesses thee to think that I knows anythin' about Frenchies?'

'You ought to,' the crier burst out. 'That wench o' yours was playing the trollop wi' one of them in Ratcliffe's barn not two days since. I've got the bugger locked up back there, waiting for the Transport Board to get him away to the hulks down south.'

'What?' George Jenkins snarled. 'Be you trying to make sport o' me?'

He grabbed the other man's podgy wrist in one of his small hands and squeezed until the constable cried out in pain. The fat man's heart pounded in fright.

'No, Master Jenkins, I'm speaking naught but the truth ... Look, come wi' me now, I'll show you the Frenchie she was with.'

He led the way back up the hill to the minute two-celled gaol which was situated beneath the clock tower of the town hall. Going to the side of the hall, Marston unlocked the heavy nail-studded door and went inside, closely followed by the ranter. The first cell was windowless, the only light coming from the open street door.

'I usually keeps the debtors and women in here,' the Constable explained, and fumbled with his key at the lock of the second cell door. This was smaller, a low, grateless, furniture-less hole with two round barred windows facing down the High Street.

When Marston pushed the door open, Henri Chanteur was leaning against one of the windows, staring out between the bars.

'Hey Frenchie! There's a gentleman here wishes to speak wi' you.'

Henri swung to face them. Two days of worry and two sleepless, shivering nights spent lying on the sanded floor with only a ragged blanket for a bed, had already begun to take their toll, and he was haggard and drawn.

'Well M'sieur, how can I be of service?' he asked politely. George Jenkins strutted up to him and growled harshly.

'Does you know a woman by name of Sarah Jenkins?'

'But of course.' Chanteur felt sudden anxiety. 'Why? Has anything happened to her?'

The tiny ranter shook his head. 'Not yet,' he said grimly. 'Tell me, what's the wench to thee?'

Chanteur hesitated, then told him. 'I love her, and wish to marry her.'

Jenkins' red-rimmed eyes blinked furiously and grew murderous. Without another word, he turned and pushed past the constable and went out of the cell. Marston made haste to lock up and go after him. He found his man waiting in the street.

'Well, George Jenkins?' The constable's voice demon-strated his smug sense of vindication. 'Does you believe me now?'

'Aye, that I does, Marster Marston,' Jenkins replied, seem-ing deep in thought. 'But I'll tell you this,' he continued, almost absently. 'That Jezebel shall bitterly repent the day she played the harlot.'

The constable looked at him doubtfully. 'I must speak fair, George Jenkins. I'm not going to say that your wench was ever rogered by that Froggie in there,' he said hastily, trying to mollify the man, in whose eyes he read an instinct to murder. With all his faults, Marston was not a vicious man, and had no wish to be the cause of Sarah Jenkins being ill-treated by her father. In fact he was already regretting the outburst of bad temper that had caused him to taunt the blacksmith with his daughter's behaviour.

70

'Thee still arn't told me whether the twenty-five guineas is to be paid if the other Frenchie is found lying dead somewheer?' the ranter surprisingly asked at a tangent.

Marston seized the chance to change the subject.

'I should recommend to the council that it should be, Master Jenkins.' His tone was placatory. 'Especially if the man who was to find the body, was such a one as yourself ... I mean of good standing and repute in the town.'

The blacksmith nodded curtly. 'I bid thee good day.' He swung on his heel and strutted away, leaving the other staring after him.

'Goddam me! But you'm a nasty little bugger, Jenkins,' Marston muttered. 'I feel sorry for that poor wench of yours ... I really does ...'

'And I say that we break the door down.' Jethro was vehement. 'It's two days since Jenkins left, and I'll not stand by any longer while that Frenchman dies like a dog in there.'

The argument had raged for hours between Turpin Wright and Jethro. The older man's answer was equally vehement.

'And I say that the door stays locked. You knows as well as I does that theer's enough water and bread in theer to last for a week. I put it in meself.'

'It's not bread and water the man needs, it's a doctor!' Jethro shouted. He jumped to his feet and stormed out of the room and across to the forge.

Turpin followed him. 'Now wait, Jethro boy. Wait for another hour or so. If Hellfire arn't back by then, I'll help you break the door down meself. Theer! Is that fair enough for you?'

Jethro ignored him. He picked up a sledgehammer from the anvil and went out of the forge. At the nail-studded door of the hovel, Turpin Wright grabbed the younger man by the shoulders and wrenched him around so that they stood face to face.

'Doon't you understand, you bloody fool?' Wright shouted. 'If he comes back and finds that door battered in, he'll shop us to the traps in double quick time.'

'That's a chance I'll take,' Jethro told him angrily. 'Better that, than be a murderer.'

'It arn't us who'll have killed the Frog,' Wright answered.

'Indirectly we will have.' Jethro pulled free of the restrain-

71

ing hands and lifted the hammer.

'Doon't do it, cully,' the older man almost begged him. 'You'll have us both swinging from a gibbet.'

'I should have done it two days since,' Jethro retorted. 'I pray to God that I've not left it too late as it is.'

He lifted the hammer and sent the great iron head smashing against the barred door. The sound of the blow brought Sarah Jenkins hurrying from the brewhouse. With wide eyes she gasped, 'What's happening? What are you doing.'

'Me mate's gone bleedin' soft in the head, that's what's happening,' Turpin told her disconsolately.

Jethro ignored them both and with another smash burst the hovel door opened. He threw the hammer down and ducked under the low-lintelled doorway.

Jackie Smith huddled trembling in the corner, his hands about his head. 'Doon't kill me,' he whimpered over and over. 'Doon't kill me.'

Jethro ignored him and went to the still form of the Frenchman. The thin body was cold and rigid.

'You poor bastard,' Jethro muttered aloud to the dead face staring sightlessly upwards. 'And I helped to kill you, Goddam me for a coward!'

A faint scream came from the doorway. Sarah Jenkins stood there, horrified shock in her eyes and her hands at her mouth.

'Don't make such a show of your grief,' Jethro told her harshly. 'You would have done better to make that murdering dog you call father, fetch a doctor to this man.'

She shook her head. 'I knew naught of this, I swear I didn't, Master Stanton ... On my dear mother's grave, I swear it.'

Jethro went to the girl and for some moments studied her face. With a shock he realized that she was telling the truth.

'Then I have wronged you, Mistress Sarah,' he said quietly. 'And I am sorry for it.'

'Is that why you have been so cold and distant towards me?' she asked. 'Because you thought that I knew of this man being here?'

He nodded.

'Oh no, Master Stanton.' The tremble in her voice caused by the shock lessened, and the tone grew firm and even. 'I knew that that man there,' she pointed at Jackie Smith, 'was being held prisoner here, but I knew nothing of this poor creature. I suspected that my father had something, or some-

72

one hidden here even before you came. But when I saw the three of you in the forge that night, I assumed that it had been one of you in here all along.'

'Why did you not tax your father with your suspicions?' Jethro wanted to know.

She smiled bitterly. 'George Jenkins is not a man who takes kindly to questions, least of all from a woman ... in truth, Master Stanton, I meant to have it out with him when I first heard someone in this room, but when the opportunity came, I was afraid to,' she finished simply.

'And you had good cause to be afraid, you harlot of Gomorrah!' George Jenkins had come into the yard unseen by either of the men or the girl. His small bloodshot eyes were rabid as he inspected the smashed door and then entered the hovel to confront Jethro.

'By whose permission did thee enter here?' His huge voice boomed in violent anger from his tiny frame.

Jethro pointed to the dead Frenchman. 'Look there, Jenkins! You murdered that poor devil as surely as if you had stabbed him in the heart,' he accused.

The ranter made no reply, his breath hissed between his teeth and he went out into the yard.

'Turpin, bring me that sledge that's out there, will you,' Jethro called.

'What dost thee intend to do wi' that?' George Jenkins demanded furiously.

'I intend to release Smith,' Jethro answered, bending over the chained convict and feeling for the staples that held the fetters to the wall. He heard the ranter say threateningly:

'Doon't thee put hand to that sledge, Turpin Wright. Or it'll goo hard wi' thee.'

Turpin's reply was contemptuous ... 'Bollocks!'

There came a dull, meaty thud and Sarah screamed aloud, 'No father! No!'

Jethro hurled himself out of the hovel and into the yard. Turpin Wright was lying face downwards in the mud, and even as Jethro burst into the open he saw the ranter's iron-shod boot drive savagely into the prostrate man's genitals. Jenkins saw Jethro and in the same instant he stooped to snatch up the sledgehammer from Turpin's open hands.

'I'll kill you, you bastard!' he bellowed and came forward in a rush whirling the sledgehammer at Jethro's head.

The younger man jumped to avoid the blow and tripped,

sprawling in the filth.

Sarah's eyes went wide with horror, and a terrible fear for Jethro flooded her senses. 'No!' she screamed. 'No! No! No!'

She ran and grabbed her father's arm trying to wrest the hammer from him. He threw her brutally away as if she were weightless, and swung to catch Jethro lying helpless. But the second's interruption had been sufficient and Jethro had come catlike to his feet. Jenkins came in again and the hammer head swung once more in an effort to crush Jethro's skull. This time Jethro fought with his brain as well as his body. He timed the swing and ducked under it, then smashed his right fist into the blacksmith's mouth, fetching the blood spurting out over the black whiskers. The force of the blow jolted the smaller man back on his heels and Jethro's left and right hands flashed in a blur of movement to batter the senses from the ranter. Jenkins' eyes rolled up in his head and the hammer fell from his nerveless hands as he dropped stunned to the ground.

Panting with shock and exertion, Jethro stepped forward and picked up the tool.

'Oh please Jethro,' Sarah Jenkins pleaded. 'Don't kill him.'

'I don't intend to,' he snapped curtly, and re-entering the hovel he battered at the staple holding Jackie Smith's chains until it snapped. He lifted the whimpering convict and carried him bodily outside.

'Now get you gone, Smith,' Jethro pushed him roughly. 'I've no wish to set my sight on scum like you ever again, but I'll not leave you to die here, worthless hound though you may be.'

The whimpering convict scurried away, crouching low to the ground like a terrified animal.

'What will you do now Master Stanton?' Sarah's green eyes were dark with apprehension. 'My father will want revenge for what you have done to him, and I fear that the evil in him will stop at nothing to obtain it.'

Jethro stared at her beauty and his anger left him as he realized that but for her intervention, when he had been helpless on the ground, he would have been a dead man by now.

'I'll be on my own way, mistress,' he told her quietly. 'I've no wish to remain here and cause you any further trouble with your father.'

Turpin Wright clambered to his feet and came towards the

74

couple, his breath wheezing through his open mouth and his face grey and clammy.

'Rot my balls, Jethro! But you'm a bloody wildcat in a fight aren't you?'

Jethro didn't answer him, instead he went to Sarah Jenkins. 'I'm sorry that I doubted you over the Frenchman, and that I was forced to serve your father so,' he told her. 'I'd no wish to harm anyone of your blood.'

She smiled wanly at him. 'Don't worry about that, Master Stanton, for truth to tell, I was more concerned for your safety than his. I feared that he would kill you.'

He returned her smile and touched her cheek gently. She lifted her hand to cover his fingers and he felt a wave of tenderness for her well up in his heart.

Turpin's voice broke the spell that held them both. 'Come on, cully, we'll ha' to decide what to do.'

Jethro sighed and turned from Sarah to face his friend.

'Aye, you're right,' he said, and tried to clean some of the mud from his clothes with his fingers, but was forced to abandon the task as hopeless. 'We had best get straight away, Turpin,' he said, 'before Jackie Smith brings the dragoons on our necks.'

The older man shook his head. 'He'll not goo wi'in a mile on 'um. He'll be too scared for his own neck now.' He paused and regarded both their soiled rigs doubtfully. 'But for sure we can't goo like this, Jethro. They 'ull lift us both for thievin' beggars afore we'se gone a mile.'

'I can help you.' Sarah Jenkins touched Jethro's arm. 'My father's got a chest full of clothes in the house. Oh don't worry,' she hastened to add. 'They're not his though, God alone knows where he got them from. They're all too big for him by yards.'

The two men exchanged looks and each could clearly read the other's thoughts.

'Ahr!' Turpin nodded sagely. 'I see you thinks the same as me, cully. They'll be dead men's clothes, I'll warrant.' He cleared his throat noisily and spat on to the ground. 'No matter! It'll not be the first time I've worn a dead 'un's britches.'

With no more hesitation they followed the young woman into the house.

While they had been talking, George Jenkins' senses had returned. Too cunning to move, he had lain feigning uncon-

75

sciousness, though when he had heard Sarah's offer of help he had been forced to bite his smashed lips to stop himself bawling out in fury.

'I'll pay thee out for this, you hell-damned strumpet!' he raged silently. 'For this and for being a Frenchie's harlot ... I'll pay thee out till thee begs for mercy. Whore! Dirty whore!' He waited until the three went into the house and he heard the door slam shut behind them, then slipped out into the lane, using a scrap of rag to try and staunch his bleeding mouth.

The clothes were musty and those at the bottom of the chest had become mildewed. The two men put on one side those garments that would fit them, while Sarah stretched a rope across the room and hung the remainder over it.

'I'll tell father that I opened the chest to air the clothes,' she told them, as they stripped off their muddied breeches and coats and put on those they had sorted out. When dressed, they made a sombre pair: black breeches, black coats worn over dark plain shirts and with dull stockings on their legs.

'Rot my balls!' Turpin Wright chuckled. 'They'll take us for Methodys from the looks on us.'

Jethro turned to Sarah. 'We owe you our gratitude, Mistress Sarah, but I'm not happy about leaving you here alone with your father.'

She smiled, pleased at his concern. 'Don't worry about me, Master Jethro,' she told him. 'I'm well able to look after myself.'

The young man frowned. 'I think in all truth that your father is a madman ... There's no telling what he may do. Why not come with us? We could protect you until you found a place where you could be safe from him.'

'I would like to come with you, Jethro, but I cannot,' she said soberly. 'There is an old friend of mine who, because of me, is in grave trouble. I must stay here and help if I can. But I thank you for your offer, and I shall pray for your well-being.'

Moved by sudden impulse Jethro took her hand and lifted it to his lips. 'I wish that we might have met under different circumstances, Sarah,' he murmured, 'for I feel that there could have been a good regard between us; and perhaps even more than that.'

Her eyes were soft. 'I also feel this, Jethro.'

He smiled. 'God willing, there may yet be a day on which

we will meet again, and I hope that it may not be long in coming. Goodbye, and thank you for all your kindness.'

With a nod to Turpin Wright to follow, Jethro went from the room. As the door closed behind the two men and the sound of their footsteps died away, Sarah felt an overwhelming desire to run after them and go with them on their journey.

'You know well that you cannot go,' she reproved herself angrily. 'You owe it to Henry to stay here and try and help him.'

She busied herself in cleaning the room and drove her wayward imaginings from her mind.

CHAPTER EIGHT

'Hark how the drums beat out agennn,
For all true soldier gentlemennn,
The King commands and we'll obeyyyy
Over the hills and far awayyyyyyy ...'

Trooper Macarthy's tuneful tenor carried across the crowded taproom of the Black Lion tavern, and the veins swelled and throbbed in his throat and forehead as he strained to draw out the last note.

The room was packed with white-smocked countrymen, wild-looking drovers and tail-coated yeomen farmers, and thick with the blue fug of the tobacco fumes that puffed out from the long churchwarden pipes that most of the men were smoking. The rattle of brass dominoes cracked down hard on the scarred dark-wood tables mingled with the hubbub of talk, argument, and laughter; and the squeals of the serving wenches being pinched on rounded buttocks and plump thighs as they moved through the thronged room were counter-balanced by the sharp reports of the slaps they dealt the offending pinchers.

Corporal Ryder raised his pewter mug and hammered its dented base upon the table.

'That's good, Paddy! That's a rare good tune, that is,' he applauded.

At the next table a heavy-bodied yeoman farmer drew the sleeve of his brown tail-coat across his ale-wet lips and, winking at his companions, shouted, 'Well, I rackons it to be a damned poor thing, meself!'

The room stilled and hushed suddenly and all eyes switched to the corner where the farmer's and soldiers' tables adjoined.

Corporal Ryder's hard, hatchetlike face became wary. 'Does you know a better song then, my fine bucko?' he questioned, his voice still croaking from his injured throat.

'Ahr, that I does, lobster.' The yeoman got ponderously to his feet and with one thick forefinger he tilted his low-crowned beaver hat back from his sweating brows. 'It 'ud be a strange thing if I couldn't sing a better 'un than that.' Without waiting for an answer, he began to bellow out in a deep bass the words of a song.

'Come all you sweet charmers, come gi' me your choice ...
For there's nothin' can compare wi' a ploughboy's voice.
For to hear the little ploughhhhboy sweetly singnnng ...
Makes the hills and the valleys around us to rinnnggg.'

A shout of acclamation burst from the countrymen and as the farmer raised his hands and beckoned, they came roaring in to join him.

'For it's up you little ploughboy, get up i' the morn,
    Move alooonnngg, jump alooonnngg.
Here drives the ploughboy wi' spark and beauty bearing.
    Good Luck! We will cheer him as he moves along
    For we are the laaaddss who can keep along the plough
    For we are the laaaadddsss who can drive along the plough
    ...'

The chorus finished to a tumult of cheers and laughter. Grinning triumphantly, the farmer slammed his great calloused hands on the table.

'Theer lobster! That's summat loike a song that is! Bain't that true lads?' He addressed the crowd who bellowed good-natured agreement. 'That's a song for true Englishmen. Them that stands four-square and bows to no one ...' The farmer's tone became aggressive. 'It bain't a bloody tune for bloody slaves loike you lobsters be.'

'What d'you mean by calling us slaves?' Ryder asked truculently.

'Just what I says, surry,' his tormentor shouted. 'Damn thee for bein' poor pitiful scoundrels what sells yourselves for a shillin' a day to goo and be shot at like Shrovetide cocks at the bidding o' any stuffed popinjay wi' a big feather in his cap and a bit o' bloody gold on 'is shoulder. Thee hanna got a spark o' spirit in your body, or thee 'uddent goo and do it.'

Ryder glanced about him. The rest of the men in the room had lost their original good temper, and the happy tipsiness of a few moments before had changed to a threatening sullenness.

'Ahr, gaffer, you'm roight theer.' A ruddy-faced ploughman

got up from his seat in the inglenook and came across to stand over the seated soldiers. 'You bloody lobsters does whatsoever that pack o' thieves in London they calls a parleyament tells you to do ... Even if it means shootin' your guns at poor starvin' labouring men.'

A growl of assent came from a dozen throats. Ryder measured the standing man's well-fleshed body with his eyes and sneered contemptuously.

'You doon't look as if you'se bin missing any meals of late.'

The farmer jumped to his feet and came to stand by the ploughman.

'That's neither here nor there ... Theer's a sight o' poor buggers as is starvin' to keep the loikes o' thee swilling drink, when you should be fighting the French across the seas. That's what you'm paid for ... I'd loike to know what you buggers am adoin' in this town, anyway? Thou'rt bin here for nigh on a week now ... What for? To spy on us, in case we talks o' rebellion?' His face flushed darkly and his great hands clenched into fists. 'Does you rackon we'em a lot of barmy yokels, lobster? That we dinna know what's agooin' on in this country? ... Men being taken and put in gaol, hung even some on 'um, because they dares to speak out agen bad rulers and empty bellies ...'

'Ahr, that's it, Tom!'

'You tell um, Tom.'

'Speak out surry, we'em with you!'

'Bleedin' lobsters?'

Shouts of support for the farmer came from all sides and the rooms' atmosphere became charged with menace. The innkeeper intervened, wiping his hands nervously on his grimy apron.

'Now Tom, lad ... Now Tom,' he said placatingly. 'For the love o' God make no trouble in here, Tom. Or I'll lose me permit and be closed up.'

He turned on the soldiers, furious in his fear. 'Get out o' my house, you lobsters! Get out this minute!'

'All bloody lobsters are bloody cowards!' the big farmer shouted. 'I'll fight any o' you for a farthing ... Ahr! I'll box the bloody lot on you, one arter the other for a farthing!'

Corporal Ryder's body shook with rage. He was afraid of no man and every atom of his being clamoured to beat the big farmer before him into pulp. But, old campaigner as he was, Ryder recognized the hopelessness of his position. If he or his troopers made one aggressive movement, the whole room would be on them, swamping them in a flood of fists and boots. He jerked his head at Timpkins and Macarthy and under a constant barrage of jeers and cat-calls the three soldiers put on their shakoes, adjusted their uniforms and accoutrements and went from the tavern. Out in the street Ryder hawked, spat and cursed in futile anger.

'Come on, you two,' he growled in disgust and led the way towards the town hall.

'Hey you, soldier?' a voice called behind them.

'God rot me! I'll slit the barstards' throats!' The corporal cursed and swung round, his hand dragging at the hilt of his sabre.

George Jenkins hurried up to the dragoons, not appearing to notice their threatening manner.

'I must speak wi' thy officer right away,' he panted, his voice muffled by the rag he held to his bleeding mouth.

'What for?' Ryder demanded belligerently.

'Listen soldier, doon't delay me, or you'll be sorry.' Jenkins pulled the rag from his mouth and spat the words from his smashed lips. 'I knows thou'rt here lookin' for runaway convicts!'

'So? And if it were true, then what of it?' The corporal was poker-faced.

'Well, I'se got them for thee,' the ranter snarled. 'But you'd best look sharp about it ... They'll not be theer much longer.'

William Seymour was sitting in the Three Tuns' parlour sipping hot rum spiced with cinnamon, when Corporal Ryder brought the ranter to him.

The N.C.O. saluted with a jangle of accoutrements and barked, 'Beg pardon for disturbing you sir. But this man's got summat he wishes to tell you.'

The captain's cold eyes measured the bleeding, muddied spectacle before him and he sneered openly. 'Are you mad, corporal. What could a filthy thing like this have to tell me that could be of any importance? Kick his arse and send him on his way.'

The blacksmith's eyes glowed redly, but he beat down his rage and forced himself to say fawningly, 'Please to listen, yer honour. I've news o' them escaped convicts you'm alookin' for.'

A few tiny flecks of blood sprayed from his lips and fell on the table, one or two of the scarlet spots splashing into the

81

glass set before Seymour. But Seymour didn't notice them. His whole attention had alerted to the man's words. His manner became perceptibly more civil. He drew his breath in sharply and said, 'Sit down my man, and tell me what it is you know. If it's the truth you speak, then you'll not lose by it, that I promise.'

The ranter's insane grin flickered across his face and leaning forward he slapped the table with both hands to give urgency to his words. 'Theer's not a minute to lose, Captin, iffen you wants them hell-spawned hounds. Just come wi' me now and I'll deliver them straight into your hands.'

Seymour took the measure of the man's veracity instantly. 'Get my horse, corporal, and jump to it! Blast you, man move!'

In the lane Jethro and Turpin Wright walked side by side. It was Jethro who broke their silence. He sighed and said unhappily, 'Well friend, where do we head for?'

Turpin grinned and began to caper about, singing at the top of his voice:

> 'Oh wilt thou go wi' me, sweet Tibby Dunbar,
> Oh wilt thou go wi' me, sweet Tibby Dunbar,
> Wilt thou ride on a horse or be drawn in a cart,
> Or walk by my side, sweet Tibby Dunbar?'

Jethro scowled, then burst out laughing, and his regret at leaving Sarah Jenkins lifted from his mind. The end of the lane was in sight and Jethro pressed his companion for an answer.

'Come, Turpin, we must turn either left or right at the top of the lane there ... which is it to be?'

At the very moment he finished speaking, a dragoon crashed through the overhanging hedgerow on their right and aimed a carbine at Jethro's chest.

'Neither left nor right, bully!' a voice jeered from their left, and Corporal Ryder stood upright from a concealed ditch. He, too, aimed a carbine at Jethro. Before either of them could properly recover from the shock of ambush, there was a clatter of horses' hooves and William Seymour rode into the lane together with the constable, Thomas Marston, and the third trooper.

'Goo on, bully boy, make a run for it,' Corporal Ryder invited. 'I'd like nothing better than to let a bit o' daylight into your tripes.'

Seymour's lean cruel face was alight with pleasure. 'Well done, Ryder! Well done, Timpkins!' he congratulated the soldiers.

George Jenkins came hastening behind the horsemen.

'God be praised! You've caught the villains, God be praised!' he kept repeating.

'Why you dirty preachin' bastard,' Turpin Wright snarled, and a sharp crack on his head with a carbine barrel cut him short. He subsided into silence, but his expression boded ill for the ranter if the opportunity should ever arise.

'I'se got the Frenchie chained up in my smithy, Master Marston,' Jenkins said. 'I 'opes he's still alive, but you never know, these two murderin' devils might ha' done for him.'

'There'll be no "might" about me doin' for you!' Wright shouted, and received another crack across his head from the carbine barrel.

'You there,' Seymour leaned from his saddle and tapped Jethro's shoulder. 'What name do you bear?'

Jethro stared back defiantly at the cruel handsome face above him and made no reply.

Seymour's white teeth glistened wolfishly as he smiled.

'So! It's a dumb animal, is it? Well, animals can be trained to perform tricks and I know ways in which they can even be taught to speak.' Without warning he slashed the back of one gloved hand across Jethro's face, causing his head to rock under the force of the blow.

Jethro's face reddened with anger, but he disciplined his impulse to hit back and kept his mouth firmly closed.

The dragoon officer chuckled. 'I see it's a mettled beast!' he taunted. 'With fire in its belly ... But never fear, I've not yet encountered the fire I could not douse down.'

While Seymour had been baiting Jethro, the third trooper had fetched the other horses from their tether points behind the hedgerows and, taking ropes from the saddlebags, had trussed Turpin Wright's arms behind his back. The dragoon now did the same for Jethro, tugging hard on the ropes so they bit deep into muscles and sinews.

'I think we'll give these fine gentlemen a lodging in your gaol until we leave the town,' the captain said to Marston. He nodded in answer, then said, 'I shall go up and get the Frenchie, Captain.' He spurred his horse towards and into the smithy, only to return almost immediately.

'The bugger's dead!' he said shortly. 'I'll have to come up with a carter to fetch him, he's stiff as a board, so he can't be slung across my mount's back.'

'Dead? Did you say dead, Master Marston?' George Jenkins questioned incredulously.

'I did,' the fat man told him curtly.

The little man's red-rimmed eyes brimmed with tears. 'The poor young boy,' he intoned dolefully. 'May the Saviour who sits at the right hand of the Lord Most High have mercy on his soul. May its black sins be washed white in the Blood of the Lamb ... I'll goo and pray for his salvation right this minute.' Head bowed and hands clasped prayerfully in front of him, the ranter walked to his smithy.

'Bleedin' stinkin' hypocrite!' Turpin Wright raged, and ducked to avoid another blow.

'Mount up,' Seymour ordered, and the group moved off, Jethro and Turpin Wright each being led behind a dragoon by means of a rope lashed to the saddlehorn and noosed around their necks.

William Seymour was jubilant. It seemed that his luck had turned at last, and now alternative paths of action were opening to him. As the little procession entered the outskirts of the town, he plotted in his mind his next moves.

First he must get Wright on his own. The man was tough and full of hatred, but Seymour knew what a skilfully applied whip could do to tough men, and he cared nothing for any man's hate.

Then he would deal with the other man, the handsome one who refused to give a name to himself. Seymour smiled pleasurably. Before he was done, the man would recite his whole life's story, let alone a name. Then, once he had forced the whereabouts of the hoard from the pair ... Seymour's mind gloated on what the possession of wealth could mean. To begin with, there would be no court martial, he had re-captured the convicts after all, and money judiciously spent would ensure that he would be allowed to exchange into another regiment ... Perhaps there might be sufficient for him to purchase his own command ... A colonelcy! Colonel William Seymour ... He savoured the sound of the title, it had a fine ring to it.

So deeply engrossed was he in his daydreams, that he failed to notice the drunken man who came reeling from the front door of the Black Lion tavern.

The man's white smock flapped up about his thighs as he stumbled over the gutter and his broad-brimmed straw hat slipped forward across his eyes. In a fit of drunken temper, he snatched it off his head and threw it from him. Its wideness caught the wind and it sailed straight into the muzzle of Seymour's horse. The startled beast snorted and reared violently, pitching the unprepared officer from the saddle. Seymour's body cartwheeled through the air and thumped on to the cobblestones. He heard, rather than felt, the crack of breaking ribs, then white-hot shafts of pain lanced through his chest.

'You stupid bugger!' Without stopping to think, Corporal Ryder spurred his mount to crash into the man and send him toppling. The commotion brought the rest of the tavern's customers to the doors and windows of the building. Big Tom, the yeoman farmer, his mood already belligerent after the vast amounts of gin and porter he had poured down his throat, let his temper break.

'Stinking lobsters!' he bawled. 'You'm only fit to ride over honest men ... Well, thee shall not do it here. Come on, lads, let's teach the red-bellied pigs a lesson they'll not forget in a hurry.'

The hotheads among the drinkers bellowed their support, and the next instant they came boiling from the tavern, wielding bottles, jugs, pots, and chairs as weapons.

Thomas Marston, who was bringing up the rear of the party came to an instant decision. He felt no liking for the military, indeed at times a positive hatred for the arrogant Seymour. The men pouring from the tavern, on the other hand, were his fellow townsmen, and he must continue to live his life among them. He swung his horse and headed away from the erupting brawl, drumming his heels on the gaunt ribs beneath him to drive the broken-winded wreck faster.

A bottle shattered against the wall behind Ryder and he drew his sabre, sending the bright blade whirling through the air and causing the men coming at him to jump back in alarm. The other dragoons did the same and the narrow street became a frantic mêlée of neighing, snorting, trampling horses, shouting men, and flying bottles.

Fortunately for Jethro and his friend, there was a quick-thinking man amongst the brawlers. Seizing the moment when the dragoons were totally occupied in keeping their attackers at bay and dodging hurled missiles, he darted behind the horses with a knife and hacked through the neck ropes of the prisoners. Some more rapid slashes, and both men were free of their bonds.

'Goo on, lads,' the man urged. 'Run for it.'

They needed no second bidding and took to their heels, soon leaving the howling mob out of earshot. Half a mile from the town, the pair left the road and plunged through the hedgerows, making for the woodlands which lay to the south-west.

Back in the narrow street, the fury of the mob was slackening, particularly when the drunken man whose downfall had caused the trouble, clambered to his feet and staggered away singing to himself, completely unaware of what was happening around him. Big Tom, the sweat running in streams down his face and his wind gone from dodging the sabres of the dragoons, shouted in a voice which could plainly be heard above the tumult,

'By God, lads, but this is thirsty work. I'm as dry as Old Nick's arse!'

It caught the mob's humour and roars of laughter swept through them.

'Let's goo for some more drink, lads!' a man shouted, and scuffling and cheering, the crowd began to push back into the tavern, demanding more drink and leaving the badly shaken soldiers staring bemusedly after them.

After a pause, Corporal Ryder realized that it was all over. He sheathed his sabre and checked himself and his friends for injuries. They had been lucky, a few bruises and a bloody knee where Trooper Timpkins' horse had scraped him against the wall, were the sum total of their hurts.

It was otherwise with William Seymour. He lay motionless, his face bloody and already swelling from the trampling he had received as the crowd had stamped backwards and forwards across his body. One arm was bent at a peculiar angle and as he breathed, his rib-cage felt as if it had been crushed completely. The agony he suffered was such that he could only lie with tight-shut eyes, and struggle to stop from screaming aloud.

'What 'ull we do now, Corporal?' Timpkins' simple face was utterly perplexed. He lifted the cut end of the rope trailing away from his saddlehorn and showed it to Ryder.

'They'se got away agen!'

'I can see that, you bloody fool!' the corporal shouted at him, and pointed to the injured officer. 'We'll get him to a surgeon, he looks as if he were near dead. Then we'll goo back and rejoin the regiment.'

'Be Jase! We'll get a flogging if we go back wi' out any prisoners,' Macarthy protested.

Ryder smiled grimly. 'Not now we wun't, Paddy. Not arter I'se told you what we'em all going to tell Major Hickey and the Colonel.' He stared at Seymour's broken body, his expression a mixture of hatred and gladness. 'We'll tell 'um as how this barstard here brought the mob about our ears by acting like a bloody loony.'

'But it was you who knocked that cove over,' Macarthy said. Ryder grinned at him. 'I was actin' in defence o' my orfficer, warn't I? That's a soldier's duty, that is ... But who was it who attacked that cove fust, for no reason? And who was it who 'uddent raise the hue and cry for them pair o' buggers? And whose fault is it that we'se lost 'um agen and all bin near killed?'

As his friends got his meaning, they returned his grin. 'Shure, that's the truth of it, Corporal dear,' the Irishman laughed. 'But how about that fat ould sod who run off? D'you think he'll agree wit out story if the major should ever come to question him?'

The corporal nodded slowly. 'He'll agree all right, to save his own skin, especially if this bugger dies, and he looks as though he might ... There's one thing sure, he'll not be able to save hisself from court martial now, even if he recovers from this little battering. Told you I'd settle with the bastard, didn't I?'

'You shurely did, Corporal dear, you shurely did,' Macarthy agreed happily.

Seymour heard all that was said and cursed inwardly at the realization of his own impotence. He feigned unconsciousness while the dragoons roughly bundled him on to a crude litter fashioned from rope and carbines. He bit the inside of his mouth until it bled, to stop himself screaming out in agony and giving them the satisfaction of knowing what tortures they were inflicting on him, tortures that intensified with each slow, jarring step they took.

CHAPTER NINE

On the evening of the day of the brawl in which Seymour was hurt, a sheriff's officer came by post-chaise from Shrewsbury to escort Henri Chanteur on the first stage of his journey to the hulks at Portsmouth. A small group of his fellow prisoners-of-war came to the town gaol to wish him well, and to give him the few guineas they had been able to collect. Henri heard very little of what they said to him, he was too intent on searching for some glimpse of Sarah in the darkness of the street.

Not unkindly, the sheriff's man ushered him into the closed carriage and to the waves of his comrades, Henri's journey began. He sat numbed and unhearing and felt only a great emptiness at the thought that he would perhaps never again see the woman he loved.

Thomas Marston locked the thick door of the now empty gaol and stood in the street, absently gnawing at his finger-nails as he watched the post-chaise, drawn by its two mares in tandem, rattle away. He had had an earlier visitor in the shape of Corporal Ryder and had come to an agreement with the soldier regarding the story they would tel labout the incidents concerning Seymour, who was lying unconscious in the doctor's dispensary.

'Taking all in all, it's ended pretty well,' the constable thought. 'And I must remember to goo wi' Binns the carter, up to Jenkins' shed to fetch that dead Frenchie. I'll pop up to the Castle and tell him now. Perhaps I'll have a tot o' brandy while I'm there.'

Happy at the comforting notion, he went waddling up the short steep slope to the Castle Hotel. A slender, shawl-covered figure slipped out from the shadows to confront him.

'Pon my soul! What a shock you gave me, wench. What is it you want?'

The woman slipped the shawl from her head, revealing herself as Sarah Jenkins.

The constable frowned. 'Well, young woman? I'm not in the mood to bandy words wi' you,' he snapped, 'so stand from my way.'

'Not before you answer a question I have,' she told him boldly.

'I'll save thee the trouble of asking it,' he puffed. 'Your French friend has gone to Portsmouth. That was the post-chaise that come and fetched him to Shrewsbury to catch the wagon.'

Sarah drew in her breath sharply. 'Oh God! And he went thinking that I didn't try to help him, I'll be bound,' she thought, then recovered herself and asked. 'Is it the hulks he's gone to?'

He nodded, then, softened a little by her obvious distress, he said, 'Now don't you worry your pretty head, my wench. That Frenchie will be treated well enough. We're not a nation that tortures its prisoners-of-war. Why, they do say that the hulks can be quite pleasant places, especially in the summer wi' the sun shining and the sea airs ablowing, and all the fine ships to look at.'

Without answering, the young woman pulled the shawl back over her head and left the fat man still talking.

'Wheer's you bin?' In the flickering light of a solitary candle, George Jenkins sat at the table, an open Bible lying before him. 'Sit down theer,' he pointed to a footstool placed in the centre of the room. Sarah hesitated.

'Do as thou'rt bid, you harlot!' His voice was cold and expressionless and the glow of the candle shining into his face highlighted the glowing pinpoints of madness in his red-rimmed eyes.

Sarah shivered in sudden fear. She had come back to the smithy expecting her father's usual roaring display of tantrums. This strange control and his manner made her afraid. Silently she obeyed his command and seated herself.

'Put that shawl off,' he instructed. 'And look straight at me.'

She slipped the garment to her shoulders and steeled herself to meet his insane glare.

'Listen well, whore!' he boomed at her, and a trickle of saliva dribbled from one corner of his mouth, trailing slime across his black whiskers. 'Listen to the words of the Holy

Book.' He began to read aloud, tracing the sentences with his fingers. 'But if this thing be true and the tokens of virginity be not found for the damsel,' his voice grew excited, 'then they shall bring out the damsel to the door of her father's home, and the men of the city shall stone her with stones that she die, because she has wrought folly in Israel to play the whore in her father's house.'

Jenkins' voice thundered the words and his hands gripped the edges of the heavy brass-bound tome, kneading the leather covering as if they would tear it to pieces.

'Does thee understand that, whore?' the ranter glared down at her, hysteria in his tone. 'To play the whore in her father's house! And the Lord tells us, so shalt thou put evil from amongst you.' He slammed the book shut and rose to his feet. 'The Lord has come to me in a vision, and commanded me as to what I must do. Praise to the Lord for His infinite mercy!'

At first Sarah didn't fully understand, but as her father rounded the table she suddenly realized with a shock of horror what he intended doing.

'No!' she screamed. 'No, father! Please! Nooo!' She sprang towards the door, but before she had taken more than two steps, he was on her. His hands locked into her thick hair and he heaved her back, dragging her off balance. She twisted her body, clawing at his face with her nails and trying desperately to sink her teeth into his hands. Jenkins began to growl deep in his throat like a savage dog and he shook Sarah violently, lifting her from the ground as though she were weightless. The girl felt her wits leaving her and she shrieked in hopeless terror. The sounds reverberated through the room, going on and on and on and on and on, and the last thing she heard was that appalling shriek tearing at her senses and filling her being, until it blotted out all else around her and became a mass of blackness into which she fell.

'There now, lass, rest easy. Rest easy.' The rustic burr of Binns the carter's voice came faintly to Sarah's ears and when she opened her eyes, his seamed face smiled reassuringly down at her. She recovered her senses with a surge of fear and tried to struggle up from the bed she was lying on.

'My father? Where is he?' she asked anxiously.

The man's strong hands held her shoulders. 'Doon't you fret, lass.' Binns calmed her fear. 'He'll not harm you. Marston the constable has took him to the lock-up in the town.'

The girl blinked in puzzlement. 'But how did you come here? The last thing I remember is my father catching me by the throat.'

With her fingers, she gently explored the bruised soreness of her neck.

'Me and Fat Thomas was coming up to fetch that dead Frenchie you got here,' the carter explained. 'Well, we comes up the lane and we 'ears you ahollerin' and screamin' enough to wake the dead.' He gave a long tuneless whistle. 'I thought twas the Devil hisself had got you.'

'I think perhaps it was,' she mused, half to herself. 'For I've never seen such evil in a man's eyes before as my father had in his.'

The man sighed heavily and released her shoulders. 'The pity is, lass, there's naught the constable can do to him. Oh e's' going to lock him up for the night for causing a disturbance, but that's all 'e can do. There's no law says a man canna gi' his own daughter a beating . . .'

'What hour is it?' Sarah asked.

'Nigh on half past ten o' the clock, I should rackon,' the carter told her.

Sarah's head ached, but it was now clear and she was collecting her thoughts. 'I thank you for your help, Master Binns; and please convey my thanks to Master Marston. I don't doubt but that you saved my life by coming when you did,' she told him gratefully.

' 'Tweren't nothing, lass.' The man's simplicity was embarrassed by her gratitude. 'Soon as he 'eard us coming through the door, he let go on you.' He shook his head with reluctant admiration. 'Ahr he's an artful bugger, is old Hellfire. He said as 'ow he was just agoin' to gi' you a whipping acorse you'd bin gooing wi' that Frenchie. O' course me and Fat Thomas both rackoned that if we hadn't come when we did, then the bugger would ha' done for you. But there's no way o' proving it, is there?'

'No,' Sarah agreed. 'But he'll not get an opportunity to try again. I'll make sure of that.' She sat up and swung her legs to the floor. 'I'll not detain you further, Master Binns,' she said quietly. 'And once more I give you my heartfelt thanks. Tell me, at what hour will my father be released?'

The carter pondered the question, rubbing his hand on his bristled chin. 'Well, Fat Thomas doon't loike to rise too early from his bed, so I should rackon he'll let Hellfire out at about nine in the morn ... 'Ull you be all right now, lass?'

'I'm very well.' Sarah smiled at the man.

''Ud you loike me to fetch the doctor to have a look at you?'

'No, Master Binns, I'm truly recovered, I thank you. I shall manage very well.'

'Ahr! All right then. If you'm sure you're all right, I'll be getting on home. Me old 'ooman starts thinking I'm a laying drunk in the ditch if I arn't home about this toime.'

He left Sarah alone in the room and she listened to the rumble of his cartwheels fade to silence before she moved from her seat on the bed. She wasted no time in beginning a search of the living quarters. An hour later, Sarah was forced to admit defeat. Her father had left no money or valuables for her to find.

'That crafty old devil.'

She threw the stripped covers back on his plank bed and sat down on it to decide what to do.

'I cannot go anywhere without money,' she realized, and then the memory of Turpin Wright's words came to her. The old squire's grave! Something of value was buried in the old squire's grave!

A wave of apprehension threatened to discourage her. She would be committing a terrible sin, it was sacrilege to disturb the sleep of death. She fought to overcome her fears and scruples, and gradually a determination to do whatever was necessary to get far away from the father she now knew was a madman, steeled her mind and nerves. From her cubicle she took a canvas sack and in its capacious folds placed her toilet articles wrapped up in a spare dress. The only other things she took with her from the smithy were a shuttered lantern and a triangular-bladed, long-staved shovel.

The wind had risen high and rain fell steadily. In the churchyard of St John Baptist, the branches of the ancient yew trees creaked and rustled eerily before the buffeting of the wind, and an impenetrable darkness hid Sarah from curious eyes. There was hardly any danger of anyone seeing her though, the weather had driven any late revellers indoors and the town seemed abandoned by all living things.

Once among the graves in the churchyard, Sarah lifted the shutter of the lantern and by the lance of light it poured out, she found the grave mound she sought. She closed the shutter and in the darkness began to dig. Long years of heavy work had strengthened Sarah's body and built into her muscles a great endurance. She worked rapidly and well, handling the shovel with a dexterity and ease to equal a good many men. The piles of earth heightened and spread. The rain, still falling, made the earth soft and soggy, and soaked through her dress. It gathered in the thickness of her hair, causing its hanging strands to stick to her neck, and moisture trickled down her forehead and cheeks, mingling with the salt sweat that the mauling work caused to flow freely. Deeper and deeper she went, finding nothing but earth, clay, and stones until finally she drove the metal edge of the shovel down and felt it thump with hollow dullness against wood. She leant against the side of the deep hole, feeling nauseated.

'It must be inside the coffin,' she thought, and despite the heat of her body, she shivered violently. 'Dear God forgive me for what I'm doing,' she prayed silently. 'Forgive me, I beg of you.'

Summoning all her courage, she cleared the earth from the top of the coffin and placed the lantern with its shutter opened, so that she could see clearly. She lifted the shovel and with all her strength drove it down. The wood, half-rotted by long years in the damp earth, jarred and cracked with an unnerving drum-like sound and a stench of corruption erupted from its interior. Sobs dribbled from Sarah's lips and she pressed against the clay sides of the grave, moulding her body to its wetness until she had regained some control over her mounting fear. Into her mind's eye there swam the murderous face of George Jenkins and she seemed to see in the darkness above her, the trickle of saliva sliming his black whiskers and hear once more the reading from the Testaments that he had given her.

'No!' she panted aloud. 'No, I'll not be here tomorrow, he'll not catch me.'

In sudden resolve, she lifted the shovel again and again, driving down blow after blow, until the wood splintered and holes gaped. She dropped the shovel and with both hands tore at the gaps, hurling the strips of wood over her shoulders. As she tore the last hanging piece free, the lantern suddenly tilted as the earth beneath it slipped and the light shone fully into the hole she had made. Sarah's muddy, blood-streaked hands crushed against her mouth forcing back the screams which came wrenching from deep in her chest. A rotting, snag-toothed, eyeless skull grinned up in hideous delight at

93

her horror. She bit back the screams and looked close into the coffin.

On each side of the skull, metal gleamed dully. Platters, spoons, goblets, knives, bowls ... with the stench of ancient death filling her throat, and with her stomach heaving and retching, Sarah snatched at the silver, cramming it into the open bag that lay at the grave's edge. As soon as she had cleared the objects surrounding the skull, she scrambled out of the grave and snatching up the bag, began to run.

She ran and ran until it seemed that her lungs would burst in her chest and her legs were a torment of anguished flesh ... then flopped to the ground and rolled over on to her back to face the sky, arms outstretched and palms opened in supplication. The rain lashed across her body and Sarah surrendered in utter thankfulness. Letting its chill freshness wash the blood and mud from her hands, gratefully she opened her lips so that it could obliterate the vile taste of the grave from her mouth and clean it from her nostrils.

CHAPTER TEN

Jethro Stanton and Turpin Wright spent a cold wet night deep in the ancient heart of the Clun Forest. Piles of dead leaves and armfuls of ferns made a comfortless bed for an hour or two, and before daylight came they went on southwards, following the winding foresters' tracks through the almost impenetrable woodlands. At dawn they came to the swift-running River Clun and, stripping off their clothing and rolling it into bundles, they plunged across the icy flow. Emerging with teeth chattering and skin blue with cold, they dressed and went on. The blood-heat engendered by their hard travelling quickly dried the wetness of their bodies and supplied the stiff muscles of legs and torso.

When naked, Jethro had seen that Turpin Wright's back and shoulders were criss-crossed with welts of scar tissue that corrugated the white skin like coarse darned threads. When they paused at the top of a slope to catch their breath the young man said,

'I see you're no stranger to the lash, Turpin.'

The convict bared his broken brown stubs of teeth savagely. 'Have you sighted such a badge afore then, cully? On your own dad's back maybe?'

Jethro's memory flew back across the years to a day when, as a small boy, he had watched cavalry troopers of the King's German Legion tear the flesh from his father's back with their cat o' nine tails until the ivory of living bone could be glimpsed beneath the red curtain of blood and tattered flesh. He nodded grimly.

'Yes, Turpin, my father carried such a badge on his body ... And what was worse, he carried it on his soul.'

'You'm right theer, matey,' the other's hard leathery face was bitter to match his tone. 'When I first met your dad, he told me summat of Ely. Peter was a captain o' the Luddites when I met him; and I become the same arter talking wi' him.'

'You?' Jethro was incredulous.

'Yes, cully. Me! Old Turpin Wright, the biggest rogue that's ever worn holes in his britches' arse ... It was up in Nottingham I was, doing a bit o' the Low Toby for me rhino ...' He noticed the puzzlement in Jethro's eyes and explained. 'That means I was a footpad, knocking coves on their heads and stripping 'um ... Still, never mind about that now. I met your dad in a beer-ken and we got talkin'. He mentioned that he was a needle-pointer in Redditch town and I told 'im as how I was an old pointer lad years ago ... To cut the story short, me and him hit it off together. Ahr, he was a fine man, your dad was, Jethro, and a great one as well. Because o' what he said to me, I joined the Army o' Redressers ... Ahr!' He shook his head and smiled reminiscently. 'They was brave days for a bit, I'll tell you ... We thought we was agoing to change the world and make it fit for men to live in. Even bad buggers like me 'ud be able to change their ways and make an honest living. God rot my balls!' He cursed in sudden disgust. 'The government spies and the soddin' yeomanry cavalry soon changed our ideas about that, blast their black hearts!' His voice became touched with a note of sad regret. 'So old Turpin takes to the flash ways agen, and if it 'adn't bin for you matey, I'd have bin dangling at the crossroads in an iron suit wi' the birds feeding orf me this very minute ... Come on, lad, let's move on our way.'

Late afternoon found them miles beyond the forest boundary and deep into the forbidding valleys of the Black Mountains. They had kept away from the places where men dwelt; the villages and hamlets whose musical-sounding names, Bettws y crwn, Beguildy, Duthlas, might in happier days have drawn Jethro to visit them. They had crossed the steep-banked Teme river by riding astraddle an old log. The stark crest of Beacon Hill, framed against the cloud-heavy skies, frowned down at them as they hurried over its western slopes; and when they entered the narrow valleys, the wind rose and was channelled by the bare mountains so that it buffeted against their faces and tugged at their garments as if it would tear the protecting cloth from their bodies. They met no one and saw only kestrel hawks, and black carrion crows which swooped fiercely cawing outrage and defiance at these unwelcome trespassers.

Jethro's breath came in short gasps and his legs ached from forcing his heavy boots through the tussocks of marsh grass on the valley floor. Unlike the hill heather, this did not surrender easily to the thrust of strong muscles, but tangled its rank-smelling roots around the feet and calves of the travellers and fought tenaciously to deny them passage. A red film began to form at the edge of Jethro's vision and his exhausted body threatened to come to a halt, despite his mind's determination to go on. Suddenly, without warning, Turpin Wright's iron physique abruptly failed him, and he tumbled face downwards on the soggy grass.

'I'm done, Jethro! I'm done!' he gasped out.

The young man knelt beside him. 'We must find food and shelter,' he panted. 'This damned wind would beat giants to their knees.'

He passed his hand across his eyes, wiping the sight-blurring wind tears from them. Even as his vision cleared, he felt the first spatter of raindrops come hurtling against his face, propelled like bullets by the hammering gusts of the gale.

'Goddam it!' he exclaimed. 'We really will be finished if we stop here.'

He got to his feet and peered forward in the rapidly deepening gloom, searching for some sort of shelter. He felt a growing anxiety. The air had become bitterly cold and the rain would soak through their sparse clothing in minutes. Jethro knew that this combination of elements could mean the death of both of them from exposure in this bleak hostile land. He bent and helped Turpin Wright to clamber up.

'Come on Turpin,' he urged. 'We must find shelter. We must!'

Half-pulling, half-carrying the older man, Jethro battled along the valley against an onslaught by wind and rain that seemed bent on giving both men to these cruel mountains as a sacrifice.

It seemed an eternity had elapsed when Jethro stumbled into a low stone wall fashioned, in the manner of the hill people, of flat rocks cunningly interwoven without mortar or binding. Beyond the wall, the ground had been cleared and in one corner was a lopsided fabrication of wood and rock. Jethro climbed over the wall and, exerting his remaining strength, he dragged Turpin with him. When they neared the man-made object, Jethro saw dimly the pale huddle of a flock of sheep packed under its low roof. He felt like sobbing in relief.

'It's a sheep-fold, Turpin,' he shouted. 'We're safe now.' The wind, as if understanding him, redoubled its fury and hurled great sheets of sleet and rain at the staggering men. Jethro and Turpin pushed in amongst the woolly acridity of the animals which, after some plaintive bleating, seemed to accept that these humans had not come to harm them, but only to share their life-giving warmth.

'Let's rest here, Jethro ... Please let's stay here and rest.' Turpin Wright's voice sounded old and utterly weary.

Jethro felt a rush of compassion for this convict, who for all his brave spirit and toughness was, by comparison with himself, an elderly man.

'Don't worry, friend,' he answered. 'We'll stay here ... We'll not move any farther this night.'

They lay full-length amongst the sheep and pillowing their heads on their arms, gave in to their exhaustion and slept.

Many hours later, just past daybreak, the sheep milling about and trampling upon their bodies roused Jethro and his friend at the same instant. They came to their knees pushing the smelly, woolly masses away from them and, crouching low under the sagging roof, forced their way to the open end of the fold.

'It's a bloody dog that's disturbed them,' Jethro called over his shoulder and swung his leg across the low gate that blocked the entrance. Immediately his foot touched the ground outside, the small black and white collie that had frightened the sheep, hurtled at Jethro and sank sharp fangs into the meat of his calf.

'Damn and blast you!' Jethro, astraddle the gate, was forced to endure the tearing pain until he could get clear. Then he bent and grabbed the dog by the back of its neck, using both hands and digging into the corded tendons under the rough fur with his strong fingers until the animal squealed with pain and released its grip. With all the strength of his well-muscled arms and shoulders, he flung the dog bodily from him, and it hurtled through the air to thud squirming and howling on to the turf.

'*Pwy ydech chi?*'

The angry shout coming from directly behind caused Jethro to start in shock. He swung round to confront a blue-smocked, heavily-bearded man, wearing a sack over his head and shoulders as protection against the drizzling rain.

'*Pwy ydech chi? Beth ydych eisiau?*' the man shouted again and brandished the long shepherd's crook he was carrying in threat.

'Take it slow, Jethro.' Turpin Wright clambered out of the fold to join him. 'He's speakin' in the Welsh tongue. He wants to know who you be, and what you wants.'

The convict chuckled and winked at his friend's expression of surprise.

'Ahr, you didn't know I could understand the mountain lingo, did you, cully? It's easy explained, I used to have a woman who come from these parts, she taught me a bit on it.' He held up both his hands placatingly at the shepherd. '*Saeson!*' he said, pointing first to himself and then to Jethro. '*Saeson!*'

The man's mean features scowled, and in thickly accented English, he said. 'Oh, so it is English you are, is it? What are you wanting here?'

'We had to take cover 'ere for the night,' Turpin told him. 'If we hadn't, we'd ha' bin dead men by now.'

'Would you indeed!' The shepherd was still highly suspicious. 'Was it offer the mountain you came?'

Turpin nodded. 'That's right, Taffy.'

While Wright was talking with the man, Jethro looked about him. Above the small area of walled pastures the thick purple-brown carpet of gorse and heather billowed upwards in folds to the rounded heights of the dark green and grey-black mountains that hemmed in the narrow valley from all sides, and were now half-hidden in the early morning murk of drizzle. Beneath where they stood, a stream dashed down the steep slopes in a succession of tiny waterfalls to lose itself in the vast peat bog which covered the valley floor.

On the near bank of this stream, less than a hundred yards away, was a row of low-built turf bothies, their roofs fashioned from ancient brown canvas stretched across trimmed branches and held down by rocks and lashed cords. From one or two of the bothies, coils of grey smoke escaped upwards through the crude rock chimneys to mingle with the veils of fine mist that drifted through the breezeless air.

Even as Jethro stared at the huts, a red-cloaked bent old woman with a man's worn-out beaver hat on her head came hurrying through one of the canvas-hung doorways and began to climb up the slope. Her cracked old voice came clearly to their ears.

'*Pwy sydd yna? Y bwytyr pechod?*'

'What's she saying?' Jethro asked Turpin Wright, and for reply got a sharp elbow in the ribs.

'Keep quiet, cully! Just leave this to me.' The devils of mischief danced in the convict's bright blue eyes.

The wrinkled old crone reached them, her dark eyes flicking from one to the other and her long jaw almost hitting her thin hair-tufted nostrils as her toothless mouth chewed indignantly.

'*Y bwytyr pechod? Lle fuoch chi? Rydych yn hwyr!*' The words were meaningless to Jethro, but the irascibility in her voice was plain to understand.

'That's right, grandmother,' the convict nodded gravely. 'I'm the Sin-Eater ... I know I'm late, but the storm last night made us lose ourselves.' He spoke in English and at the sound of the alien tongue the old crone's face filled with doubt.

She poured out a torrent of Welsh to the shepherd who, at Turpin Wright's words had begun to look at the Englishmen with awed fear. The convict raised his voice in seeming impatience.

'Now you listen to me, Taffy,' he went to the shepherd and prodded him in his smocked chest with a forefinger. 'You tell the old woman that the Welsh Sin-Eater couldn't come ... Tell her that he had a bad fall yesterday and 'e's alaying in his bed wi' a broken leg ...'

While the man tried to comply with these instructions, Turpin said in an aside to Jethro. 'God rot my balls! Doon't stand theer wi' your mouth gaping like the village loony. Try and look as if you knows what's agoin' on ... Just leave it all to me, and say nothing. But for Christ's sake! Close your chops up!'

Jethro collected his wits and tried to hide his hopeless puzzlement at what was taking place.

'*Rwan, rwan, Nain, tawelwch eich hyn.*' The shepherd tried to soothe the old woman's uneasiness. 'There there, grandmother, calm yourself.' He turned apologetically to Turpin Wright. 'It is the first time my old Nain has effer met a *Saeson* who eats the sins, do you see ... It is a bit upset she is ... But neffer mind, I've told her that it's not too late ... She will be quiet in a minute, look you. Please would be good enouff to come down, shentlemen.'

The shepherd took the still chattering old woman by her arm and led her towards the turf bothies, leaving the Englishmen to follow.

'Will you tell me what in hell's name is happening?' Jethro demanded in a whisper.

'We'se struck lucky, matey,' Turpin whispered back, and his eyes twinkled in wicked glee. 'These buggers be up 'ere to get their sheep collected in for the winter. They's got a stiff 'un down theer, might be man, woman or babby, I doon't know yet.'

'Well, what's that to us?' Jethro hissed.

'It's a full belly, a warm fire, and rhino in our pockets,' Wright told him happily.

Jethro was still mystified. 'I don't understand. What do you mean by telling them you're a sin-eater? Whatever is that?'

'It's like this,' the older man took pity on his ignorance. 'If these buggers dies wi'out having their priests give 'um pardon for their sins, then they believes they'll goo into hell's fires because their souls am black wi' sin. Well, there's coves who goes around these mountains, atakin' the sins o' the dead on to their own souls, so that the buggers who croaks it wi'out a priest or suchlike to give 'um pardon needn't goo to hell at all, but goo's straight up t'other way into bleedin' heaven.'

'And you ... ?' It suddenly all became clear to the young man.

The convict nodded, and his leathery face lit up with delight ... 'That's it, cully. You'se got it in one go. I'm agoing to ate this dead bugger's sins. It's money for old rope, arn't it!'

Jethro felt a quick stab of superstitious horror and his expressive features mirrored his feelings.

Turpin Wright stared at him for some seconds, his lips jerking, apparently in paroxysms of agony. Then he stopped in his tracks and, burying his face in his hands, gave vent to a series of muffled groans.

Jethro felt an instant concern. 'Look, Turpin, don't upset yourself so. There's no need for you to do this awful thing. We'll find some other way of getting food and money.'

'Upset?' Wright's voice was strangled. 'Bugger off ahead o' me, you barmy young bugger, afore I busts out laughin', and spoils the whole thing.'

Kicking himself for being so taken in by the hardened old sinner, Jethro walked on. Turpin could never feel apprehensive before God or devil. By the time the pair had reached the bothies, Turpin Wright had composed himself and wore an expression of pious gloom. Jethro suppressed a smile at his companion's brazen deceit. He also composed his features to appear suitably sombre and grave.

The old crone went into the largest of the bothies and the shepherd followed her. There was a sound of voices raised in argument, and the old crone cackled angrily.

'*Yr hen cythrel Saesneg! Yr hen cythrel Saesneg!*'

Turpin chuckled aloud. 'The old bat's calling us dirty English bastards.'

'She's none so clean herself, judging by the smell of her,' Jethro answered.

The shepherd pulled back the canvas cover to one side and stuck his head out, beckoning for the Englishmen to enter.

The thick smell of the interior was almost a tangible substance. Jethro felt its hot, sickly reek filling his nose and mouth and as he swallowed, his throat threatened to choke upon it. The bothy was dark and close, its only light coming from a smouldering, spitting peat fire in the corner hearth and two tall wax candles, one at the head and one at the feet of the dead man lying on the dirt floor in the centre of the room. The corpse was naked, its arms stretched by its sides, while two gold sovereigns glinted upon the closed eyes. The protuberant bones of the ribs and hips caused shadows to fall across the sunken gut. When the candle flames wavered, the shadows moved, and it looked to Jethro's queasy gaze that the belly was rising and falling in quick, shallow breaths.

In a wide circle around the grimy, pale cadaver, crouched or seated on the earth, were the men, women, and child mourners, and the white fleeces of the sheepskin coats that many of them wore caused Jethro to remember the stories of the spirits who came to guide the dying to the next world. He jumped nervously when a terrible scream cracked the murmurous silence.

It was the old crone. She fell to her knees, her gnarled fingers tearing at her wispy hairs and rocked backwards and forwards in manifestation of her grief.

'*Fy mab! ... Fy mab! ... Fy mab! ... My son! ... My son!*' She crooned the words over and over again

The women among the mourners started to keen and wail in unison, their shrieks rising and falling in ever more strident echoes and several of the babies and smaller children squalled and sobbed in fear. A giant of a man beat his shaggy head upon the dirt with skull-jarring thuds, then lifted both arms above his head and roared, '*O Fy nuw da! Arbed ni oll ... Oh my good God! Save us all!*'

'*Fy mab! Fy mab! Fy mab!*' the old crone screamed, and the women tore at their hair and necks and breasts, and chorused, '*Bachgen druan! Bachgen druan! Bachgen druan!* Poor boy! Poor boy! Poor boy!'

The shepherd pushed his way through the crowd and knelt by the side of the corpse. In one cupped hand he held a small heap of salt, in the other a lump of bread. He let the salt dribble through his funnelled fingers and form a cross on the bony, sparse-haired chest. Then, taking the bread, he broke it into five separate pieces and carefully placed one piece at each point of the salt cross, and the final piece in the centre of the cross itself.

'Let the sin-eater come forward,' he called out in his own tongue, and the mourners vented a concerted howl of apprehension which charged the air with tormented noise and made the candle flames shiver violently.

Then all became hushed. Turpin Wright moved forward. He took the candles from their mounts and holding one in each hand he knelt above the corpse's head, staring fixedly at the bread and salt.

'Oh God and Satan both ... pay heed to me!' The deep tones of his voice trembled with strain and Jethro looked at his friend to see with astonishment, rivulets of sweat streaming down his face and the flickerings of fear in his eyes. The atmosphere tensed as the mourners waited for this dread-inspiring sin-eater to take the blackness from their kinsman's soul and release it from its purgatory.

'Oh God and Satan both ... pay heed to me!' Turpin Wright intoned once more. 'I, the eater of sins, have come to take the sins from this soul.' In a sudden swift motion he bent, and with his lips and tongue he took the bread from one point of the cross, gulped it down, then licked the salt of the arm of the cross from the clammy flesh beneath his bowed head ... 'Oh God and Satan both ... pay heed to me. One fifth of this soul's sins are now mine own. As I took the bread and took the salt, so took I the sin.'

The convict's face was a harrowed mask of suffering, and his breath rasped audibly in his lungs. Three more times he repeated the words and the actions, until only the one piece of bread remained in the centre of the cross. In the light of the candle's flames, Turpin's skin glistened with sweat and his head twisted from side to side as he battled with some nameless inner agony.

The mourners sat silent, transfixed with frightened awe by the spectacle of this man damning his own soul for eternity, even the smallest babies had hushed into stillness. Dragging the words from his dry throat, Turpin Wright repeated the formula for the final time, then shouted:

'And now Satan, King of Hell! To seal my bargain with thee, I take the thrice-cursed payment for my newly gotten sins.'

He bent and again using only lips and tongue he lifted each gold coin in turn from the corpse's eyelids and held the coins in his mouth. As the weight left the lids they slowly opened and the dead eyes stared into his. The mourners moaned softly and a single sob forced itself from Turpin Wright's throat. Then he appeared to clamp a rigid control over his emotions, and said slowly in a peculiar tone, as if it were not himself speaking. 'See how the dead man wishes to recognize the benefactor who has set him free from torment.'

A gasp of utter relief gusted through the room and the tension fell away. Wright, as if in a dream, placed the candles at each side of the corpse's head and rose to his feet. His body began to shake uncontrollably and he stumbled from the room and out to the freshness of the open air. Jethro went after him and found the convict lying flat on the bank of the stream, frenziedly dashing his head beneath the icy rushing torrent again and again and again.

CHAPTER ELEVEN

Loud hammering on the rickety door woke Henri Chanteur. He opened his eyes reluctantly and stared upwards. The room was dark and freezing cold, and beside him in their shared truckle bed the sheriff's officer stirred restlessly, muttering unintelligibly in his dreams. The flimsy panels resounded again.

'Yes, what is it?' Chanteur called.

'It's three o' the clock, zur ... The horses be coming out for the Portsmouth coach shortly.'

'Very well ... thank you.' Henri sat up and tugged at the fetter chain which secured his ankle to that of his companion. Grumbling and scratching, the man also sat up. 'It's time to rise,' Henri told him. 'Will you unlock the chain?'

When they had arrived at the Bush coaching inn, Bristol, the previous night, the sheriff's man had insisted on locking them together before they slept, in spite of Henri's assurances that he would not attempt to escape. Their bedroom was in the main part of the inn and Henri's lavish distribution of the money his friends had given him ensured that the room was reserved for them only, which avoided the continual disturbances of travellers coming and going from their beds. Henri's money had also enabled the journey to be made in the comparative comfort of an inside berth on a crack Royal Mail coach, instead of being perched on top of a lumbering stagewagon exposed to all the vagaries of the suddenly worsened weather.

The porter bustled into the room, carrying a jug of hot water and an open razor, and shaved both men by the wavering light of a smoking, floating-wick oil lamp. He caught the shilling Henri tossed to him and bit it sharply before slipping it into the pocket of his leather waistcoat. 'Thank you, your honour. The ordinary's being served now.'

Together with his escort, Henri went down to the ground

floor dining-room. The number of people sat at the long table in the dimly lighted room was small. Two or three civilians, merchants by their prosperous appearance, a blue-coated naval officer, several officers of the Militia and two officers of the Royal Marines. Henri regarded the latter's headgear with interest. They both wore the distinctive girdled and cockaded top hats of their famous corps, which were only worn by some Norwegian and Belgian troops in the Emperor's army.

Served grudgingly by a sleepy-eyed slovenly maid, the shared breakfast dishes were not appetizing to the Frenchman's taste. The rest of the party, however, set to voraciously and soon made great inroads into the roast leg of mutton, the broiled pigeons, the meat pies and fish, the cold cuts of tongue, brawn and ham, and the pile of potatoes boiled in their skins which dominated the centre of the greasy-topped table in their huge earthenware dish.

Henri contented himself with toasted buns and a dish of milky coffee, then paid the reckoning for both himself and his companion and went into the courtyard to watch the bustle of preparation for the journey.

As always he was forced to smile at the self-important airs of the English coach driver. This one was short and stout, wielding a long-stemmed, long-lashed whip and dressed in the very height of coaching elegance. A many-caped greatcoat was slung across his shoulders, opened to show off a brilliantly brocaded pair of waistcoats worn one over the other, and the most enormous frilled cravat Henri had ever seen. The whole ensemble was set off by a feathered, three-cornerd hat, far too small, perched on the bullet head, and a pair of embroidered white silk gloves.

'What a fine dandy you are, my Jehu!' the Frenchman murmured to himself.

The four matched horses were now in harness and were having the final brush applied to their glossy coats by a swarm of ostlers, while the coach guard was busily checking the priming of his blunderbuss, and the pair of long horse-pistols he carried slung from a sash hanging from his shoulder. He too was elegant, uniformed like a soldier in a gold-laced scarlet coat with blue lapels, and a blue waistcoat topped off by a beaver hat with a gold lace band around its base.

With surprising nimbleness, the stout little driver swarmed up the side of the yellow-painted coach, seated himself on the high box in front, and nodded to the guard. The man blew a long blast on his copper horn and shouted, 'Now, gennulmen, if you please! The *Celerity* is ready to leave for the Blue Posts Inn at Portsmouth Point. Travellin' by way o' Bath, Warminster, Salisbury, and Southampton. The *Celerity* leaves in three minutes exact, gennulmen, and we carries 'Is Majesty's mails ... No delay can be tolerated ...'

Joined by his escort, Henri surrendered their tickets to the guard and took his seat inside the coach. The leather seats were damp and cold to the touch and he was grateful when the other four seats were filled by the three merchants and the elder of the two marine officers. Their close-sat bodies would help to warm the air. The other marine officer joined three of the militiamen on top of the coach. As the elder marine took his seat, his dark blue boat cloak fell back from his shoulder and disclosed an empty sleeve pinned to the chest of his scarlet tunic, half-concealing its blue facings. The solitary star on each of his fringed golden epaulets denoted his rank to be that of major. Once settled he stared hard at the young Frenchman. The only light inside the coach came from a small horn lantern carried by one of the merchants, and the marine leaned across to ask the man,

'By your leave, sir. I'll take the glim for a moment.'

Without waiting for assent he took the lantern and held it so that its light fell fully across the young man. Henri opened his own cloak.

'Let me satisfy your curiosity, Major,' he said quietly. 'I am a French officer.'

The marine's stare did not waver. 'I know that already, monsieur,' he barked the words gruffly. 'But I wanted a good look at your face.'

'Why?' Henri was puzzled.

'Because I wanted to know who it was who as a prisoner-of-war has the gall to ride in comfort inside the coach at the Government's expense, while officers of His Majesty's forces must ride on top of the damned thing, and pay their own fares to boot!'

'The fare has been paid with my own money,' Henri replied quietly. 'So I suggest, Major, that if it offends you to travel in the company of a French soldier, who has had the misfortune to be captured when wounded, then you get out and wait for another coach.'

The major's wine-red face mirrored his surprise, then, unexpectedly, he threw back his head and laughed heartily.

'God blast my eyes! But I like that reply, monsieur. I perceive that you're a regular Gallic cock, who crows bravely even when he's on his way to have his feathers plucked and his neck wrung.' He tapped Henri on the knee and told him jovially, 'I admire your spirit, sir, for if I'm not mistaken, you'll be on your way to the hulks, will you not?'

'You are correct, sir,' Henri told him curtly.

The marine nodded his satisfaction. 'I thought so. Well, my young Gallic cock, allow me to tell you who I am. My name is King ... Major Harry King of His Majesty's Corps of Royal Marines. At present, I command the garrisons of the hulks *Fortune* and *Ceres*. They lie moored in Langstone Harbour under the guns of Fort Cumberland. You may well, one fine day, find yourself sent to one of those magnificent vessels. Yes indeed ...'

The young Frenchman smelt the reek of brandy fumes on the other's breath, and realized that the man was drunk. To avoid getting into a pointless dispute with someone not in his senses, he contented himself by merely nodding in answer. Closing his eyes he leant back his head on the seat and shammed sleep.

The time of departure had come and the driver cracked his whip to signal the ostlers to release the lead horses' heads and jump aside. Plumes of smoke-like breath jetted from the nostrils of the team as they took the strain and the coach lurched into motion. The whip cracked again, one, two, three, four times. The guard blew an ear-splitting blast on his horn and the driver deftly steered the heaving team through the archway of the inn courtyard, and out of the tangle of winding streets and half-timbered houses to the broad, newly gravelled turnpike highway which stretched, like a white ribbon in the moonlight, towards the city of Bath. The horses settled into an easy stride and at a good nine miles an hour the coach swayed along to the creaking of wood and leather, the jingle of metal, and the rhythmic drumming of ironshod hooves.

It was on the wide, fertile plains of Wiltshire after the change of teams at the market town of Warminster, that conversation started inside the coach. The leather curtains had been fastened up from the side windows and the crisp morning air brought a bracing cold freshness into the fusty interior.

The three merchants produced from sack-wrapped bundles, great golden-crusted pasties and several black-glassed bottles of gin. Nothing would satisfy their good nature but that the remainder of the party should share in their provisions.

'I insist, good sir! If you don't accept, you will mortally offend me.'

The fattest of the three would not hear Henri's polite refusal and pressed him until the young man took from him a huge chunk of rich meat-filled pasty and a crock tumbler full of the heady gin. The touch of food on his lips caused Henri's stomach to rumble in acknowledgement of its emptiness, and he bit deeply, savouring the delicious taste.

The merchant watched the enemy soldier chewing eagerly at the food, and his heart held pity as he thought of where this fine young man was destined for. As soon as the chunk of pasty had disappeared, he pressed more on Henri.

'Go on, boy ... eat hearty,' he smiled kindly. 'I'll warrant there's a good many of your countrymen now in Russia who would give a year of their life at this time for a pasty like this.'

Henri felt a sense of foreboding. News of Napoleon's invasion of that country had reached Bishops Castle, but he had heard nothing more for some time.

'In Russia?' he queried, and swallowed the half-chewed piece of meat in his mouth. 'But I thought that the Grande Armée had defeated the Tsar's troops and were in winter quarters around Moscow.'

The merchant shook his head. 'No, my friend, not any longer. Your Emperor is in full retreat, and, according to the latest despatches received in London, the Russians are everywhere attacking your troops and causing the deaths of many many thousands.'

The young man's appetite abruptly left him. '*Le Bon Dieu!*' he breathed ... 'And it is now full winter there ... *Bon Dieu!*'

'Yes, young sir,' another of the merchants joined in the conversation. 'It is said that the sufferings of the French soldiers are hideous. Whole regiments are said to be dying from the effects of the frost and snow, and the army is starving because the Muscovites have destroyed all food-stocks and shelter in its path.'

'And Spain?' Henri questioned. 'What is happening in Spain?'

The fat merchant smiled ruefully. 'Well, my friend, unhappy as I am to tell you, our Duke of Wellington is once more falling back to Portugal. The seige of Burgos has failed

... The Frogs are ... I beg your pardon! The French are in hot pursuit. Also, it grieves me to add, our General Hill has been forced to abandon Madrid ... so you see, the war is still undecided ...'

'Oh no, sir! Dammee! Not at sea it ain't undecided,' the major of marines interjected forcefully. 'No matter that the Yankee frigates have taken a few prizes, the Royal Navy still rules the oceans of the world and will never cease to do so, I might add, sir! Not while there's an Englishman can still lay a cannon and swing a cutlass.'

'Bravo! I concur with that sentiment wholeheartedly, sir,' the fat merchant applauded. 'And while not wishing to be offensive to this unfortunate young man here, I am honour-bound to say that I do not think the nation has been seen yet as could beat old England, once the blood is up.'

'Here, here!'

'Well said, sir! Well said!'

His companions agreed vociferously, and began to toast each other's health in large gulps of gin.

Henri stared unseeingly at the rich grazing country the coach was passing through, and dwelt miserably on what he had been told. He could not accept it ... The Grande Armée under the personal command of the Empereur himself, in full retreat? The conquerors of Europe running from the in-efficient, ill-equipped armies of the Tsar? The heroic victors of Marengo, Wagram, Jena, Austerlitz and a hundred other fields of glory being beaten by the crowd, knout-driven slaves of a barbaric tyrant? ... And yet, in spite of all his emo-tional rejection of the news, his logic told him that it was the truth.

It took twelve hours for the crack *Celerity* to make the ninety-six-mile journey from Bristol to Portsmouth, and it was a few minutes before four o'clock in the afternoon when the horses toiled at a walking pace over the crown of the Portsdown Hill; and the driver halted them to rest for a while before beginning the descent to the sea.

'Does you gennulmen wish to stretch your legs?' The guard opened the coach door and let down the folding steps.

Only Henri and the marine major took advantage of the offer. The others, gin-fuddled and sleepy, burrowed deeper into the high collars of their greatcoats and stayed in their seats.

A sharp wind whistled in from the sea and brought the

strong tang of ozone to Henri's nostrils. The sky was clear of clouds and the sunlight glinted upon the wide expanse of foam-flecked blue-grey waters. The major came to stand by Henri's side. His tone was jocular, as he asked,

'Admiring your new home are you, my Gallic cock?'

The young man remained silent, gazing down at the flat peninsula below them. It was cut off from the mainland by marshy creeks which at high tide filled with the sea to create a moat. This moat was spanned by a causeway which on the island side cut through the earthworks of the Hilsea defence lines, with its garrison of square huts lying half a mile beyond the fortifications. Henri judged the peninsula to be five miles in length and perhaps three and a half in width at its widest point, the seaward end. On either side, were great natural harbours and the town and dockyard lay on the west side of the island. While, separated by a five-mile channel, the gently rising, green wooded hills of the Isle of Wight acted as a shield to the harbours, protecting them from the full fury of the English Channel gales.

'Look there, my fine fellow,' the marine pointed to the dockyard, filled with great black- and yellow-banded ships, made toylike by distance. 'Look beyond them men o' war, look farther out.'

Henri's gaze followed the line indicated by the scarlet-clothed arm with its elaborate blue and silver laced cuff. A line of dark humps sunk low in the water, with wisps of smoke rising from them which curled and dispersed in the sea breezes was all he could see. Another line of humps lay at right angles a little distance from the first, and between the two lines tiny specks of light craft moved to and fro.

'There's your new quarters ... Those are the hulks!' the marine told him. 'And over there,' the scarlet and blue arm swung eastwards, and Henri saw at the end of a curving spit of land that jutted from the eastern extremity of the island, a star-shaped structure, 'is Butcher's Fort.' The major's voice grew strained. 'Or to give it its proper title, Fort Cumberland ... See there, moored close inshore to it?'

Henri made out two low humps.

'They're my command.' The strain in the major's voice was now so marked that Henri looked sideways at him in surprise. The man's face was twisted in torment and he burst out, 'There they lie! The *Ceres* and the *Fortune*, and I curse God for taking my damned right arm from me that day at the Nile, and leaving me with my life, so that I was only half a man! No longer considered to be fit for battle!'

He glared at the distant hulks and lifting his remaining arm he shook his fist furiously.

'I curse the God who brought me down to acting as a filthy gaoler on those stinking hell-holes!' Swinging on his heels, he stumped back to the waiting coach.

Henri drew a deep breath. 'You poor devil, Major!' he thought. 'You are a soul in purgatory!'

The long oars creaked in the brass rowlocks and the boat crept past the towering yellow and black walls of the men o' war anchored close to the dockyard. Seamen working on board the warships came to look over the taffrails and through the open gunports. Their tarred pigtails hung to the sides of their weather-beaten, ear-ringed faces as they peered down. Their expressions were neither friendly, nor hostile, merely curious.

Henry Chanteur sat in the waist of the longboat with a small party of other Frenchmen all facing the stern, where a minute midshipman sat by the side of the helmsman and squeaked the rate of stroke in his high childish treble. The men o' war fell behind and once out of their shelter the wind hit the boat on its starboard beam, causing it to wallow and roll over the foam-flecked waters. Henri's blond hair ruffled wildly and his fair skin was reddened and wetted by the spray blown off the dripping oars before the longboat came into the lee of the nearer line of prison hulks. The Frenchmen stared with interest at their first close view of their new quarters.

They saw a long line of black-tarred hulls, tied bow to stern, seven in number. The once-tall masts had been cut to stumps and on the top decks wooden housing had been built fore and aft. Some of the housing was raised above the rest by thick wooden stilts, and from the forrard end, tin chimneys jutted out of the roofs of the stilt housing, each one belching clouds of dark smoke. Dangling from the stern of each hulk, a huge red or blue ensign flapped in the wind, as if giving the time to the festoons of drying clothing whipping backwards and forwards on lines slung across every available space. While, adding to the rhythm, the hulks themselves rose and fell, their water-logged timbers straining and complaining to the swell that constantly shifted them.

'There you are, messieurs,' the tiny midshipman smiled mockingly at the French prisoners. 'There's the *Prothee*, *Crown*, *San Damaso*, *Vigilant*, *Guildford*, *San Antonio*, and the *Vengeance*. You should feel at home on them, because every one of them once carried the colours of France and her friends, and there's plenty more of such-like vessels in the harbour as well ... It don't pay to challenge the Royal Navy, do it?'

'With all respect, *mon petit enfant*, the American frigates seem to make a profit from it,' a grey-mustachioed Corsican naval lieutenant said aloud.

The child flushed and for a moment made no reply, then said triumphantly, 'Perhaps, monsieur, your old Boney should have employed Americans to man his fleet. You might then have been able to put to sea.'

The rowing British sailors roared with laughter and the middle-aged Corsican acknowledged his verbal defeat with a rueful grin.

Henri gazed at the blue-uniformed boy who carried the dirk of his rank at his belt, and marvelled that from such children as this came the redoubtable British admirals and sea-captains who ruled the oceans of the world.

The boat changed course and headed towards the second hulk in the line, Around its sides just above the waterline ran a gallery with a guardrail and openwork flooring from which two gangways rose up to the top deck. At the head of each gangway Henri could see marine sentries, distinctive in their girdled, cockaded top hats. While on the gallery itself, more red-coated, white-breeched, cross-belted marines tramped round and round the hull with muskets at the shoulder.

'Ahoy the *Crown*?' the midshipman squeaked.

A scarlet-sashed sergeant of marines came to look over the fo'c'sle rail, then bellowed, 'Prepare to receive prisoners aboard,' and came clattering down the gangway to the gallery. He stood at rigid attention, a rattan cane held horizontally under his left arm, and brought his right hand to the brim of his hat in salute.

'Only one body for here, Sergeant,' the midshipman squeaked and ordered the rowers to ship oars. The blades flashed upwards and the longboat bumped gently against the gallery entry port. 'Hey! You there, in the green rig.' The child tried to frown ferociously. 'Get inboard! And jump to it smartly, ye French lubber!'

113

With a nod of farewell to his fellow prisoners, Henri stepped on to the gallery and the longboat drew away. Immediately he was conscious of an almost overpowering stench. A compound of rotted wood, putrid offal, human rancidness and excreta. The burly marine sergeant grinned as he saw the young Frenchman's nose wrinkle in disgust.

'Not to worry, Frenchie,' he said jovially. 'You'll get used to the stink ... It's a bit raunchy at first, ain't it, but you'll soon think it to be the smell o' roses ... Come on, follow me.'

He led the way up the gangway and Henri's heart momentarily sank within him as the black-gaitered legs moved upwards on a level with his eyes.

On the poop deck a dozen marines with bayoneted muskets lounged about in various attitudes, trying to get what shelter they could from the cutting wind, while scattered about the top deck half a dozen barefoot, tarpaulin-jacketed sailors busied themselves at different tasks, with a rope-end-wielding boatswain's mate stalking amongst them to make sure they didn't shirk their work.

'You'm in luck, Frenchie ... Cap'n Redmond ain't aboard at the moment,' the sergeant grinned. ''E likes to greet all the new prisoners in person and to gi' 'um half a score o' strokes wi' a cane to make 'um feel welcome ... You'll still ha' to take a bath though, afore we gis you your slops and shows yer y' new berth ... that's unless you got some rhino wi' you. Iffen you 'as, and you'm inclined to part wi' some on it, we might be able to forget the bath.'

Henri shook his head. 'I've no money,' he answered, and cast about in his mind for some means of hiding his few remaining coins from the greedy eyes of the guards.

The sergeant's beefy face scowled and his jovial manner changed abruptly.

'Get stripped off!' he shouted, and swished the rattan cane through the air a bare inch from Henri's head. 'And look smart about it, ye damned swab! You, Wilkins! Get some slops for this Frog.'

'Aye aye, Sarn't!' The marine jumped to his feet and ran to obey.

Henri let slip his warm cloak and while removing his uniform and underclothing managed to slip his money into his mouth unseen. He tucked it underneath his tongue with a facility born of long practice. Without clothing his smooth skin goose-fleshed and he began to shiver. The sergeant pointed to a huge wooden tub which was placed by the taff-rail at the stern end of the poop.

'Theer's your bath,' he barked. 'Get in it and make sure you scrubs yourself proper, Froggy. We doon't want any dirt or vermin brought on to our nice clean ship.'

The marines laughed at the N.C.O.'s joke, and watched with mocking, cruel anticipation as Henri went to the tub. It was almost full of a turgid mess of greenish-black scummed liquid that erupted constantly with tiny, foul-smelling gas bubbles.

'Gerron wi' it!' The rattan cane swished and a thin streak of living fire burned across Henri's shoulders. He took a deep breath and stepped into the icy-cold tub. The disturbance caused the gas to rise in a froth and he gagged uncontrollably.

'Get your head under, Froggy!' the sergeant bawled, and the cane swished once more. Henri's fury at this treatment overcame all his apprehension. He stepped out of the tub and boldly faced the N.C.O.

'I am an officer, not some criminal. If you continue to abuse me in this manner, I shall lay complaint before your superiors.'

The beefy face in front of him lit with glee. 'Oh, will you now, Froggy? Well, if that's the case, I'll gi' ye summat to complain about.' He stepped forward and swung one meaty fist.

Henri was a practised exponent of 'La Savate' in which the French use the feet instead of fist. He easily ducked the ponderous blow and jumping high, lashed out with his feet. The side of his foot sank deeply into the sergeant's plexus, doubling him over. In the next instant, the Frenchman slipped to the sergeant's rear and, placing one foot on the tight-breeched rump, he pushed gently. The marine, already unbalanced, fell forwards and went head-first into the tub. His top hat floated, cockade upmost on the layer of scum and his black-gaitered legs somersaulted over and disappeared beneath the surface with the rest of his body.

The faces of the marine privates were momentarily blank with shock, then the quicker-witted men howled with laughter, and the others followed suit. Some rolling across the deck helpless with merriment, while others leant against the taffrails weeping tears of joy. The uproar brought other marines and sailors running, and as the sergeant surfaced, spluttering water from his mouth with his regimentals plast-ered with green scum, they too burst out with shouts of enjoyment.

The sergeant used both hands to rub the filthy mess from his eyes and blinked furiously, his face purple with temper.

'I'll bleedin' kill you for this, you Frog bastard!' he raged. 'You dirty mother-shaggin' Frog bastard!' And began to clamber from the tub.

Henri stood waiting, his arms held loosely in front of him and his body poised in perfect balance upon the balls of his feet.

'I'll take three to one on Johnny Crapaud!' a sailor shouted, and was instantly bellowed down by the marines.

'Goo to it, sarn't!'

'Gie it to the barstard, sarn't!'

'Ten to one on the bootneck!'

'Show 'im how the old Jollies can fight, sarn't!'

The burly N.C.O., streaming water on to the deck, tore at his cross-belts and stripped off his sodden scarlet waist sash and tunic. He lifted his shirt over his head and threw it aside.

'Now then, Johnny Crapaud,' he grunted. 'I'se 'eard about you Frog bastards a boxin' wi' your feet. Let's see 'ow you makes out agen English fists.'

A cry went up ... 'Form a ring. Form a ring!' And sailors and marines jostled and pushed into a rough square. The sergeant moved forward, left arm held high and extended, the right tucked against the chest. His pasty body carried a roll of fat about the midriff, but his shoulders and arms were thick and heavy with muscle. He prodded out his left and as Henri started to duck under it, the sergeant swung grunting with his right. His fist caught the young Frenchman on the shoulder. Henri let his body ride with the blow, then, like an acrobat, he spun and fell forward on to his hands, jack-knifed his body and kicked back with both legs as a mule would. His heels thudded up and under the sergeant's rib-cage and sent the man hurtling back into the packed bodies forming the ring. A dozen hands propelled the marine forward and Henri went to meet him, throwing his agile torso horizontal. Scissoring his legs to front and rear of the black gaiters, Henri twisted his body with them. His opponent went thudding head first and his face crunched against the oak planking. The Frenchman disentangled his legs and sprang upright. The sergeant pushed himself off the deck and struggled to his feet. He faced his elusive enemy once more, blood oozing from a cut on his forehead and dribbling from his broken mouth.

He again blinked furiously to clear his sight, then lumbered towards Henri, his breath snorting from his flattened nose.

'He sounds like a hog back home, rutting for truffles,' Henri thought, and began to feel a grudging respect for the toughness and fighting spirit of the Englishman. But before another exchange could take place, a sailor shouted,

'Look out, cullies ... 'Ere's the bleedin' captin coming back.'

From in between two of the men o' war moored by the dockyard, a gig came in with fast-sweeping oars towards the line of hulks. The marine sergeant bawled a series of orders, then using the tub water splashed the blood from his head and chest.

'You'm a tricky bugger in a set-to, Frenchie,' he told Henri, and there was respect in his voice. 'Well, you needn't fret none over this. I ain't a cove what holds a grudge agen a man who stands up to me and fights back. T'ain't your fault you doon't know how to use your dukes, but 'as to use your feet instead. You'll hear no more o' this.'

Henri felt a surge of gratitude at the other's sporting words. He slipped a gold guinea from beneath his tongue and pushed it into the marine's hand.

The man looked at the coin and grinned. 'You'm a fly cove, ain't you? You'll survive these damned hulks, never fear.'

He picked up his clothes and bundled them together.

'Corporal Bower!' he shouted. 'I'm going to me berth to get changed. Gi' this Frenchie his slops and get him below.' He looked back at Henri. 'I'll gi' you a word o' warning, cully,' he spoke in a low gruff tone so that no one else could hear. 'Be careful while you'm on this damned hell-ship. The cap'n's half-mad, and the other bastards am about the same. Youse best keep a still tongue and a careful eye, and if you gets the chance, then get orf the bloody thing one way or another.' He winked and tapped the side of his nose. 'I'm being drafted back to a ship o' the line shortly, so I wun't be able to 'elp you, except by gie'ing you this word o' warning.'

With that, he tucked his hat under his free arm and went along the deck to disappear into the forward housing.

''Ere, Froggie!' The corporal handed Henri a jacket and trousers. 'Get these on quick, afore the captin gets aboard.'

Henri put on the ill-fitting clothes reluctantly. They were a garish orange-yellow in colour, thick with dirt and grease and on the back of the jacket were two big black letters, T.O.

'What do they stand for, these letters?' Henri asked.

'They means Transport Office, cully,' the corporal explained. 'You'm their property, d'you see.'

He took the young Frenchman down a ladder and on to the lower deck, where an armed sentry was standing looking through a loophole in a barrier. The barrier stretched from deck to deckhead and at first glance appeared to be metal, so thickly were the nails driven through the stout wood, so that their points protruded through to the prisoners' quarters. Other loopholes flanked the sentry's and through them could be heard a tumultuous hubbub, while the stench that Henri had first encountered on the gallery was here so strong and overpowering that it seemed to force its foulness through the very pores of his skin.

'Cop these.' The corporal took a hammock, a thin ragged coverlet and a long narrow hair mattress weighing perhaps two and a half pounds, from a heap at one end of the sentry walk and gave them to Henri.

'Take care o' these,' the man instructed. 'Because you'll get no more.'

Three marines came down the ladder and stood with muskets aimed at a low hatch-cover, now barred and bolted, which rose only a couple of feet from the deck. The corporal unbarred and opened it and Henri crawled through, pushing his scant bedding in front of him. The hatch slammed shut and the bars and bolts rattled into place.

Henri got to his feet and stared unbelievingly at the scene before him. In a space barely 130 feet long, 40 feet broad and 6 feet high, with the only light that which seeped through a few narrow iron-grilled scuttles set at the sides of the deckhead, hundreds of men milled and surged in chaotic ear-deafening commotion.

To Henri, they looked like dead people risen for a brief time from their graves. Hollow-eyed, earthy-complexioned, their thin wasted bodies were barely covered by the yellow rags they wore. Round-backed and unshaven, with fetid breath, rotted teeth, and vermin-ridden hair and skins. The young man stared at them in horror as they haggled and quarrelled, sang and shouted, wept and laughed with maniacal, feverish clamour.

'Ah oui, m'sieur! Ils sont vraiment les enfants d'enfer.' The musical cultured tones came from the shorter of two cadaverous caricatures of human beings standing at one side of the hatchway, looking with interest at the new arrival.

Henri summoned his wits and bowed politely to the creatures. 'Indeed, *m'sieur*, you speak truly. These poor men do resemble our vision of the children of hell.'

The human wreck laughed delightedly and returned the bow. 'Permit me to introduce myself ... Colonel Gaston de Chambray, of the Third Cuirassiers, and this gentleman is my friend, Captain Nathan Caldicott of the American Merchant Service.'

The American was an exceptionaly tall and skeletal forty years old, without a tooth in his mouth or a hair on his head. He was a New Englander and spoke with the nasal twang of his home state of Maine.

'Welcome to His Britannic Majesty's Ship, *Joy* ... Some may call it by its given name, the *Crown*, but I know better,' he said and held out his hand. His eyes twinkled merrily in the gravity of his face. 'I'll be most happy to shake your hand, monsewer, for I've not yet mastered the art of bowing graceful.'

Henri liked the man instantly and shook the proffered hand, then bowed to both men and introduced himself.

'*Eh bien*, Henri. There is no need for the formalities here, so I will call you by your forename ... What do you think of our charming abode?' the colonel asked pleasantly, as if they were in the best of hotels.

The newcomer shook his head confusedly. '*Mais c'est affreux!* I never believed that soldiers of the Empereur could fall as low as this.'

The colonel's skull-like face smiled, showing surprisingly good white teeth. 'But, mon cher, you do not yet fully understand. On this deck are only the privileged ones. The men of some consequence ... *les officiers and les messieurs ou bourgeois*. Down below there,' he tapped the decking with the knotted stick he leant heavily upon, 'down there in the lower battery is where the fallen ones live ... *les raffales*! And below their deck, is another one called the Orlop. You'll find there the people who even *les raffales* despise ... *les manteaux imperiaux!* Why, on this deck, we enjoy a comparatively gracious existence. You must endeavour to do your utmost to remain here with us, *mon jeune ami*. To go down below is indeed to descend into hell. This deck ...' he gestured with courtly gracefulness at the bedlam in front of them, 'this deck is merely the ante-chamber of Purgatory ...'

CHAPTER TWELVE

It took some days after the happenings in the shepherd's encampment for Turpin Wright to recover his customary light-heartedness.

'God rot my balls!' he told Jethro repeatedly. 'I'll tell you this, cully. It fair shook me up, so it did. Does you know summat? I felt the Devil's hands in that hut. He was reaching for me, his fingers aclawing into me body like burning coals and trying to wrench me immortal soul from me.'

The convict insisted on stopping at every church and chapel they passed, and praying before the altar, then splashing himself soakingly with holy water. He even persuaded a travelling parson, somewhat the worse for drink, to exorcize the evil spirit that he insisted had come to dwell within him. Inevitably as the days passed and Satan made no attempt to snatch him down into the fires of hell, Turpin's mood lightened and his superstitious dread left him. He began to taunt the Devil when in his cups and challenge the demons of hell to appear.

'Come on then, Old Nick, and the rest on you hairy-arsed buggers. Come out and face me.'

When nothing occurred he would laugh and dance a jig, saying to Jethro, 'Theer, matey, what did I tell you? It takes more than Old Nick to beat Turpin Wright. I'm too sharp for the bugger. As sharp as one o' Abe Morrall's needles I be, and that's a fact.'

Jethro would smile to himself, pleased to see the older man happy again.

The pair were heading in a roundabout route back to Redditch, Jethro's home town. It had been his idea since it was obviously out of the question to risk returning to Bishops Castle for the hidden hoard.

'We'll lie low in Redditch for a time,' Jethro said. 'We can always find work on the canal with the navvy gangs, if there's naught else to be had. I'm well thought of there, and I've friends who will help us.'

Turpin had initially demurred, giving as his opinion that it would be better for them to keep moving.

'Nonsense.' The younger man was dogmatic. 'We're objects of curiosity in these remote country areas. You should know that only too well by now. It's better that we should be in a place where people at least know me, and then we'll not stand out from the crowd.'

'But what if I'm recognized in Redditch?' Turpin asked.

'How long was it since you were there?' Jethro wanted to know.

'Over a score o' years now,' the convict informed him.

Jethro laughed at his doubts. 'I should think that your own mother would not know you after that length of time ... It's not as though you've aged well, is it?'

'You cheeky young bugger!' Turpin Wright cursed him, but was forced to admit the truth of what Jethro said, and agreed to follow his plan.

They were now on the road between the ancient Severn river port of Bewdley, and the weaving town of Kidderminster. It was midday and the sky was overcast with black clouds, while underfoot the previous night's frost still rimed the dirt road.

'How far are we from Redditch now?' the convict wanted to know.

Jethro knew the road well, having travelled over it many times when he worked as a carter. 'We're about a mile and a half off Kidderminster,' he answered, and indicated the thickly wooded hill in front. 'Once we get over that, we'll be nearly in the town, and Redditch lies about fifteen miles beyond, as the crow flies.'

'We'll not reach it this night, then,' his companion said. 'It 'ud be silly to wear ourselves out hurrying to it.' He jingled the coins left from the two corpse sovereigns he had earned in Wales and went on, 'Let's stop and get some vittles, cully. I'm fair clemmed wi' hunger.'

'All right, there's an alehouse just over the hill that I used to stop at sometimes. We'll fill our stomachs there,' the young man agreed. 'But mind now, Turpin, let's have none of your tricks. We want no hue and cry raised for us in these parts, and no attention drawn to us either, in case there's already been inquiries made.'

'Does you take me for a loony wi' straw in his 'ead?' Turpin asked irritably.

'Only sometimes,' Jethro teased, and saved his breath for the steep climb ahead.

An hour later, their stomachs comfortably full with boiled bacon and cabbage, and their thirst quenched by several jars of porter, they were on the point of leaving the small roadside inn, when a commotion higher up the hill took their attention.

A young farmgirl came running screaming down the rough road, her sackcloth apron and skirts billowing and her mobcap hanging by a solitary hairpin at the side of her distraught face. They ran to meet her, together with the innkeeper. She threw herself into Jethro's arms and slumped against him, panting hoarsely and gasping in terror.

'The French are come! The French are come!'

'What's that thee says?' the bald-headed, lean-shanked innkeeper blanched in fear. 'The French? Here?'

'Doon't talk so bloody soft, man,' Turpin jeered. 'The nearest Frog to her is a dead bugger we saw in ...'

Jethro's elbow jabbed sharply into his friend's ribs and stopped him short. The convict rubbed the painful spot and glared at the younger man, then took his annoyance out on the innkeeper.

'You'm a real booby, you am. Bloody French 'ere? Achh!' He spat on the ground in scorn. 'There now, my pretty, calm yourself ... No one shall harm you.'

Jethro gently comforted the frightened girl. 'What do you mean by saying the French are come? There's none within two hundred miles of here, except for a few prisoners.'

She stared wildly behind her and screamed faintly.

'Theer they be ... Acoming arter me!'

A troop of weirdly clad men were approaching from over the brow of the hill. Their clothing was adorned with coloured streamers and around their tall beaver hats were strings of paper flowers, and more ribbons which fluttered about their heads as they walked. Each man set up a tuneful tinkling, as he moved, from the frills of tiny bells tied to the knees of his breeches, and to one side of the troop capered a fantastically dressed clown who brandished a long whip with an inflated bladder attached to the end of its thong.

Jethro burst out laughing. 'Lord save you, girl. Those men aren't the French. They're Cotswold Morris Men, I've seen their like many times before.'

Recovering from her fright, the girl became angry. 'Then

what be they adooin', gooing' about the land loike that, afrightin' poor honest wenches loike me?' she demanded indignantly, and when the party reached her, she assailed them shrilly. 'You oughter be shamed! Afrightin' me loike that. I'm a good honest girl, I be, arsk anybody in these parts ... It's not deserved what you done ... It warn't deserved!'

The tall ruddy-faced man, who appeared to be the leader of the group, stared at the irate girl in amazement. 'What's that you says, wench? We'se done nothin' to 'ee.' The soft vowels of the Cotswold hills made his voice restful to listen to.

'It's all right, master,' Jethro intervened. 'The poor girl took you for French soldiers.'

'Whaaat? French? ... We 'uns?' The men began to laugh.

'God bless you, wench. Iffen my old 'ooman 'eard you acallin' we 'uns French, her 'ud have your guts for garters, so her 'ud,' the leader grinned broadly. 'We'em Cotswold men we'uns be, and proud on it too.'

Unabashed, the girl kept up the attack. 'Then why must you goo round dressed so outlandish, then?'

'Toimes be hard, wench, and bread costs high, as you well knows I shouldn't wonder. Theer's no work to be had in our villages. We'uns goes around dancing and earning a few coppers to fill the babbies' bellies back home.'

Refusing to be mollified, the girl re-arranged her mobcap on her disordered hair and flounced away, calling angrily over her shoulder, 'You oughter be 'shamed! Grown men gooin' about dressed loike 'eathen savages. It's wicked, so it is. Wicked!'

Shaking his head, the Morris man turned to Jethro. 'How far be it to the next town, marster?'

For all their gay finery of ribbons and bells, the Morris men looked tired and drawn. Their bodies lean and underfed and their faces deeply etched with the lines of long years of hard toil and constant want. Jethro regarded them sympathetically. He knew only too well the grinding hardship and terrible poverty that were found inside the picturesque honey-coloured cottages of the Cotswolds' farming villages and hamlets.

'It's a little above a mile,' he answered. 'If you wish my friend and I will show you the shortest way there.'

'My thanks marster, that'ud be civil on you.'

Side by side they walked on.

'I lead the lads 'ere. We calls a bunch o' dancers a "side" and the one who leads 'um, like meself, be called the "squire",' the man told Jethro in reply to his questions. 'We'uns bin on the roads for nigh on three months. We'em heading home now, so we con spend the Yuletide wi' our kin.'

They passed by rows of cottages from whose interiors sounded the clicketing of hand-driven looms, and their progress brought hordes of sickly-looking weavers and their families out from their damp unwholesome dens.

'What be thee?' men shouted.

'Dancers,' the squire bawled back. 'Come to gi' you'uns a show.'

Immediately the work was abandoned and the people swarmed after the troupe. The town itself was a close-knit, unhealthy jumble of red brick and timber-framed wattle and daub houses, some of the latter having their upper stories built jutting far out over the malodorous Stour river which, replete with dead cats, sewage and assorted offal and rubbish, ran through the town. The rapidly increasing procession of excited shouting men, women, children and yapping stray dogs crossed a hump-backed stone bridge and came to the triangular junction of streets called the Bullring.

Abutting on to the narrowest egress of the cobbled triangle was the ancient greystone Guildhall, under which was the town gaol, and standing on the steps of the hall was a resplendent figure. His name was Henry Perrins and he was the bellman or crier of the town and also the head gaoler. A florid-faced burly man dressed in blue coat and breeches, white stockings and a black bicorn hat, the whole set off by huge red and gold epaulets and facings resembling an exotic naval officer. He watched the arrival of the Morris men with great interest. The squire glanced about him and decided that the Bullring was an ideal spot.

'Right ho, lads,' he shouted. 'Let's gi' 'um a turn.'

The bellman heard the words and came down the steps, but instead of joining the eager crowds of spectators he turned left around the corner of the building and went hurrying up the crooked gabled High Street towards the Lion coaching inn which stood at the very end of the street. Its ornate four-pillared entrance had a large statue of a lion astride it, growling silently at the Guildhall.

In the room above the inn's entrance, a group of men were engaged in heated dispute. There were six of them, all seated around a circular table. Three were army officers and the others prosperously dressed civilians, muffled in costly great-coats, their low-crowned beaver hats crammed down on heavy bucolic heads. The spokesman of the civilians, high bailiff John Best, brought his hand sharply on to the table. 'And I tells you gentlemen, that we cannot fulfil the ballot yet . . . maybe next month . . . ?'

The centre officer of the three, who all wore scarlet coatees with yellow facings and silver lace, rose to his feet. For a moment he toyed pensively with the white frontal plume of his shako, which was set in front of him on the table, then sighed impatiently and answered.

'Very well, sir, you leave me no choice. I shall inform the Lord Lieutenant of the county that you three, the high steward, the recorder, and yourself Mr Best as high bailiff of Kidderminster, have refused to obey the lawful commands of your sovereign.'

Best's drink-purpled face turned greenish with apprehension. 'Now that arn't true, Captain Ward,' he said hastily. 'We drew the ballot nigh on two weeks ago. 'is no fault of our'n if the men drawn are not fit for the militia service.'

Captain Joseph Ward ran his hand through his close-cropped, lightly powdered brown hair, which even now in his forty-sixth year held no tints of grey. His high-cheek-boned face was calm, belying the anger in his eyes. When he spoke his speech was clipped and controlled.

'Mr Best, I am the Captain of the Grenadiers company of the Third Worcestershire,' he indicated his silver shoulder epaulets, each with its flaming grenade insignia and white fringes. 'I am not a silly young ensign. Surgeon Purpost here,' he nodded to the officer on his left who wore an enormous black-feathered cocked hat of his military profession, 'is a highly experienced medical man. The people of this town who were drawn for the militia have been buying substitutes to go in place of themselves. I do not particularly object to this practice, unpatriotic though it may be, if those substitutes are young men sound in wind and limb. But I do object when they are the very dregs of the weaving trade, consumptives who can hardly draw breath, let alone march and drill. It will not do for me, Mr Best, and it will not do for the Third Worcestershire Militia. Surgeon Purpost has quite rightly rejected the last batch of offered recruits as being totally unfit for the service.'

'I have indeed, sir,' the surgeon's bluff red face was set and stern, 'and might I add to what you have said, Captain Ward?'

Ward nodded. 'You may, Matthew.'

'Thankee.' Purpost directed himself to the high bailiff. 'I may tell you, sir, that I regard it as an insult to my professional capabilities when attempts are made to pass into the army such pitiful wrecks of men as those that this town has presented for examination and induction during the past weeks.'

'But what can I do, gentlemen?' the high bailiff almost pleaded. 'The men originally balloted are many of them the sons of respectable tradesmen, and others are yeoman farmers. Then there are the married men with families and positions and properties to maintain. What can I do?'

'Do, sir?' The surgeon gave no weight to the other's excuses. 'Do, sir? Why, send me men who are fit and agile, and who have some strength in their bodies. I am no quack sawney to be fobbed with rubbish, sir. I know my craft, and take a pride in it. It won't do, it won't do at all.' He shook his head firmly.

Captain Ward took up the attack. 'We should have been back in Portsmouth with the new recruits more than a week since, Mr Best. The battalion is carrying the main burden of the garrison duties there, and is badly under strength as it is.'

The officer sitting on the right-hand side of Joseph Ward laughed scornfully. 'God dammit, sir! You must either find good substitutes, or them damned pot-bellied respectable burgesses o' the town must do their own soldiering, and be damned to them!' Captain Josiah Patrick was not noted in his regiment for his diplomacy.

'In God's truth, sir!' the bailiff exploded. 'The cursed militia will bleed this town of every decent man we have.'

'In God's truth, sir!' Josiah Patrick flung back at him. 'The militia has troubles enough of its own with being bled of men for the regulars. The Quota Act is destroying the Army of the Reserve, sir. Destroying it!' While they glared at each other across the table, Henry Perrins knocked on the door.

'Come in, blast you, whoever you be,' Best shouted.

The bellman removed his hat and bowed obsequiously. 'Might I have the honour of a private word with you, high bailiff?' His manner was fawning.

'Damn your eyes, man! Cannot you see we are in conference here?' the bailiff shouted blusteringly.

'Indeed, high bailiff, I most humbly beg your pardon for intruding, but I assure you it's a matter of the gravest urgency.'

'Oh very well, blast you,' Best grumbled, and excusing himself went to stand outside the door with the bellman.

The men left inside sat silently, each immersed in his own thoughts; and the only sound was the measured ticking of the great grandfather clock that, apart from the table and chairs, was the only other article of furniture in the room. The low murmur of voices sounded for a little time through the door then Best's voice came clearly, raised high in excitement.

'God's truth, Perrins, but you're a good fellow! I'll not forget to see you rewarded for this. Go to the petty constable straight this instant and tell him what he must do, tell him that my orders are that you be obeyed in this matter. I'll follow on to the Guildhall myself directly.'

The door opened and the bailiff re-entered the room, grinning broadly. 'How many men do you still have to take from here Captain Ward? Seven was it not? Well, be of good heart, Captain. We shall have them for you in a very short time, and all prime specimens, you may be assured on it.'

Back in the Bullring, the dancers had made ready to begin. Three of the men were ranged to one side: a fiddler, a drummer, and a man with a tin whistle. The remainder of the group formed two lines facing each other and produced white kerchiefs which they held in each hand. The squire checked the lines then called, 'Come, lads, let's start wi' the Maid o' the Mill.'

The tin whistle trilled out a jaunty tune which was taken up by the fiddle and the drum stacccatoed the tempo. The men began the dance, moving lightly and gracefully in and out of intricate formations. The knee-bells tinkled musically and the ribbons swirled in cascades of bright colours as the dancers performed the age-old half-gipsies, hooks, capers, and galleys which were the steps of the dance. More people gathered to watch and the Morris men warmed to the work. They symbolically beat each other with the kerchiefs, then broke away and pirouetted around a circle, stamping and leaping high, then formed and stamped, broke and formed again. The watchers clapped their hands to the beat of the drum and hardly without pause the squire shouted the melodic names of fresh dances as each one ended. 'Bobbing Joe'. 'The Lads o' Buncham'. 'Jockey to the Fair'. 'Constant Billy'. The whirling kerchiefs gave way to short sticks and the air clattered to the rapping of the mock fights.

Jethro felt himself drawn into the ancient ritual of colourful flowing movement that had taken place in this land of England from times immemorial. There were those who said that John of Gaunt had brought the dance back from the Moors of Spain in the Middle Ages. But men, whose roots were deep in the rich black earth of England, sensed that the dances were older by far. That they were born in the vast green forests that shrouded the mysterious tribes of Albion long ages before the empires of Rome, or even Egypt, ever existed.

The fantastically clad clown went through the spectators, collecting the copper coins, pathetically few, for hunger was no stranger in these mean streets. Then he capered back amongst his fellows, belabouring with his bladder any that faltered or flagged.

The ritual finally ended. The fiddle and tin whistle died away and the drum ceased beating. Panting for breath, the exhausted dancers halted and stood staring at each other, and in spite of the strained faces and tired muscles it seemed to Jethro that these men were experiencing a triumphant joy. A recognition that the spirits of their forefathers were in communion with them, and that no matter what alien manners had been imposed upon the people of England, the ancient ways still lived on.

The squire took the collection from the clown and counted the coins.

'We'uns 'ull not get rich in this town, lads,' he told his side.

'No, cully, and neither 'ull we, and we lives here,' a young weaver shouted waggishly.

The crowd and dancers laughed together and then the spectators began to disperse, most going back to the looms where they spent so many weary hours.

The squire saw Jethro and came over to speak with him.

'Will you show we'uns the way from here, marsters?' he asked.

'Aye, that I will,' the young man told him. 'For our roads run the same for a few miles and we'll be glad of your company ... How did you do for wages here?'

Before the squire could answer another voice broke in, 'They did well enough I'm sure, and they'll need to ha' done to pay the fine.'

A tall man dressed in grey and carrying a long staff with a wooden crown carved on its top end, pushed between Jethro and the squire. Behind the tall man followed Henry Perrins; he too carried a similar staff.

'What's that you say?' the squire's worn, honest face was puzzled. 'What's this talk about fines?'

'You'll know soon enough,' the tall man replied brusquely. 'You lot must all come along o' me. You'm all under arrest.' He pointed the crowned staff at Turpin Wright who was trying to sidle away. 'That means you an' all, my buck. There's no use you trying to run. We'se got every road covered.'

Jethro looked about him. Small groups of cudgel-wielding men blocked every exit from the Bullring. He tapped the tall man on the arm.

'Who might you be?' he questioned.

The tall man's face was arrogant as he held his staff up in front of Jethro's eyes. 'I be Gregory Watkins, petty constable o' this town,' he said loudly. 'I'm the King's Law here, my buck and I want no sauce from the likes o' you. You might be dressed like a preacher but Gregory Watkins knows your sort ... You and these coves in their heathenish gewgaws and ribbons. You'm a load o' gypsies, that's what you be, a load o' rogues and vagabonds. I can tell!'

Jethro's resentment came powerfully. The petty constable's smug, stupid face seemed in that moment to epitomize all that Jethro had been taught by his father to hate and struggle against. Lifting his arm he struck the crowned staff away from him.

'You stupid bugger!' he swore. 'These are not rogues nor vagabonds either, but honest men, driven to dance in the streets for a pittance to feed their families. At least they are trying to support themselves and not applying to the poor rates for money.'

'That's only what you say, and anyway it means naught to me,' the petty constable scoffed.

'Oh yes it does,' Jethro told him forcefully. 'Because if the government and the gentry couldn't find stupid fools like you to do their bidding, then perhaps we could create a just system in this land and good men like these would not have to beg for pennies, but could find well-paid work in their own districts.'

Henry Perrins poked his staff into Jethro's ribs. 'You'm talkin' like one o' them bloody Radicals,' he said threateningly.

'And we knows how to deal wi' such nonsense in these parts, I'll warn thee.'

Jethro's patience snapped as the wooden crown again thrust painfully into his chest. He snatched the staff and lifting it with both hands brought it down across his knee, cracking and snapping it in two parts. He flung both halves at Perrins' protuberant stomach, causing the man to cry out in pain.

'The next man to lay hand or stick on me will get his head broken,' Jethro warned, and stood poised and ready to put his threat into effect. The tall constable abruptly retreated a couple of paces.

'You'm making things a lot harder on yourself, young man,' he blustered. 'And on your mates here as well. It 'ull goo a lot easier on you all, if you comes along quietly.'

The squire and his team of dancers stared anxiously at Jethro. He met their frightened eyes and his anger fell away, to be replaced with a sense of hopelessness. These men had had all spirit driven from them by their lives of poverty and toil. The landowning gentry and farmers, aided by enclosure acts and penal laws, had ensured that the once wilful and turbulent rural peasantry of England had become for the most part a docile breed of forelock-tugging beasts of burden.

'And what right have I to blame the poor devils for being as they are?' Jethro silently castigated himself for despising these countrymen. 'I've no wife or children living in a tied cottage, dependent on the whim of some cider-swilling pig of a farmer for the very roof over their heads and with only the poorhouse and a pauper's grave to look forward to when the strength to slave like a brute has gone from their bodies ...'

'Very well,' he said aloud. 'I'll come with you. There'll be no trouble from me, providing you keep tongue and hand to yourself.'

The palpable relief in the Morris men's eyes was such that for an instant Jethro had the overwhelming urge to shout at them ... 'Don't be so damned slavish. Get off your knees and stand on your feet like men, for once in your miserable lives.' Then the memory of the wives and children waiting in those distant villages calmed him once again. He shrugged his shoulders and allowed the constable's deputies to shepherd him along with Turpin and the Morris men in the direction of the Guildhall.

They entered the main entrance and were chivvied down

a flight of stone steps into a short passageway cut out of the strata of sandstone on which the building stood. The passage was lit by a bracketed lantern on one wall, and facing the lantern were two barred and bolted iron-studded doors. Henry Perrins bustled self-importantly forward and taking a ring of keys from the pocket of his blue coat, he made a great racket in opening the nearer door.

'Get in theer, you lot,' he ordered, and stood to one side, watching the Morris men file through the opening. When it was Jethro's and Turpin Wright's turn to enter, the petty constable, who was standing under the lantern, intervened.

'Not you, young man ... or your mate. I reckon you'm a different kettle o' fish from these others.'

Jethro met Watkins' nervous gaze steadily. 'Oh do you now? And what makes you think that?' he asked.

The man's stupid face held more than a trace of fear, trapped as he was by the remaining dancers blocking his helpers at the end of the passage. He swallowed hard, not liking what he read in Jethro's expression.

'Now don't get excited, young man,' he said hastily. 'I means only that you strikes me as being summat of a gentleman, by your manner and the way you talks.'

Jethro's tone was contemptuous of this man, armoured only in his petty authority. He shook his head slowly and answered, 'I'm no gentleman, cully. I'm a labouring man.'

The other dancers had by now entered their door and Henry Perrins slammed it shut behind them. The constable visibly relaxed when he saw that his helpers were now directly behind this pair of dangerously insolent men and as his fear lessened, his manner grew more confident.

'Well, I've not time to argue the toss about that, young man. No doubt it 'ull all come clear when you goes afore the magistrates.'

'And when is that to be?' Jethro wanted to know.

The constable smirked. 'Well now! That arn't for me to say, is it. Arter all, I'm only a humble servant o' the law in these matters. It's not my place to question my betters as to what they intends to do, or when they means to do it.'

'No, that's the trouble with this country,' Jethro's disgust was plain to see and hear. 'There are too many arse-crawlers like yourself who are too afraid to question what their so-called "betters" are doing.'

The man's face reddened, and for a second he seemed about

to make an angry retort, but instead he only shouted at Perrins.

'Get this bloody door unlocked, will you, and let's finish this business.'

The second door crashed open and Jethro and Turpin went through it.

The room they entered was about five yards long and three to four yards wide and high. Directly opposite the door was a barred aperture that led upwards and let in air and daylight. It was unfortunate that directly beneath this aperture stood a large iron pot half full of urine and excreta which abominably tainted the incoming air. On the sides of the room, benches were bolted to the walls and on the floor were scattered heaps of straw, thick with greenish mould. Two men lay huddled along the benches and, squatting for warmth in the straw, two other men stared with interest at the new arrivals.

'God blast my eyes! 'Ere's two devout smashers come to visit us,' one of the men in the straw exclaimed and scrambled to his feet. 'Gi' us a prayer, Methody,' he jeered.

'Arsk that bleedin' God o' yourn to split this bastard place in two and let us out on it.'

'Ahr, and tell him to cause that bleeder Perrins' balls to rot and drop orf,' his companion added.

One of the sleepers on the benches stirred and cursed angrily. 'Damn your mouth! Can't a cove get some sleep in 'ere? Shut your noise, damn you!'

The man who had first spoken was short and stocky, roughly dressed and wearing the leather badge of a drover on his jacket arm. Beneath his shaggy mass of hair, his face bore the marks and scars of a fist fighter, and his nose had been broken so badly at some time that it spread wide and flat across his dirt-grimed face. He rushed across to the man on the bench and dragged him from it so that his body thudded on to the sandstone floor.

'Doon't you shout at me, cully,' the flat-nosed drover stood over the fallen man, snarling like an animal. 'Or by the Christ! I'll kick your bleedin' head in.'

The other made no answer, only rolled to cower against the wall under the bench, his arms wrapped about his head.

'We'll ha' trouble here, Jethro,' Turpin Wright whispered warningly.

Jethro by now felt he had stood enough harassment for one day. He nodded. 'If there's trouble coming, then I'm ready to meet it,' he replied, his voice ringing out clearly.

His challenging words brought all eyes on him. The man still lying on his bench rolled over and sat up, and the one cowering on the floor peeped out from under his arms. The drover's face was momentarily surprised, then he laughed mockingly.

'God blast my eyes! We'se got a Methody bruiser come among us in these palace halls.'

He strutted to stand a yard from Jethro and made a great show of examining the newcomers from head to toe.

'Well, they doon't look like Jolly Boys to me,' he told his friend, who now shook the straw from him and disclosed that he too wore a drover's badge and, apart from his face, was the other's twin.

'What does you rackon they be?' he asked.

The flat-nosed man appeared to be considering the question. 'They might be fences,' he mused aloud. 'Or maybe workin' the flimsies. Is that it, you coves? Be you in the bank-note business?'

'What we are is for ourselves only to know,' Jethro answered evenly.

The drovers laughed uproariously.

'God blast my eyes! Doon't he talk proper,' the flat-nosed one jeered. 'He must be in the collecting way ... On the road wi' a loaded pop in each hand and a grey mare like Sixteen String Jack had under his arse.'

'No, that ain't possible,' his friend protested. 'They'll be doing a little in the crack line, this pair o' nancies 'uil. Abreakin' into old women's houses to rob 'um o' their ha' pence,' he baited.

'Ahr, you might be right at that, Billy Boy,' Flatnose agreed, and held out his hand menacingly. 'Come on, nancy, let's be havin' a divvy-up o' your rhino.'

'Why should we give you money?' Jethro wanted to know.

'Becos I'm the king o' this bloddy palace, nancy. They calls me the Battlin' Drover. I'se met some o' the best pugs in the land I 'as ... Tom Blake, Ikey Pig, Jack Carter, Young Powers ... I'se met 'um all. So if you'm wise, nancy, you'll bail up.'

Turpin Wright went to speak, but Jethro winked at him, then turned to the drover and shrugged.

'Well, I don't like the idea of fighting with a man of your calibre,' he said, and told Turpin, 'You'd best give me what money we've got friend. I've no wish to feel the weight of this man's fists.'

The convict cursed under his breath and handed Jethro the few coins left to them.

'Here,' Jethro glumly proffered the money. The drover grinned.

'Now that's a good girl,' he jeered. 'I can see that you and me am going to be real sweethearts.'

As his hand closed on the coins, the toe of Jethro's boot crunched hard and heavy against his kneecap. The drover bellowed out in shocked agony and his leg gave way beneath him. He fell sideways, but before his body reached the floor, Turpin Wright was on him like a wildcat. One strong hand digging into the shaggy mop of hair, the other spread across the flat nose, its rigid thumb pressing hard under the eyeball.

'Make a move, cully, and you'm short one eye!' Turpin hissed.

'No!' the drover gasped in terror. 'No, doon't blind me. Please doon't blind me!'

Jethro jumped at the second drover, but after seeing the rapid overthrow of his friend, he had no stomach for a fight.

'I wan't no trouble cully!' he shouted in alarm. ''Twas not me who told you to bail up ... I want no trouble!'

'Then sit down and keep your mouth shut,' Jethro warned grimly. 'Or by God! You'll find out what trouble is.'

The man cowering beneath the bench sprang to his feet. 'Bugger me, if I didn't see you was a pair o' flash coves all right,' he chortled gleefully. 'I knew the minute I saw you come through the door that that flat-snouted sod theer 'ud cross the wrong 'uns if he crossed you two ... I knew it!'

He was a tiny, bald-headed, bright-eyed sparrow of a beggarman whose clothing was one mass of assorted rags and whose filthy feet poked through flapping, broken boots as he executed a grotesque dance up and down the cell.

Jethro smiled at his antics and spoke to Turpin. 'Let that soft lump of dung go free, cully. He'll do no more fighting while we're here.'

Turpin obeyed and the drover scrambled to the far end of the cell and crouched by the side of the privy pot, nursing his damaged knee and moaning softly to himself.

The tiny beggar finished his jig and grinned up at Jethro. 'Tell me, marster? I means no offence, but tell me how you come to be here? Fine gennulmen like you and your mate?'

Jethro softened to the cheeky, infectious grin of the tiny

man, and after a moment he related what had occurred in the Bullring. The tiny man cocked his bald head to one side, increasing even further his resemblance to a bird, and tapped the side of his beaky nose with a long black fingernail.

'So that's what the buggers be up to, is it?' he observed with satisfaction in his voice. 'I knew it, so I did ... I knew it all along. Specially when they fetched in old Flatsnout there and his mate, and that other cove what's a sittin' across from us.'

Jethro looked at the man referred to. He wore a decent suit of fustian with good plain linen, and appeared a respectable artisan.

'What is it you know, little 'un?' Turpin Wright questioned.

'Why, it's plain to them as con see, ain't it sir?' The beggar-man grinned. 'These buggers in this town 'ad the ballot drawed for the militia nigh on three week ago. The buggers as was drawed wants to send substitutes and con get none. That's what they'll do wi' us lot, I'll wager my life on it. They'll send us to the army to be made sodgers on, so they 'ull.'

'To the army? Us?' Jethro was incredulous.

The tiny beggar nodded vigorously. 'Well, they ain't agoing to send fine men like us to Botany Bay, be they sir? Specially now they wants substitutes ...' he chortled and began his jig again, singing in a high-pitched voice as he hopped about,

'Suppose the Duke be short o' men ...
    What would Old England sayyyy?
They'd wish they'd got those lads agennnn ...
    They sent to Botany Bayyyy ...'

'Oh God help me!' the artisan groaned, and buried his face in his hands. 'I've got a wife and little 'uns. What's to become o' them if I'm sent to the army?' He started to sob loudly.

'They cannot do it, surely?' Jethro remonstrated.

'Oh yes they can, matey,' Turpin Wright said bitterly. 'It's bin done to thousands o' coves. I knows it from first hand. It 'appened to me once afore, down south theer in Berkshire, but I was a bit too sharp for 'um that time, and scarpered double quick once I'd done me drills and was sent to duty.'

'But we can't be made to substitute! We haven't been drawn in any ballot, so we've no legal obligation to serve,' Jethro insisted.

The beggarman halted by the sobbing artisan. 'Damn you for a big soft Jessy, dry your eyes,' he scolded. 'It ain't so bad. Them that wants the substitutes pays well. Anythin' up to forty gold 'uns.'

'What if we refuse to be press-ganged in this way?' Jethro persisted.

Turpin smiled wryly. 'We'em under arrest as rogues and vagabonds, matey. The bloody magistrates and the constables fix it all up between theirselves. If we refuses to 'list, the traps swears our lives away in the court, and the beaks sends us up for a laggin'. That's unless you'se got friends or family wi' influence to spake up for you ... How long d'you reckon we'ud last in gaol, cully?' he asked rhetorically. 'And doon't forget, it arn't only the goal-fevers and suchlike that we'se got to worry about. If we refuses to do what they calls our patriotic duty, and 'list, they'll start asking questions about us. And you knows what that 'ull mean, doon't you?'

The younger man knew very well what it would mean. His mind whirling, he lay down on the bench and tried to collect his thoughts to meet this new development. The rest of the men in the cell arranged themselves as comfortably as they were able and eventually all was silence. Except for the mutterings and snorings of the sleepers, the soft moans of the injured drover and the rustle of straw as bodies stirred restlessly under the onslaught of the swarming vermin.

Jethro himself began to feel sleepy and drifted into a shallow doze. Later, when all was cold and dark, he awoke and lay staring into the unrelieved blackness. The sleep in the foul, over-used air of the cell had not refreshed his body, but it had resolved his mind. He remembered his father once telling him that all men should at some time or other experience the life of a soldier, if only to test their courage and learn the skills needed for successful armed rebellion.

The young man muttered inwardly, 'Perhaps you're guiding me in this matter, father. From wherever your soul now dwells.' He smiled to himself. 'Maybe I shall emulate Peter Stanton and gain the King's commission on the battlefield as he did.' Resigned to his fate, Jethro composed himself to sleep.

Lying awake in the straw Turpin Wright also pondered this sudden change in his fortunes. 'Ah well! It wun't be the first time I've followed the drum,' he thought resignedly. 'At least I can show young Jethro the ropes and save him a deal o' grief as a 'cruity.' He grinned in the darkness. 'The young sod's learnin' fast what life is all about, I'll be buggered if he arn't. He's a man now, that's for sure ... A real son of his father.'

Beside him in the straw, the beggarman broke wind loudly and foully. Turpin kicked him hard on the backside then turned away on his side and closed his eyes. 'I hopes they doon't gi' me this little bastard for a bedmate in the barracks,' was his last thought before he slept.

CHAPTER THIRTEEN

In Bishops Castle the days had passed so slowly for William Seymour, that at times he had feared his mind would give way in sheer frustration. His broken bones were knitting together and his body regaining its strength and vigour with remarkable speed, considering the severity of his injuries. But, burdened as he was with anxiety, the time dragged by with an awful slowness. As soon as he was able to hobble about, William Seymour began to exercise secretly; punishing his lean frame mercilessly and driving his muscles to the very limits of their endurance so that he might be ready the sooner to carry out the planned course of action he had decided upon during the (seemingly endless) tedious days spent helpless upon his sick bed.

The discovery of the old squire's open grave had caused a sensation of horror in the small town; and the finding of some silver goblets that Sarah had overlooked in the broken coffin only added to the mystery for the vast majority of the local people. 'For surely any grave robbers would not have left behind such valuable objects,' they argued.

Two men, however, had a shrewd notion of what had occurred. George Jenkins and William Seymour. When the tools that Sarah had abandoned by the graveside were put on show in the old market hall, the ranter recognized them immediately, but kept his own counsel and swore to himself that some day he would find his harlot daughter and tear the life from her with his bare hands.

When William Seymour was able to move about on crutches, he spent hours in the local alehouses, sipping brandy and listening quietly to the talk and gossip around him. His agile mind also arrived at a conclusion, and that was that George Jenkins could, if he wished, make clear the mystery of the open grave. Grimly the cavalry officer set to the painful task of recovering his full strength. Orders came

138

periodically from Major Hickey, via the post boy, for Seymour to report back to his regiment as soon as he was fit enough to move. Seymour's eyes were cold as he scanned the messages and he cursed,

'God blast your mealy mouth, Hickey! I'll not report back for my own court martial, be damned if I will.'

Each time the orders came, he cunningly inveigled the local surgeon who was treating him, into writing to Major Hickey and informing him that, 'William Seymour is not in my considered opinion as a medical doctor, yet fit enough to travel, and indeed it will be many weeks before he will be able to do so.'

So, in public, Seymour struggled painfully along on his crutches, his face a mask of pain as he gasped for breath. While in hidden places in the Forest of Clun, the cavalryman exercised his lean hard body and measured gladly the strength that came flooding back to it.

The rest of the month of November passed and Seymour began to feel he was now ready to put his plans into action. On the second Sunday in December he started to do so ...

It was morning and at the smithy of George Jenkins a group of men, women, and children had gathered. They all wore sombre clothing and the women and girls had kerchiefs tied like turbans about their heads. Following the instructions Jenkins had given them, each person wore on their headgear a cockade of white feathers and on their left breasts they had pinned small stars fashioned from yellow ribbands.

The tiny ranter's red-rimmed eyes were satisfied as he inspected his faithful followers in the smithy yard, and led them in the hymn-singing that always initiated their meetings. When he judged the mood of the group was sufficiently exalted, he fetched from his living quarters two flags of blue silk and a brass trumpet decorated with blue ribbons

'Edward! Thomas! You take these and wave them proudly.'

Jenkins handed a flag each to two of the boys with the party. Then he began to address the group in his booming voice.

'Oh ye blessed children of the Lamb of God,' he exhorted them, 'the day of the revelation ... has come!'

'Blessed be the Lord our God!' a fat smelly woman shouted. 'HALLELUJAH! HALLELUJAH!' her companions exulted.

The manic gleam came to Jenkins' eyes and he blew a loud

blast on the trumpet. 'Last night I had a vision!' he proclaimed. 'The Holy Joanna Southcott, the Prophetess herself, came to me ... and brethren! There came with her a vast multitude of the Lord God's angels clad in bright raiments, and the light of glory shone down upon them and they cried out my name and it sounded to mine ears like the thunder of the storm ... Ay! And the light of glory poured down upon me also ... UPON ME! ... GEORGE JENKINS!'

The listeners groaned ecstatically. 'PRAISE BE! AMEN! AMEN!'

Some of the women and children started to weep, overcome by the emotive atmosphere.

'Oh blessed Joanna, come to us! Come to us!' 'Hallelujah!' 'Hallelujah!' 'Honour the Prophetess!' 'Amen! Amen! Amen!'

'Now hear my words, brethren.' Jenkins held high the trumpet with both hands and closed his eyes, as if in pain.

'The light of glory burns my sight even now, Brothers and Sisters! It burns deep into my soul! MY VERY SOUL!'

'Hallelujah!' 'Amen!' 'Amen!'

'You'm blessed, George Jenkins! You'm blessed o' the Lord, so you be!' a young gap-toothed woman shrieked, sweat streaming down her pockmarked cheeks.

The ranter raved on ... 'Joanna Southcott and the Legions of Heavenly Angels brought to me, George Jenkins ... THE VERY WORDS AND COMMANDS OF THE LORD GOD MOST HIGH!'

The fat smelly woman screamed aloud and threw herself at the tiny ranter's feet, wrapping her flabby arms about his ankles and slobbering with froth-flecked lips at his dung-caked boots. She crooned hysterical, unintelligible gibberish and pressed her mouth to the hard leather.

Jenkins ignored her, possessed as he was by his own maniacal fancies, and kept his arms raised and his tightly closed eyelids lifted to the cloud-covered sky.

'Tell us, marster,' a sharp-featured little man in the front of the group begged frantically. 'Tell us the commands o' the Lord.' He slumped to his knees in the thick-layered mud and animal dung of the yard and, clasping his hands in front of his slack-mouthed face, wrung them beseechingly.

The others followed him and their chorused pleas rang out louder and louder, until Jenkins opened his eyes and looked blankly down at them as if he did not know what they did there. The madness glared from his eyes and a trickle of saliva wriggled from the corner of his mouth and lost itself in his black beard.

'Hush my children ... hush!' He spread his arms above their heads and his voice became muted and soft. 'Hush, blessed army of martyrs ... hush and be still.'

They obeyed as if mesmerized and soon only the choked sobs of the fat woman still clasping the feet of the ranter could be heard. The tiny man's chest swelled out like a pouter pigeon, and he felt a giant among pygmies as he savoured the spectacle of these people slavishly obeying him.

'The blessed Joanna Southcott told me that the Lord Most High has entrusted me to be his Prophet here on Earth!' his voice boomed out suddenly, and he sawed his arms rapidly back and forth in the air and went on, his voice charged with hysteria. 'The Lord Most High has commanded me, His Prophet! To proclaim to the world that the Shiloh comes once more! The Prince of Peace leaves his seat on the right hand of God and comes for the second time to earth ... AND I, GEORGE JENKINS, AM TO PROCLAIM HIS COMING!' he boomed.

His face suddenly suffused with blood and was almost purple in colour as he bellowed out again and again, 'WOE! WOE! TO THE INHABITANTS OF THE EARTH BECAUSE OF THE COMING OF THE SHILOH! WOE! WOE!'

His followers scrambled to their feet and began to shout with him. He led them from the yard and down towards Bishops Castle. The flag-carrying boys flanked him on either side and every few paces he blew a great blast on the be-ribboned trumpet while the whole group chanted resoundingly, 'WOE! WOE! TO THE INHABITANTS OF THE EARTH BECAUSE OF THE COMING OF THE SHILOH. WOE! WOE! TO THE INHABITANTS OF THE EARTH BECAUSE OF THE COMING OF THE SHILOH!'

William Seymour and Thomas Marston, both dressed in wide-brimmed hats and civilian greatcoats, were sat together in the bar-parlour of the Three Tuns inn haggling quietly and acrimoniously about money.

'I tell you truly, Captain Seymour. I do not have any money

to lend you.' The fat constable managed to convey his indignation at Seymour's reiterated demands for a loan without slowing the tempo of his gin-sipping. The expression on the soldier's face plainly showed his disbelief. The nerves at the side of his left eye began their erratic twitching and, leaning farther across the narrow table he wrapped his long, strong fingers about the other's podgy wrist and squeezed viciously until the fat man squeaked in pain.

'You great fat turd.' Seymour hissed. 'I've given you near fifty pounds in gold and notes since I've been here. I do not ask you to return that. All I ask is for a loan of some of it.'

'Captain, I swear to you I have no money,' the fat man bleated pitifully. 'It's all gone, all the money you gave me has gone ... I swear it! May God strike me dead if it ain't gone!'

Seymour's unstable temper erupted. 'I'll not wait for God to strike you dead, you fat pig. I'll save him the trouble by doing it myself,' he snarled.

Marston's gin-reddened folds of complexion became a sickly puce.

'Now don't you be so hasty, Captain ... I beg you not to be so hasty. I'll try and get some money for you, I will. I take my oath, I'll try.' As he finished his anxious assurances, the blasts of a trumpet and shouts muted by distance came from the west of the town.

'What the devil's that trumpet blowing for?' Seymour demanded. 'Are you expecting recruiters here?'

Marston shook his head in mystification. 'No, Captain, I've had no word about soldiers coming here.'

As he spoke, a small boy burst through the door of the bar-parlour and gabbled in nervous excitement, 'If it please you, Marster Marston, me Dad says can you come up to the Black Lion. Me Dad says he afeered there might be some trouble ... Me Dad says that them bloody ranters am causing an upset ... Me Dad says they'm ablowing trumpets and such-like and me Dad says that it's a terrible sin to do that on the Sabbath day, that's what me Dad says ...'

'And who, in hell's name, is your Dad?' The constable's fear of his companion vented itself in aggression against the child.

'If you please, Marster Marston. Me Dad keeps the Black Lion,' the small boy answered breathlessly, and took to his heels.

'God's curse on those damned lunatics!' Marston's grumbles were more relieved than angry as he snatched at this opportunity to get away from the dangerous-tempered soldier. 'You'll forgive my leaving you, Captain Seymour, but there'll be a riot if I don't get over there this instant.'

William Seymour's pale eyes were filled with contempt and loathing. 'I well recall another riot that you failed to prevent, fat man, and you were there when it started.'

He once more put pressure on the constable's sore wrist. The man grunted at the renewed ache and begged almost tearfully, 'I must go, Captain, I must!'

Seymour smiled savagely. 'And I must have some money. A small loan only, to stay me until my pay arrives from the regiment.'

The constable's many chins quivered as he nodded his head.

'I'll see what's to be done, Captain Seymour. I promise you faithful, I'll see what's to be done.' He tried to smile confidently and reassuringly, but the other man's expression halted the attempt. 'I'll bring you some money tonight, Captain. That's a promise.'

Seymour grinned again and released the captive wrist. 'Make sure you keep that promise,' he whispered menacingly.

The constable, his breathing coming in short shallow gasps, nodded, and without another word went quickly away. Left to himself, William Seymour took a sip from the half-full tumbler of brandy at his elbow and abruptly realized the import of the small boy's message about the ranters ...

'Goddam me for a slow-witted fool,' he muttered. 'That means George Jenkins will be with them ... Excellent! That gives me the chance to have a quiet look about his quarters before I have my few words with him.'

The captain finished his brandy in one gulp and went painfully on his crutches from the tavern and up in the direction of the smithy. Once out of sight of the town's buildings, he hefted his crutches across one shoulder and ran quickly and easily towards his objective.

At the Black Lion, George Jenkins blew a long trumpet blast and ordered his companions to halt.

'WOE! WOE! TO THE INHABITANTS OF THE EARTH BECAUSE OF THE COMING OF THE SHILOH!' he shouted.

The group formed a circle around him and the two flag-carriers which all but blocked the narrow street.

'In the blessed book of Joel, chapter two verse twenty-eight, we are told ... "In the latter days your old men shall dream dreams and your young men shall see visions ..." '

George Jenkins' booming tones carried to the ears of the drinkers inside the Black Lion. Big Tom, the yeoman farmer who had started the fight with the soldiers, was in a genial mood. He opened the leaded bay window that fronted the street and retorted.

'You'm bound to dream, Jarge Jenkins, specially when thee's had a drop o' drink.'

His fellow topers joined in the bantering. 'Ahr, that be roight, Tom. But you couldn't call they buggers wi' old Hell-fire, a set o' visions, could you now?'

'Noo, more loike bloody bad dreams or nightmares oi should rackon.'

The ranter blinked furiously and putting his trumpet to his lips began to sound blast after blast, until the echoes bounced along the entire length of the street and women left the fires where they tended the stewpots for dinner and came to their cottage doors to see what was happening. A stray dog sat down in the gutter outside the inn and started to howl in concert with the trumpet blasts.

'Theer Jorge, thee'st made another convert!' Big Tom jeered, and the onlookers laughed uproariously, women throwing their white aprons up before their faces and men, choking, spitting out the mouthfuls of drink they had been taking when the big man spoke. Gangs of urchins flocked to see the free entertainment and as the news of what was happening spread, customers at the dozens of other ale-houses and taverns in the town left their seats and hurried to the Black Lion. By the time Thomas Marston had fetched his staff of office from his house and reached the scene, a dense mass of people and dogs hemmed the ranters in from all sides.

'WOE! WOE! TO THE INHABITANTS OF THE EARTH BECAUSE OF THE COMING OF THE SHILOH! ...'

The chant echoed again and this time the crowd mockingly joined in.

Marston selected some of the more sober, steadier men and directed them to aid him. Then he began to push his way through the close-packed, strong-smelling mass, using his heavy staff to belabour the backs and shoulders of those who were reluctant to move.

'Clear the way in the King's name,' he ordered officiously. 'Clear the way, I say ... in the King's name, clear the way!'

'Watch out, Jarge!' Big Tom shouted above the tumult of excited jeers and insults. ''Ere's the conquering 'ero himself, acoming to get you!'

'Ahr, that's roight,' a blue-aproned gardener laughed at Big Tom's side. 'Here's the Champion o' Salop acomin' ... the Tom Cribb o' Bishops Castle.'

The crowd good-naturedly hectored the constable, most of them liking him well enough. All through the baiting and heckling that George Jenkins had been subjected to, his temper had steadily risen, until now, when the constable had nearly broken through the crowds, it at last overwhelmed him and he lost control.

'YOU ARE ALL ACCURSED!' The tiny frame shook violently from head to toe and, pouring from the whiskered mouth, the mighty voice overtopped all the noise from the gleeful masses, while the small clenched fists flailed the air above the bushy-haired head. 'YOU ARE THE GADARENE SWINE!'

A roar of cheers greeted the booming insult.

'YOU SHALL ALL PERISH LIKE THE MISERABLE SINNERS OF SODOM AND GOMORRAH!'

'HURRAH! HURRAH! HURRAH!' A hundred throats bellowed their mocking plaudits.

Jenkins red-rimmed eyes bulged from their sockets and the blue veins in his forehead swelled and throbbed like thick twisting worms. 'MAY GOD STRIKE YOU DEAD!' his voice cracked into a hoarse scream. Blood-streaked froth bubbled down from his lips. 'MAY HE STRIKE YOU DOWN AMONGST THE FILTH THAT BEGAT YOU! MAY GOD DESTROY YOU AND ... GGGHHH ...' The hoarse scream gurgled in his throat and the ranter suddenly staggered and pitched face foremost into the gutter, sending a stray dog yelping. For brief moments there was a hush, then the fat, smelly woman shrieked and cried shrilly, 'The Lord's struck 'im down! He's bin struck down!'

Instantly the superstitious fears that dominated most of the people there took effect. Men walked quickly away, and mothers came running in a flurry of skirts to grab their children and hustle them into the cottages. Doors slammed shut and bolts rattled home. In only seconds, all who remained in the street were the constable, his helpers and the followers of Jenkins, all staring in mute horror at the small form lying motionless on the cobbles. Thomas Marston, like the rest, could not help thinking that the preacher had indeed been struck down by God. Summoning all his resources of courage, he carried out the bravest action of his life. He went to the motionless Jenkins and turned him over. Marston's bated breath whooshed from his lungs in one great gust.

'He's alive!' he uttered.

The ranter's face was calm and peaceful. There was a discoloured, fast-rising swelling on the cheekbone that had struck the ground and some small bubbles of saliva around his mouth, but that apart, the man might merely have dozed off. Big Tom the farmer came from the inn, with his cronies creeping nervously behind his broad shoulders.

'He's alive, is he, Marster Marston?' The big man's normally florid face was pale and tense.

The constable nodded, and for once in his life felt strong and confidently in command of the situation. Jenkins stirred and his eyes opened. They held a peculiar fondness of expression.

'Mammy?' the ranter crooned the word doubtfully, and then smiled suddenly in delight, holding up his arms. 'Mammy! Mammy! Mammy!' he crowed like a baby, and curling himself up, he started to suck noisily at his thumb.

There was a sharp gasp of horror from the people standing about him, and Marston shook his head gravely.

'The poor bugger's mind has gone,' he said quietly. 'He's fit only for Bedlam now.'

'What? What's that you say?' the smelly fat woman asked, hesitant and afraid.

The constable scowled at her. 'I means that he's gone mad. As mad as a bloody hatter, and he's got to go to the madhouse!' He swung his staff at Jenkins' followers. 'Get you gone from here!' he shouted angrily. 'I'll lock you up, if you ever comes to cause such disturbance in this town again ... Get you gone!'

Silently, they obeyed him, the men shocked and frightened at the terrible downfall of their prophet, the women sobbing bitterly and their children wailing in sympathy with them.

Marston turned to his deputies and to Big Tom's group of friends. 'You men carry the poor sod down to the lock-up.

146

l'll put him in there and watch over him while one of you fetches the doctor to him ... But it'll do no good. He's a loony now and bound only for Bedlam, that's for sure.'

'Ahr, oi rackon you'm roight theer, Thomas Marston,' the big farmer sighed. 'Mind you, he's bin halfway theer for years, arn't he?'

Between them Marston and Big Tom lifted the thumb-sucking preacher and carried him gently to the town gaol.

William Seymour searched every inch of the smithy, even sounding all the walls and floors for hidden, hollowed-out spaces, but found only a soiled one-pound banknote and a few silver and copper coins. He slipped those into his pocket then sat on one of the rickety chairs in the living room to think.

'That hoard of Turpin Wright's is not here,' he decided. 'But I would stake my life on it, that George Jenkins knows where it is. It's clear that it was hidden in the grave, but who the devil took it out? Surely Wright and his friend could not have done so. It must have been Jenkins ... Or?' Another possibility occurred to him. 'I wonder now? Could it have been his daughter?'

At first Seymour thrust the idea from him as preposterous, but the longer he pondered, the more it persisted. He went back over the news he had gleaned from the gossips in the taverns and alehouses. Jenkins had attacked his daughter and she had fled the town. The grave had apparently been opened while Jenkins was locked up. Could the attack on his daughter have been part of a carefully contrived plan between them? A hundred different possibilities raced through Seymour's mind. Where could Sarah Jenkins have gone, assuming she had the hoard? ... Could it be to Portsmouth? To be near her French lover? What better place to dispose of valuables of any kind than a bustling seaport, with rare and costly objects continually changing hands as ships brought home prizes of war and captured cargoes?

'But I must be sure!' Seymour told himself. 'I must force the truth from that poisonous little rat, Jenkins.'

He decided to return to the smithy later that night when the town would be sleeping and the streets deserted. He wanted no interference when he tackled the blacksmith. Seymour went slowly back to the Three Tuns and found the bar-parlour full of excited townspeople discussing the events of the morning. Seymour listened intently to the disturbing news and then made his way discreetly to the town gaol. A small crowd was hanging about the open door watching the doctor examine Jenkins in the first of the cells.

The ranter kept muttering to himself and then gurgling and waving his arms and legs in the air like an infant. Seymour leant against the open doorway, ostensibly to rearrange his crutch pads more comfortably beneath his armpits. He caught only one snatch of Jenkins' apparently meaningless rambling, but that was sufficient.

'Her's took me pretty things, Mammy ... Her's took me pretty things,' the ranter grizzled.

Thomas Marston came to the open door. 'You'd best be off about your business,' he ordered the inquisitive loafers impatiently, and then sensed Seymour's cold regard. A flash of apprehension crossed his eyes. 'I haven't forgotten our talk, Captain,' he said nervously. 'I'll be seeing you tonight, never fear, and I'll have with me what we talked about.'

Seymour was pleased at the other's obvious misunderstanding of why he was there.

'You had better have it, Marston,' he snapped, and hobbled away up the steep slope of the hill.

Inwardly, Seymour felt a warm glow of satisfaction, and a certainty that he now knew what had become of Turpin Wright's hoard. 'At last my luck has changed ... I'm sure it will hold for me now,' he exulted fiercely. 'When I get some money from that fat pig tonight, I'll be on my horse and away to Portsmouth,' he promised himself, and smiled in anticipation. 'Who knows, I might even take some pleasure with Sarah Jenkins ... God knows, I deserve a little honey after all the vinegar I've been forced to swallow these last months. ... She's a tasty piece right enough, and would make a rare sweet bedmate for a while.'

CHAPTER FOURTEEN

Portsmouth, December, 1812

'Yes, good voman? Vot can I do for you?' Shimson Levi opened the small hatch let into the fretworked iron grille that surmounted his pawnshop counter and protected his goods from the thieving hands which abounded in Broad Street, the main artery of Spice Island, Portsmouth.

Sarah Jenkins took a large silver spoon from her canvas sack and showed it to the young Jew. Unlike his father, old Shimson, the pawnbroker did not favour the wide hat and gaberdine, with the long ringleted hair and beard of his fellow Hasidic Jews. Instead he was clean-shaven, with hair trimmed short and he dressed in elegant cutaway square-tailed royal blue coat, with tight breeches and gold-tasselled Hessian boots. Shimson took the spoon and turned it over and over in his be-ringed hands, while his brown, slightly protruding eyes evaluated it. He finished his scrutiny of the metal and then gave his full attention to the woman, openly admiring her shapely body and handsome face.

'Vell, my pretty, vot does you expect me to give you for this?'

'Only a fair price ... no more, and no less,' Sarah boldly met his avid stare. 'Come now, Hebrew! Give me your offer, for I've no time to waste here.'

Shimson toyed with the large diamond pin that he wore stuck in the folds of his fine lace cravat, and his wide thick-lipped mouth grew suddenly dry. This woman disturbed him, the sexuality she exuded so powerfully almost caused him to offer a generous price. With an effort, he recovered his customary poise and stated a ridiculously low figure. Sarah immediately took the spoon back and went to leave the shop.

'Vait! Vait a moment, young voman ... I was only teasing you.'

She paused with her hand on the doorlatch that opened on to the street.

'Come back here ... Please ... I'll give you a good price,' Shimson wheedled, overcome by the desire to know more about this handsome girl.

Still without speaking, she released the latch and came back towards the counter. He poked his head and shoulders through the hatch and she caught the fragrant scent of the oils of Macassar that glistened in his abundant raven curls. He smiled at her, his teeth white and perfect, and for all his fleshy nose and thick straight eyebrows he was not unhandsome.

'Have you more things to show me?' he asked. 'If you have, I can give you a better price for the spoon ... That is, so long as you let me have first choice of the rest of your goods.'

His tone gave a double-edged meaning to the words, but Sarah disregarded that.

'Give me a good price for the spoon, Hebrew, and I'll bargain with you for what's in here.' She jerked her sack causing the silver plate inside to clunk dully. 'But that won't be to-day,' she added.

'All right, my pretty one,' he nodded, and doubled his price. 'There? Is that fair enough? I'm letting you rob me,' he joked.

She took the money and again went to the door.

'Don't forget, pretty. Come and see Shimson Levi very soon.'

'I will, Hebrew. You may count on it,' she told him, and left the shop.

He knew with a powerful certainty that he would indeed meet her again. His father, who had been sitting on a tiny stool in the darkest corner of the shop, clucked his tongue scornfully.

'The boy is a fool!' he stated firmly to an invisible audience. 'It's no wonder I haff vhite hairs, and a head mad vith worry. He'll be the ruin of the bissniss, he vill.'

His son ignored him and dwelt upon his memory of the young woman, who in spite of her shabby travel-stained dress had carried herself like a queen. 'Ve'll meet again, my pretty. I know it,' he thought, and went back to his ledgers.

Sarah paused beneath the overhanging three gold balls of the pawnshop and drank in the scene that curved away from each side of her. On both sides of the street, the crooked, ramshackle ancient buildings were crammed one against the other as if they battled for the very ground they stood upon.

Liquor shops, contract taverns, tailors, chandlers, grocers, watch-jobbers, eating houses, ordinaries, drapers, pawnbrokers, cook-shops, beer- and gin-kens, all clamoured with garishly painted signs and strident-voiced shopmen to be allowed to serve and entertain the passers-by. At one end of the street she could see the arch and drawbridge of King James Gate, that cut off the Island from Portsmouth proper, with the vivid scarlet, white and gold of its military sentinels standing watch upon it. At the other end was the open sky, where the buildings ended and the road ran into the shingle of the beach. The masts and rigging of anchored merchant ships and men o' war lying at their moorings of the Portsea dockyard presented a brave show of flags and buntings fluttering in the wind.

In the street itself civilians were in the minority. They were mostly ticket-porters with the fantail hats and leather shoulder cushions attached by straps to their foreheads, waiting to carry the chests of travellers and Royal Navy men coming ashore at the Spice Island Point, where the lighter men ran their boats up on the shingle beach to unload. Dozens of bell-bottomed, loose-jacketed sailors, their round flat-crowned hats perched jauntily on their tarred pigtailed heads, swaggered by arm-in-arm with women of every conceivable shape and colour. Ragged, gin-sodden hags who for a penny or two would allow any perversion to be practised upon their raddled flesh. Young fresh-faced girls newly come to their age-old profession, who gloried in their tawdry finery of feathered turbans and bonnets and breast-revealing gowns; and who for a few brief months would command high fees and gentle treatment. Older women, still retaining some attractions of face and body, but thin-lipped and hard-eyed, knowing too much of the cutting knives of abortionists, the blows and kicks of drunken clients and vicious ponces, and the slow insidious rot of syphilis and gonorrhoea.

From the ground floors of the taverns sounded the stamp of feet and the wailing of fiddles as the matelots gaily danced, drank and sang their precious hours of freedom away. In the upstairs rooms, blue- and white-uniformed naval officers also entertained their women; and though the food and wines were finer the songs, dances and the urgency of hands seeking warm, soft flesh were the same.

In the gutters outside the foodshops and inns, beggars plied their pitiful trade. Some armless, some legless, some blind, and some all three. Their hoarse pleas for help mingled with the shouts of the street urchins that swarmed shoeless, half-naked, ragged, hungry and neglected, few knowing a mother, even fewer a father.

Periodically a file of soldiers shouldering muskets with fixed bayonets and led by halberd-carrying sergeants patrolled the area, sharing that task with mixed parties of armed marines and cudgel-swinging, hard-hatted ships' petty officers. Whenever men's voices bellowed oaths and curses, and women screamed as glass shattered and furniture crashed over in the taverns and beer-kens, the patrols suddenly appeared and battered down the doors. Minutes later, bloody broken-headed men and women would be hauled out bodily from the rooms and flung into the stinking, refuse-thick gutters, to await the rough justice and draconian punishments of the town's military Provost Marshal.

The very vitality and bustle of the street acted as a magnet, and as Sarah Jenkins stood absorbing this new world, her heart thudded within her breast. 'This is the place ... This is where I'll make my fortune and become a fine lady,' she promised herself exultantly.

'Spare a copper, spare a penny piece for a bold tar, 'oo lorst 'is eyes and legs at Trafalgar Cape wi' immortal Nelson.' The whining voice came from ground level and Sarah started in shock as a grasping hand tugged her skirt.

Propped against the wall of the pawnshop was a grotesque figure, dressed in rags so filthy that no trace of original colour could be discerned. The stumps of thighs jutted out from the base of the torso and the ends had been left uncovered to show the hideous lumps of putrid-hued flesh, created by the surgeons' knives and saws, and the cauterizing boiling tar. The beggar's head was wrapped in greasy swathes of cloth which hid all but the gap-toothed mouth and pimpled, bristled chin. Sarah shuddered as the blackened hands, taloned like claws, tugged insistently again and again on her skirt.

'Spare a copper! Spare a penny piece, for a bold tar as lorst 'is eyes and legs wi' immortal Nelson at Trafalgar Cape.'

She fumbled in the pocket of her skirt and, finding a coin, pressed it into one of the groping hands.

'Bless yer kindness, lady. Bless yer a 'undred times!' The gap-toothed mouth grinned and spittle dribbled down the bristled chin. 'Bless ye good 'eart!'

Sarah pulled free and walked on slowly towards the seaward end of the street. Behind her the beggar stealthily lifted a fold of the cloth covering his face so that his bleary yellowed eyes could examine her clearly. He vented a low whistle of appreciation and beckoned one of the street urchins playing in the foul-smelling gutter before him. The child came and the beggar whispered urgently.

'Run and tell Moonlight Annie, that theer's a fresh partridge afluttering up to'ards the Point.'

The child disappeared into an adjoining beer-ken, and the beggar grinned and let the fold of cloth drop over his eyes once more. Then resumed his plaintive whine. 'Spare a penny! Spare a copper for a bold tar 'oo ...'

Sarah dawdled along the road, absorbed in the sights, scents, and sounds that surrounded her. Brilliantly-feathered parrots hung in tiny cages before a small shop, and they preened and groomed their plumage, spreading their wings, cawing and screeching in constant cacophony, while one cackled almost humanly. 'Rot my bollocks! Pretty! Pretty! Rot my bollocks! Pretty! Pretty!' Sarah laughed at the gorgeous white-and gold-feathered bird, and a passing sailor, struck by her beauty, stopped to speak.

'Wheer bist wandering, my lovely?'

Sarah smiled at him. 'I'm walking for my health,' she replied.

He grinned, showing strong teeth stained brown from the cud of tobacco he had tucked in his cheek. The skin of his pleasant face was deeply suntanned, and his long tarred pigtail snaked over one broad shoulder and down the front of his short open blue jacket.

'You don't want to walk alone in this street, gal,' he told her. 'Some o' these drunks 'ull be athinkin' you'm not the good, nice wench I can see you am ... If you gets my meanin'.'

Sarah side-stepped him and went on, saying in passing, 'My thanks for the warning, but I'm well able to steer a safe course.'

'Come inside for chops and rumpsteaks, lady,' a short, fat white-aproned man invited from the doorway of a cook-shop. 'Just smell that loverley pie I'm acookin' in the oven this very minute, will you.'

The savoury scent of roasting meat and baking pastry and thick rich hot-spiced gravies billowed out in almost tangible clouds from the shadowed interior.

'Only the finest, tenderest and freshest meats here, lady,' the shopman continued to cajole her. 'Ate enough on it and it'll keep that fine body o' yourn as firm and juicy as a capon.'

She fended him off with a shake of her head, then stepped close to the wall to give way to a pair of half-drunk marines who had their scarlet-sleeved arms wrapped around the waist and shoulders of the young, fresh-faced girl between them. She wore the plumed-turbaned finery and deep-slashed colourful gown of a successful whore and was laughing shrilly, responding to the rough banter of her companions. But Sarah saw that above the laughing mouth the thickly kohled blue eyes were bleak and hopeless.

Sarah pursed her lips. 'That's one trade I'll not be following,' she told herself silently. 'No matter how empty my belly might become.'

Another shop window caught her attention. Behind its bow-fronted diamond panes, a jumbled profusion of ornaments and jewellery glittered and sparkled. She pressed her nose to the distorting glass and gazed at the strange barbaric trinkets garnered from the four corners of the earth.

On she went, half drunk with the salt tang of sea, wet sand and stone, fresh-cut timbers, tarred ropes and cables, spiced with the scents of cinnamon, nutmeg, cloves, peppers, coffee, rum, brandy, tobacco, snuff, and a myriad other smells of a great maritime port. Her pleasure was suddenly marred by a sense of loneliness. A longing for someone dear to her to share all this with.

'I wish that Jethro were with me,' she thought, and her whole being pulsed with a hungry yearning for him to be there. Walking by her side, smiling with her and sharing her delight in this treasure-house of new experience. Half-angrily she thrust the thoughts from her mind. 'It's no use my wishing for what cannot be,' she told herself, and tried to ignore the tiny voice in her mind, which would not be silenced but kept on repeating, 'Yes, but how wonderful if it could be so.'

She had reached the shingled Point, and was standing looking at the rows of boats drawn up on the pebbles when the Negress came from behind her and said, 'God save me, my honey, but you were hard to find.'

Sarah swung in a surprise which deepened when she saw the magnificent figure now standing at her side. The Negress was a glossy plum-black in colour and stood a full six feet in height. The curves of her body, accentuated by her flowing

154

green robe shot with shimmers of gold, were huge at breasts, hips and shoulders, and yet so perfectly proportioned that they were beautiful. She wore no hat and her thick woolly curls were tight to her well-shaped head. Apart from one thick silver bangle on her plump wrist, her only jewels were the great gold chains which dangled from her ears and which glinted as she moved.

'Moonlight Annie bids you welcome to Spice Island, my honey.' The voice was deep and musical and the splendid white teeth flashed in the purple-painted thickness of curved lips as she smiled at Sarah. 'Don't you take fright, my honey, I know you're new come here. It's Moonlight Annie's business to know these things.'

Sarah had recovered from her surprise, but not entirely from a faint sense of awe at being confronted by such an overwhelmingly outlandish creature.

'What do you want with me?' she asked, a trifle nervously. The Negress chuckled and rolled her long-lashed eyes so that the whites seemed to rotate around the axis of the jet black centres.

'Only to talk, my honey. Only to talk.' Her deep voice was warm and friendly. 'Come in here with me and take a glass of wine.'

Impelled by loneliness and curiosity, Sarah allowed herself to be gently ushered into a small tavern that fronted the shingle, and within moments found herself sitting in a tiny room sipping sweet heady wine with her new acquaintance.

Shimson Levi had watched Sarah's departure through the grilled windows of his shop. He saw the beggar accost her and then the small boy being sent on his errand. When the big Negress came out of the beer-ken and spoke to the beggar before hurrying away up the street, Shimson scowled to himself. 'Oh no, Moonlight,' he muttered. 'This vench isn't for you.'

From a hidden drawer under the counter he pulled a small silver-mounted pistol and slipped it into the waistband of his breeches.

'Vatch the shop, old 'un,' he told his father, and went into the street.

The Negress was far ahead of him, but her height and exotic colouring made her an easy mark to follow. By the time he reached the shingle, however, the two women had already disappeared. He looked about him at the huddled row of ramshackle taverns and houses and, beginning with the nearest, began to prowl through them.

The warmth of the room and the strength of the wine, coupled with the effects of her hard travelling, combined to relax Sarah and make her drowsily careless. Although expecting that the giant Negress would eventually make her some sort of proposal, for the time being Sarah was content to sit and rest in the Negress's congenial company. Moonlight Annie's high spirits and friendly manner were a welcome change from the loneliness of the past weeks. But Sarah retained enough awareness to say after a time,

'Listen, Mistress, I'll pay the score here. For I've heard that sometimes, penniless girls are recruited into bawdy houses and with all respect, I have no wish to be.'

The Negress threw back her head and laughed uproariously, her massive breasts and shoulders heaving with her enjoyment. When her mirth had subsided she wiped the laughter tears from her plum-black cheeks and answered, 'Oh my honey, don't you know? You've already bin recruited.'

Sarah's head rang with alarm. She made to rise but the vast black hands clamped on her two wrists and pinned them to the table-top.

Sarah's wits raced. 'If you do not release me this instant, then I'll scream for help,' she threatened.

Moonlight Annie's golden earchains swung and clinked as she slowly shook her head. The smile on her thick purple lips momentarily lost its warmth and became vulpine.

'Oh no, my honey. You won't scream, because there's no one to hear you.'

'The landlord will,' Sarah retorted defiantly.

The Negress laughed amusedly. 'The landlord is an old friend, my honey. So stay still, and let's talk some more.'

'I'm no sixpenny whore!' Sarah's temper had risen and it overlaid her fear of the other's great size.

The big eyes facing her widened in mockery. 'I know you're not, my honey. I wouldn't be interested in you if you was ... No, I like you because you looks like one of the gentry, a real lady. My gentlemen friends will pay a high price, and gladly, for a fine-mannered piece like you.' Her voice softened. 'And you'll do well out of it, my honey ... Moonlight Annie knows how to treat her girls proper. You'll earn more money than you've ever dreamed on. Why, in a few months you'll be riding in your own carriage, with servants to wait on you hand and foot, and that's the truth, I swear it on my soul!'

The Negress grimaced. 'Listen, my honey. One shout from me and there'll be two of my bully-boys here in a second. They'll not be gentle with you, I'll tell you that. They likes to give the girls a rough handling, them two does.'

Sarah screamed, and tried to jerk free. Her body was strong and agile and the Negress, for all her bulk, was forced to close with the smaller woman to stop her escaping. She shouted aloud, 'Morry! Beddo! Get in here!'

Two burly, rough-looking men burst into the tiny room and in seconds their brutal hands had smothered Sarah's cries and pinioned her struggling body across the table. The Negress put both hands on her big hips and stared at the girl's full heaving breasts.

'You're a rare sweet prize, my honey, no doubt on it.'

'And so are you, Moonlight!' Before anyone could react to his shouted words, Shimson Levi hurtled through the door to clutch the Negress's throat with one hand, and with the other ram the barrel of his pistol between the thick lips.

'Let the girl loose, or I'll blow this nigger sow's head off,' he hissed at the men holding Sarah.

The bully-boys gaped open-mouthed at Moonlight Annie, who nodded as best she could.

Levi swung the Negress so that her body was half between him and the men, then said urgently to Sarah, 'Take your bag, girl, and get along to my shop. I'll be there straight behind you.'

Sarah, trembling and flushed, her mind reeling from the impact of so many violent events, did as she was bid. Shimson Levi wrenched the pistol barrel from Moonlight Annie's mouth and thrust it brutally under her chin, gouging the soft folds of flesh so that she winced in pain.

'That vos my vench you'd got there, Moonlight, you black sow,' he told her menacingly. 'I've a mind to blow your brains out.'

The Negress was badly shaken. 'I didn't know that, Shim. I swear on my soul, I didn't know!'

'Vell, now you do,' Levi growled. 'And don't try any more o' your tricks with her, Annie, or I'll see that you svings for it.' He glanced at the two bully-boys. 'That means you two as vell ... Don't any of you forget that Shimson Levi knows enough about you lot to get all of you hung from Vapping Valls ... And if anything should happen to me, then my

family up in London vill lay the info in front o' the beaks ...
Remember it vell.'

Once satisfied that he had cowed them, Levi released the
Negress's throat and slipped the pistol back into his waistband. 'And now I'll bid you good day,' he told them, and
walked casually out from the tavern.

Back at the pawnshop, Sarah was standing waiting. Already her resilient spirit had thrown off the effects of her un-
pleasant experience. When Shimson Levi returned she started
to thank him, but he silenced her.

'No, my vench, don't thank me,' he grinned. 'It's only that
I'm not a man to let a bunch o' vharf rats like them come
between me and a bit o' good business. Let's see the rest o'
that stuff you're acarrying now, shall ve?'

Sarah's face hardened. 'So that's your game, is it, Hebrew?
I'm to give you the stuff for helping me, am I?'

He shook his macassared curls and said gently, 'No, my
pretty. You've not understood me right. I intend to give you
a fair price for it.' His moist, protruding eyes were kindly and
his sincerity so patent that she softened immediately.

'Forgive me,' she said, and poured out the silver from the
sack.

Levi whistled softly as he calculated a rough total of its
value. 'That's a handsome sight, my pretty, and truth to tell
I've not sufficient here in the shop at present to cover it.'

Sarah studied him carefully for some minutes while his long
knowing fingers lifted and fondled the pieces of precious
metal. Ideas which had been burgeoning in her mind during
the long trek south came to sudden fruition. She wanted desperately to help Henri escape. She wanted, equally desperately, to establish herself as a woman of means. She came to
a decision and asked, 'Is there sufficient price from those to
set me up in a business here?'

The man looked up at her and pursed his lips judiciously
while he considered the question and its possible implications.
Then he nodded.

'Yes, surely there is. But vot sort of a business had you got
in mind?'

'A club,' she told him. 'A gaming club.'

His surprise showed clearly, and he started to shake his
head. Then his agile mind saw the idea's potential, and he
followed his instincts.

'You'll need tvice or three times vot's here, to do the job

proper,' he told her, while his thoughts clarified. 'And you vouldn't be able to do it on your own. You'd need a good man vith you. One that you could trust and who knew all the capers.'

Sarah's determination had now reached white heat. 'Do you know where such a man might be found in this town?' she pressed.

After a long pause, during which his steady regard of her did not waver, Shimson Levi finally grinned and told her, 'You're alookin' at him, my vench.'

CHAPTER FIFTEEN

All through the night, the heavy boots of the marine sentries clumped along the catwalk of the *Crown* hulk. Every fifteen minutes, the hoarse shouts of 'All's well!' 'All's well!' 'All's well! 'All's well!' rang out from ship to ship, reassuring each guard commander that the men he had posted were alert, and the prisoners battened below decks were quiet.

Henri Chanteur lay on his back in his narrow hammock and listened to the sounds of the night. The hammocks were slung in rows across the battery, so closely that the sides touched and if his neighbour, Gaston de Chambray, moved arm or leg, then Henri could feel that movement. He calculated that there were almost four hundred men on this deck, snoring, breaking wind, muttering and crying out in bad dreams ... The neighbour on Henri's other side did none of those things. He had died some hours before. Henri had listened to the gurgling death rattles and had roused Gaston de Chambray. The cuirassier colonel had shrugged.

'Just forget it, Henri. The poor devil will die before morning and will then be happier than we are. Try and sleep, there's nothing you can do for him.' ... And so the young Frenchman had lain listening to the man's life-force struggling to free itself from the diseased bone and flesh that entrapped it, and had prayed for a speedy end to the suffering.

'All's well!' 'All's well!' 'All's well!' 'All's well!' The shouts echoed across the calm harbour and as those echoes grew faint and far away, Henri heard a peculiar scratching across the deck beneath the hammocks. At first he disregarded it, thinking it to be just another of the many strange ship noises as the old timbers creaked and the waves gently lapped and gurgled against the hull.

'It's probably a rat,' he told himself, knowing that at night when all was quiet, myriads of the rodents came out of the bilges to forage. The scraping and scratching persisted and came nearer.

'It's too damned heavy for a rat,' he thought, and listened hard. The scraping suddenly ceased, to be followed immediately by a loud and distinctive smacking of lips masticating food. This also ceased and for a few seconds nothing more occurred.

Gaston de Chambray snorted and turned his body and Henri was momentarily distracted by the pressure of his new friend's knees and elbows through the thin canvas wall of the hammock. He moved his own body to escape that pressure and as he settled upon his side, facing the dead man's hammock, he felt that hammock suddenly drop silently down. Unable to see anything at all in the pitch darkness, he felt with his hand. There was only empty space. A spasm of fear caused his heart to thud and he held his breath to stop himself shouting aloud.

He lay tensed and still, and sensed rather than heard, movement at his side. Cautiously he slid his arm out from his hammock and searched the blackness with his fingers. They suddenly touched warm, living flesh and he cried out in shock.

Instantly Gaston de Chambray was awake. 'What is it, Henri?' he asked urgently.

'Someone's meddling with this dead fellow,' Henri told him.

'*Aux armes! Aux armes!*' de Chambray bellowed. 'Block the ladder! The Imperial Mantles are here! Block the ladder! Imperial Mantles! Imperial Mantles!'

The shout was taken up all through the battery as men were torn from sleep. Then abruptly, there was silence once more. A clattering of booted feet and weapons sounded from behind the guard barrier and from two of the loopholes beams of light streamed into the prisoners' quarter and a voice roared, 'Stop that bloody noise, you Frog bastards, or you'll be fired on.'

From somewhere in the battery a man screamed in terror, '*Aidez-moi! Aidez-moi!*'

'Here he is! Get him!' other men shouted in excitement. There was a brief scuffle in the darkness and the piteous screams for help were cut short.

'I'll not be tellin' you buggers agen,' the threatening voice behind the barrier roared. 'One more sound and we open fire.'

All was still and silent and after a time the lights disappeared from the loopholes and the boots clumped back up the ladder and dully across the deck above.

'What has happened?' Henri whispered. 'Who was the man who was screaming?'

'You'll see in the morning, when it gets light,' de Chambray whispered back. 'But now get some sleep, there's nothing more to be done tonight.' With that, the older man settled himself back in his hammock and in seconds was again snoring softly.

His mind a jumble of puzzlement, Henri also tried to rest. The battery again filled with the murmurous sounds of sleeping men and he dozed fitfully.

The stars wheeled about the poles and slowly the sky lightened in the east. At eight o'clock in the morning, a seaman went forward and rang the ship's bell. The burly marine sergeant saluted the naval lieutenant who commanded the night guard.

'Eight bells, sir. Permission to open portholes.'

The lieutenant, a thin sallow man nodded in affirmation. 'It's fair weather, sergeant. You may leave open port and larboard.'

'Aye aye, sir.' The sergeant stamped to the taffrail and shouted to the night sentries, seven in number, on the gallery.

'Open portholes, port and larboard!'

The marines, aided by some sailors, hurried from portlight to portlight unbolting and wrenching them open, taking care to jump back from the apertures to avoid the rush of foul gases that had built up in the pressure from so many lungs in such a confined space.

'Eight bells! Eight bells! Lash up and stow! Lash up and stow! Eight bells! Lash up and stow!'

Henri was roused by the orders hurled through loopholes and portholes by a dozen leather-lunged men. He felt bleary-eyed and stale in mouth and body. He rubbed his eyelids to clear the gum of sleep and scratched hard at the vermin he had already begun to give unwilling shelter and nourishment to. Gaston de Chambray sat up and grinned at him.

'You did well last night, *mon ami.*'

The memory of the previous night's events flooded back and Henri peered over the edge of his hammock. The dead man was lying face down, arms stretched above his head. His jacket was half off and his legs and lower torso naked.

'Never mind him for the moment,' Gaston instructed. 'You must get your bedding stowed away.'

He showed the younger man how to roll his hammock about his covering and mattress and use its hanging ropes to thread through the brass eyelets along the length of the canvas and truss it so that it resembled a long thick sausage. From his neatly fashioned canvas waist-pouch, Gaston fished a piece of chalk and handed it to Henri.

'Write your name, rank and regiment on the canvas, so that no one else will take it.'

Once their hammocks had been placed with the others against the bulkheads, the cuirassier examined closely the pale body of the dead man, paying particular attention to the lean buttocks and thighs. He nodded to the men watching him.

'It's all right. The bastard either wasn't hungry or didn't have time.'

A collective sigh gusted in relief, and at Henri's elbow Nathan Caldicott chuckled bitterly and muttered, 'On the other hand, maybe after spending so much goddam time in this Limejuicers' floating palace, the poor devil's flesh was no longer fit for human consumption.'

Henri hardly heard the American. A veteran of the pursuit to Corunna and the savage winter guerrilla warfare in the bitter mountains of Spain, he knew well enough what de Chambray had been searching for. When men grew hungry enough, and desperate enough, then the tenuously enforced restraints and mores of civilization were rent asunder and any type of food became desirable.

'All right boys.' The colonel evidently wielded great authority in this sub-world. 'Take out the blanket and mattress and tie him up nicely in the hammock. Not that these misers of English will bury him in it, I know. Still, let him go decently from here. Are there any more?'

'Non, mon colonel, not yet. But I don't think old Léfèvre will last the day out,' a man answered.

De Chambray nodded. 'Very well. Put this poor devil by the hatch when you've done ... Now go about your normal business while we deal with the animal.'

'He is over here, Colonel de Chambray.' A skeletal Parisian pushed through the crowd.

'Good! I want at least twenty men with knives. We'll deal with him down on the Orlop deck. Trust the cursed English to leave the portholes open and give us too much light when we didn't want them to.'

'It's a beautiful morning, *mon Colonel*,' the skeletal Parisian tried to joke. 'Perhaps the noble Captain Redmond wishes us to enjoy the balmy airs.'

'*Merde!*' For a moment the colonel's customary good manners deserted him. He beckoned Henri. 'Come, you must give testimony.' Then led the way to the wide ladder at the far end of the deck which connected the upper and lower batteries.

The captured man presented a sorry spectacle. He was naked, his body caked with filth, and lice could be seen moving amongst the long matted hair that grew low on his forehead. His hands were tied behind him with rope cunningly lashed also around his bearded throat, and another piece of rope held a wad of rag crammed into his mouth as a gag. Dried blood liberally plastered his hairy chest and shoulders and his eyes were mere slits in a badly swollen, bruised, and cut face.

'I see *les enfants* were not gentle with him,' de Chambray chuckled. He issued a series of rapid orders and a large body of knife-brandishing men acted as an advance guard, pushing the surly-faced inhabitants of the lower battery away from the bottom of the connecting ladder. Henri could see no apparent difference between either the quarters or the men that lived in them.

De Chambray quickly explained. 'These men on this deck are *les raffales*. They don't want to work or try to escape. They are nearly all private soldiers and junior N.C.O.s. All they do is gamble and laze around all day and steal whatever they can. They don't consider that the war is any concern of theirs any longer. We, *les officiers* and *messieurs ou bourgeois*, on the other hand, are still soldiers of France and wish to serve the Empereur. You will learn what I mean and see the differences between them and us as time goes by.'

The party traversed the lower battery and came to yet another ladder, narrow and steep, that went down into the very bowels of the ship. De Chambray issued further instructions and from somewhere stubs of candle were produced and lit. The colonel leant and shouted into the fetid darkness below.

'Move away from the ladder. Any of you scum that are within five metres of the ladder will get your throats slit.'

He held up his hand for silence and listened carefully. From below could be heard low-pitched mutterings and then the padding and shuffling of bare feet over the planking. De

Chambray smiled his satisfaction and jerked his head. A candle-bearer swiftly descended the ladder, followed by three of the biggest men in the party. They disappeared from view for some moments, then one reappeared at the foot of the ladder.

'It's all clear, *mon Colonel*.'

The remainder of the party, dragging the prisoner with them, quickly descended. As Henri put his feet on the Orlop deck he felt his stomach turn over. Despite his sense of smell having accustomed itself to the stench of the upper battery, the sheer putridity of the air down here, with only a single layer of planking separating the Orlop from the bilges, made him feel faint.

'Behold, Captain Chanteur ... the empire of the Imperial Mantles!' Colonel de Chambray gestured at the space illuminated by the wavering candle flames ... 'And these animals were once the soldiers of Napoleon Bonaparte!'

In a half circle, blinking in the weak light, the Imperial Mantles stared sullenly at the intruders. They were, every one of them, naked. Shaggy headed and heavily bearded, their bodies corpselike in both smell and appearance. Many wore draped around their shoulders the single torn filthy blanket from which they derived their nickname. Henri inwardly acknowledged its justice. The Empereur's robes of state had swarms of bees worked in pure gold thread as decoration. The blankets of those who possessed them also had small patches shimmering in the candle glow; silvery-gold patches of lice and their sticky eggs.

The deck itself was thick with tiny delicate bones, scraps of bedraggled half-chewed fur and skin, and soggy with human excreta. Even as Henri stared in horrified disgust, there was a movement amongst the refuse and with a shout of glee one of the Imperial Mantles flung himself forward to snatch up a writhing, struggling, squealing black rat, which he held high in triumph before neatly breaking its back with his thumbs.

'At least we've made one of these creatures happy, gentlemen,' de Chambray observed quietly. 'We've provided him with a fine dinner. Now listen to me all of you,' he shouted. 'This animal here,' he indicated the bound prisoner, 'last night attempted to rob the body of a dead officer. We permit a few of you to wander our decks at night and pick up any scraps of food that you find there. I do not wish to stop this custom. But you all know well the penalty for stealing from either the living, or the dead ... Captain Chanteur, give your evidence,' he ordered sharply. 'Come on, man! Tell what happened.'

Henri stepped forward and related what had occurred.

'Do you recognize this man as the guilty person?' de Chambray demanded.

Henri's jaw dropped in sheer surprise at the stupidity of such a question. '*Mais non!* How could I?' he burst out. 'It was pitch black at that time. I couldn't possibly recognize anyone in such conditions.'

The colonel frowned. 'Sergeant-chef Malet. Step forward,' he ordered curtly.

A barrel-chested, shaven-headed man, the sergeant-chef spoke in the thick argot of the Marseilles waterfront.

'At your orders, *mon Colonel.*'

'Give your statement,' de Chambray told him.

'Oui, *mon Colonel.*' The man stared straight ahead, expressionless and rattled out, 'I have the hammock directly in front of the ladder to the lower battery. The instant the alarm was raised I and my *copains* blocked the ladder. It was impossible for any living creature to pass without us knowing ... And no one did pass.'

'Good.' The colonel's deepset eyes lost some of the anger that had entered them when Henri had spoken. 'We shall waste no more time. This man was the only one on the upper battery who did not belong there. Without doubt he is guilty of attempting to rob the dead. Commandant de Malvoisin, Commandent de Thierry, Captain Arnaud, what verdict have you arrived at?'

The three men so addressed had been standing opposite the prisoner regarding him closely. They whispered together briefly, then one after the other replied with a single word, 'Guilty!'

The bound man began to shake his head frantically from side to side and tears squeezed out of the slits of his eyes.

The colonel's face was grim. 'The verdict is guilty! The penalty is death!' he stated curtly.

Choking sounds came from deep in the prisoner's throat and his knees buckled. De Chambray pointed at two of the Imperial Mantles before him.

'Put him in the bilges,' he told them.

With no hesitation they sprang to obey, while a space was

cleared amongst their fellows to disclose a trapdoor. The trap was opened and the prisoner dragged to the opening and heaved head-first down it. There was frantic splashing and thudding and both Imperial Mantles followed feet-first down the black hole.

'This is murder!' Henri ejaculated angrily. 'There is no proof that he was the man. Where are the trousers that were stripped from the body? He didn't have them.'

'Hold your tongue,' de Chambray barked at him. 'I will remind you, Captain Chanteur, that this is a military tribunal.' His face was merciless, and Henri felt the sickening realization that nothing he could do or say would alter the course of events. He remembered the words of the marine sergeant after the fight. 'Indeed it is the truth, what you said, Englishman,' he thought helplessly. 'They are all mad on board this hulk.'

After what seemed endless hours, but in reality only a few minutes, the flaccid, steaming wet corpse of the drowned prisoner was lifted from the bilge hatch and thrown to land soggily at the feet of de Chambray. He nodded and pressed on the dead stomach so that a spout of water gushed from the gaping mouth.

'Let this be a lesson to the rest of you,' he warned, and amidst a frightened silence the party returned to their own quarters.

When they reached them, the colonel spoke to Henri. His manner was once more courteous and his voice pleasant-toned and gentle.

'You are shocked and disgusted, I know, my young friend. But when you have been here a little longer, you will realize why we have to do such terrible things.'

'I realize already why the Englishmen here treat us with such contempt,' Henri said hotly. 'It can only be expected when we behave like savages.'

The cuirassier's eyes were kindly, he had felt a great and instinctive liking for this young man from the first moment he had met him.

'What right have the English to despise us for behaving like savages, Henri?' he asked softly. 'It is they who have imprisoned us in this vile jungle ... We are its victims, not its creators.'

The words sank deep into Henri's mind, and he could find no answer to them.

CHAPTER SIXTEEN

The twelfth day of December was almost springlike in the warmth of its air and the softness of the southern breezes. The sails of Ballard's windmill which stood close to the shore near the abandoned Southsea Castle circled slowly, occasionally creaking to a halt when the fitful wind dropped. Each time the millstones stopped grinding, Samuel Ballard the miller would curse horribly and berate his long-suffering wife as if it were her fault when God stopped the winds. Close to the mill was the miller's house and outbuildings, and in between the castle and the mill stood a small windowless building known as the Firebarn. It was here that ammunition was prepared for the practice of the Portsmouth garrison.

Lieutenant the Honourable John Coventry, adjutant of the Third Worcestershire Militia, leant negligently against the open doorway of the Firebarn and watched, without much enthusiasm, the white-jacketed fatigue party inside the building make up blank cartridges. The young adjutant was something of an 'exquisite', with his fair hair cropped in the upswept 'à la Titus' mode, and his side whiskers curling across his cheeks. His civilian dress was the very epitome of gentility; single-breasted, cutaway olive coat, striped waistcoat, white gaiter pantaloons strapped over polished shoes and an extremely high-wrapped pink cravat. In one hand he held his curly-brimmed high-crowned brown hat, while the other constantly toyed with the quizzing glass he wore dangling on a silk ribbon around his neck.

'Goddemmit! Cannot your men hurry it along, Corporal?' he drawled lazily. 'I've no wish to spend the entire dammed day here.'

The corporal saluted the brim of his cap and shouted at the men, 'Gerra move on wi' it, you idle dogs!'

There was a brief flurry of quickened movement, then imperceptibly the pace of the work slowed back to the original tempo.

The Hon. John yawned and, pushing himself languidly erect turned to look across the flat Southsea Common at the skyline of Portsmouth, a mile distant, dominated by the tall square semaphore tower on its shore side. All over the common, squads of soldiers were at drill and the shouts of the drill sergeants and corporals mingled with the blaring sounds which came from the sheltered area beneath the castle ramparts, where Mr Charles Quinton, the Bandmaster of the Third, badgered his twenty-odd yellow-coated musicians through the scales of their bassoons, cor anglais, oboes, trumpets, fifes, serpents, tambourines, cymbals, triangles, and drums in tuneless cacophony.

The Hon. John yawned again and stretched wide his arms, causing the hard muscles of his deceptively languid-looking body to tense and contract. Then suddenly he noticed something which made him forget his boredom. Approaching him was a pony and trap. It was on the occupants of the trap that the adjutant focused his interest. Two young women sat side by side, one handling the reins very competently, while on a small dicky seat behind them was perched an older woman. The Hon. John lifted his hand in greeting and went smiling to meet them. The trap halted and he bowed low, with an elegant flourish of his hat.

'La, sir! How gallant we are this morning,' a laughing voice teased him. He straightened and caught his breath. The girl handling the reins had honey-coloured hair and large brown eyes, and the young man thought her to be one of the most beautiful women he had ever seen. Her companion was also blonde, but he found her plain and disagreeable in expression. Both girls were clothed alike in black close-fitting helmet hats with white ermine edging and long grey cloaks trimmed with the same fur. The pretty girl who handled the reins was Jessica Ward, and she nudged her companion, Dorothea Burd.

'What do you think, Dotty? Is not the Honourable John Coventry both looking and behaving very gallant?'

Dorothea Burd sniffed crossly. 'Cannot we drive on, Jessica? I thought that you wished to watch the *Vulcan* come in.'

'The *Vulcan*, Miss Jessica?' John Coventry raised his eyebrows quizzically.

'Yes, Lieutenant Coventry ... The *Vulcan* frigate! Jessica

has a friend on it, returning from Portugal,' Dorothea snapped at him, and added maliciously, 'He is a real soldier.'

The adjutant flushed. It was a sore point with the militia that most people regarded them only as play-soldiers.

'Miss Dorothea,' he said stiffly. 'I'm quite sure that your father regards the men in his regiment as "real" soldiers also.'

Dorothea's father, Major Thomas Henry Burd, was commanding the Third Worcestershire in the absence of its Lieutenant-Colonel.

Coventry went on, 'We may be classed as the Army of the Reserve, but we stand ready to meet any French assault on these shores, and are trained well enough and have bravery enough to give a good account of ourselves.'

'I do not anticipate that Boney and his hordes will come at that time, Lieutenant Coventry,' she said scathingly. 'According to the latest gazette, he and his Grand Army are even now perishing in the snows of Russia ... It hardly seems likely that he will suddenly swoop down like an eagle upon the fair city of Portsmouth, does it?'

Jessica's red lips trembled as she struggled not to smile at her friend's acid treatment of the languid exquisite. She liked the Honourable John well enough, but at times his affectations irritated her and she thought it only just that his vanity should be occasionally pricked a little. The young man made no reply to Dorothea's attack. Instead he spoke to Jessica.

'If you wish to watch a ship come in, Miss Jessica, the castle is certainly the best vantage point. Might I have the pleasure of escorting you there?'

'Why? Is there a danger of French pirates carrying us off?' Dorothea scoffed.

Jessica's brown eyes softened at the sight of John Coventry's obvious embarrassment, and she smiled at him sympathetically.

'It would please me greatly, Lieutenant Coventry,' she told him.

The older woman perched on the dicky seat was her maid Joan, who had come to wetnurse Jessica as a baby and had stayed to look after the girl ever since. Jessica handed the reins to her and told her to wait with the trap.

'It's such a lovely day,' she told them all. 'I feel like strolling for a while until we hear the signal gun.'

The two girls and the man walked slowly towards the ramparts of the castle, chatting as they went. Even Dorothea lost some of her tartness and joined amicably enough in the conversation. Coventry was utterly happy as he looked down at the lovely Jessica, who was so petite that the top of her head came only to his shoulder.

A hollow thump came loudly from the earthworks of the Lumps Fort battery, farther east along the shoreline, and Jessica clapped her hands in delight.

'They must have sighted the *Vulcan.*'

'May I inquire who is the friend you expect?' the Hon. John asked, jealousy beginning to torment him.

'His name is David Warburton. He was my very dear childhood playmate,' the girl answered, her soft eyes shining in excited anticipation. 'He was wounded July last, at the battle of Salamanca. One of his fellow officers brought news some time ago that he was now recovered sufficiently to be sent home to recuperate. It's almost certain that he will be on the *Vulcan.* It will be such a surprise for him to find our family here in Portsmouth.'

'Why should that be, Jessie?' Dorothea Burd asked.

'Well, he left for the Peninsula more than four years since, and my mother and I were then at home in Worcestershire. I've written to him of course, but not since we came here to be with father, and then after David had been wounded we knew naught of his whereabouts until his friend called to tell us that David would be coming home, and naturally we were still at Holt End when that occurred. He has no way of knowing that we are here in Portsmouth.'

'Has he a family of his own?' the adjutant wanted to know, thinking that if the wounded man had, then he would not stay long with the Wards.

'No, the poor boy has no one. He was orphaned as a child and came to live with his uncle, George Seymour, at our village. His uncle died some time past ... George Seymour had a son, named William ...' She paused, and her eyes took on a faraway look as memories dominated her thoughts.

'William was a very strange boy. He was much older than David or I, and although I think he loved David well enough, yet he had a streak of cruelty in him which sometimes frightened me very much ...' She shivered slightly.

'And his cousin, William Seymour? Will not your friend wish to go and visit him for a while?' Coventry broke in, clutching at straws.

Jessica smiled and shook her head. 'William went into the army years ago, and no one has heard from him since, to my knowledge. He could be in India, or anywhere. Perhaps even dead. But it doesn't matter. Davy will stay with us until he is completely recovered.'

The Hon. John's heart sank.

'Naturally I would have preferred to go to the dockyard and meet him myself,' the girl went on happily, not realizing the effects her artless pleasure was having on John Coventry. 'But Mama would not hear of such a thing. She says that a young lady must never be seen in such low places amongst the riffraff that congregate there. So instead we have to send one of the servants to meet every ship, and bring David to our home when he arrives.' She looked up into the adjutant's face. 'Do you think it will help Davy to recover more quickly if he is amongst friends?' she appealed.

The young man nodded slowly. 'To convalesce under the same roof that you live beneath, Miss Jessica, would ensure a recovery from any wounds.' he said sincerely.

They entered the castle and mounted the ramparts.

'There she comes,' Jessica called out excitedly. 'Is she not most beautiful?'

The frigate was under full canvas, her white ensigns spreading bravely and the waves creaming back from the slicing impact of her black- and yellow-striped hull.

'What a fine thing it must be, to be a man and have command of such a noble creation as that ship,' Jessica murmured half to herself, as her romantic imagination was sent soaring by the sight. 'Why, it resembles a very tiger of the sea.'

The Hon. John stared down at her small, wrapt face and envied with all his heart the fortunate David Warburton. His Britannic Majesty's Ship *Vulcan* fired her cannonades in reply to the salutes of the shore batteries and swept through the narrow harbour entrance, under the frowning cannon muzzles of Fort Blockhouse on the Gosport side and the Point Battery of Spice Island on the other. Glazed-hatted boatswains' mates shouted oaths and swung knotted rope-ends, starting the seamen up the rigging like agile monkeys and out along the yardarms. There they lay across and in concerted effort began to haul up and furl the salt-stiff sails by sheer strength of hands and muscles. The ship lost way and her great anchors dropped plummeting to the sea bed where their curved, barbed flukes gouged, dragged, gouged and then bit deep, sending clouds of muddy sand swirling up from the rocky bottom. The seamen gazed hungrily at the land while they finished furling, then lashing and trussing the folds of canvas, and grumbled bitterly to each other about the captain's harshness in prohibiting shore leave.

'Eighteen months at bleedin' sea and not even a bleedin' foot on the bloody beach, let alone inland,' was the overriding grievance. On shore the lookout high up on the square semaphore tower overlooking the harbour entrance, snapped his telescope shut and bellowed,

'The *Vulcan* frigate's in, sir.'

A tiny midshipman wearing a cocked hat three sizes too large for him, ran to bring the news to the hoary-headed old lieutenant commanding the signal station, and within seconds the signal pennant rose to the mast head and the two arms of the semaphore-post began to twirl and set in their evolutions. From High Street, Portsmouth the message was picked up and relayed by other men peering through telescopes and shouting letters to operators at the stations on Southsea Beach, Portsdown Hill, Compton Down, Holder, Haste, Bannick and Pearly ... On and on it flashed, to Chatley, Coopers Hill, Kingston, Putney, Chelsea, to arrive finally at the Admiralty House in Whitehall, London. From the dropping of the frigate's anchor in Portsmouth Harbour, it took only fifteen minutes for the august Lords of the Admiralty 73 miles away in London to be informed of its safe arrival.

It took far less time for the news to spread through the narrow twisting alleyways and lanes of Spice Island, old Portsmouth, and Portsea. From dozens of beer-kens and taverns, cook-shops, and chop-houses, back-street brothels and main-street gambling hells, hundreds of pedlars, bumboat men, touts, ponces, bully-boys and ladies of easy virtue hastened to the beach.

Sarah Jenkins and Shimson Levi stood quietly to one side on the Point beach at Spice Island and observed the happenings. A trio of paint-plastered, wrinkled hags, clad in torn dirty dresses and bedraggled feather bonnets approached one of the boatmen, a big, peg-legged ex-petty officer. Their spokeswoman's toothless red gash of a mouth curved wide in grotesque coquetry.

'Come on dearie, take us out to the *Vulcan*. We'll pay well.'

The boatman shifted the quid of tobacco he was chewing from one cheek to the other and spat a long stream of brown juice on to the shingle.

'Sod orf!' he growled. 'You'm too bleedin' old!'

The hag drew herself erect and swore at him in fury. His mahogany-brown face remained stolid and he spurted another stream of juice from his dark-stained mouth and said unheatedly,

'It's no use you agooin' on at me, you old cow. I'd not be able to sell you to the *Vulcan*. I takes only tender wenches that I con get three shillin' apiece for ... I'd not get three pence for the likes o' your withered bilboes. Look at 'um!' He pointed at the shrivelled breasts displayed by the torn gown.

All along the beach similar scenes were enacted as the other boatmen haggled with the crowding whores. Each man trying to select the youngest, most attractive and best-dressed women, knowing from past experience that they would only get paid if the women were accepted on board the ship. The three hags withdrew a couple of paces and whispered together, then the spokeswoman came back to the boatman.

' 'Ere, dearie,' she whined placatingly. 'We'll gi' you four shillin's each to take us out.'

He shook his head. 'I'se told you once, you stupid cow ... You'm too bleedin' old and too bleedin' ugly. Now bugger orf, afore I catches you a belt in the chops.'

The woman's raddled face was tragic beneath the thick mask of rouge, enamel, and powder.

'Lissen, cully, things 'um terrible hard wi' us. We'll gi you the rhino now if you'll take us out.'

The boatman hesitated. 'You'se got the sale-money, 'ave you?' he questioned doubtfully.

'Yes, we 'ave,' the hag nodded excitedly and with a great show of grimy petticoats she fumbled beneath her skirts and produced some coins.

'Get in, and look sharp about it.' The man jerked his head, and, laughing with the feverish gaiety of heart-felt relief, the three women clambered aboard. The man pushed the boat off the beach then jumped in and rowed out to the frigate, which lay less than fifty yards offshore.

Sarah watched it go and when Shimson Levi would have spoken to her, she hushed him to silence.

'Let me see what happens, it's necessary that I know these

things,' she explained.

A gangway had been lowered along the frigate's side and already several boatloads of women were waiting their turn to draw alongside its bottom platform. Eager, excited seamen and marines were clustered along the taffrails, cheering and cat-calling invitations at the women, as some deftly and others clumsily scrambled on to the platform and mounted to the deck where they were immediately besieged by the sex-starved crew. The three women's boat joined at the end of the queue, but unfortunately for them a brazen-voiced naval officer, armed with a speaking trumpet was overseeing the gangway from a vantage point on the quarterdeck taffrail. The officer did a double-take at the new arrivals and raised the speaking trumpet to his lips.

'Ahoy there! You, lubber wi' the timber foot ... Sheer away, blast you!'

The boatman cupped his hands around his mouth and shouted back, 'What's the matter, your honour?'

'Damn your eyes, Timber Leg! It's that load of ugly ducks you've got wi' you that's the matter. I'll not let any of my men get between their spindle shanks, be damned if I will!'

'We'em all right, yer honour,' the hag's spokeswoman interjected. 'We'em clean decent bodies, so we be,' she started to plead desperately. 'Please let us aboard, yer honour, please!'

'Be damned to ye, for a poxed-up old bitch!' the officer roared. 'Now sheer off, or I'll bloody well sink you.'

The seamen and marines jeered at the three women, and the pedlars in the bumboats, waiting to sell drink, eatables and trinkets, once the overwhelming urges of the flesh had been satisfied, joined in the catcalling.

'What price the one in the blue?' 'Sheer orf, Mother Gammy!' 'Aye, clear the way, old bitch!'

A young whore in another boat stood up and shouted to the officer.

'Hey there, Jack Tar?' She was a strapping, well-built girl with bold eyes and gaudy finery.

'What does you want, my pretty? Is it to share my berth?' the officer teased her, and a storm of lewd invitations and compliments came from the crew.

The young whore let slip the shawl she wore and pulling down the front of her low-cut gown she used both hands to free her firm, shapely breasts. She lifted and fondled the smooth white-skinned mounds with their dark-ringed jutting nipples and flaunted them before the avid, hungry eyes on the ship.

'Be these sweet enough for you, my fine bucko?' she asked.

An ear-splitting outburst of cheers and whistles came from the onlookers and the officer ran his tongue across his wet lips.

'You're in luck today, my pretty,' he grinned lasciviously. 'I've taken a fancy for you.' He waved his arm at the other boats. 'Clear the way there, you lubbers. Let the girl's craft through.'

'Don't bother!' the young girl shouted angrily, and laughed into the officer's lustful face. 'If them three poor wenches you just told to sheer off ain't good enough to be rogered by you poxed-up bleeders on the *Vulcan*, then neither am I.' She suddenly bent and tossed up her rear skirts, displaying her naked buttocks. She slapped the temptingly rounded flesh so that it quivered. 'You can kiss my arse *Vulcan*!' she shouted scornfully. 'Row back to the shore,' she ordered her boatman.

He began to argue, but she out-shouted him. 'Damn your stinking hide! I'll gi' you the sale-money meself, you broken-down sand-rat,' she cursed, and sullenly he obeyed her.

Sarah watched the young whore closely as the craft beached on the shingle, and she touched Shimson's arm.

'Bring her to me, Shim. She's the sort of girl we need ...'

'Vot's your name, girl?'

The whore was busily retying the garter of her black cotton stocking above one dimpled knee, oblivious to the comments and lustful stares of the boatmen and loungers on the beach. Without lifting her dark, curly-ringleted head, she answered,

'T's Molly, my bucko.'

'Molly vot?'

For the first time she looked at her questioner. She saw what she considered a well-dressed flash cove, with jewelled rings on his fingers and a great diamond stickpin in his lacy cravat folds. She met his admiring stare with a contemptuous smile and dropping her skirts she straightened, using both hands to toss her long hair back from her flushed face.

'It's Molly Bawn, Jew-boy.'

His swarthy complexion darkened and anger momentarily hardened his eyes. Even after almost a lifetime spent in England, Shimson Levi, still fiercely resented the arrogance that even the lowliest English showed towards all who were not of

176

their nation. He forced himself to smile back at the whore.

'I've a friend who vant's a vord vi' you,' he said.

Molly Bawn stared at him suspiciously. 'Listen, Old-Clothes, I'm not a girl who fancies men who won't speak to me direct, but must send others to pimp for them.'

Shimson bit back his burgeoning anger. 'My friend is not a man.' He pointed back to Sarah. 'She is standing there ... And if I vos you, girl I vould come and talk vith her. It might be the makin' of you.'

The girl looked where he indicated and her eyes widened. The handsome woman along the beach was dressed like a gentlewoman. She wore a green satin habit trimmed with swansdown, a sealskin hat and huge muff of the same material. A swansdown-trimmed black cloak hung casually across her shoulders and on her small feet were expensive black kid half-boots. Beneath her hat, her glossy hair was arranged 'á la Madonna' with a centre parting and loose flowing waves which showed her emerald and gold earrings, all in the very height of fashion. It took some moments for Molly Bawn to recover her customary bravado. Then, holding her shoulders well back so that her fine breasts were displayed to their best advantage, she went walking proudly to meet Sarah Jenkins.

'She calls herself Molly Bawn,' Shimson Levi said aloud and Sarah nodded, her eyes not leaving the girl.

'What age are you, Molly? she asked pleasantly.

'I don't know for certain, mistress,' the girl smiled ruefully. 'I was a foundling, d'you see, and brought up by anybody who 'ud feed me for a few weeks ... I think I'm about eighteen years though.'

Withdrawing one hand from the recesses of her muff, Sarah touched the girl's smooth cheek with her fingers.

'I'd like to ask you a question or two, Molly,' she said. 'I'll pay you for your time. I'd not want to see you lose a chance of making some money from the *Vulcan*.'

The girl tossed her long hair and her bold eyes flashed.

'There's no call for you to gi' me anythin', mistress. There's only the *Vulcan* in to earn any rhino from and I'll not go on board that bloody dung-heap.'

Sarah chuckled in amusement. 'I didn't really think you would. I saw what happened.'

The girl spat her scorn. 'That bastard Jack Tar angered me! He'd no call to treat them poor old drabs in that way. 'Tis no fault o' theirs that they'm agetting a bit long in the tooth, is it. He could have let 'um on board. Some one o' them bleedin' poxy deck-apes would ha' rogered the wenches and given them a few shillin's ... Why! Once they'se swilled enough grog down 'um, some o' them would roger their own grandmas, and I tell no lie.'

'Tell me, Molly, and I mean no offence by asking. But are you clean and free of disease?'

The young whore's laughter was loud and unrestrained, but beneath it was an undertone of great bitterness.

'I am now, mistress. But a bloody marine gi' me my first dose o' the clap, when I was no more than a bit of a kid. It taught me a lesson ... I takes great care now, and that's for sure. I've no wish to end up dying blind and mad in some stinkin' midden, like a good many o' my pals ha' done.'

'Good,' Sarah nodded, and went on. 'Would you like to come and work for me and my partner here, Molly?'

Instantly suspicion veiled the girl's bold hazel eyes. 'I've no mind to work in a brothel, mistress ... I likes me freedom.'

'I'm not asking you to work in a brothel, Molly,' Sarah told her quietly. 'My partner, Mr Levi here, and myself are going to open a gaming club. We need girls to help attract the men with money into the place, to help serve and entertain them. If you do not wish to bed with the men who come there, then you do not have to. In fact I do not wish any girl to sell herself while she is working for me, but I do know something of human nature, and I'll not forbid what I cannot hope to prevent. The only thing I do insist upon, however, is that the girls will be honest and obey me during the hours of work. After their work is completed, they are free to do whatever they wish. But I'll make it plain to you now, that if any girl becomes diseased, or steals from men they have met at the club, then we want no more of that girl, whoever she may be.'

Molly Bawn's hazel eyes searched the candid green eyes before her and what she read in them eased her suspicions.

'What exactly would I have to do in this club of yourn?' she asked.

'I'll not try and give you a host of worthless tales,' Sarah answered. 'Nor try to hide from you the truth. You and the other girls I shall be recruiting will be at the club for one reason only ... To attract the men, to encourage them to spend heavy on food and drink and, most important of all, to get them to gamble at the tables. Some of the cleverer girls we'll train as dealers, and one or two of the really knowing ones we'll teach how to watch out for the flash coves and sharps who'll be trying to cog the dice and pack the cards.'

'And how much money will I be making?' Molly questioned.

Shimson Levi winked at Sarah from behind the girl's shoulder. Sarah frowned at him and shook her head.

'Shim! I'll not begin by haggling over wages,' she snapped, and told the girl, 'In all honesty, Molly, I do not yet know myself. This is a new venture for me and it's Shimson's cousin from London, the one they call the Hebrew Star, who will be running the gaming to start with ... But I will promise you that I'll see you get a fair return on whatever you persuade the flats to wager or spend ...'

For the first time in many years Molly Bawn found herself trusting another person completely. She smiled gaily.

'What's your name, mistress?'

'It's Sarah, Sarah Jenkins.'

'Very well, Mistress Sarah, when do I begin working for you?'

The handsome face returned her smile. 'Right away, girl ... We must first go and get some refreshment, then we'll buy you some new clothes, and after we'll look for more girls.'

The young whore laughed in delighted anticipation. 'It'll be wonderful not to 'av to lie under some drunken Jack Tar or bootneck for a few measly shillings. I'll find more girls than you can ever use ... For there's very few on us who really like bein fancy pals.'

Shimson Levi mentally calculated what new clothes for this girl and the others would cost, and groaned in real pain. Sarah chuckled at the girl's reaction to the groan.

'Don't worry yourself, my dear. It's only his pocket that's hurting him, and it shouldn't do because half o' the outlay is mine.' She took the other's arm. 'Come, we'll find some beautiful clothes for you, no matter what they cost.'

At the Portsea dockyard there were no excited whores awaiting the *Vulcan*'s passengers. No crowds of eager touts and bumboat men. No smiling faces or friendly voices. Only a silent and morose dockyard official and a red-coated major of the Commissariat department.

Lieutenant David Warburton of the Twenty-Fourth Foot, sat on his leather-covered military chest and watched the groaning wrecks of invalided soldiers being lifted roughly, like so many pieces of inanimate baggage, out of the rocking lighters and on to the cold wet-slicked cobbles of the landing jetty. He was a medium-sized young man, his thin face drawn and pale and his grey eyes shadowed by much suffering. Dressed in a badly faded scarlet coatee with frayed green facings, a battered black shako tilted on his short brown hair, and the silver lace and epaulets of his uniform tarnished almost black by wind and weather, he was a far cry from the dashing resplendent officers who swaggered through the streets of Portsmouth. Now his lips twisted in anger as a hulking seaman dragged a ragged-clothed legless soldier from the lighter, ignoring the wounded man's cries of pain, and dumped him carelessly on the greasy stones.

'Hey, you there! That sailor!' the young officer shouted irascibly.

The man's vacuous face stared at him in puzzlement.

'Did you mean me, sir?' he asked.

'Yes you! You great oaf!' Warburton shouted. 'Take care with that man. He's not a lump of wood to be tossed about.'

The sailor's puzzlement deepened. 'I've done naught to him, sir,' he protested. 'Just lifted 'im to the jetty, that's all.'

'Oh, what's the use of it?' David Warburton asked himself disgustedly, and turned away. He stared about him at the shores of his native land and could only feel a great weight of lonely depression pressing down upon him.

'God help me! But I'd have preferred to remain in the Peninsula,' he thought despondently. 'For there's none to bid me welcome home.'

The Commissariat Major, a plump fussy hen of a man, bustled across to him, waving his lists of names and goods importantly.

'You'll be Lieutenant Warburton of the Twenty-Fourth, will you not?' he flustered.

David got to his feet and clicked his heels, half-bowing to the man. 'The same, sir,' he told him.

'About these invalids you've brought back.' The major's tone was hectoring.

'What of them, sir?' The young officer was curt. He was contemptuous of the gentlemen of the Commissariat.

'Well, there's a good half score on 'um not yet here on the jetty,' the man said aggrievedly.

Warburton's resentment of the other's manner deepened.

'Nor likely ever to be, sir,' he snapped. 'For they're feeding the fishes in Biscay Bay. They died for lack of medical attention and decent treatment.'

The major's tiny mouth opened and closed as he ingested this news. ''Pon my soul!' he grumbled finally. 'It's most damnably remiss of you not to have informed me of this before I made the list out.'

The young man's resentment boiled over. 'Not half so remiss as the damned commissaries who loaded the poor devils on board without medicines, or blankets or decent provisions,' he said heatedly. 'There was not even a Hospital Sergeant on board to tend them, never mind a surgeon.'

'That's no concern of mine, young man,' the major retorted. 'And I'll thank you to show a civil manner when you're addressing a senior officer.'

With an effort of will, David clamped down on the angry words that clamoured to spill from his lips. Satisfied that he had won the day, the major went on.

'You yourself will be staying with your family no doubt, until you go before the Medical Board.'

'My family?' David thought sadly. 'Now that my uncle is dead, my only living relative is William, and I've not seen or heard from him in years. He could also be dead, long since.'

'Well, Lieutenant?' the major pressed him. 'Do you intend to stay with your family? I have to know for entry in my records.'

'I shall be staying here, in Portsmouth, for a time,' David told him. 'I shall take rooms here.'

'Very well,' the major puffed. 'You may leave now, if you wish, Lieutenant. I'll see to these invalids.'

David looked pityingly at the rows of grey-faced wretches lying moaning and shivering in misery on the cobbles without coverings or mattresses. He looked at their blood-stained filthy bandages, at the rag-padded stumps of arms and legs, at the raw empty eye sockets and swore softly to himself. 'God help you, you poor devils!' Aloud he said, 'I trust that you'll have these men moved immediately to hospital, sir?'

The plump cheeks of the other blew out petulantly. 'That, young man, is easier said than done,' the major grumbled. 'No one ever stops to consider the difficulties that we poor fellows of the Commissariat face. Dammee no! I've now got to try and obtain carts from somewhere to shift the buggers, and the Lord only knows where I'm to find them from. Perhaps He can help me to do so.'

The young lieutenant's face grew suddenly very bitter.

'I've seen precious little evidence of the Lord helping these poor devils in their sufferings,' he burst out. 'So I'm damned if He's likely to help you find carts.'

The major stared hard at him and demanded querulously, 'What d'ye mean by that statement, sir?'

David turned from the man in disgust and called a loitering sailor to him.

'Here, Jack Tar. I'll give you a shilling if you'll carry my trunk.'

'Aye, sir.' The sailor came forward and grunting with effort swung the trunk to his shoulders.

The young officer walked slowly to the dockyard gates and was passing through them when a soldier wearing a white canvas fatigue suit and red- and yellow-banded forage hat accosted him and saluted.

'Beg pardon, sir. But might you be Lieutenant Warburton o' the Twenty-Fourth.'

'That is my name,' David told him.

'Well sir, I musk arsk you to come along o' me, if you please.'

David stared at the man in surprise. 'No, I do not please, my man. I have many pressing affairs to attend to.'

The man's bovine features were wooden, and he continued as though the officer had not spoken. 'Things 'as all bin arranged for you, sir. My marster, Cap'n Joseph Ward, told me to tell you that you'm agoing to stay wi' 'im and his family.'

The young officer's jaw dropped. 'Captain Ward? Do you mean Joseph Ward of the village of Holt End, in Worcestershire?' he asked incredulously.

'The very same, sir,' the soldier affirmed. 'Only it's Cap'n Ward, now sir, o' the Third Worcestershire Militia. We 'em in garrison 'ere, sir.'

'Good God above!' David breathed the words. 'And Mrs Ward and Miss Jessica, are they here also?'

'Aye, sir,' the man grinned. 'And powerful anxious they be to welcome you back 'ome to England, sir.'

'Jessica! Sweet Jessie!' A vision of his one-time playmate whom he had grown to love so deeply as they grew up together, and who had never been absent from his thoughts for a single day during all the long years in the Peninsula, flashed across the young man's mind, and he felt his heart begin to pound.

'My lovely Jessie, here! Here in Portsmouth! My Jessie!' David could hardly breathe, so intense was his emotion. 'Lead on, man,' he blurted out. 'Lead on this instant!'

Once the *Vulcan* had entered the harbour, Jessica had made her good-byes to John Coventry and then rushed back to the house that her parents had rented in Portsmouth High Street. Dorothea had refused her friend's invitation to tea and returned to her own home, saying a trifle maliciously,

'Now do not overwhelm the poor invalid with your ardour, Jessie.'

The blonde-haired girl blushed and made no reply. Now she waited impatiently in the hallway of the house for the sounds of his footsteps. At last the door swung open and the soldier servant came in, carrying the much-travelled trunk across his shoulders. Behind the man followed a slender boyish figure carrying a cockaded shako in his left hand, whose right arm hung somewhat stiffly at his side.

'Oh Davy! It is so good to see you again.' Jessica's beautiful face glowed with pleasure and she ran to hug the young officer. As her soft arms crushed around him David grunted in pain. Instantly the girl released him and scanned his face anxiously.

'Are you ill, Davy?' Her brown eyes grew shiny with the threat of tears. 'Oh Davy, my dear Davy, what has this cruel war done to you?' she exclaimed softly, and could have wept with pity over his thin tired face, patterned with faint lines of suffering around eyes and mouth. With one soft hand she traced those lines and trailed her other hand across the tarnished silver epaulet on the right shoulder of his badly stained and faded scarlet coatee. He fumbled with both hands at his battered shako and smiled fondly at her.

'I'm very well, Jessie, really I am. It's only that my right arm is still a little stiff and sore. The wound became infected, d'you see ... but it's almost healed now,' he assured her.

She brushed away the tears in her eyes and returned his smile. 'Mama is in the salon. She's waiting to take tea with us.'

She led him through the green baize double doors to where her mother, an older, plumper version of herself, sat at the round table which was placed before the window of the richly furnished room.

'Welcome home, my dear boy,' Mrs Ward smiled. 'For this is to be your home whilst you are in England.'

David felt that it was all a dream. That the delicately cut morsels of white bread and rich golden honey and butter, the savoury hams and potted meats, the thickly-iced fruit cakes and the scented fragrant dishes of China tea were all figments of his fevered imagination. The feather-light opaque porcelain dishes, saucers, plates, and cups seemed things of no substance; and he found himself repeatedly pinching his patched grey-trousered thighs to reassure himself that the expensive oil-paintings on the walls, the rose-coloured carpets and hangings, and the pastel brocade chairs and chaise-longues were all real. As real as were the two women who fussed over him and pressed titbits upon him. The warmth of the log fire in its decorative grate made him drowsy and he smiled bemusedly at his companions. At Jessica, so sweetly beautiful with her blonde hair dressed in the Grecian style, and her flowing high-waisted peach gown whose almost sheer folds showed off to perfection the dainty curves of her shapely body; and at Mrs Ward, her mother, so like his lonely boyhood dreams of what a mother should be, in her vast snowy mobcap and white lace-ruffled dark dress smelling of lavender and rose-water.

David finally managed to convince both of his hostesses that he could positively eat no more of the cherry cake, and drink not a single sip extra of the tea or the fine Madeira wine which they offered him. His inner and outer comfort filled him with a sense of tremendous well-being, but also made him very very sleepy. He forced himself to remain awake and asked,

'And the Captain, where is he at this time?'

'Papa is due back at any day,' Jessica told him. 'He has been in Worcestershire. There was some difficulty in obtaining the Ballot men.'

'He is well, I trust?' David beat off a wave of tiredness and went on politely. 'I look forward to meeting him again.'

'Indeed he is well, David,' Mrs Ward told him. 'And will be most disappointed that he was not here to greet your arrival himself.'

'Tell us about the war, Davy,' Jessica begged eagerly. 'Were you in many battles and sieges? Have you ever seen the Iron Duke in person, or spoken with him? Are the girls very pretty in Spain and Portugal?'

He held up both hands in laughing protest. 'Please, Jessie. One question at a time.'

'No questions at this time!' Mrs Ward's kindly face was concerned. 'For I can see clearly that the poor boy is most dreadfully tired. I insist that you go to your room and rest for a while, David my dear.'

'Oh but Mama!' Jessica pouted.

'Be silent miss,' her mother told her sternly. 'I think it most inconsiderate of you to pester and badger poor David when he has only just completed a most arduous journey ... No! I will brook no argument from either of you. You will have all the time in the world to talk, now that David is to stay with us.'

'But I cannot impose upon your kindness in this way,' David began.

'Young man,' Mrs Ward would not let him continue. 'If you do not stay with us for as long as you are here in England, I shall be mortally offended ... You have no other family now that your poor guardian is dead, therefore we are your family now. So off to bed with you and not another word! Not one!' she scolded fondly.

Gratefully the young man surrendered to her kindness and also to his bone-deep weariness. He followed the soldier servant who came at the summons of the table bell, up the stairs to his allotted room. David lay back on the soft lemon-scented bed covers and before the servant had finished unstrapping and removing his boots, David was sunk in a sleep of utter exhaustion.

CHAPTER SEVENTEEN

It took William Seymour days of hard travelling to reach Winchester, hampered as he was by the constant rain and sleet which turned the muddy, rutted tracks he used into quagmires. Nevertheless, he was not dissatisfied. He had managed to average over twenty miles a day, and that was cross-country for the most part. He kept well away from the turnpike roads and stage-coach routes, not wanting to risk being seen, and perhaps remembered, in those places where news travelled fastest and was exchanged. An officer who deserted his regiment, as he had now done, would be bound to create a stir of interest and speculation through those circles whose business it was to know of such things, and undoubtedly inquiries would eventually be made concerning him. Therefore, after extorting some money from the reluctant Thomas Marston, Seymour had headed overland for Portsmouth, using drovers' lanes and bridle paths and avoiding the towns. He had slept in isolated farmhouses and hedge-inns, where people normally asked no questions, so long as a man had money to pay for his needs.

It was midday when he sighted the town and he reined in his horse to consider his next move. He knew that Winchester lay about twenty-five miles from his final destination—Portsmouth—and with the miserable weather, which even now, at high noon, blanketed the horizon in dark drizzle and cold mists, he did not relish the prospect of travelling on. He touched his spurs to the muddied flanks of his horse and went slowly towards the town. Keeping to the side streets, he made his way to the southern districts where, in a twisting alley, he came upon a small black and white half-timbered inn.

'Dammit! I'll get food and a bed here and go on to Portsmouth tomorrow,' he decided, and dismounted, shouting as he lifted his bulging saddlebags from the crupper, 'Ostler? Ostler? Where are you, damn you?'

A small ragged barefoot boy came at a run.

'Take my horse,' Seymour ordered. 'I want him well rubbed down, then fed and watered.'

The boy knuckled his forehead and led the tired beast to the stables at the rear of the building.

The landlord was bowing in the doorway. 'Good noonday, your honour. Is it good food and drink you're wanting? If so then the White Swan is the very place to get it.'

'Indeed?' Seymour stared frostily at the innkeeper. 'Then perhaps I'd best go on to the White Swan, for this place resembles nothing more than a dung-eating carrion crow.'

For a moment the man's broad fat face was nonplussed, then he laughed ingratiatingly. 'Oh, but you've a ready wit, your honour! That's easily seen.'

Seymour brushed past the man and entered the low-roofed taproom, leaving the man bowing behind him. The innkeeper followed, still bobbing his head. The cavalryman found the man's manner increasingly irritating.

'Is trade so bad, that you must jerk about me as if you were a marionette and I a puppet-master?' he snapped brusquely.

The obsequious smile never faltered on the innkeeper's features and he moved to stand beside the long mahogany counter that half-filled the small room. Inwardly he was cursing . . .

'Yes you haughty bastard! Trade is damned bad, or I'd show the likes o' you the bloody door, and sharp about it too.'

The only other occupants of the room were two men who sat in the high-backed wooden settle to one side of the blazing fire, opposite the counter. At Seymour's entrance, they exchanged a meaningful glance and studied the newcomer with covert interest.

Seymour removed his high-crowned beaver hat and unclasped his military riding cloak from his shoulders, throwing both articles together with his saddlebags, carelessly across the nearest of the several small tables that were dotted about the room.

The two onlookers mentally evaluated the cost of the clothing the newcomer was wearing. Well-cut plum-coloured coat and waistcoat, dove-grey breeches, gold-tasselled Hessian boots, his linen and cravat lace-ruffled and fine. One of the men nudged the other and said, so low that only they could hear, 'He's a well-heeled 'un, John.'

The other winked one shrewd eye in reply.

Seymour walked to the fire and warmed his hands at the flaring, spitting logs. Then, for the first time, looked at the men on the settle.

'It's cold, nasty weather, gentlemen,' he remarked.

Like Siamese twins they nodded and smiled in concert. 'Indeed it is, sir ... Indeed it is.'

'Landlord?' Seymour shouted. 'Bring me a glass of your best brandy.' Then invited politely, 'Will you gentlemen join me in a glass?'

'That's very civil of you, sir.' The speaker rose to his feet and bowed. 'Allow me to introduce myself and my friend.' His accent had a slightly foreign intonation. 'My name is Aaron Levi, and may I present my friend, Juan da Costa.'

The second man then rose and bowed. Seymour bowed back.

'My compliments to you both, gentlemen. My name is William Seymour.'

'Delighted to make your acquaintance, sir ... Delighted! Please!' Aaron Levi waved a beringed hand at the chair facing the settle-seat across an oblong table. 'Will you do us the honour of joining our company?'

Seymour accepted. His two new acquaintances were very similar in build and features. Both wore their grey hair fairly long, smoothed down on to their heads with sweet-scented pomades ... Both had plump, swarthy, clean-shaven faces dominated by large fleshy noses and small black eyes. Both wore many-jewelled rings and large diamond-studded cravat pins, and their sombre clothing, with pantaloons trapped beneath high-low boots, was of excellent quality. Seymour put them down as rich merchants. In the first respect he was correct. Both men were wealthy. In the second respect he was very wrong. Aaron Levi and Juan da Costa were notorious in the gambling hells of London, where they were better known by their sobriquets as the 'Hebrew Star' and 'Portugal John'. They were two of the most ruthless and skilful cheats and sharps ever to flourish in the haunts made fashionable by the Prince Regent and his profligate circle.

The landlord brought in the glasses of brandy and the three men toasted each other.

'Do you reside locally, sir?' Portugal John asked politely.

'No, I'm travelling through. I have some business to attend to farther south,' Seymour told him, and in turn asked the pair what they were doing in the area.

'We are merchants in gemstones and jewellery,' Aaron Levi smiled disarmingly.

'You are not English, are you?' Seymour pressed them, his agile mind wondering already if this meeting could be used in some way to fatten his own very slender purse.

'No, sir, we are not,' Portugal John smiled, showing false dentures fashioned from gold and ivory, then continued smoothly. 'At present we reside in Amsterdam, but we are "Marranos". That is to say we are Spanish Jews whose forefathers were expelled from the Iberian Peninsula many years ago by the Catholic monarchs, Ferdinand and Isabella.'

'Most interesting,' Seymour nodded, and finished his drink. 'Will you have another, gentlemen?' He pointed to their glasses.

They accepted, and in return when those brandies were gone invited Seymour. Some time went by in this pleasant way and then, when in his turn Seymour called for more drinks, Aaron Levi objected.

'No, no, good sir! You must allow me to call the drinks. It is my turn.'

'Nonsense!' Seymour ejaculated. 'It's my turn.'

'No indeed, sir!' Aaron Levi expostulated. 'I really must insist that it is mine.'

They began to wrangle over it, and Portugal John entered the argument by claiming that it was no one's turn but his. Seymour laughed aloud, the flow of brandies and the warmth of the room making him feel relaxed and careless.

'Let us not quarrel, gentlemen,' he said expansively. 'There is no need for dispute. We have the ideal means of deciding who is to pay, right here on the table beneath our noses.'

Both men regarded him with puzzlement. He laughed again at their expressions and pointed to a small round leather cup standing on the end of the table.

'The dice, gentlemen! We'll throw the dice and the loser shall pay.'

His companions looked doubtful.

'I don't know ... You see our faith does not allow us to gamble,' Portugal John began.

'Come now, gentlemen?' Seymour feigned amazement. 'How can it be called gambling? A little hazard between ourselves for a glass or two of brandy ... Goddammee! I'd not call that gambling!'

The more reluctant they appeared, the more determined

Seymour became that they should play, and he badgered them until they finally agreed.

'Very well, sir. We will play, but only for this one drink,' Aaron Levi said.

They all threw the dice in turn and Seymour lost. Portugal John shook his head.

'I feel, Cousin Aaron, that we really should give this gentleman another throw. After all, when we are the guests of a nation of sporting men, it is only common courtesy to comply with their customs and habits.'

'But the Rabbi Sholem?' Levi demurred. 'What would he say?'

Portugal John winked roguishly. 'The Rabbi Sholem, good old man that he is, is many miles from here across the German Ocean. What he does not see will not hurt him. Besides, I find that I am enjoying this sport. It is a change for us to take a little risk with the laws of chance, is it not? And exciting also ... I like it.'

'Well said!' Seymour applauded. 'Spoken like a sportsman, dammee!'

'Yes. Perhaps you are right ... Surely there cannot be anything sinful in indulging in such a harmless practice and taking amusement from it ... We will play for a while,' Levi agreed.

'Good! Come, gentlemen!' Seymour scooped the pair of dice into the leather cup ... 'And just to make it even more interesting, why don't we wager a few shillings on each throw ... It will add savour to the game.'

The two men opposite him exchanged shocked stares, then, as if taking a big decision grinned at each other and nodded.

'I agree!' Portugal John exclaimed, then added jokingly, 'That is, if my Cousin Levi here will promise me that he won't tell the Rabbi Sholem what we have done, when we return to Amsterdam.'

Levi chuckled, his face aglow with his sense of daring to pluck forbidden fruits. 'Very well, Juan, it is a bargain. I will say nothing, if you won't.'

They playfully clasped hands to seal their pledge, and Seymour, impatient with these two timid fools, shook the dice so that the ivory cubes rattled hollowly inside the leather cup.

'A crown piece says that I shall throw the highest score, gentlemen.' He cast the cubes to bounce across the stained wood of the table.

His companions glanced at each other, their eyes showing their contempt for this new victim and then gave their full attention to the fallen dice.

The play followed the classic pattern with Seymour winning a little, then losing more, then gaining the advantage in throw after throw. All the time the stakes rose higher and higher. Portugal John appeared to be losing heavily and at last he burst out angrily,

'*Madre mia!* I think God must be angry with me. My luck is terrible. Absolutely terrible.'

Aaron Levi, who was winning a small amount, chuckled with pleasure. 'It does my heart good, Cousin John, to see you lose at something for once in your life ... This is a good lesson for you. I haven't forgotten that business in Antwerp when you did me down.'

Portugal John reacted furiously to that statement. 'What do you mean by saying that, Cousin Aaron? Tell me, what are you trying to insinuate?'

Levi also grew angry. 'Insinuate? I insinuate nothing, cousin, I speak openly. You cheated me in Antwerp and now I am having my revenge.'

'Why you ...' Portugal John lunged at the other man and, grasping him by the cravat, shook him violently. Levi fought back, gasping and coughing for air as the linen tightened about his fat neck. Seymour rose from his seat and bent across the table to thrust the scuffling pair apart. As he did so, Aaron Levi's hand slipped unseen under Seymour's chest and substituted another set for the dice in the leather cup. Once the switch had been completed, they allowed Seymour to force them back into their seats, flushed and panting from their exertions. Levi was the first to speak.

'I know a way to settle this, Cousin Juan.'

'Oh, do you indeed?' Portugal John sneered.

'Yes I do.' Levi took from an inside pocket a flat leather wallet and opened it to display some folded papers. 'There!' he said triumphantly. 'There are notes drawn on banks in London, in Amsterdam and in Antwerp ... Call any amount you wish and I will match it and cast the dice for it. I think you cheated me that day in Antwerp, and I believe that God above will give me justice by letting me win the wager.'

William Seymour could not take his eyes from the well-filled wallet. His mind raced as he computed what could be done with such an amount.

'Very well, I accept the wager!' Portugal John's excited voice broke the cavalryman's train of thought.

'Then name the amount,' Levi challenged.

'Now gentlemen, I trust this wager is to be open for all to join in?' Seymour queried.

Both men were so intent on each other that they barely glanced at him.

'Of course Mr Seymour. If you wish to participate, you are very welcome,' Portugal John answered. 'I do not mind who wins, so long as it is not Cousin Levi.' The last sentence was uttered with vehement dislike.

'And I feel the same way about Cousin da Costa,' Aaron Levi retorted.

William Seymour felt wild joy swell within him. Always a reckless gambler, today he felt that the dice were his to command. The brandy had increased his habitual readiness to take risks to an almost insane degree. He went to his saddlebags and took from one of them the purse of gold coins that Thomas Marston had given him. Twenty sovereigns clinked in the soft pouch, and he put them with his pile of winnings and pushed the entire total into the centre of the table.

'There are forty-seven pounds, gentlemen. Will you meet it?' His companions nodded grimly and each laid out notes and coins for similar amounts.

Aaron Levi took the cup, and shook hard and threw.

'A trey and a six,' he shouted happily. 'That's nine, gentlemen, and hard to beat.'

He passed the cup to William Seymour. The cavalryman's lean features were completely relaxed, so confident was he that his luck would hold. Smiling easily, he shook and threw.

'A six and a five ... That totals eleven, gentlemen,' he said quietly, and felt as if a supra-natural agency was at his elbow, influencing the fall of the dice in his favour.

'My congratulations, Mr Seymour,' Portugal John told him affably. 'In all honesty I do not mind if I lose now, for to me the greatest satisfaction is seeing that that accusing cousin of mine has been already bested,' he sneered viciously at Levi. 'I thought you said that God would cause the dice to fall for you so that you would win, Cousin Levi. It proves what a liar you are.'

Levi raised his small plump fists, as if to strike the other, forcing Seymour to intervene again, and as he did so, Portugal John switched the dice once more for yet a third set.

'You see how he reacts, Mr Seymour,' Portugal John said, when Levi was pushed back into his seat. 'He hates to be beaten, this one.' Carelessly he rattled the dice once only and tossed them on to the table.

Seymour watched them bounce once, twice, three times, four times, five times and come to rest directly in front of him.

'Two sixes!'

Even as he breathed the words a stunning unbelief at what he saw overwhelmed him. 'Two sixes! A score of twelve! But I was meant to win!' a voice screamed in his mind. 'It was I who was meant to win! This isn't possible! It's not happening! It's not happening!'

'Twelve! I've thrown twelve!' Portugal John crowed in delighted surprise. 'Now, Cousin Levi, what do you say to that? Tell me, who did God protect, you or I? That shows you that I did not cheat you in Antwerp, does it not? If I had cheated you as you thought, then God would not have allowed me to win, would He?'

With a great show of reluctance and with very bad grace, Aaron Levi grudgingly admitted he might have been wrong in his suspicions.

'Now let us please forget the entire incident, Cousin da Costa,' he said grumpily. 'And see. It is almost dusk outside. We must get on if we are to reach Hurley this night.'

'My goodness, you are correct! I had forgotten.' Da Costa pulled his large gold pocket-watch from his waistcoat fob and examined it. Then said anxiously, 'We must leave this instant, or the gentleman we have to meet will be gone.' He turned to William Seymour. 'Please forgive us for leaving you so abruptly, Mr Seymour, but my cousin and I have a very important business appointment in a village some miles from here ... The game was so exciting, that I quite forgot the passage of time, but we are already late and must go immediately.'

Seymour, filled with the sickening knowledge that because of his own reckless stupidity he was again left with just a few shillings, gave only a small portion of his attention to what the man was saying. Before he had fully realized what was happening, the pair of them, muffled in their many-caped greatcoats and broad-brimmed slouch hats, were outside in the yard chivvying the stable boy to harness their horse into their small open gig.

The cavalryman sipped at his brandy and absently toyed with the dice in the leather cup. He rattled and threw and watched without interest the ivory cubes roll across the table. The crunching of iron-rimmed wheels over gravel marked the departure of his erstwhile companions and through the bullseye window panes he saw the flickerings of their already lighted carriage lamps disappear around the building. He sighed deeply and berated himself mentally for his failure to control his instincts.

'If only I had stood aside for the last wager,' he thought. 'I'd have had more funds than enough to stay me until I can find Sarah Jenkins.'

He stretched out his hand and tapped his forefinger on the dice. He noticed that he had thrown two sixes, and he grimaced. 'One throw too late to save me.'

Lifting the cubes Seymour dropped them one at a time into the cup and cast them again. Two sixes appeared uppermost.

'God rot my eyes!' he cursed and snatched the dice up. Three times more he threw them, and three times more the sixes came uppermost.

'I've been gypped, Goddammit! The dice are cogged.' The nerve beside his left eye began to throb and jerk.

'I'll blow their bloody tripes out for this day's work,' he promised himself, and shouted ... 'Landlord?' The man entered, bowing and smirking.

'Get my horse saddled and made ready,' Seymour ordered, and to allay any suspicion added. 'And prepare me a room for the night. I'll be coming back to sleep here ... If anyone should come inquiring for me, tell them I'll be returning directly.'

The man hurried away and Seymour tried to judge what direction the two cheats had gone in. When the stable boy brought his mount into the yard Seymour asked him,

'Would you like to earn a shilling, boy?'

The child's eyes glistened eagerly. 'Ahr, zur ... I 'ud.'

'Then tell me boy. Which way did the two gentlemen in the gig go, north or south?'

'They went south, zur.' The boy pointed at the stable loft. 'I knows for sartin' they went south, becos' I was watchin' 'um from up theer.'

'Good!' Seymour tossed a coin on to the muddy gravel for the boy to pick up ... 'And listen, boy.' The child stared up at the tall-hatted, cloaked figure towering above him. 'Say nothing of what I asked you ... Understand?'

The urchin's brain was nimble enough for all his vacuous expression. 'I shanna, zur. I shanna open me mouth.'

Seymour nodded in curt dismissal and mounted. He kept his horse at an easy canter, not wishing to cause the beast to stumble and fall upon one of the many potholes in the rutted road. Also he had no wish to come upon his quarry at a gallop. That, he knew, would only arouse their suspicion and give them cause for alarm.

In a remarkably short time he sighted the gig-lamps flickering in front of him. He dropped his pace so that the gap narrowed only slowly and once he was near enough to be reasonably certain that the gig's occupants were the men he sought, he allowed his horse to walk and the distance to widen once more.

The sky had cleared and the stars gave sufficient light for the cavalryman to gauge the lie of the land. Seymour knew exactly what he was looking for and was content to wait for it to show itself. Soon it did so. The road swung in a wide curve around a stretch of wild bush-covered heath, and Seymour guided his mount across it, using the cover of the clumps of bushes to shield him from the gig. The short-cut brought him to the roadside once more a good hundred yards ahead of the gig and he used the intervening time to prime and load the brace of horse pistols he carried in his saddlebags, and to wrap his handkerchief around his lower face. The gig came nearer and Seymour heard clearly the clip-clopping of the horse, the crunching scrape of the iron-shod wheels and the loud laughter of the two men.

'Did you see his face when we left?' Portugal John's voice was loud in his enjoyment. 'What a bloody Joskin he was, to be sure.'

Aaron Levi chuckled beside him at the memory, and Seymour scowled in the darkness.

'Joskin, is it?' he muttered under his breath. 'Country bumpkin, am I? You hell-damned sharps!'

When the gig came nearly abreast of his hiding-place in the bushes he spurred his horse out in front of it.

'Pull up!' he shouted. 'The first to move gets a ball in his tripes.'

'Whooaa! Whooaa, blast ye!' The gig horse snickered high with fright and with its ears laid back flat to its skull tried to baulk and turn away. 'Whoooaaa! Easy! Be easy now!' Aaron Levi, holding the reins managed to steady the animal.

'What d'you want wi' us, cully?' Portugal John blustered. 'We'em flash coves like yourself, not bloody flats.'

'Shut your mouth!' Seymour came a little nearer the gig, the long-barrelled pistols pointing unwaveringly at the men in it. 'Shut your mouth and bail up!' Seymour shouted, his voice muffled in the folds of the handkerchief across his mouth.

'What if we says no to bailing up, cully?' If Portugal John felt any fear, he hid it admirably.

Seymour didn't argue. With a touch of his spurs he drove his mount to the side of the gig and his tall body swayed in the saddle as he slashed the pistol barrel across Portugal John's plump cheek, gashing the tender flesh deeply.

'Bail up, or you're a dead man!' he spat out.

The two sharps slowly and reluctantly took small purses from their pockets and held them out.

'Pitch them on to the ground,' Seymour told them. 'And let's have those wallets you're carrying.'

Aaron Levi suddenly grasped who the highwayman was. His features, however, showed no sign of recognition. He had been trained in the vicious criminal underworld of London and had learnt long before not to let his face show his emotions. At the mention of the wallets Portugal John had also drawn his conclusions, but like his friend kept his features from showing anything but fearful indignation and the biting pain of his bleeding cheek. The wallets were tossed on the ground by the purses.

'Get those rings off, and I'll take the timepieces as well ... and those cravat pins.'

'Goddam and blast it! Would you strip us naked?' Aaron Levi complained bitterly, but wisely obeyed the instructions. When the heavy gold watches and the pieces of jewellery had joined the rest of the booty, Seymour jerked his head.

'Be on your way!'

After a slight pause, Aaron Levi cursed long and loudly and shook the reins. 'Giddup! Giddup!'

The gig had barely begun to move when Portugal John turned swiftly and fired the tiny flintlock gun he had taken from a hidden pocket in his coat. Fortunately for William Seymour, the gig hit a pothole in the very instant that Portugal John pulled the trigger. The ball went high and hummed over the cavalryman's head. Reacting instinctively, Seymour fired one of his own pieces and the ball tore through the soft top of Portugal John's shoulder. As the explosions sounded, the gig-horse squealed and reared in fright then bolted. The vehicle bucked and careered along the track with its occupants hanging on desperately to avoid being pitched headlong from its narrow seat.

Seymour waited until the clatter of the wheels and flying hooves grew faint, then gathered up his booty. His thin hard mouth curled in a savage smile.

'A joskin, am I?' he said aloud, and burst out laughing.

CHAPTER EIGHTEEN

The new recruits formed a ragged line on the parade ground of Colewort Garden Barracks, which stood tucked into the corner of the fortifications of Portsmouth nearest to the Gun Wharf. Jethro Stanton was standing second from the left in the line, engrossed in the contemplation of his new home. To either side were two-storied brown-bricked barrack blocks with long balconies fronting each storey. Behind him were the blocks of workshops, stables and stores, while before him was the officers' mess, with its fine-stained entrance flanked by captured French cannon from Marlborough's wars. The conducting sergeant who had brought the recruits into the barracks that mid-morning used the stave of his halberd to dress the line.

'Blast you bloody 'cruities! Try and look as if you'm fit to be soldiers!' he swore irascibly.

The man on Jethro's left hawked noisily and spat a gob of phlegm on to the ground.

'SERGEANT TURNER TAKE THAT FILTHY ANIMAL'S NAME!'

From the side of the parade-ground a tall resplendently uniformed figure erupted. Under his right arm, with its four gold chevrons, he carried a long, brass-headed cane and a sword hung at his side.

Turpin Wright was standing at Jethro's other elbow and he whispered from the corner of his mouth,

'It's the sergeant-major. Just keep your head up and eyes front, lad ... and don't move.'

The sergeant-major reached the group of recruits and strutted along the ranks. They were only seven in number and to each one he gave a cursory inspection. His thin-lipped mouth beneath his great hook of a nose curled in distaste.

'God rot me, Sar'nt Turner! From what butcher's midden did you rake out this offal?' he inquired contemptuously.

He reached the end of the line then turned and came back to halt in front of the man who had spat. It was the flat-nosed drover.

'What's this bugger's name, sar'nt?' he barked.

'It's Deane, sir.' The sergeant hovered anxiously to one side of his superior.

The sergeant-major used the heavy brass knob of his cane to rap the drover sharply on his broken nose.

''Ow did you come by this flat snout, you filthy-habited animal?' he questioned, but didn't pause for an answer. 'One o' the "Fancy", was you? A pug? Well, Flat-Snout, my name is Gresham, Sergeant-Major Gresham, and this is my drill-ground that you'se just gobbed on, you dirty bleedin' pig! Now I care not a tinker's knacker for a hundred o' you bastards, pugs or no, and if you upsets me agen I'll ha' you on the triangle and let you meet the Drummer's Daughter. UNDERSTAND?'

The drover nodded sullenly.

'SAY, YES SIR ... YOU SCUM!' Sergeant Turner screamed at the man.

'Yus sur,' the drover grunted submissively.

Gresham glanced at Jethro, who had remained steady, with his eyes to the front, and then looked more closely.

'What's your name, my lad?'

'Jethro Stanton ... sir.'

'Have you served the King afore, lad? You've the set of a soldier.' The sergeant-major's tone was almost pleasant.

'No, sir, I've not,' Jethro answered.

'Well, lad, you've got the height and build for the Bacon Bolters, that's if you're quick and smart at your drill, o' course. D'you know what they be?'

'No, sir.' Jethro successfully resisted the instinct to shake his head.

'They're the Grenadier Company, lad! That's what I've allus bin ... a grenadier! Not one o' your jumpin' and duckin' Light Bobs, and never, never, a Bum Tool ...' He paused and sardonically surveyed the blank, uncomprehending faces of the recruits. 'For the greater increase o' your knowledge, and because for once in a blue moon I'm feeling well disposed towards you bleedin' Johnny Raws, I'll tell you that the Light Bobs is the Light Company o' the battalion, and that the Bum Tools be the Line Companies.' His shrewd eyes fastened on Turpin Wright and took in the lengthening bristles of his once-shaven head. They also read something in the convict's expression.

'Sar'nt Turner!' the sergeant-major bawled, and pointed his cane at Turpin's face. 'Mark well this man ... I've sin a lot like him in my time,' he chuckled grimly. 'What's your name?'

'Wright, sir.' The convict was rigid.

Gresham chuckled again. 'You're a right 'un as well, I'll wager. You could tell a few stories, I'll be bound; and I'll wager you're no stranger to the drill and the drum. No! Nor to the Drummer's Daughter, neither.' Turpin made no reply, only stared blank-faced ahead. 'Well, I'll say no more than this, Wright,' the sergeant-major told him. 'I'm not worried about your past as long as you keeps your nose clean in my battalion.'

The next man in line was the tiny, bald-headed beggar, still in his filth and rags. He cocked his head and grinned at the sergeant-major, as if recognizing an old and dear friend.

'Oh my good God!' Gresham moaned the words, and passed immediately by both the beggar and the Morris men's squire beside him. The second drover brought no comment and the last man, the respectable artisan would not have evoked any if he had not stepped out of line to confront the sergeant-major.

'Can I speak wi' you a moment, cully?' the artisan's face was tense and strained.

The sergeant-major halted, the cropped grey hair on the back of his neck bristled, and the eyes beneath the shiny peak of his elaborately braided, chained and feathered shako flashed in outrage.

'GET BACK IN YOUR PLACE, YOU STUPID BASTARD!' Sergeant Turner bellowed in rage, and using his halberd like a quarter-stave he struck the artisan hard across the chest.

'BACK INTO LINE! DAMN YOUR STINKING HIDE!'

'AND DAMN YOU AN' ALL!' the man shouted back. 'I'se got my missus and kids to think on ...'

'SHUT YOUR MOUTH!' The sergeant savagely backhanded the man across the lips.

'I'll speak my piece!' The artisan was half-sobbing with rage and torment.

'That's enough, Sar'nt Turner!' Gresham restrained the

N.C.O. when he would have struck the man again. 'Calm down Johnny Raw, and tell me what's the matter ... Speak up, man, say your piece.'

The artisan rubbed his bruised chest where the halberd stave had caught him and glared in hatred at both N.C.O.s.

'It's me missus and kids,' he babbled the words tearfully. 'I was promised twenty-five pound to be a substitute, and another two guineas from the King when I took me oath in front o' the magistrates, and I'se not bin gi'ed a penny piece on it. ... Not even a brass farthing, and me missus and kids back home in Cleobury Mortimer, they doon't even know I'se bin took for the army. What's to become on 'um, that's what I'd like to know? I only come to Kidderminster to find work, for we'd none at home and no money for food ... Them bloody magistrates and constables tricked me into the army, so they did ...'

'Get on wi' your grievance about the money, man,' the sergeant-major said impatiently.

'He can have no grievance, sir,' Sergeant Turner put in. 'Most of the money these lot got for being substitutes was took by the magistrates to pay the sums they was fined for bein' rogues and vagabonds.'

'Well, if that's the case, I've no wish to hear any more o' this bellyachin' about it,' Gresham snapped.

'I wants to know why I arn't bin paid loike I was promised?' the artisan apparently refused to hear what Sergeant Turner had said about the fines and the substitute bounty. 'I saw that cove I went as substitute for, gi' the money to one o' they bloody orficers who was asittin' in the courtroom wheer we was took. If I'd ha' bin paid loike I was promised, I could a sent the money to me missus. But I'se had nothin! Nothin' at all! And my kids could be bloody starvin' by now ... starvin'!'

'They can go to the parish overseers for relief,' the sergeant-major told him harshly. 'Other woman ha' done so when they've lost their menfolk.'

'Ahr, and other women ha' bin put in the poorhouse for doing such and have lost their home and everything else that belonged to 'um,' the man retorted hotly, and rubbed his hand across his eyes, as he stepped back into line. 'What be you agooin' to do about my money? That's what I wants to know!' He began to shout in temper. 'I'm not a man who'll stand to be cheated by the loikes o' you red-coated villains, I'll tell you straight! You'm a load o' bloody thieves, you redcoats be! You'm bloody scum, so you am. Scum! Thievin' scum! Bloody scum!'

As the tirade echoed about the square, soldiers in a variety of drill and fatigue dress, and slatternly-looking women and children began to cluster by the barrack blocks to stare curiously at what was taking place.

The artisan was not conscious of the commotion he was causing. He was not conscious of anything except his terrible anxieties about his wife and children which had been slowly driving him half-insane ever since his arrest and induction and through all the weeks of the long march south.

He stepped out of the rank again and advanced shouting upon the sergeant-major. 'When be you agooin' to gi' me my money so that I con fill my babbies' bellies?' he demanded, raging and shaking his fists. 'I wants me money ... It's me entitlement and I wants it! I wants it!'

Gresham's patience snapped. 'Knock him down and put him in the guardroom, Sar'nt Turner,' he ordered. The heavy halberd stave swished through the air and cracked sharply against the side of the advancing artisan's head. The man staggered, then came on in a rush. The sergeant dropped the halberd and grappled with him and they rolled biting, punching, gouging at each other across the parade-ground.

'Call out the guard, damn you!' the sergeant-major roared at a drummer-boy who was gaping open-mouthed at the scene from the nearest balcony. The child ran, and within seconds, more soldiers came doubling across the parade-ground with muskets at the slope.

'Take that bugger to the guardroom, and don't be gentle with him.' Gresham's cane indicated the struggling artisan. Musket butts rose and fell with dull, soggy thuds and the senseless body of the artisan was dragged away, feet first, his bloody head bumping limply across the stony ground.

'Are you hurt, Sarn't Turner?' Gresham asked.

The sergeant's face was bloodstreaked and his uniform dirtied. 'Not really sir,' he gasped.

'Then stay here with this lot until the adjutant's seen them. After that they can draw some stores and be detailed off for their quarters. You'll take them for drill tomorrow ... Goddamn this for a day! I don't know how long you'll have to wait here, the whole bloody battalion is out on a field exercise on Southsea Common. Still it won't hurt 'um to learn how to stand still and quiet for a few hours, will it?' He tucked his cane under his right arm and marched stiffly away, leaving the new recruits standing at awkward attention behind him.

The morning slowly passed. At midday a small drummer-boy marched out to the centre of the parade-ground and beat a call which was, the sergeant told them, the dinner call.

'And if it warn't for you lot, I could be eating my dinner,' he grumbled.

Having been marched breakfastless from a small village some miles away, well before dawn, the recruits were also feeling hungry and tired. Periodically the sergeant walked up and down in front of them to break the monotony, and occasionally from the barrack blocks the sounds of children at play and women's laughter were heard. But with the regiment away, a torpor overhung the barracks that could not be dispelled by these happenings.

'Permission to speak, Sar'nt?' Turpin Wright finally broke the silence early in the afternoon.

'What d'you want, Wright?'

'When do we get our bounty money Sar'nt ... what's left on it, that is?'

The N.C.O. grinned, showing badly discoloured teeth. 'You'll get it, never fear ... What little's left on it.'

'Yes, I knows that Sar'nt ... but when?' Turpin persisted. 'Arter all Sar'nt ... wi' respect. There's more than us stands to benefit when we does get it.'

The sergeant winked at the convict. 'The Sar'nt-major was right about you, warn't he, cully. For all you'm dressed like a Methody pisspot, you'm a flash cove ... It's as plain as daylight that you'se follered the drum afore.'

'Well, I arn't admitting to that, S'ar'nt, but I will say that I knows how to look arter them gennulmen who looks arter me,' Turpin Wright winked back.

'That's fair enough, Wright,' the N.C.O. told him. 'You should be drawing ten guineas of it, this afternoon. Captain Ward will ha' give all your bounties to the paymaster, Lieutenant Garmston, and he'll advance you ten guineas on it.'

'What about the rest of it Sergeant?' the Morris dance squire asked shyly.

'It'll be kept safe for you, cully, doon't you fret. Not that there'll be much left. But the colonel doon't like the 'cruities to 'ave too much money all at once. It gi's men funny ideas, and apart from that, there's a lot o' the knowing lads who'll soon strip the Johnny Raws o' their rhino, wun't they Wright?'

the N.C.O. joked heavily.

'Ahr, that's for sure, Sar'nt,' Turpin laughed.

Eventually a pair of mounted officers trotted through the main gate behind and to the side of the officers' mess, and, negligently returning the salutes of the gate sentry, headed towards the stables. Sergeant Turner called the recruits to attention and hurried to present them to the adjutant.

'Goddemmit,' the Honourable John Coventry drawled. 'Cannot a man get any peace at all in this demmed regiment?'

Even in uniform he continued to look like a dandy. His crimson waistsash a little finer and its dangling tassels a little curlier than other's. His silver braiding and epaulets a trifle richer and heavier. His shako plumes a little longer and more swaying, and his clothing a fraction better cut and tighter. Beside him, Matthew Purpost was drab in his plain braidless coat and black feathered cocked hat. The surgeon chuckled at his companion's droll manner and said,

'Now, John, it will only take a moment or two to look them over. They are all in good physical condition, I examined them myself,' his gaze strayed to the tiny beggar and then the flat-nosed drover, 'though I must confess that there's one or two of them ain't as pretty as they might be.'

By this time they had reined in their mounts directly in front of the line of recruits, and the smell of the men's unwashed bodies and clothes reached them powerfully.

'Phhheeewww! Devil take me!' The Honourable John wafted a finely laundered scented handkerchief in the air and put it to his nostril. 'They ain't so sweet smelling as they might be, either.' He glanced along the rank and then wafted his handkerchief in the direction of Jethro and Turpin Wright. 'What are those two tall 'uns? Methodist praters? Demme! They're dressed dull enough and look sour enough to be, don't you know!'

Jethro didn't catch the quip the surgeon made in answer to the young exquisite's scathing comment, but his resentment and anger rose quickly at the mocking laughter the two officers indulged in at his expense.

'What gives useless fops like these the right to sneer at men who are powerless to make any reply?' he demanded of himself, and the answer came rapidly enough to his mind. 'No right, that is justly earned.'

'March this rubbish away Sar'nt, for God's sake,' the adjutant drawled. 'I'm sure Sergeant-Major Gresham would not wish his beloved parade-ground to be soiled a moment longer than is absolutely necessary ... Take them to the stores and give them their necessaries, or throw the buggers into the sea ... I care not a demm either way ...'

Chatting and laughing together, the two officers rode away. The sergeant hurried the recruits from the parade ground and into a large, freezing cold, bare room in one of the stores buildings.

'Strip off,' he ordered, 'and put all your clothes in one pile and all your shoes in another ... Not you, you little turd!' he told the beggarman. 'Your'n will all ha' to be burned.'

'What happens to our clothes?' Jethro, still smarting beneath his humiliation on the parade ground, didn't bother to sound humble. The sergeant looked at the young man speculatively, and said slowly.

'I'll gi' you a word o' warning, Johnny Raw. I was watching you when the orfficers was by you. You wants to keep that temper o' yourn under control. The Sar'nt-major liked the look of you, you could do well in the army, if you works hard at it ... But you looks to me as if youse got a bit o' the rebel in you,' he paused and shook his head warningly. 'It doon't pay to show a rebel spirit here, my lad ... It doon't pay at all.'

'With respect Sergeant,' Turpin Wright spoke up. 'This is my mate, and he's a good 'un, wi' plenty o' fire in his belly. He's got a hot temper, I know, but there's no harm in him, and he's as sharp as a needle, I'll tell you. He'll not put a foot wrong, if you leaves him wi' me.'

While Turpin spoke, Jethro's thoughts had been racing towards the realization that now he was in the army, he must act as the army expected. Also, after witnessing what had happened to the artisan, he knew already that he could not hope to challenge the system of discipline, and survive.

He swallowed hard, and said civilly, 'I meant no disrespect, sergeant.'

The N.C.O. nodded his satisfaction and his manner softened.

'All right lad, that's a better attitude to take ... Your clothes 'ull be sold to the Jew pedlars and you'll get the money for 'um,' he grinned, 'that's if you'm lucky.'

Once the clothes had been piled and the men were stripped to the skin, the sergeant opened the door leading into the stores proper and bawled,

'Barber get in here. There's some 'cruities to be cropped.'

There was a clumping of boots across the dusty wooden floorboards and one of the biggest men Jethro had ever seen, clad in a brown canvas smock and pork-pie forage cap, entered the room. In his vast hand he carried a pair of clippers such as were used to shear sheep.

'You lot get into line and kneel down wi' your heads bent to the front,' the sergeant ordered, and told Turpin Wright and the bald-headed beggarman, 'No, not you two. There arn't enough grass on your 'eads to fill a sparrow's belly.'

The big man worked along the line, attacking the bowed heads as he would have attacked a sworn enemy. Brutally pushing and twisting them this way and that and cursing foully as the locks of hair fell. Jethro, feeling curiously vulnerable in his nakedness, hissed in pain as the hair was almost torn from his scalp by the blunt shears and wondered why men who were expected to fight for England should be treated as if they were criminals.

Shorn, sore-headed and shivering they were then herded into a long high-ceilinged room where rows of shelf racks were packed with every conceivable necessity of clothing and equipment. An elderly, pot-bellied quarter-master sergeant with a gin-nose presided there, aided by white fatigue-jacketed acolytes.

'The adjutant says that they'm only to draw the necessaries now, and the rest tomorrow,' Turner stated.

The quarter-master sergeant was half-drunk and bleary-eyed. He belched in greeting, spreading gin fumes liberally around him. 'Stand agen the wall theer, you 'cruities. Readman?'

A thin weedy 'chosen man', or lance corporal, with a pimpled tallowy face appeared from some hidden recess.

'Look arter these men, 'ull you, Readman. Me and Sar'nt Turner 'ull be in my office if you needs me. And you'd better not had.'

The blue-nosed man then stumbled away between the racks of shelves. Before following him, Turner warned the recruits, 'Any noise or skylarking, and it'll be the Black Hole for you. Arsk Wright theer what that is, no doubt he'll know.'

The weedy chosen man started to make a great show of authority, shouting at and abusing the recruits. He ordered them one by one to the tall desk he sat at where, aided by a private who fetched and carried for him, he threw on the floor

206

for each man in turn, two coarse shirts, two pairs of stockings, one pair of shoes, one pair of grey trousers and a black leather neck-stock with brass clasps attached to it. Turpin Wright touched Jethro's shoulder and indicated that he should stand last in the line and follow himself. Jethro obeyed without a word and watched with mounting indignation the stores clerk's bullying of the other men.

'Step lively you! What's your name?' Readman's pale face was mean and spiteful as he ordered the Morris dance squire up to the desk.

'My name is Wilder, zur ... Isaac Wilder,' the squire answered docilely. His simple honest face was still as confused now as it had been when he had been the only member of the dance side to be taken for the militia. Readman, a product of a lifetime spent mainly on counting stools, mimicked the countryman's thick accent. 'Oi-m a hayseed, oi be, an' moi name is Izzzaaac Wilder, zzzur.' He sneered. 'Can you write your name, Chaw-Bacon?'

The countryman's face burned with shame and he shook his head. 'Oi canna, zur. I never 'ad no book-learnin'.'

'Then make your mark here, yokel. Where I'm pointing my finger, you bloody numbskull.'

When Isaac Wilder had with great concentration and effort, made a crude cross against his name in the ledger, Readman took the gear from his helper's arms and tossed it on to the floor. 'It's easy for these damned yokels to bend their backs, ain't it. That's all they'm good for, to bend and pick turnips and such-like all their lives. Get dressed over there, Chaw-Bacon.' He jerked his thumb at the corner of the room where the others were getting dressed.

Bemused and intimidated by what they had seen since entering this new environment, no one had the audacity to challenge the bullying of the stores clerk, or to question why they should be given the worn-out dirty clothing he had issued them, and not the new clothes that were on the racks.

'You! Get up here!' Readman pointed at Jethro, but Turpin Wright's arm came across the younger man's chest holding him back, and Turpin went forward himself.

The chosen man's spiteful face twisted in anger. 'I called the dog, not his vomit,' he said.

Turpin smiled pleasantly at the clerk. 'Did you now, Spindle Prick? Well, I'se come instead.'

Readman's narrow jaw dropped and his eyes widened in

shocked surprise. Turpin went round the desk to meet the private coming from the rear of the shelves with an armful of clothing.

'Hold hard, cully,' the convict growled, and stiff-armed the small-statured private to an abrupt halt. He picked up the articles of dirty worn clothing one by one, and after examining them, hurled the lot to the rear of the stores. When he had done that he came back to the desk where Readman sat as if transfixed and snarled menacingly.

'Does you take Turpin Wright for a bleedin' flat, you spindle-pricked little bastard? I'll not take "dead men's" clothes.'

The clerk tried to recover himself and blustered. 'What d'you mean by saying that I'm—'

Turpin's clenched fist slammed on to the desk top causing the pewter inkwell to jump and the black ink to spill across the neat columns of the open ledger.

'I means that I takes you for a slimy, arse-crawlin' turd,' he growled. 'Well, you might be able to mount a rocking horse and play king wi' these others, but I'm no Johnny Raw.' He swung to tell the other recruits. 'Theer's three kinds of issues, mateys ... Theer's what you get from the King, hisself. And that's just your musket, bayonet, and pouch. Then the colonel kindly gives you your breeches, coats, caps and shoes. But! Everythin' else you gets, you pays for yourselves out on your bloody stoppages! This skinny turd here, is trying to come the flash cove wi' us. He's giving us what's called "dead men's" gear, that was first give to coves who'se since run, or died.' He pushed his hard fierce face against the weak features of the chosen man, and hissed, 'Who's pocketing the rhino, cully? And how much does you cheat the sar'nt out of? Becos' it looks to me as if he's drunk most o' the time and doon't know what's agoing on from dawn 'til dusk. I reckon I ought to report this to the lieutenant quarter-master hisself, and to the adjutant.'

Readman looked stricken. 'Now hold hard, matey,' he croaked. 'Hold hard, I'll see you'm all right. There's bin a mistake made, that's all ... Just a mistake.'

'I know well there has.' The menace left Turpin's manner and he beamed benevolently at the frightened man. 'But then, a small mistake like that is easy to put right, arn't it, cully?'

The clerk's face was a sick mixture of relief and disgust as he nodded agreement and beckoned to his helper.

'Get some new stuff for this man.'

'For all on us, cully ... For all on us,' Turpin Wright reminded him pointedly.

Readman smirked in anguish. 'For all on 'um,' he croaked to the private.

When Sergeant Turner reappeared, alone and stinking of gin, the recruits were waiting quietly for him. All dressed alike in new shirts and trousers. Their leather stocks strapped chokingly around their necks and their stout new boots already beginning to pinch their feet. Their outer clothing was folded under their arms and there seemed to the sergeant's experienced eyes to be more there than there should have been. Turner hid a grin and spoke to Turpin Wright.

'You'll go far, you 'ull, my bucko ... You'll go far.'

The day was nearly done when Jethro and his fellow recruits were finally taken to their various barrackrooms. When the paymaster had given them enough silver coins and paper banknotes to make up their ten guineas advance, Jethro had noticed Turpin Wright slip some money to the sergeant. Afterwards, the convict whispered to Jethro, 'You and me 'ull be put together in the same quarters now, matey. You just follow what I does and you wun't goo far wrong ... Give us a guinea.'

'What for?' Jethro asked.

'Becos' I just gi' the sergeant two guineas from the pair on us, so that he could drink our health ... He's to be our drill instructor, see, so you wants to keep on the right side of him.'

'You men am to goo to number four company's quarters, at present commanded by Captain Josiah Parker,' Turner told the recruits before he dismissed them. 'Now he's not a bad officer as far as it goes ... He's away from the battalion more than he's wi' it. You'll each on you be put as bedmate wi' a steady man who's done some time, when you gets to your rooms. He'll look arter you and show you the way to do things ... You'll parade behind your barrack block when the assembly is beaten tomorrow morning.'

'Wun't we be on the parade ground then, Sar'nt?' Deane the flat-nosed drover asked.

'What?' The sergeant was contemptuous. 'Does you think that we lets bloody wapstraws like you on our parade ground when you carn't even stand proper, let alone march. My oath we doon't! Now gerroff to your quarters ... GOO ON! AT

209

THE DOUBLE! Wright? Stanton? You stay here a minute.'

When the others had gone running and the sergeant was alone with the two of them, he winked at Turpin.

'T'se put you in the same room as your mate,' he told him. 'You'll show him the ropes, I don't doubt.'

'Thank you very much, Sar'nt,' Turpin answered smartly, and added, 'Oh, by the way, Sar'nt. The rest o' the 'cruities asked if you'd do 'um the honour o' drinkin' their health. I explained the old custom to 'um, d'you see, Sar'nt.' Turpin had taken money from each recruit by a mixture of warning and cajoling and this, minus a sum he had secreted to compensate his trouble, he now passed to the N.C.O. Turner laughed admiringly.

'You'll goo far, cully, you 'ull.' Still chuckling he left them. Their quarters were on the second storey. It was a long wide room lined on each side with double-sized box beds each filled with straw and covered by a coarse sheet with the blankets folded upon it. Above every bed was a row of wooden pegs with a shelf above them. A large black-iron firegrate with engraved royal ciphers upon it was set into one side wall midway along its length, and at the far end of the room, beneath a small barred window, was a long wall-rack for the muskets. The centre space between the lines of beds was dominated by narrow trestle tables placed end to end to form one whole, and on their scrubbed wooden boards were arranged small earthenware bowls, assorted pothooks, fire-irons, candlesticks, and long barbed flesh-forks. On either side of the musket rack, stood a huge crock pot each with a wooden cover. Turpin nudged Jethro and pointed.

'Be careful when you wants to take a piss at night, matey.'

'Why?' Jethro was curious.

'Because one o' them pots is for pissing in, and the others wheer they keeps the salted meat ... And salt though it might be, a drop o' piss doon't improve the flavour.'

Each corner of the room was partitioned off by blankets hung from ropes, and at the sound of fresh voices one of the blankets was pushed aside and a woman looked out. Her body was fat and shapeless and her hair hung in an untidy mess about her broad, pudding-like face.

'Sadie! Charlotte! Bertha!' she yelled stridently. 'We'se got some Johnny Raws come.'

To a muffled accompaniment of curses and children's wails, the blankets at the three other corners were pushed aside and more frowsty women appeared, with small, snot-nosed, tow-headed children about them.

The woman addressed as Sadie, a blonde, statuesque creature, grumbled, 'Fine bloody time to come, ain't it. Only bleedin' chanst we 'as to get some sleep, and these bleedin' Johnny Raws 'as to come disturbin' us.'

'Now then, my pretty,' Turpin remonstrated good-naturedly. 'That's no way to welcome good men and true, who're come to buy a drop o' the Mother's Comfort for friends ... And all paid for wi' the bounty money that's ajinglin' in me pockets.'

At the mention of 'bounty money' a change that was almost magical in its immediacy came over the women. The three named ones came smiling and simpering to welcome the newcomers. While the first woman dropped the blanket and bent over her sleeping, sweat-smelling husband in the bed, whose coat, hung on its peg above his head, bore the white chevrons of a corporal on its upper sleeves.

'Wake up, Charlie, ye lazy pig!' she whispered urgently, shaking his shoulder hard. 'There's 'cruities here, wi' bounty to spend.'

'Uhh! Wha! Uhh! Wha's that you say?' He sat up on the bed, yawning wide and scratching his hairy naked body. 'God rot yer bleedin' eyes, Annie! Ye fat pig, ye!' he spoke with the harsh twang of a Northern Irishman. 'Haven't I bin on the piquet all night, blast ye! And you ashakin' me for I don't know wha' ...'

'Hush yer blether, damn ye!' His wife clapped her hand across his mouth. 'Will yez lissen to what I'm tellin' ye,' she hissed. 'There's two Johnny Raws come, wi' the bounty in their pockets.'

Her husband's pale blue eyes filled with glee and he dragged her fat grimy paw from his mouth. 'Why couldn't ye say that in the first place, ye stupid sow!' he swore at her in a jocular tone, and getting off the bed he dragged on a pair of trousers and slipping his tunic upon his bare torso went out through the blanket.

'Well, well, well! Welcome boys to Corporal Rourke's room,' he greeted them smilingly.

Jethro and Turpin examined him closely. He was as big as them and well muscled, with a swarthy complexion and thick black curly hair. Very handsome in a brutal, coarse way.

'Where is it ye're from, lads?' he wanted to know, and ushered them to sit on the benches flanking the tables.

'From Worcestershire,' Jethro answered for both.

'Ahr, to be shure, ye would be, wouldn't ye ... this being a Worcestershire recruited battalion ... I'm from Ulster, me-self, transferred from the North Antrim Fencibles about a year since?' He laughed with a great show of strong white teeth. ' 'Twas transferred I did to get away from that ugly fat ould sow there, my missus ... But she found out and follered me. Ah well, 'tis the cross I have to bear for me sins, not to mention me utter stupidity in marrying her like I did.' He laughed again. 'Faith! There's me owld Ma would turn in her grave so she would, if she knew that her fine boy, Desmond, brought up to be a good Catholic had married a Protestant ... And it's not even as if my missus had the looks to recommend her, is it?'

'Hold yer blether, ye Papish bastard!' his wife cursed him spiritedly. 'I was pretty enough for ye when ye was beggin' and pladin' wi' me to marry yez ... I could have taken me pick o' plenty. I'll tell ye. And they was all good, clean-living, God-fearing Protestant boys. Not a bleedin' Roman like ye ... burning y'candles for the Pope.'

His pale blue eyes hardened and he swung to her and said warningly, 'Now ye've said sufficient for the day, my jewel.'

'Oh have I now?' she warmed to her task. 'Twelve bloody kids that Pope lover has put in my belly! Twelve on um'! And seven still livin', so help me God! That's all he's good for, that and getting drunk! He calls me a fat sow and all the badness he can get his tongue to when we'em in front o' people, but he calls me summat else at night.' She nodded her head until her flabby cheeks shook, 'Ahr, and it's every night wi'out fail as well!'

Turpin Wright had sat watching quietly and he sensed that there would be physical violence between man and wife in a very few seconds. He stood up and taking some money from his pocket threw it on the table.

'Can we get a couple o' bottles d'you think?'

The big blonde, Sadie, snatched up the coins instantly.

'We'll get more than a couple, my handsome,' she exclaimed delightedly. 'Come on, Annie, and help me carry 'um. We'll not be long away, Johnny Raw!'

She started to walk past Turpin, but he grabbed her upper arm and swung to face him.

'I'm only gooin' to say this the once, my pretty.' His voice was soft and low, but there was in it a note that caused all at the table to look at him nervously. 'I'm no Johnny Raw! So you'd best make good and sure that them bottles comes back here in double quick time and that what's in 'um arn't bin helped to spread itself wi' water, or anythin' else ... Understand?'

The blonde gazed at his hard tough features and a spasm of fear crossed her own. 'I will, cully ... I will,' she muttered.

Turpin grinned, and released her arm to fondle her large firm buttocks with the same hand. 'I rackon you an me 'ull grow to be real good friends, my pretty,' he told her pleasantly, 'now fetch that drink, I'm fair parched.'

The tension eased and the two women went on their errand. The corporal had read correctly the danger that had threatened in the room, and now his pale eyes held a hint of caution as he regarded his two new recruits.

'You'se took a fancy for Big Sadie, I see, cully,' the Ulsterman remarked.

'Ahr, I likes big women, wi' summat for a man to get ahold of,' Turpin told him, then said. 'Is she one o' your bits o' fancy then, Corporal Rourke?'

The thin, haggardly attractive woman named Bertha, who was sitting at the table suckling a swaddled baby at one of her flat breasts, cackled with laughter. 'If you knew Paddy, you'd know that anything in skirts is his bit o' fancy ... Ain't that so, Charlotte?'

Her friend next to her, a toothless, prematurely aged woman of about thirty shared the enjoyment. 'He's a rare hot 'un, our Paddy is ... Ain't you darlin?'

The corporal took their bantering in good part. 'Aye! I'm a rare 'un for me weemin,' he smiled complacently. 'If the good Lord ever created anythin' better than a bit o' rogerin', then I've yet to find it ... An spakin' about it makes me feel like a bite o' the apple right now.' He leant against the skinny Bertha who was next to him and slipped one hand over her shoulder and into her open bodice to clasp the free breast. The other hand he used to fondle her bony thighs.

'Get away wi' you!' she cackled in delight. Then the baby disturbed from its feed began to squall loudly.

'Theer! Look what you'se done, you randy Irish goat!' Bertha shouted in annoyance. 'I'll not be able to get the babby back to sleep for hours now and my man 'ull bloody half-kill me so he 'ull, if the babby keeps acrying.'

The Ulsterman's coarse handsome face was heavy with lust and he continued to knead her flat breasts and thin flanks with his hands.

'Come on, honey, let's have ten minutes behind the curtain.' His manner was joking, but his eyes were serious.

Jethro didn't know whether to feel pity or disgust at the spectacle of a man so dominated by the desires of the flesh. He was, he admitted, of an ardent temperament as regards women himself, but could feel no desire for the worn-out sluts at the table. He found himself comparing them with Sarah Jenkins. 'By God! I'd like to see her again,' he thought, and was surprised at the strength of his longing for her.

The other children who, up until now, had played quietly enough began to squabble and scuffle and the baby cries redoubled their intensity.

'Arggrrhh be damned to ye!' the corporal exclaimed and withdrew his hand. 'For the love o' God, get them kids quieted, will ye.'

The thin woman was now very angry. 'Why doon't you do it, cully?' she jeered. 'Most on 'um be yours anyway.'

'Can't you shut that brat up?' A short squat man entered the room wearing the tall hairy mitre cap and the yellow uniform with red and silver facings of a drummer.

'Theer! I bloody well said I'd get the blame for the bloody babby crying, didn't I?' Bertha swore.

The drummer, who was Bertha's husband, unslung the deep-bodied drum and handed it to one of the children ... 'Put it away in my corner,' he grunted, and scowled at his wife. 'If that little barstard keeps on bawlin', I'll throw it through the bloody window!' he threatened.

She stood up clasping the baby tightly to her and faced him unafraid. 'You wants to think about that when you'm pumping the bloody kids into me,' she retorted.

He raised his hand and aimed a blow at her, but she evaded him and scurried away behind the curtains of the corner bed. The drummer slumped on to her vacated seat and said to Rourke,

''As these 'cruities got their bounty?' He didn't look at the men he was talking about.

Turpin winked at Jethro and said loudly, 'In the army, Jethro, the drummer is a man o' great importance. He's equal to a corporal and gets a corporal's pay. But there's one thing you oughter know about drummers. They'm give the drum because they'm either too weak to carry a firelock, or too blind to shoot wi' one ... Now as to 'um being blind, you con see the truth in that straight away, can't you? This bleeder can't even see far enough to look at us, when he's atalkin' about us. But I con see well enough to reach him, Jethro ... And if he comes the flash cove wi' us, then I'm agoing to take his bloody drumsticks and shove 'um right up his arse!'

The drummer's hairy mitre cap turned so that its brass-badged front plate caught the last of the daylight from the window. He stared long and hard at both Turpin Wright and Jethro, then held out his hand towards them.

'Welcome to our humble abode, mateys,' he grinned. 'Theer's allus room here for "knowing lads" such as your-selves ... Specially if they'se got the price of a dram, and they'se travelled these sort o' roads afore.'

Turpin Wright grinned back and took the outstretched hand. 'We'se already sent out for the dram,' he replied, then shivered exaggeratedly. 'Jesus! But it's cold comfort here, arn't it! Have you no coals for the fire?'

'No,' the corporal told him. 'We used our allotment up pretty quick this time, and bedad! There's hardly a candle stub to be had in the room, let alone anythin' for supper.'

'Say no more,' Turpin said, looking the very picture of geniality and as soon as the women returned with the bottles of gin, the drinking began.

The battalion returned from Southsea Common and the barracks became a hubbub of shouting, cursing, boot-clump-ing men. Corporal Rourke's room suddenly filled with soldiers in full drill kit and every one of them took a swig or two of gin, until in a very short space of time the bottles were empty. Turpin Wright, by now half-drunk, commandeered the whole of Jethro's money and, putting it to his own, grandly proposed to buy food, drink, candles, and coals for the whole room. His offer was eagerly accepted and by the time the gun to signal sunset was fired from the platform of the seaward-facing Duke of York's bastion, to be followed by the din of muskets, drums, fifes, bells and trumpets from all over the town's barracks and establishments, the festivities in Corporal Rourke's room were in full swing. Turpin Wright had ap-pointed himself chairman of the gathering and since he was paying for the ale, gin, meat-pies, and bloaters being toasted by some of the men and women at the roaring fire, no one had objected.

Some of the older daughters and young women of the company had come to join the party and they and their men packed the benches along the trestled tables. The entire length of the tables was thick with stone jugs and raw gin, and the smell of toasting bloaters spitting their rich juices on to the flaming coals overpowered even the fug of the harsh, strong-tasting tobacco that was puffed in the short clay pipes by both men and women alike. Clasps were undone and neckstocks removed. Tunics and bodices unbuttoned and opened as the heat of fire, candles and dense-packed bodies caused sweat to run from hot red faces and across hairy chests, and to trickle down the clefts of plump white breasts. Wailing babies were given scraps of bread-filled rags soaked in gin to suck and they quickly became fuddled and slept.

Turpin Wright, wearing a shako back to front on his head, sat on a stool placed on top of the extreme end of the tables. His face was shiny with greasy sweat, and in one hand he held a stone jug of gin, while in the other a clay pipe waved to and fro, its burning ashes threatening to spill over the heads of those who sat directly below him. On the left were Corporal Rourke and Jethro. On the right lolled Big Sadie, slack-mouthed and glazed-eyed, her vast melon-like breasts spilling from her loosened bodice so that their big brown-ringed nipples were in plain sight.

There was no room for dancing, so the gathering sang instead, accompanied by the shrill tin whistles that some of the men produced. They roared the words of the Rogues March ...

> 'Fifty I got for selling me coat,
> Fifty for sellin' me blannnnnket ...
> If ever I 'list for the army agen,
> the devil shall be my seeerrrgeant!'

Feet stamped in unison and sinews stood out stark in muscular throats as they bellowed the chorus ... 'Poor owd sodger! Poor owd sodger!' and the tin whistles thrilled jauntily on in counterpoint. 'Poor owd sodger! Poor owd sodger!' To thunderous applause the best singer in the room, a freckle-faced Scotsman, gave them the haunting melody called 'Love Farewell', with its words of men dying in violent battle and mourning, as they died, the women they had loved and left. Fists

216

hammered on tables and men and women wiped tears of laughter from streaming eyes in tribute to the saucy innuendo-laden ditties that Turpin Wright himself obliged them with.

As chairman, he would call the party to order after each contribution and, pointing with his pipestem at some man or woman sitting at the tables, would shout,

'The honourable chair calls on you to sing a song, or dance a jig, or tell us a tale!' And all present would bellow, 'and the company desires it also!'

Mainly they sang. The sentimental,

'Farewell, my lovely Nancy, farewell I must away ...
For I hear the drums abeating and no longer can I stay ...'

All who knew the song would join in. The sadness inherent in its verses bringing maudlin tears to drunken eyes as they sang softly,

'For we've orders out from Portsmouth town, and for many
    a long mile ...
For to fight the French and the heathens, on the baannks o'
    the River Nile!'

The tune would die away and the mood abruptly change as someone would start to beat the rhythmn of the rollicking 'Girl I left behind me,' or 'The British Grenadiers,' or 'The Parliaments of England ...' Men hurled the words at the rafters and drank great gulps of ale and gin and kissed and mauled the women beside them; and the children watched, and wondered, and learned.

One or two of the younger girls, whose bodies were still firm and shapely enough to arouse any man's lust, hoisted their petticoats above their knees when called on by the chair, and mounted upon the table top to dance a heel-tapping, dextrous-toed hornpipe, or high-kicking jig. The sight of full breasts bouncing, smooth haunches swaying, and well-formed calves and thighs peeping from under the froth of petticoats brought greedy hands stretching and reaching, and the dancing women laughed in delight and tormented the men even more with the soft promise of their bodies. The drink kept flowing and the songs and laughter, the jeers and kisses, and slaps and cuddles and promises went on and on.

One greyheaded old soldier, a one-time play actor, insisted continually on getting to his feet and quoting the 'Crispin Day' speech from Shakespeare's *Henry the Fifth*. Each time he was overwhelmed by a torrent of good-natured abuse, and he would bow gracefully and give way before the storm, only to rise again at the next call by the chairman and start to declaim ... 'And gentlemen in England now abed, shall think themselves accursed they were not here, and hold their ...' It was at this point, stupefied by drink, that he finally fell, crashing backwards from the bench, and was rolled under the table by his neighbours. He lay uncaring and unfeeling of the stamping feet, the gobs of tobacco juice and phlegm, and the rough hands of two of the older children who had crept under the benches and were now tugging at his clothing in search of money.

Drummer Morrison, Bertha's husband, had been forced to leave the party to join the other drummers and fifers of the battalion in the Beating of the Retreat on the Grand Parade in Portsmouth. Bertha Morrison herself had been covertly watching Jethro Stanton for a considerable time. The gin she had drunk made her feel amorously inclined and the new recruit was a fine-bodied handsome young man, she thought lasciviously. She waited until Jethro rose from the table to go to the latrine sheds which were some distance behind the barrack blocks, and slipped out of the room after him. She hid in a darkly-shadowed corner of the perimeter walls near the sheds, and as the young man began to make his way back to the barracks she reached out and clasped his arm.

'Come 'ere a minute, dearie,' she whispered invitingly, and, in his surprise at this encounter, Jethro allowed himself to be drawn into the shadows. She pressed her body against him and crushed her wet-lipped mouth to his, whimpering in her hungry need. Jethro fuddled by the drink he had taken, found himself responding to her squirming body, and as her practised hands sought for and found his manhood, the long weeks of enforced celibacy caused him to forget all but the aching desire for a woman's body. His hands lifted her skirts and caressed her hips and buttocks. She guided him into her moistness and they clung together panting and moaning softly as he urgently thrust her against the rough cold brickwork of the wall, and climaxed with almost unbearable pleasure. Spent, they remained tight-clutched in the shadows. She lifted her face from his neck and whispered, 'That was nice, cully ... Really nice.'

The young man's fuddled senses began to clear rapidly and the fetid sourness of her breath in his nostrils sickened him. He pulled away from her and fastened his trousers, not looking at the woman, and felt a shamed self-disgust at his animal response to her. Bertha's thin arms clung to his neck and again her lips came seeking his mouth. Jethro stepped back from her, and a quick sense of rejection caused her to curse.

'What's the marrer wi' you, you bastard? You was hot enough for what I got a few minutes since?'

'Aye, that's true,' Jethro replied, and tried to find words so that he would not hurt and offend her. 'I'm sorry about it ... I don't know what came over me ... It must have been the drink,' he offered lamely.

'It must 'ave bin the drink, he says!' she aped his well-spoken accent with savage mimicry.

'Now don't be angry,' he told her. 'There's no harm been done.'

'Oh no! No harm at all!' She tossed her matted, stringy hair indignantly. 'Only that now you'se had what you wanted, you reckons you con treat a wench like a bit o' dirt ... Who does you reckon you be, Johnny Raw? Does you reckon that I opens me legs like a bleedin' tanner-a-go whore for any bleeder that's got a hard on?' Her voice rose and her drunken rage became more apparent with every word she spoke.

Jethro cursed himself for drinking so much that he had lost control of his actions. His silence only increased her fury.

'I ain't good enough for you, you fancy-spoken barstard! Is that what you thinks?'

He cast about desperately for something he could do or say to calm her ... 'No, I don't think that at all,' he began, and she clutched at him again.

'Then why wun't you be nice to me, cully? I could give you a pleasurin' whenever you wanted ... I'se took a liking for you, my handsome, a big liking!'

He fended off her questing hands and tried again. 'Listen, woman, it's naught that's wrong with you ... But I've no wish to become involved with anyone; and there's your husband as well. What would happen if he found out that you and I had done this?'

'Him?' she ejaculated scornfully. 'He doon't care a bugger about me, nor what I does ... He'd not gi' a damn even if he did find out, and he ain't likely to do that anyway.'

'No,' Jethro said quietly, but very firmly. 'I'm truly sorry for

219

what happened between us. I blame myself for it. But it'll not happen again.' He turned from her and walked quickly towards the barracks, from whose dark bulk broken only by the flickering light coming from some of the windows, the faint sounds of revelry in Corporal Rourke's room could still be heard.

Bertha Morrison leant back against the wall and a terrible hatred for Jethro Stanton took seed within her mind. Hardened as she had become to humiliation and degradation at the hands of men, yet she still possessed deep down, a conviction that she was still as desirable as she had undoubtedly once been as a girl. Sober, she would have shrugged off the rejection, only one of so many in her hard life. Drunk as she was now, the seeds of resentment and hatred that men had planted and caused to grow within her by their brutal mistreatment over the years, suddenly flourished and came to full flower. She glared after the receding figure of Jethro, and shook her fist.

'I'll get even wi' you some day, you proud-stomached bastard!' she vowed. 'I'll get even, I swears it!'

CHAPTER NINETEEN

Crown *hulk, February 1813*

'Eight bells! Eight bells! Lash up and stow! Lash up and stow!' The shutters crashed open and the smoking steamy clouds of foul air belched out from the lower decks.

Captain Arthur Redmond of His Britannic Majesty's prison ship, *Crown*, added his own coarse shout to the chorus of bellowed orders from the guards and answering curses from the prisoners.

'Sergeant Belton?'

'Aye aye, sir.' The burly marine ran aft to report. 'All portlights open, sir.'

The N.C.O. studied the face of his commanding officer closely.

Of late Arthur Redmond had been unusually mild-tempered and the marine, experienced in the ways of his naval superiors, was puzzled.

' 'Tain't natural for the mad barstard to be so quiet and gentle,' he thought to himself.

'My thanks, Sergeant,' the captain nodded pleasantly. 'Have my boat lowered, sergeant. I've business ashore.'

'Aye aye, sir.' The marine saluted smartly and, at the other's gesture of dismissal, stamped away to carry out his orders. Arthur Redmond breathed deeply and with great satisfaction of the crisp morning air, and his mood grew increasingly festive as he thought of where he intended visiting once ashore. His heavy-browed square features under his black bicorn hat were placid, and he rubbed his fingers across the purple drink blotches on his nose and cheeks as he waited.

The boat dropped from its davits on the hulk's stern and its six oarsmen brought it smartly to rest at the foot of the gangway. The white-crossbelted, scarlet-coated marine quarter guard, carrying muskets with fixed bayonets formed up at the head of the gangway, flanked by a drummer and a fifer.

Sergeant Belton's bull voice sounded. 'Honour Guard ...

Attention! Dress!' Their cockaded top hats swivelled to the right and their boots stamped a broken riffle as the line straightened. 'Eyes front! Shoulder arms!' Muskets were thrown up smartly and hands slapped wood and iron in unison.

The sergeant, halberd rigid at his side about-turned, and as he also snapped to attention and saluted, the drummer beat a soft rhythmn and the fife fluted the mournful notes of 'Roslyn Castle'. Captain Redmond went down the gangway. The boat rocked under his weight and drew away towards the shore. Once he was sure that the captain was out of earshot, the sergeant growled,

'Belay that bloody funeral march,' to the musicians, and ordered the guard to fall out.

'Has he gone for long, d'you think, Sarn't?' a lanky private asked.

'Aye, we'll not be seeing the captain back here this day, I reckon,' Belton told the man. 'Good riddance to the mad pig!' his inner voice echoed.

'What's he gawn ashore for?' the same private went on. 'Is it a doxy he's tailin', d'you think?'

'I think you're heading straight for a few days in the Black Hole, Dibbins! That's what I think!' Belton roared at the man in sudden anger. 'Who the 'ell does you think you'm atalkin' to, you poxy lubber?'

The private quailed visibly. 'I meant nothin', Sar'nt,' he stuttered.

'Then be silent about your officers in future,' Belton threatened. 'You stinking-hided bilge rat ... I'll not stand any insolence from scum like you regarding your betters. Is that understood, dammee?'

'Aye aye, Sar'nt,' the private croaked, and inwardly prayed that something would intervene to deflect the wrath of the N.C.O. Something did. It was the approach of a broad-beamed barge, rowed by a motley collection of pig-tailed sailors and cropped-headed soldiers. At the stern next to the helmsman stood a pair of men wearing black-feathered cocked hats, and black-faced red coatees. The sergeant recognized who they were without needing to see the silver epaulets and buttons that were their distinguishing insignia.

'Goddam and blast my bleedin' eyes!' he swore. 'I'd forgot what day it was ... Theer's the bleedin' purveyors acoming.'

The marines around him groaned audibly. The ration

barge meant for them a lot of heavy toil, manhandling the casks of salted beef, herrings and small-beer inboard and storing them.

Sergeant Belton grinned wickedly. 'Goo and get your slops on, my beauties ... You'se got a bit o' work ahead ... That'll keep you out o' mischief, wun't it?'

Below decks the hammocks had by now been lashed up and stowed away. Henri Chanteur, who was the orderly this week for his mess of six men, went to join the orderlies of the other messes at the hatchway that opened into the sentry walk. The weeks he had spent on the *Crown* had had their effect, and now he resembled all the other prisoners in his unshaven ragged dirtiness. At the hatch the men stood silent and morose. The first hour of the morning was always a bad time for each individual as he faced the grim reality of yet another day of seemingly endless captivity somehow to be survived. Henri had by now come to know the majority of the men on his deck by sight, if not by name, and he constantly marvelled at their polyglot nationalities and infinite variety of backgrounds. There were on the *Crown* alone, French, Dutch, Pomeranian, Danish, Swedish, Polish, Spanish, Italian, and American captives.

It was to one of his friends among the latter that Henri now spoke.

'Good morning, Nathan. You slept well, I trust.'

Nathan Caldicott smiled at him.

'Good morning, Henry. I slept extremely well. I thank you for inquiring.' His tired eyes were faded to a light, indeterminate colour and his complexion very pale beneath the grime. 'I wonder what gourmet's delight these limejuicers have for us this morning ... Some tasty little delicacy, I don't doubt,' the American mused whimsically, and Henri felt a glow of warmth for this redoubtable man suffering, as he was, from debilitating illness, yet whose dry humour never failed him.

'I heard a rumour that they're going to issue our beloved brethren from the Carolinas some black-eyed peas, because some of them are unaccountably becoming a mite homesick, and getting uppity about it ... I do not, for the life of me, understand how any man cannot enjoy living here in England ... I declare that I for one, have never been so content in mind and body, as since I've resided here on the dear old *Crown*,' the New Englander joked mildly.

The Frenchman smiled. 'There's an easy remedy for the

223

Carolinian's malady, Nathan. The United States government should inform King George that the War of Independence was all a mistake, and that they want to become a colony of England once again. Then you Americans would go free.'

The tall man chuckled wryly. 'I should not care to be at your side if you stated that opinion in Boston, my friend.'

The hatch bolts rattled as they were drawn and a voice ordered, 'Come on. Let's be having you.'

One by one the prisoners crouched to hands and knees and scrambled through the opening into the sentry chamber where they were searched rapidly and expertly by two sailors, while the loaded muskets of marines covered them; and then allowed up the ladders on to the top deck.

The crisp cold air tasted so exquisitely fresh as to be intoxicating, and Henri drank huge mouthfuls into his body until he felt giddy and exhilarated with it. On deck he never gazed with hungry longing at the town of Portsmouth, as did most of his fellows. Instead, Henri always turned towards the harbour mouth and the rolling greenness of the Isle of Wight. It was beyond that island barrier that his beloved Normandy lay, and he wished with all his heart that a second Conqueror's ships would swarm from its harbours and inlets and bring his ordeal to an end.

The sounds of an altercation drew him back to the present. One of the housings built on deck was the prisoners' cooking galley. Inside its crude wooden walls, was a row of huge iron cauldrons built into a brick oven. Under each cauldron a fire was lit with trays of wet sand placed beneath to catch any falling coals or sparks. To one side of these ovens some planks had been nailed across barrels to make a table, and on this table was bolted a tall, spring-loaded, metal weight scale. Nathan Caldicott was standing in front of this scale in hot dispute with one of the English cooks who prepared the prisoners' food.

'And I'm telling you, Limey, that you're not going to cheat my mess outern our bread ration. I want eight pounds, and there's nary but six here.' The American's bony chest rose and fell rapidly beneath the ragged orange-yellow jacket and his prominent Adam's apple jumped up and down in his wasted throat as he continued indignantly, 'Now, I don't arsk any man for more than what is my due and proper portion. But Goddamm it! I will have what is mine and my friends' by right.'

The cook, a fat, squat one-eyed London Cockney, sniffed long and loudly and dragged the back of his greasy hand across his wet mouth and nostrils.

'Look 'ere, matey,' he began, and pointed towards a pile of bulging jute sacks that were heaped on top of the table. 'The bleedin' ration barge ain't got to us yet. And that there is all the bleedin' bread we got to gi' you, until the barge gets 'ere.' He sniffed loudly and again wiped his nose with the back of his hand. 'I'se got to gi' each mess the same, ain't I matey? And if I ain't got sufficient to gi' you eight pound apiece, then I cawn't gi' you eight pound apiece, can I?'

'That's not my concern,' the New Englander told him. 'My messmates will expect their proper apportionment.'

'Wot's that mean?' the Cockney's fat face was suspicious.

'What's what mean?' Caldicott demanded.

'That wot you just said then ... That larst word ... Wot was it naow? Appo ... or somefink?'

Henri was forced to hide a smile under his hand at the un-conscious comedy of the dialogue between the two. The cook put his hands on his hips and pushed his belly forward.

'Look matey, I'm a busy man and I've no time to argue the toss wiv you ... Besides! You'se got a pot o' burgoo for your breakfass as well, ain't you? Fink yerself lucky I'm dish-ing out the bread naow. On the uvver bleedin' ships they 'as to wait until their bleedin' dinner afore they gets it ... They ain't all as bleedin' soft-'earted as me, I'll tell yer.'

Nathan Caldicott's shiny bald pate flushed bright red. This was another peculiarity of the American's that endeared him to Henri. When the New Englander grew angry, his face and neck remained corpse-pale, but the scalp of his bald head always crimsoned with temper.

He threw out his long stick-like arm and pointed trembl-ingly at the foul-smelling greyish liquid bubbling in the cauldrons.

'Do you have the gall to call that goddamned piss, break-fast?' his voice rose to a near screech on the last word. 'My Gahd, Limey! Back home in Maine we wouldn't feed that to the hogs. A man would feel too shamed to face the poor beasts if he fed them piss like that.'

The Cockney rocked on his heels in outrage. ''Ere, cully, you just watch your bleedin' marf,' he spluttered. 'I'se bin makin' burgoo for a good many years and that's good stuff there. Four parts barley to one part o' finest oatmeal, wi' meat juice and spices and such ... I'se never had no complaints afore about my burgoo, I'll tell yer.'

By now the ever-increasing queue of waiting prisoners were impatient at the delay.

'*Scheissen! Was machst du hier?*' a Pomeranian shouted.

'*Oui, bien dit! Bouge ton cul, sale cochon d'un anglais!*' a Frenchman echoed the German's complaint.

A chorus of shouted oaths and jeers came from the long queue which brought Sergeant Belton to the galley.

'What's the delay, you fat swab?' he demanded of the Cockney.

'It's this bleedin' Yankee, Sar'nt Belton. He says he wants the full eight pound o' ration. I'se told 'im we got no more 'til the barges come, but 'e wun't lissen.'

The burly marine stared hard at the New Englander. 'Is this true, what he tells me?'

Nathan Caldicott nodded vigorously. 'You're darn right it's the truth,' he answered heatedly. 'I want what is my messmates' entitlement, eight pounds of bread per mess per day. Now I ain't complaining about this stuff being a mite stale.' He hefted one of the round loaves and tried without success to depress the crust with his fingers and thumbs. 'It's a mite musty as well!' He brushed at the thick layer of mildew that covered it. 'But that can't be helped these days. I do insist, however, on being given the official ration scale, not the six pounds only, that this fat-gutted bastard has issued.'

Belton's face was expressionless, and his tone even.

'Take what you've bin give, Yankee Doodle, and draw your burgoo and then get them bones o' yours back below.'

'Now just a moment ...' Caldicott started to argue, and Belton stepped to him and thrust his beefy red face close to the other's.

'Doon't talk back to me, Yankee Doodle,' he hissed. 'A bloody good mate o' mine was killed on the *Macedonian* afore she struck to one o' your men o' war. I'se got a bit o' respect for you Yankees as fightin' tars, but my mate meant the world to me and when I thinks about him, then I feels like shoving' a bayonet through every bloody Jonathan's guts. So while I'm still holding me temper, draw your rations and get below!'

Nathan Caldicott drew a deep breath and shook his head slowly.

'Sar'nt, while I have all due sympathy for your sad loss, yet

I must refuse to obey your order. A matter of principle is involved here.'

For long moments, the Englishman's big ham-like fists clenched and unclenched as he fought to control himself. Henri Chanteur, who had already felt the weight of those fists, feared for his friend, whom he knew would stand no chance against the marine. At last the man spoke.

'You leave me no choice, Yankee,' he raised his voice and shouted, 'Corporal Noakes ... Git in here wi' two files o' men.'

Almost immediately the galley filled with armed marines. The mood of the prisoners, which as the argument proceeded had become increasingly noisy and belligerent, subsided abruptly into muttering apprehension. Sergeant Belton grabbed Caldicott by the front of his ragged jacket.

'You can thank your lucky stars, Yankee Doodle, that I've got pity in me for brave men such as yourself who are here in these damned hulks. I'm putting you in the Black Hole for the rest o' the day; and I'll gi' you fair warning, that if you ever gets uppity wi' me agen, I'll knock seven sorts o' shit out o' you and put you in front o' Captain Redmond. Take him away!'

Erect and proud, Caldicott was marched away between two marines.

The sergeant shouted at the rest of the prisoners, 'Draw your rations and get below. If I 'as any more trouble from any one o' you, then that man will regret it to his dying day ... And that's a promise!'

Henri collected the bread and a leather bucket full of burgoo for his mess and went below. His messmates were in their usual spot, crouched or sitting on the deck beneath one of the iron scuttles. Six small tin bowls and the same number of pannikins were arranged in a row before them. The prisoners were not issued with knives, forks, or spoons and each man either ate with his fingers or bought, begged, or stole implements of bone or wood that those men who possessed tools and knives had carved. Gaston de Chambray smiled at Henri.

'You have been a long time, *mon ami* ... What caused the delay?'

Henri told them about Nathan Caldicott's dispute.

'Some of these Americans have a great deal of fire in their bellies,' the cuirassier colonel observed admiringly. 'It's easy to have spirit when you have only been here a little while,' one of the other men pointed out. 'If these Yankees had been prisoners for as long as most of us, or had fought and suffered for as long as we French, then I doubt that their spirits would be so high.'

'Very true,' de Chambray agreed mildly. 'A few years in this damp atmosphere soon deadens the fire in any man's belly!'

The meagre breakfast was soon consumed and the bowls wiped clean with scraps of bread. Henri put the remainder of his bread together with his bone spoon into the sack, sewed from rags, which in common with most of the prisoners he wore on a cord around his waist. Then he went with Gaston de Chambray for a fencing lesson.

All about the battery, men were busily engaged in their occupations. For one sou an hour a man could be taught by their fellow captives, masters of fencing, stick play, mathematics, languages, logic, drama, and literature. Manufacturers of tobacco shredded, dried, and blended different types of grass and weeds which they had bribed the guards to bring them. Cobblers cobbled shoes, and tailors sewed busily. Merchants of all kinds abounded, striding up and down the battery calling their wares. Some were vendors of marvellous models carved from animal bones and lumps of wood, or moulded from iron-hard bread. They offered miniature ships with cannon, rigging, and sails. Tableaux of the Passion. Sets of dominoes and chessmen. Crucifixes and rosaries. Rings, bracelets, necklaces, and brooches. Two or three supreme craftsmen even offered animated groups of tiny fiddlers, drummers, and dancers which moved and swayed, and spun round and round when tiny wheels were turned to operate minute pulley systems of wood and catgut.

There was always brisk bidding and haggling for favoured hammock positions that were constantly being bought, sold and bargained for. Just as there were always bidders for the portions of stale cheese, butter, and cone sugar that the richer captives eagerly sought and craved. But few craved the ragged, stinking jackets and trousers that some naked men offered for sale. Henri himself supplemented his last few coins by giving lessons in the art of 'La Savate', and this brought him a few sous from week to week.

On the deck below *les raffales* gambled and quarrelled the hours away, or lay entwined in dark corners and tried to find brief oblivion from their misery in each others' bodies.

228

In the rancid depths of the Orlop deck, the Imperial Mantles hunted for rats amongst the filth they slept on, and some went boldly into the noisome bilges in pursuit of their prey. Others merely lay staring blankly into the darkness, their minds empty and stultified beyond redemption.

Henri Chanteur and his friend Gaston de Chambray took the slender foils, made from whippy bamboo canes and began their practice. Changing and counter-changing, thrusting, disengaging, thrusting, parrying, riposting, counter-riposting, counter-counter-riposting, while the short fiery-mannered fencing master strutted about his pupils exhorting, encouraging, abusing these would-be exponents of his art.

The bored sentries stared through the loopholes or tramped in endless circles on the gallery. They watched and listened to the tumultuous vitality that filled the prisoners' quarters and asked themselves yet again who it was who really found captivity the most irksome and enervating. Those who were guarded? Or the guards themselves . . . ?

Deep in the very bowels of the hulk, in a wooden box six feet square, whose only opening was a series of tiny airholes, Nathan Caldicott lay naked on the rough planks in the pitch blackness. He could hear only the gurgling lapping of the poisonous bilge water, and the soft pattering scurrying pads of the rats. His eyes wide and filled with blindness, he lay on his back and fought desperately to retain his sanity.

CHAPTER TWENTY

Sarah Jenkins was at breakfast in her chambers when her maid announced that Captain Arthur Redmond RN had called. Sarah smiled at the gaunt old woman in her widow's weeds.

'Show the gentleman in, Anna.'

The old woman bobbed a curtsey. 'Yes, mum.'

For Sarah the thrill of having a maid to serve her, a cook to prepare her food, and women to wash and clean her luxurious chambers was still a novel and exhilarating experience.

The gambling club which she had opened in partnership with Shimson Levi had been an instant success, and now halfway through February 1813, the officers of the army garrison, the navy, and the dockyard together with the local gentry and rich merchants flocked there nightly to eat and drink to excess, to ogle and flirt with the abundance of beautiful young hostesses. Most important of all they came to gamble at the card tables at rouge-et-noir, whist and French hazard; or throw dice across the green baize, or risk their money on the newly introduced roly-poly wheel, which the French termed roulette. Hebrew Star and Portugal John had sent for two or three croupiers from London and had also found that several of the young girls recruited by Sarah and Shimson Levi were no mean hands as card sharps. These the two experts had trained, and now the club boasted some of the most attractive dealers in the whole of England.

What had ensured the rapid success of the club had been the attendance on its opening night of the doyen of the local *beau monde*, General the Earl Harcourt, the Governor himself, a man with an eye for a good horse, and an insatiable appetite for women, gambling, and drink. The money flowed so freely that Shimson Levi lost the worried frown he had worn as Sarah had insisted continually on purchasing only the finest furnishings and appointments for the large three-storied house in the Barrack Row, near the King James Gate at Spice Island which had become 'The Golden Venture'.

Sarah's chambers were on the top floor of the house and could be reached only up a narrow steep staircase and through a heavy oaken door. Arthur Redmond found that the climb up the stairs taxed his lungs and legs, but counted the discomfort as nothing. He still could not believe in his good fortune. That a near-penniless, rum-soaked old sailor such as himself should have attracted the interest and fond regard of the beautiful woman he was calling on. It had been two weeks since he had first met her, and during those two weeks Arthur Redmond had fallen, like any callow addle-pated midshipman, head over heels in love.

Sarah heard the heavy footfalls on the stairway and smiled to herself. Her motives in ensnaring the officer could be summed up in two words ... Henri Chanteur. With the help of Shimson Levi, who by now was so besotted with her that he would indulge her every whim, she had distributed some discreet and judicious bribes amongst the clerks at the transport office in the dockyard, and discovered that Henri was imprisoned on the *Crown*. Although she did not love Henri, yet she felt a great affection for him, and a responsibility for his imprisonment and had determined that before all else she would ensure his escape back to France. She had also determined that Arthur Redmond should unwittingly aid her to gain this objective. The door opened and the captain entered. He bowed deeply.

'My compliments ma'am!' he grunted, the sight of her affecting him so that all the gallant phrases he had practised in the privacy of his cabin aboard the *Crown* fled from his mind. Straightening, he feasted his eyes on the woman and felt his mouth grow dry with longing. She wore a brown and yellow striped sarsenet gown, which was cut low to show off the smooth roundness of her breasts and shoulders. Her chestnut hair was drawn back over her small ears, its rich colouring accentuated by her delicate lace mobcap. She smiled at him and his heart began to thump against his ribs.

'Good morning, Captain Redmond. Will you take breakfast with me?'

He bowed again. 'Delighted to accept, ma'am ... delighted,' he said gruffly.

The gaunt maid took the bicorn hat from his nervously twisting hands and questioned,

''Ow about that sword, Capting? Will you be wanting it?'

'Ohhh!' He blushed furiously and flustered as he unslung his sword and gave it to the woman together with his white gloves. Then, hot and uncomfortable in his best blue uniform coat with its heavy gold epaulets and braid, and his tight white breeches and stockings, he perched stiffly on the edge of the graceful chair that Sarah invited him to take by her side. He sat flushed, sweaty and quite unable to think of anything to say. Sarah chattered constantly to try and put him at his ease, and he ate the savoury, hot-spiced kedgeree, the tender juicy lamb cutlets, the cold brawn and pickles without even being conscious of their taste. In a euphoric daze, Arthur Redmond gazed at the woman he loved and could not recall ever feeling quite so happy before in his entire life.

It was while they were both sipping hot sweet chocolate that Sarah reminded him of the drink-fuddled promise he had made to her the night before.

'You will take me on the hulks today, won't you, Captain?' she smiled sweetly at him. 'You do remember assuring me that you would do so, don't you?'

Redmond at first said he didn't recall saying it. But the tightening of her sensual lips and the slight frown that appeared between her flawless eyebrows warned him that he had better recall the promise if he wished to continue to bask in her smiles.

'Very well, ma'am. I will take you,' he told her gruffly

She dazzled him with her gratitude, touching his cheek tenderly. 'I know that you may think it most unbecoming for a lady to wish to visit such horrid places,' Sarah said demurely. 'But I do declare I have the most overpowering desire to see at first hand those dreadful Frenchmen. And I know that with you I shall be perfectly safe from them.'

Stimulated by the soft touch of her fingers, and the fragrant nearness of her perfumed body, Redmond's overpowering desire was to take the woman in his arms and possess her there and then.

Sensing the strain she was subjecting him to, Sarah withdrew her fingers and rose from the table.

'Wait here for me, Captain. There are household matters I must attend to before we go.'

Redmond grinned bemusedly. 'What a wife she'll make me,' he told himself silently. 'Beauty and practicality in the same woman ... What more could a man ask for?'

He rose also and when she had departed, seated himself on one of the three flowing-lined chaise-longues in the room and gave himself up to his pleasant imaginings, visualizing in his mind's eye the joys of matrimony with such a magnificent creature, the nights of ecstatic pleasure with her naked body in his arms, and the days and evenings of good food, drink and sport, both indoor and out, that her income from the club would obtain for him.

'I am indeed a fortunate man,' he sighed contentedly.

At two o'clock in the afternoon, the iron bars began to sound against the walls and gratings of the *Crown*. The sailors wielding the bars released some of the frustrations and resentments of their harsh life by hammering the wood and metal with all their strength and yelling oaths and execrations at the tops of their voices. The prisoners' leaders started to muster their messes, for one hour after the din had subsided they would be driven up on deck for the daily count and if any man was absent from a mess, then the mess leader was held responsible and punished.

Henri Chanteur reported to Gaston de Chambray, and the cuirassier ordered, 'Lay out your fish.'

One by one the men pulled from their waist-sacks long black and brown strips of vile-smelling salted herring and cod. De Chambray counted them. One man had produced only three fish instead of the four every other man showed. De Chambray regarded him sternly.

'What has happened to the fourth fish, Second-Lieutenant Archard?'

The lieutenant, who was little more than a boy, shuffled his bare feet on the planking and hung his head in shame.

'Please *mon colonel* ... I ate it,' he whispered nervously.

Henri felt a surge of pity for the youngster. He looked at the deeply ulcerated, pus-trickling legs and feet, and the awful thinness of the wasted body and felt an impulse to spring to the lad's defence. Henri smothered that impulse. He knew by now that Gaston de Chambray imposed an iron discipline upon his mess for a very good reason ... survival. Without that discipline, men quickly lost all vestiges of self-respect and ended inevitably amongst the ranks of the Imperial Mantles.

The death toll was high amongst the prisoners. Scorbutic diatesis, tuberculosis, bronchial disease and a dozen different

233

fevers struck men down daily. But at least here in the messes of *les officiers* and *messieurs ou bourgeois*, a sick man would be tended by his messmates, and they would do their utmost to have him transferred to one of the hospital hulks. Among *les raffales* and the Imperial Mantles, however, a sick man was first robbed of anything he might possess and then left to his own devices and ignored. Unless he was fortunate enough to attract the attention of the guards, he invariably grew worse and died. The attention of the guards was perhaps the most difficult things to attract if one was a *raffale* or an Imperial Mantle, because when they were mustered they presented such a spectacle of verminous, filthy degeneration that the guards were reluctant even to stand near them, let alone examine them. It was no use either for a sick man to hope that he would be discovered on the Orlop deck, for the guards rarely went down to it.

De Chambray pursed his lips and appeared lost in thought. The young officer, sick and worn-out as he was, began to weep soundlessly, the tears welling from his deep-sunk eyes.

'It's too late for that,' the colonel told him harshly.

'But I was so hungry, *mon colonel*,' the youngster pleaded. 'Don't send me from the mess, I beg you. I couldn't help myself.'

'I have no other course open to me,' the cuirassier answered gruffly, more affected than he cared to show. 'You have disobeyed my strictest order. Take your fish and go from among us.' The words were uttered quietly, but with an awful finality. The lieutenant, knowing that a man expelled from his mess became an outcast in the upper battery who could expect no help from anyone, stared beseechingly at each of his messmates in turn. They either refused to meet his eyes or, like Henri, shook their heads sadly. Sobbing loudly now, the lad picked up his fish and shuffled away. He would join them at today's muster but after that would no longer be regarded as a live person by them.

Twice a week, Wednesday and Friday, occurred the 'maigre' days. On these days, instead of being issued half a pound of salt beef to go with their cabbage or turnip, each man was given two pieces of salted fish and a pound of potatoes. The tubers were usually half-rotten, the fish was always completely so. The wiser prisoners saved the fish issue and sold it back to the purveyors at a penny a piece. This money was then pooled by the mess and used to buy cheese or butter, onions or extra vegetables. The purveyors were happy with this arrangement since they drew money from the government to purchase fresh fish, and this system enabled them to issue the same old fish time after time and keep the money thus saved for their own uses. It was rumoured that some of the blackened, leather-like herring and cod had been passing back and forth between the dockyard and the hulks for the last ten years. Henri, after seeing the fish, had been forced to give credence to this rumour.

Les raffales and the Imperial Mantles invariably ate their issue, and paid a heavy price in food-poisoning, consequent ill health and even death for doing so. It was because of this that de Chambray and his fellow senior officers did all in their power to stop their men consuming the deadly putridity, no matter what agonies of hunger they might undergo.

The mess watched the young officer shuffle away and although in their hearts they pitied him, each man admitted the necessity of the sentence of banishment.

'The dockyard purveyors are here, gentlemen,' de Chambray stated. 'When we muster, Captain Chanteur will sell them back the fish. Therefore you will pass them to him after the count is completed.'

Exactly one hour after the sounding, the hatch was opened.

'All prisoners to muster! All prisoners on top for muster!' the orders rang out, and from the depths of the hulk the Imperial Mantles came blinking and stinking to pass between the lines of watchful *officiers* and *messieurs ou bourgeois* and through the hatch. It was necessary that the Imperial Mantles and *raffales* should precede the rest, because if not, then the hammocks and other possessions of the inhabitants of the upper battery would disappear below. The ship's garrison, knowing that if this happened an outbreak of such violence would explode as could well mean their own destruction, consequently left the prisoners to enforce their own procedure to and from muster. Once the parade was over the upper battery men would descend first and the rest would follow.

The muster was complete and the counting had begun when Captain Arthur Redmond returned to the vessel, accompanied by Sarah Jenkins and her pampered new pet, a spiteful King Charles spaniel. The appearance of a beautiful woman on board the hulk caused a sensation among prisoners and guards alike, and the men muttered and nudged each other excitedly and voiced audible desires about what they would like to do to this woman whose blue cloak and hood only accentuated the voluptuous curves of her breasts.

The entire ship's garrison of fifty marines, a marine lieutenant and ensign, and twenty sailors were present at the muster. A pair of canister and grape-shotted cannon muzzles gaped menacingly from the poopdeck at the captive horde, while on all sides the bayoneted, loaded muskets of squads of grim-faced marines were ready to blast the life from any potential rioters or mutineers.

After the initial surge of interest and speculation about the woman, the captives' attention mostly centred upon the plump spaniel dog in her arms. These veterans of a dozen hard-fought campaigns knew, from past experience, that with the addition of garlic and herbs the flesh of a tender young dog made excellent stew. Lips were licked and hollow stomachs patted in pleasant recollection.

Sarah and Redmond stood a little behind and to the side of the cannon with their sailor guncrews, and she shuddered in acute disgust at the spectacle before her. Nothing had prepared her for this shaggy host of human animals in their bizarre orange-yellow rags. She held a silver pomander of crushed rosemary to her nose in a futile effort to mask the overpowering stench of the mob, and her green eyes searched for Henri Chanteur, even as she felt the hopelessness of being able to pick him out from this crowd of nearly a thousand men, all made so weirdly similar in features by their hair-covered faces and dirt-caked skin.

At the bottom of the poopdeck ladder, the two cocked-hatted purveyors waited, surrounded by their helpers. Once the counting had been finished and the total reported to the marine lieutenant, who in turn reported it to Redmond, the mess orderlies formed a line before the purveyors, each man carrying the stinking putrid fish in his arms.

One at a time, the orderlies approached and under the un-blinking stares of the purveyors, counted out their fish, dropping the slimy pieces into the open mouths of the jute sacks held out by the purveyors' men. Once the prisoner had counted his fish, the teller of the purveyors handed him the coins due. Henri stood patiently in the line and waited his turn. He too had stared at the woman with interest, but her hood hid her face and hair from him and loth to torment his imagination with thoughts of warm, soft, sweet-scented womanflesh, he had turned away and ignored her. For her part, Sarah had not yet abandoned hope of sighting Henri in the dense mass. Conscious that Arthur Redmond's head was continually turning towards her, she feigned a growing indifference to the captives and petted and fussed her spaniel who snapped pettishly at her stroking fingers. But all the time her keen eyes flickered eagerly across the suffering-worn faces below. Finally her gaze came to rest on the line of orderlies, and her heart seemed to stop. It was Henry! Without any shadow of a doubt it was Henry!

Momentarily forgetting her caution she stared openly at his slender figure, and could have wept at the contrast between this grotesque, matted-haired wreck, and the handsome, lithe-muscled gallant she had pleasured herself with in distant Shropshire.

In the velvet reticule slung from her wrist, Sarah had a letter which she had written in case there should be an opportunity to contact Henri. Her agile mind now formulated a plan of action which would enable her to pass the letter to him. Stealthily, she slipped the folded paper from her reticule and crumpled it into a tight ball in her fingers. The next move was to draw his attention to herself. She moved the hood back from her face and stroked the dog in her arms. Henri was now counting the fish into the sack; desperately she willed him to look up at her. He straightened and took the money handed to him then turned. As he turned, Sarah acted. Her strong fingers dug into the fat body of the spaniel and twisted hard. The dog squealed in shock and pain and she let him fall from her arms.

'Catch my dog! Please catch him!' she shouted, and a sailor on the nearer gun bent and grabbed the animal's tail. It twisted and its white sharp teeth sank into the man's wrist.

'You little barstard!' he yelled, and sent it flying from the poopdeck with a swinging kick. Yelping in fright, the spaniel bolted into the forest of the prisoners' bare legs.

Henri's eyes went to the woman and for a second or two he thought he had gone mad. 'Sarah?' he gasped aloud. *'Ma belle Sarah?'*

Everyone else was intent on the dog and Sarah smiled and winked at him, then with a flick of her fingers sent the small ball of paper flying to his feet. In an instant he had lifted and secreted it. Not daring to risk another shared glance, he slipped back into the ranks of his mess. His thoughts were a wild chaotic jumble and he shook his head in an effort to clear and marshal them.

'Please catch my dog, Arthur. Please,' Sarah begged the captain. His face flaming with mortification, Redmond strode to the top of the ladder and bellowed,

'Bring that damned beast to me.'

The prisoners seized their opportunity with alacrity and started to mill about, shouting, screaming, singing and making barking noises. For all his slightly unbalanced mind, Redmond was no fool. He realized instantly his mistake and also saw that a first-class riot was on the verge of beginning. He snatched a musket from a marine flanking the top of the ladder and selecting the noisiest of those prisoners nearest to him, aimed and fired. The crash of the discharge was followed almost immediately by the anguished howl of a man as the ball drilled into his thigh. The shot and the scream brought the prisoners to a hushed standstill, and Redmond shouted,

'Get below, you scum! Get below this instant, or Goddam ye! I'll gi' you a charge o' grapeshot in your tripes.'

Without allowing them a moment in which to react, Redmond ordered the marines to drive everyone below decks.

'If any say nay, then blow their guts out!' he bellowed.

The marines moved quickly and efficiently, and before the threat of their long, slightly curved bayonets, the prisoners fled the deck in haste.

Unfortunately for Redmond's chances of happiness with Sarah Jenkins, the dog disappeared below with the prisoners.

'He's gone?' she stamped her foot angrily. 'You mean to tell me, Captain Redmond, that my dog has been stolen by those ... those ... savages!'

'Please ma'am 'twas no fault of mine,' he muttered in a placatory tone, and was conscious of the barely-hidden, mocking grins of the men witnessing his discomfiture.

'Of course it's your fault! You are the commander of this vessel, are you not!' she berated him. 'Of course it's your fault, so spare me your mealy-mouthed excuses, sir!'

Refusing to listen to his mumbled apologies, she stormed off the poop and down the gangway into the boat waiting there. He followed her, forgetting all dignity in his fear of losing her. Her face set and hard, she sat stiffly on the forward bench and would not look at him all through the journey back to shore, not heeding any of his entreaties or wild promises. Inwardly her heart held only contentment.

'Now that Henry knows that I'm going to help him to escape, he'll be the happiest man in all England,' she thought, and found it increasingly difficult to stop her own happiness from showing in her face.

As soon as he was below decks, Henri pushed his way through the mobs of men scuffling and disputing bitterly as to who should share in the eating of the already strangled spaniel. He settled against the bulwark under the light of a scuttle and eagerly scanned his letter. The delicately-coloured paper with the subtle scent of Sarah still lingering upon it, threatened to tear asunder between his trembling hands as he smoothed its folds.

Unusual for a woman of the people, she was literate and wrote a fine strong copperplate.

'My dear Henry,' she had written. 'I am going to help you to escape. Try to send word to me at The Golden Venture, Barrack Row, as to your needs. Do not be afraid to promise high reward to the messenger you find. I have sufficient means to pay ... Your true friend, Sarah.'

In spite of the joyful hope that the message brought him, Henri felt an underlying disquiet. She had written as one would write to a friend, not a lover.

'Is that all I am to her?' he wondered. 'Only a friend?'

His eyes burned as he read and re-read the note, but try as he would, he could not find his own deeply-felt love reciprocated in its words.

Arthur Redmond walked by Sarah's side through the narrow bustling streets as far as Barrack Row. She refused even to look at him and ignored all his entreaties to speak. When they reached the Golden Venture, the sturdy door opened to admit her and then slammed in his face. 'Doon't you fret, Jolly Jack!' an old beggarwoman cackled, and pointed to her toothless gums. ' 'Ere's a sorft 'arbour for your needs.'

He pushed her roughly aside and hurried back to the beach, a terrible fury growing within him. 'They shall pay for this! By God's blood, they shall pay!' he vowed.

Once aboard the *Crown* he shouted for the marine trumpeter. 'Give the call for the fireboats!' he ordered, and stamped backwards and forwards across the deck, not able to contain his impatience for revenge.

The brass trumpet sent the call blasting across the harbour waters, and the fire-pump barges that constantly patrolled the lines of moored shipping came ponderously rolling and dipping under the thrust of their long sweeps to the sides of the

Crown. Redmond raised a wide-muzzled speaking horn to his mouth.

'Have the goodness to flush out my lower decks, will you,' he shouted, his face twisting spasmodically, betraying the turmoil in his mind.

The four longshoremen commanding the pump-barges didn't question the order, so rare at this inclement time of the year. They were all well-used to the eccentricities of the captains of the various hulks. They rapped out commands and the stiff leather hosepipes were slung across and thrust into the port-holes of the upper battery. Teams of men manned the twin shafts of the pumps and in well-drilled unison began to push down and pull up, chanting in deep-pitched voices,

'Heave awaaay! Push awaaay! Heave away, Johnny oh!' while a red-stocking-capped boy perched astride the pump and sang out the cadence in his pure soprano.

The vacuum chambers of the engines sucked greedily at the icy green sea water, drawing it into their lungs of metal, wood, and leather and belching it through the release valves in great vomits. The masses of freezing liquid came gushing into the upper battery, soaking everything within, hammocks, clothing, men's bodies.

A tremendous howl of dismay and fury erupted from the prisoners, and hearing it, Redmond danced on his toes and howled back.

'That'll learn ye, ye hell-spawned scum! That'll cool your appetite for dog flesh, I'll warrant!' he roared with demented laughter and urged on the pump crews. 'Drive it strongly, ye swabs! Drive it hard, blast ye! Drive it hard ... !'

CHAPTER TWENY-ONE

It was the end of February before the court martial was convened to try the artisan for his attack on his superiors. During that month he remained in a cage-cell in one corner of the guardroom, and after the first anguished days of imprisonment, he lapsed into a dull apathy, obeying what orders he was given, without question or expression. The remainder of his recruit squad had proved surprisingly adept at drill, had completed their foot and musket exercises, and were well advanced in section and company drill. Two or three members of the squad were called to give evidence at the court martial. Jethro Stanton was one of them.

The senior officer, a grizzled old colonel, snapped questions at Jethro and seemed not to hear any replies.

'What's that, man? What's that you say? Speak up, damn you!' he barked after each sentence of Jethro's, and before the young soldier could repeat himself the colonel would snap,

'Oh, no matter! No matter!' and ask another question.

After giving his evidence, Jethro was dismissed and returned to his barrack room seething with anger at the charade of a fair trial he had witnessed. He took off his shako and placing it on the table sat down in front of it. Turpin Wright was room orderly for the day, and he came to join his friend.

'Now then, matey, what's the cause o' you lookin' so grumpy?' he asked.

Jethro stared down at the bright brass front plate of his shako and replied by asking quietly, 'What do you think the artisan will get?'

Wright shrugged his shoulders. 'Wun't be less than a thousand I reckon, cully, and more likely it'll be a firing squad.'

'God blast their black hearts!' Jethro burst out savagely. 'It's nothing less than murder, which ever they give him. The poor devil should never have been court martialled in the first place.'

There was a long silence as both men sat immersed in their own thoughts, then the door of the room opened and Big Sadie came in, her arms piled high with the men's dry laundry which they paid her, and the other women, three pence a week each to wash and iron for them.

'Hello, my handsome,' she greeted Jethro, and went on, 'that cove bin give fifteen hundred.'

'Who told you? The colonel hisself, I suppose?' Turpin Wright growled sarcastically.

'Doon't you take that tone wi' me,' her face mottled angrily. ' 'Tis no fault o' mine the poor bugger's bin served so.'

'I knows that you silly cow,' Turpin said impatiently. 'But am you sure o' what you says?'

'That I am,' she answered, tossing her tangled blonde hair. 'I'se just heard two o' the orfficers talkin' about it ... The sentence is to be carried out arter dinner.' She paused and shook her head. 'It's a mortal shame, so it is. Fifteen hundred 'ull kill the poor sod. There'll be a few o' the young 'uns who'll leave their dinners on the parade ground I'm thinking'. And God only knows, there's little enough in their bellies to begin with.'

'Just so, Sadie my duck,' Turpin nodded agreement. 'That's always a surety, that is.' He turned and patted Jethro's shoulder. 'You'se sin summat like a flogging parade afore, arn't you boy.'

'That I have,' the younger man said bitterly. 'I saw them flog my own father ... God's curse on them!'

Lieutenant the Honourable John Coventry was also incensed when he received the news that the punishment parade was to be held that afternoon.

'Devil take me!' he grumbled, and stared aggrievedly at the drummer who had brought him the message from the C.O., Major Thomas Burd. Both men were in the entrance hall of the Ward's house in Portsmouth, and through the slightly open door of the salon, Coventry could hear the musical laughter of Jessica who, together with her mother and father, was entertaining David Warburton and himself at luncheon.

'Inform Major Burd that I shall return to barracks presently.' He dismissed the drummer, who saluted and hurried away. The Honourable John Coventry went back into the salon.

'Why look so glum, Coventry?' Joseph Ward winked mischievously at his table companions. 'Have orders come that the French have landed?'

'Demmee, I wish it were that, sir,' the young man said petulantly, and for a moment, even dressed as he was in the full glory of his finest regimentals, he resembled nothing more than a spoiled child. 'There is to be a punishment parade after luncheon for that demned recruit who attacked the sergeant-major.'

Joseph Ward's lean features grew troubled. 'What was the sentence of the court martial?' he questioned.

'Fifteen hundred,' the adjutant told him. 'Demn the nuisance of it.'

'That is monstrous!' David Warburton stated vehemently.

A month's good food and rest had worked an almost miraculous change in his appearance, and in his good dark grey civilian clothing with its fine white linen, he was the picture of health and vigour.

'Indeed it is!' the Hon. John agreed wholeheartedly with the sentiment. 'It will ruin my plans to escort Miss Jessica and her Mama to the song recital in the assembly rooms.'

Jessica Ward's lovely eyes became unusually frosty and she said tartly, 'I think you misunderstand dear Davy's meaning, Lieutenant Coventry. For if I am correct, he thinks that it is the cruel sentence that is monstrous, not the ruination of your planned pleasures.'

'That is sufficient, miss,' her father told her sharply. 'What the court martial chose to do is no concern of yours. The discipline of the army must be maintained no matter what the cost to individuals. The man committed a grave offence, and must be punished hard for doing so. If he were not dealt with harshly, then others would seize the opportunity to profit from their superiors' weakness, and Lord only knows what would be the outcome ... Don't you agree, David?'

Warburton's gentle grey eyes were troubled but his voice was firm.

'I agree, sir, that discipline must be maintained ... But I must speak the truth, as I see it. I detest and condemn the practice of flogging, for in my own limited experience I have yet to see the man that a flogging will improve. On the contrary, in the Peninsula I have seen many good soldiers ruined both morally and physically by it.'

'Demmee! I'm most surprised that a combat veteran, such

as yourself, Warburton, should be so dismayed at the prospect of seeing a rogue's blood drawn by the lash,' the Hon. John's voice held a sneer.

David forced down his rising indignation at the other's veiled imputation and said quietly,

'Perhaps, Coventry, it is precisely because I have seen so much blood drawn by sword and bullet, that it makes me reluctant to see it spilt by the lash.'

Mrs Ward's intervention halted any further development of this theme.

'Gentlemen, please! This is hardly a fitting subject to be discussed when we are about to eat this dish.'

She indicated the bowl filled with thick slices of rare roast beef in the centre of the food-laden table.

Her husband laughed appreciatively. 'As always, you are correct, my dear,' he told her, and spoke to the two young men bristling at each other across the table. 'Gentlemen, consideration for my lady wife forces me to forbid any further mention of this matter.' His voice was light but there was in it a note which brooked no argument.

The tension that had arisen, lessened and disappeared in the pleasure engendered by good food and wine and even the heartfelt disappointment of John Coventry caused by the disruption of his plans, left him under the spell of Jessica's smiling flirtatiousness. He laughed and joked and fed Mrs Ward's pet terriers with choice titbits of tender meat and savoury gravy. Only the slightest pangs of jealousy marred his enjoyment when he intercepted the shared glances between Jessica and David Warburton.

At twelve noon, the rank and file of the battalion were dismissed from the drill they had been performing since seven o'clock that morning, and marched back to their barracks for dinner. In every room the women squabbled and pushed each other about, over who should take precedence at the cooking fires. In Jethro's quarters the twenty-odd men had divided themselves into two messes, and the same scene was repeated here as Big Sadie and Bertha Morrison haggled with Annie Rourke and Toothless Charlotte, while the swarming children wailed for food.

'My cripes!' Turpin Wright expostulated. 'I doon't know why you lot o' bleedin' fools can't come to some agreement

244

about your cooking ... Gawd save us all! You'se only got a bit o' salt beef to boil ... Why doon't you put it all in the same pot and cook it together?'

The women joined ranks and rounded on him like a pack of screaming harpies.

'Why doon't ye keep yez long conk outta our business?' Annie Rourke screeched, and thrust out her several chins pugnaciously. 'By the Christ! Iffen ye meddles wit' me, yez are going to find that I'm a match for any mon!'

'Ahr, and that goo's for the rest on us as well, right girls?' Big Sadie's great breasts threatened to spill from her unbuttoned bodice and her large fists clenched in readiness to fight.

Jethro, in spite of his bitter feelings about the court martial was forced to laugh at the expression on his friend's face. Turpin sat chewing his lower lip and contemplating the odds against him. Barrack women were a notoriously tough breed and some of them were indeed handy with their fists and boots, if it came to a brawl.

'Be you agooin' to stand shoulder to shoulder wi' me, Jethro?' the convict asked finally.

Jethro shook his head in vigorous repudiation. 'No, my friend,' he chuckled. 'It would take a better man than me to tame these beauties.'

Three of the women held soft spots in their hearts for the handsome young recruit. The fourth, Bertha Morrison, held hatred.

'Man?' she sneered. 'You calls yourself a man, does you? You'm nothin' but a bleedin' nancy-boy, you am!'

He made no reply to her taunts, knowing too well the futility of arguing against her hatred.

The trampling of many boots sounded from behind the block as the men returned from drill, and the clattering entrance of the sections sent the women scurrying to lay out the earthenware bowls and the cobs of stale wholemeal bread for each man's rations along the tables. Both Jethro and Turpin Wright were members of Corporal Rourke's mess, the other mess was in the charge of Drummer Morrison. Amid a tumult of shouting, grumbling and laughter the shakos, packs and pouches were removed and hung upon the pegs over the men's shared beds and the muskets were racked. Most of the men also took off their tunics, and while waiting for the meal to be served out, amused themselves by mocking the women and each other and playing with the excited children.

The bubbling iron pots were taken from the fire and brought to the tables. Corporal Rourke used the long flesh fork and a pewter ladle to fish the rancid-smelling lumps of yellow-fatted meat, gristle, and bone from the watery stock it had been boiled in, and carefully measured out a portion into each small bowl. The men, their stomachs rumbling with hunger, watched him closely to make sure that each portion was composed of roughly the same amounts of solids and liquids. At the opposite end of the table the surly Drummer Morrison followed the corporal's example. When all the bowls were full, Rourke handed the pot back to his wife.

'Break some bread into that for ye and the kids,' he told her.

Her fat face puckered disagreeably as she peered at the small amount of greasy mess swilling about the bottom of the pot.

'Phwat?' she spat at him. 'D'ye rackon that me and Charlotte and the babbies can live on such a wee bit o' bread and water?'

Corporal Rourke was already in a foul temper. He had made mistakes in the drill orders that morning and had felt the weight of Sergeant-Major Gresham's cane across his head. The livid welts raised by the blows still throbbed painfully and his sense of humiliated grievance rankled still more.

'Shut yer mouth, ye ould sow,' he hissed warningly. 'Ye know well enough that the meat pot's empty.'

'That I'll not!' Hands on hips she faced him boldly. 'I wants some o' that meat for me and the babbies. Our bellies 'um empty as well.'

Her husband's pale blue eyes narrowed and his voice rose high in anger. 'Is it meat ye want, ye fat-bellied whore? Here! ... Try this!'

He punched her heavily in the face and the force of the blow dropped her to the floor. He stood over her with clenched fists, his mouth snarling.

'D'ye want some more?' he demanded. 'Or was that sufficient ration for ye?'

She raised herself to a sitting posture and sat moaning and clasping her jaw. The smaller children began to wail in fright and the other women rushed to help their friend. Between them they carried the half-stunned woman to her corner, cursing loudly at the corporal and the rest of the men as they did so. Jethro had never liked to see women beaten, but it was the

246

way of his world and he knew nothing he could do or say would stop the custom. Indeed, if he intervened, then the first person to abuse him for doing so would have been Annie Rourke herself.

The corporal shrugged and told the men, 'All right, boys. Let's begin ... Turpin, will ye do the callin'?'

'Ahr, that I 'ull, and gladly for me belly thinks me throat's bin cut, it's so bleedin' empty.' The convict went to the head of the table and standing with his back to the smoking dishes of meat put his hands over his eyes so that he could see nothing.

Rourke tapped a dish at random with the flesh-fork. 'Who shall have this?' he asked loudly.

'Greener!' Turpin answered.

The designated man stepped forward and picked up the bowl and a cob of bread.

The Irishman tapped another bowl. 'Who shall have this?'

'Perkins,' Turpin answered.

The ritual went on until every man in the mess had been allotted a portion.

The system was designed to prevent unfair distribution of food by the mess N.C.O.s and worked well enough. Though if there were new and inexperienced men who joined the mess, the older hands worked out a code by means of voice tone and inflection which made sure that the newcomers always received the worst pieces of meat. Those which were mostly bone, fat, and gristle. Fortunately for Jethro, Turpin Wright's being an old soldier and the readiness of both of them to fight for their rights, prevented their messmates cheating them in this way.

The men seated themselves at the tables and started to eat. Jethro broke a piece of the hard sour bread from his cob and dipped it into the rancid-smelling gravy. He chewed it slowly, it tasted of harsh salt and rotten flesh, but he was hungry enough to disregard these details, particularly since it would be the only food he would taste until six o'clock in the morning, when he would get his pitiful breakfast of 'Tommy', a bowl of black bitter coffee with toasted bread broken into it. Once the first hunger pangs had been relieved, the men began to talk about the punishment parade that afternoon.

'Jase! But it's a hard sentence,' Corporal Rourke observed. 'No doubt about it, it's a damn tough bullet to chew on.'

'The poor barstard 'ull not survive it!' another man said.

'How d'you reckon they'll divide it, Paddy?' a third man

247

asked.

The Irishman pointed at Drummer Morrison, who was seated at the opposite end of the table. 'Arsk your mon there. He's one o' them who'll do the floggin'.'

All attention switched to the stocky drummer, who ignored the questioning stares. He sat hunched over his bowl of food chewing the tough meat with loud smackings of his thick lips and frequent belches. His brutish face beneath the bristles of his close-cropped scalp showed indifference to the prospect that faced him: the flogging of a fellow human being who had done him no harm.

Jethro felt revulsion for the man. He knew that if it were he who was to rip a man's flesh from his bones, then he would not be able to display such a hearty appetite for his dinner.

'Well, Morrison?' Jethro challenged. 'How will it be divided? I'd like to hear, if you can spare a moment from your trough?'

The drummer belched loudly and smacked his lips as his scaled tongue searched the gaps of his yellowed teeth for trapped shreds of meat. Finally, he wiped the grease from his mouth with his fingers, and cleaned his fingers on the front of his shirt, then grunted.

'Three lots o' five hundred, I should reckon. That's if the barstard lives.'

Some of the men blanched visibly at the answer, and Jethro could not contain his disgust at the barbarity of giving a man five hundred lashes, then waiting until his wounds healed before giving him a further five hundred, and repeating the procedure yet again.

'It doesn't seem to affect your appetite, Morrison. The prospect of torturing the poor bugger like that,' he said grimly.

The drummer shrugged his broad shoulders and peered about the table to see if any man had left food in his bowl.

'T'se bin flogging men twice or three times a week ever since I 'listed in the army,' he answered carelessly. 'You gets used to it, cully ... And besides, I has to obey the orders I'm give, doon't I ... or I'd be on the bleedin' triangle meself, 'uddent I?'

Jethro could find no reply to that statement, and was obliged to admit that the man had justice in what he said.

'My Good God!' he suddenly thought to himself. 'Here am I getting angered at Morrison, because he can eat hearty before he flogs a man. And I've bolted down my own food like a pig. I'm acting like a hypocrite when I condemn the bugger. In my own way I'm just as bad as he is.'

At two o'clock in the afternoon the warning drum was sounded throughout Colewort Garden Barracks. The February sky was dark and heavy with snow and a cold biting wind gusted flurries of tiny snow flakes across the parade ground. The bearded and white-aproned sergeant of pioneers marched to the very centre of the parade ground and, aided by one of his section, lashed three halberds into the form of a tripod, and two others horizontally across one face of the formed tripod to create a ladder effect.

Behind the barrack blocks, the troops mustered in their companies, wearing over their scarlet tunics long grey greatcoats which stretched to the black-gaitered ankles of their blue trousers. Their splendidly corded and plumed shakos were sheltered from the inclement weather by black oilskin covers wrapped about them, and their hands were snug in warm woollen mittens. Yet in spite of all their protective clothing, many men shivered before the buffets of the icy wind. The company sergeants called the roll, and then presented their sections to the company officers.

At two-thirty, the mace-swinging, gorgeously-uniformed drum major led his drummers on to the parade ground and their bright yellow tunics were a brilliant line of colour against the all-pervading sombre greyness, as with black-gaitered calves moving in perfect unison and their deep-bodied, gaudy-painted drums swinging, they beat the thunderous call to general muster.

'COMPANNNNY ATTENTION! SHOULLLLDER ARMS! COUNTER MARCH TO THE RIGHT ABOUT ... QUUIIICCCK MARCH!'

The high-pitched voices of the company commanders echoed through the barrack blocks and the measured tread of hundreds of men sounded in counterpoint to the throbbing drums. The long white-crossbelted columns snaked on to the great emptiness of the parade ground and formed themselves into a hollow square facing inwards towards the triangle of halberds. The officers halted their men and as the drums fell silent their voices sounded unnaturally loud in the sudden quiet.

'REAR RANKS ... TAKE OPEN ORDER ... MARCH!'

Iron-shod boots crashed down. 'RIIIIGHT DRESS!'

Sergeants moved swiftly as the hundreds of heels battered the worn cobbles and the staves of their halberds pushed roughly against men's chests to complete the dressing of the lines.

'PARADE ... ORDEEERRRR ARMS!' Mittened hands flashed in rapid movements and musket butts clattered.

In the front rank of his company, Jethro obeyed the words of command automatically, and without conscious volition. His eyes and interest were centred only upon the triangle of halberds and the drummers next to it, busily engaged in piling their drums and loosening tunics and belts prior to removing them.

All became silent and still once more, and the only sign that life existed in the rigid, motionless ranks were the pale plumes of breath jetting from men's mouths and nostrils as breathing quickened in anticipation of what was to come.

A gap had been left at one corner of the square and through it came the acting commanding officer, Major Thomas Burd, together with the regimental surgeon, whose black cock-feathered hat, together with the caped black cloaks that both men wore, gave a suitably funereal note to their appearance. Directly behind them sauntered the elegant figure of the Hon. John Coventry, who made no concession to the weather and wore his splendid regimentals without a cloak. His smooth face was made spiteful by his resentment at being there. The three positioned themselves to one side of the triangle and then, through the same gap was brought the prisoner.

He was bare-headed and dressed in an old white canvas fatigue jacket and trousers, with his arms bound behind him. In front of him slow-marched the ramrod figure of Sergeant-Major Gresham, his long cane tucked horizontally under his left arm, his right arm stretched rigidly at his side. A file of privates shouldering muskets with fixed bayonets marched at each side of the prisoner and behind the small procession, a diminutive drummerboy tapped the time of the stately paces. Two yards to the rear of the drummerboy walked the surgeon's mate in his green apron and feathered round hat. He carried a bowl of water and a strip of towelling. His satchel of drugs and dressings was slung across his shoulder and dangled low enough to bounce against one fat buttock as he waddled awkwardly, trying to slowmarch in step with the drumbeat.

To Jethro it seemed that the prisoner was not really aware of what was about to happen to him. He looked dazed, his eyes wide and blank as he shambled along between his guards with no emotion of any kind showing in his face.

At the triangle, the procession halted. The artisan's arms were unbound and the sergeant-major ordered him to strip to the waist. The prisoner's tallowy pale skin pimpled and took on a bluish tinge as the wind's freezing tentacles enveloped him. He started to shiver violently but still his eyes remained blank and his face expressionless. Drummers took him and lashed him with his wrists above his head, face forward on the ladder side of the halberds. With leather straps they secured his ankles, knees and thighs to the staves. The Honourable John Coventry took a rolled sheet of parchment from inside his tunic and, smoothing it with difficulty against the snatchings of the wind, he read out the charge and sentence. Then saluted the parade commander, and in ringing tones ordered:

'DRUM MAJOR, DO YOUR DUTY!'

The drum major signalled with his mace and a drummer hurried to him, carrying a large bucket full of brine water from which protruded the narrow handle of a cat o' nine tails. The drum major lifted the 'cat' and whistled it through the air, causing it to swish a fine spray of liquid from its long plaited thongs. Drummer Morrison took off his mitre cap and yellow tunic, and in his shirtsleeves went to stand to the side of the trussed prisoner. The drum major handed him the 'cat' and then himself stood behind Morrison while Coventry, a slender rattan cane in his hand, positioned himself to the rear of the drum major.

Major Thomas Burd looked long and hard at the paraded troops, then shouted, 'Each man present take heed. For if you should commit a similar offence, then as surely as the sun rises, you shall suffer the same penalty. Let the punishment commence.'

'Make ready!' the drum major ordered curtly, and Drummer Morrison, his brutish face impassive, drew the plaited thongs through his fingers, separating each from its fellow. He held out his thick arm to its fullest extent, so that the handle of the whip was a foot or more from the prisoner's naked back. Another drummer stepped up to the triangle and thrust a scrap of thick leather between the prisoner's teeth for him to bite on.

The drum major lifted his mace and tapped the ferrule on Drummer Morrison's broad shoulders ...

'Begin!' He shouted. 'ONE!'

The drummer drew back his arm and brought the thongs slashing across the white defenceless flesh before him with all the strength he could muster. The cords bit deep and at the final instant of impact, Morrison flicked his wrist so that the thongs dragged viciously at the skin. The artisan's body jerked horribly and his twisted face strained upwards to the grey pitiless sky. A collective gasp came from the watching troops and Jethro glanced at the men to right and left of him. The youngster to his right was deathly pale and beads of sweat stood out on his fresh face. The older man to the left had a peculiar expression half pleasure, half anger on his weathered features.

'TWO! ... THREE! ... FOUR! ... FIVE! ... SIX! ... SEVEN! ...'

The drum major's voice bellowed out the cadence and the 'cat' rose and fell with dreadful precision. The white skin broke at the sixth blow and the thin lines of blood welled jewel-like against the paleness of their setting. At twenty-five lashes, another drummer took Morrison's place and the beating continued. Until now, no sound that was audible to the spectators had been uttered by the prisoner. Only the agonized jerks and writhings of his body showed the torments he was suffering. After fifty strokes, another drummer took over the 'cat', and now with the prisoner's back and shoulders a hideous crimson jelly of torn flesh and blood, it was necessary after each stroke for the drummers to drag the lash thongs through their fingers to remove the scraps of human wreckage that stuck there. At the eighty-third stroke, the man screamed ... a terrible wrenching bubbling scream that was torn from the very depths of his outraged being. The drummer giving the lashes halted and let his whip arm drop, appalled by the choking shriek.

'God demmee, drum major! Make the dog lay on hard!' The Hon. John's petulant face flamed with anger and he beat the drum major furiously about the shoulders and hips with his rattan cane.

The drum major's mace in its turn cracked over the drummer's back. 'Lay on hard, God blast your eyes!' he bellowed, and the young drummer continued.

Now the blood sprayed out at every soggy-sounding stroke, and each drummer in his turn became splattered with the myriads of scarlet butcher's badges.

At two hundred and sixty-three strokes, the prisoner's continuous screaming reached an ear-splitting crescendo, and then halted abruptly as he collapsed. His head fell back showing the whites of his still-open eyes and his body hung slack by his trussed wrists. The surgeon beckoned his mate and went to examine the unconscious man. Jethro heard a sound of retching as a soldier in the centre rank to his left rear was violently sick. It started a chain reaction, and soon other men were vomiting helplessly, while one man fainted clean away. Jethro himself, inured though he was by years of poverty and suffering, felt an overwhelming pity for the tortured victim, and a terrible anger against the men who could order and carry out such punishments.

The administration of stimulants to the collapsed man brought him back to consciousness and the surgeon and his mate resumed their former posts. Major Burd nodded to the drum major.

'Continue with the punishment,' he snapped.

The blood-heavy 'cat' rose and fell once more and the prisoner shrieked in concert with the strokes. A muttering of rage came from the ranks and here and there anonymous voices shouted,

'Let the poor bugger alone!'

'Cut him down, damn you!'

'Yes, cut him down!'

The company subalterns searched the faces of the men for the culprits, but could find no one to blame.

At the four hundred and third stroke, the prisoner collapsed once more and this time Jethro prayed for a merciful God to intervene.

The surgeon made his examination with a grave face. He felt the neck for a pulse and then held a small pocket mirror to the nostrils and mouth of the grotesquely crooked head. A minute elapsed and not a sound was to be heard except the fitful moaning of the wind. The flurrying snowflakes settled on the prisoner's head and flayed shoulders and collected for brief moments on the blood-soaked seat and thighs of his trousers. The surgeon looked closely at the mirror, and shook his head. An explosion of released breath came from the troops, followed by a concerted growl of fury.

'Goddam the bugger for a weakling!' Major Thomas Burd cursed in temper, then shouted, 'Officers, march your men to different areas of the parade ground and give them an hour's hot drill. That'll sweat the badness and malice from them, I'll be bound.'

Commands rang out instantly and the deeply-instilled habits of disciplined obedience asserted themselves. Muskets were slapped and positioned and boots rang upon the ground in quick and double-quick time.

Four drummers each took an arm or leg and carried the limp, head-hanging dead man away with the surgeon and his mate following. Jethro watched them leave from the corner of his eye as he sloped, ordered, presented, and shouldered his musket without pause, and thought bitterly of what a tragic epitaph the drops of blood dripping from the lacerated body on to the snow-flecked cobbles made for the poor artisan.

CHAPTER TWENTY-TWO

In the first days of March orders came for David Warburton to go to London to appear before the Medical Board. At the fine old three-storied Blue Posts Inn in Broad Street, Portsmouth Point, Joseph Ward, his wife and Jessica had come to see the young officer off on his journey. It was six o'clock in the evening, and the post-coach, *Royal*, presented a glittering spectacle of polished panelling and shining brass-work under the spluttering oil-lamps of the inn's entrance.

The black horses in their traces pawed at the cobbles, striking tiny white-hot sparks from their plated hooves, as if impatient to be away. The air was damp and misty and minute droplets of moisture collected on the fur edging of Jessica's hooded cloak, framing her heart-shaped face in a shimmer of sparkling pinpoints. The guard blew his long horn and shouted for the passengers to take their seats.

'Good-bye, my boy, and Godspeed.' Joseph Ward shook David's hands and Mrs Ward kissed his cheek.

'Good-bye, sir, and you, ma'am ... I cannot thank you enough for your kindness to me.'

'Nonsense!' the gentle features of Mrs Ward belied her scolding utterance. 'Now remember that you are to return here immediately the Medical Board has given judgment on you.'

'But they may order me back to the Peninsula,' David joked.

'Then you must take ship from here!' Mrs Ward replied sharply, and her husband laughed.

'You had best obey my wife in this matter, young man. For if you do not come back to see us before you go to your next posting, then you will find her more fierce in pursuit than any Polish Lancer.'

'I will obey her, sir, and gladly ... I promise,' David said, and turned to Jessica. Their hands met and clasped tightly.

'And you, Jessie? Do you wish me to return?' he asked softly.

For answer she brushed his cheek with her lips and her brown eyes glistened with unshed tears. Unable to speak for fear of weeping, she nodded her head.

'Come now, sir ... Hurry, for the coach is leaving.' The stentorian shouting of the guard reverbrated through the street and David, his own eyes suspiciously moist, entered the coach.

A blast on the horn and the journey began. There were two other passengers, both inside; a civilian, and another army officer who, like David, wore a long black cloak over his uniform, and whose green cockade on his shako showed him to belong to a Light Company. In the dim light of the swinging overhead lamp, the civilian's appearance seemed curiously archaic to David. It was some time before the young man realized why that was. The man wore a white tie-wig with a tiny pigtail tied with a bow and very bushy about the neck-end in the style of the previous century, as were his dark coat and knee-breeches.

'Of course,' David thought. 'He's a member of the College of Physicians.'

The plump, pink-cheeked medical man was aware of his fellow passenger's interest, and smiled at him.

'Allow me to introduce myself, sir.' His voice was rich and fruity and his eyes twinkled merrily. 'My name is Thomas Marder, I am a physician and surgeon by profession.'

David felt somewhat embarrassed. 'Forgive my rudeness in staring at you so, Doctor Marder,' he hastened to apologize, 'only my interest was aroused because even now I am on my way to pass before a Medical Board in London.'

'Then we are travelling on the same errand, sir,' the doctor bowed his head. 'For I am to be one of the examining physicians on that board ... This gentleman here, also goes before them, I believe.' He indicated the other army officer, a man in his thirties who, when he turned towards his companions, disclosed that the right side of his face was a livid purplish-red mass of mangled flesh and was minus an eye.

'Patrick Flaherty, gentlemen. Captain in the Eighty-eighth Foot.'

His introduction was delivered in a soft Irish accent, with a blurring of diction caused by his injuries which twisted one side of his mouth. David bowed his head and introduced himself in return. Marder produced a silver flask from his leather instrument bag.

'Well, gentlemen, as an experienced doctor, I really must prescribe a tonic for you both ... Will you join me in a nip or two of brandy ... I carry it strictly for medicinal purposes, I do assure you.'

Cheered by frequent gulps of the fiery spirit, the three men chatted amicably as the horses laboured up the steep Portsdown Hill. The mist hung heavy on its bleak crest as the coach breasted the final rise and swung rattling over the rutted road towards the village of Havant. The doctor lifted the thin leather curtain on the window next to him and peered out into the foggy murk.'

'Dammee! But it's clammy weather,' he observed.

At that instant there came from the road ahead a loud shout. 'Pull up, or you're dead men!'

The lead horses baulked and bucked, neighing in fright as a tall, cloaked horseman suddenly loomed out of the mist before them. The driver cursed horribly.

'Whoaaa! Whoaaa! Steady yerselves, yer stupid silly barstards!' he bawled, and hauled hard at the reins.

The guard, who in the absence of any outside passengers had been sitting dozing by the side of the driver, both of them swathed in blankets, gave a jump and, still half-asleep, let fly with his blunderbuss. The bell-shaped barrel jerked and roared and the rusty nails and bolts it was loaded with went hurtling far above the highwayman's tall hat.

Inside the coach a whispered conversation was being carried on between the travellers.

'It's the Dandy,' the doctor said, 'and a most brutal and vicious dog, by all accounts. He served one poor fellow most cruelly. Not content with robbing him and breaking his head with a pistol butt, the rogue then shot him. It was only by the grace of God that he received merely a flesh wound. I treated his injuries myself. He was a foreign gentleman ... Since then, this highwayman has struck several times more.'

'Has he wounded anyone else?' Flaherty asked.

'Not seriously,' Marder told him. 'He's cracked a few heads, nothing more.'

'Why is he known as the Dandy?' David wanted to know.

'Apparently he has the speech and manner of a gentleman,' replied the doctor.

The masked, cloaked man was guiding his mount with his knees. In his right hand he carried a cavalry sabre and in his left a long-barrelled pistol. Without hesitation, he spurred his horse forward towards the coach and leaning sideways he passed along first one side and then wheeling rapidly, the other side of the team. As he passed, he slashed the beasts free of their traces with lightning strokes of his sabre. The terrified team bolted up the track and were quickly lost to view in the mist, only the fast-fading thuds of their hooves marking their flight. Laughing softly in satisfaction, the elegantly accoutred highwayman sheathed his blade in the scabbard attached to the saddlehorn and drew another pistol from under his cloak. He hammered against the coach panels with its butt.

'I'll thank all those inside to get out one at a time, using this door.' He looked up at the driver and guard who sat like two statues with their arms held high in the air. 'What do you carry in your strong box?' he demanded.

'Just letters and a few packets, your honour ... Nuthin' o' value,' the driver quavered.

'Toss it down on the roadway nevertheless ... And no tricks, if you wish to continue alive.' The pistol barrels moved to point unwaveringly at a spot directly in the centre of the guard's forehead. 'You owe me a shot, my bucko!' the masked man snarled, 'I've a mind to take it now.'

The guard groaned aloud, his eyes rolled up in his head and he fainted from sheer terror. His body tumbled from the seat and thudded head-foremost to the ground beneath. The highwayman's horse skittered nervously.

'Be still, blast you!' he growled.

By now the three passengers had got out and were stood side by side on the track with their backs to the coach. The doctor felt such a storm of indignation that his body trembled with it. Before the masked man could speak, he blurted out,

'You are a shame to the name of England, you damned rogue! These two gentlemen are officers wounded in the service of their country and they are now to be robbed by gallows' scum such as you. You are not fit to lick their boots ... Damn you for a worthless evil dog!'

The highwayman's eyes widened behind their mask when he noticed David. Ignoring the choleric doctor the man pointed the barrel of his pistol at the young officer. 'You there, take off your shako, so that I may see your face.'

Surprised at the unusual order, David obeyed. His face unshadowed by the broad flat peak was calm and unafraid as he looked steadily at the highwayman. From behind the full face mask came a sharp hiss in indrawn breath. His voice muffled, he went on, 'Give me your name.'

'Warburton ... David Warburton.' The answer was firmly given.

'God rot me!' The masked man cursed, then suddenly wheeled his horse and, spurring it to a gallop, was swallowed up by the swirling mist. The men by the coach gaped at each other in utter bewilderment.

'What in Heaven's name made him do that?' the doctor exclaimed.

The others were equally at a loss and could only shake their heads in bafflement. A moan sounded loudly from the front of the coach, and the driver's pock-pitted face peered nervously at them from behind the footrest.

'Sir, sir, 'ud you come and see to me mate, I fear he's bin sore hurt.'

The three men hurried to help tend the injured man, and as they busied themselves in finding water to bathe his bleeding head and trying to construct a makeshift stretcher to lay him on, the shock of the highwayman's strange behaviour wore off. In David's mind, as he worked, a chain of association of memories jerked into motion, and a bizarre notion as to the highwayman's identity wormed its way into his consciousness. Thrust it from him as he might, this notion persisted, growing stronger and more certain with every minute that passed. ... The elegant highwayman was his cousin, William Seymour.

Riding away from the coach, Seymour used one hand to remove his face mask and inwardly cursed the fate that had confronted him with his young relative.

'I should not have reacted as I did,' he castigated himself. 'I should have robbed them all, but that would have meant the risk of him recognizing me.' The picture of the young man's calm gentle face swam into his mind's eye, and Seymour realized with a sharp shock of resentment that in spite of himself, he could never take anything from Davy. 'He is the only person in the whole world that I have any regard for.'

The cavalryman's cold grey eyes momentarily held a warmth and softness that perhaps no one who knew him would have believed possible.

'But now what is to be done?' Seymour puzzled. 'There is

always the possibility that David will realize that it was me. And I need more funds.'

He was indeed desperately short of money. The banknotes and jewellery he had taken from Levi and da Costa were worth nothing to him here in Hampshire. He would have to dispose of them in a centre such as London, and the other robberies had netted him only comparatively small amounts. So far he had been unsuccessful in his search for Sarah, and the necessity of secure hiding places for himself and his horse meant that he paid heavily to ensure closed mouths and blind eyes concerning his comings and goings. At present, he had a hideout in a tiny fishing village close to Chichester. The hamlet was a notorious haunt for smugglers and, providing he paid the high prices they demanded for bed and board, he was safe with them, their hatred of authority being sufficient to ensure their silence when constables searching for the Dandy made inquiries about suspicious strangers in the area.

'Damn the High Toby!' Seymour decided. 'Tomorrow I'll move into Portsmouth, and this time I'll stay there until I find Sarah Jenkins. All I'm likely to find if I continue like this is a hempen rope around my neck.'

CHAPTER TWENTY-THREE

In the time she had been working at The Golden Venture, Molly Bawn had been able to save more money and acquire more possessions than in all the years she had been selling her body on the streets and ships of Portsmouth. True to her promise, Sarah Jenkins had given the girls employed at the club a fair return on the money they persuaded men to part with. Molly herself had been one of those trained as a 'priestess' or croupier by Hebrew Star and Portugal John, and her income had increased correspondingly. The sight of Molly's creamy-skinned swelling breasts in the low-cut semi-transparent gowns which all the girls wore, had caused many a gambler to lose concentration on the hand of cards he held, and in doing so to lose his stake.

Molly's sense of loyalty and affection for Sarah had also developed and grown, and when her mistress had asked Molly to carry out certain mysterious tasks, the girl had assented eagerly. For the most part these tasks had been merely to go once a week, sometimes early in the morning, sometimes late at night, to a sleazy beer-ken on Spice Island and take a sealed letter. At the beer-ken Molly would wait until a pig-tailed young sailor came to her carrying another sealed letter. Without more than a word in passing they would exchange missives and part. Molly would see how eagerly Sarah tore the letter open and read it, and would wonder what sort of lover Captain Arthur Redmond could be, to arouse such emotion in her normally undemonstrative mistress.

On the night of the second day of February, Sarah again called Molly upstairs to her chambers. Sarah's handsome face was flushed and her manner strangely tense.

'Molly, my dear. I want you to go on an errand for me.' The girl's bold eyes twinkled. 'Is it the usual place, Mistress Sarah?'

The other woman nodded. 'It is, yes.'

Molly laughed and teased. 'I rackon you're having a high old fling wi' that captin, ain't you, Miss Sarah ... Sending all these love notes to him?'

Sarah's full lips tightened in annoyance at the other's assumption that the letters were for Redmond. 'Hold your tongue, girl,' she snapped angrily. 'Don't jest of matters you know nothing about.'

The girl flushed, hurt and affronted by the rebuff.

'I'm sorry,' she retorted sharply. 'I meant no harm by it. I was only teasing you.'

Sarah was instantly sorry for what she had done. Her voice softened and she went to her young protégée and hugged her gently. 'It is I who should say sorry, for answering you in that manner, my dear,' she smiled, and released the girl. 'I could wish with all my heart that it was merely a love affair ... But there are plans coming towards completion that I can tell no one of, not even you.' Her green eyes held anxiety. 'Believe me, when I am able to do so, then I shall tell you the meaning behind these letters you have been delivering and bringing for me.'

Molly returned the smile and lost her feeling of hurt. 'Be sure, Miss Sarah, that you can trust me. You've bin real good to me. Better than anyone ever was before in me life ... I'll never fail you in anything.'

Her sincerity was so patent that it touched Sarah deeply.

'Thank you, my dear,' she said, and then from the cabinet of her French-style writing bureau she lifted with difficulty a largish parcel wrapped thickly in oilskin covers. Her expression was grave as she told the girl, 'This is the last thing I shall be asking you to take, Molly, and the most important. I must know that it reaches its destination safely, and it is vital that it reaches there tonight. When the sailor takes it from you, wait at the beer-ken until he returns, no matter how long that may be ...' She paused and then with great emphasis repeated. 'You must wait until he brings back the news that the parcel has arrived safely. Do you understand? It must get there tonight, it is of the utmost importance to me.'

The girl nodded. 'I will, Miss Sarah. I promise you faithful I will.'

'Good! Go quickly now, and take care.' Sarah gave the younger woman the packet and ushered her down the stairs and out of her private entrance into the dark street. The parcel was very heavy in relation to its size and before she had gone far, Molly was obliged to rest for a moment. Then she went on, picking her way through the narrow ill-lit alleyways made sinister by the faint wraiths of steam snaking up from the fetid gutters and sewer puddles that lay everywhere along the lengths of the cobbles.

In the pitch blackness of the upper battery of the *Crown* hulk, Henri Chanteur lay in his hammock, unhearing of the night noises of men and rats, his mind a turmoil of anxious tensions. For weeks now he had been making his preparations. First had come the task of finding a safe messenger from among the garrison of the hulk to carry letters to Sarah. Helped by Gaston de Chambray, he had been able to meet and bribe a young sailor for this. Next had been the recruitment of half a dozen daring and trustworthy prisoners who were ready to risk their necks in an escape attempt. One of these was, of course, de Chambray and between the two of them they had slowly and very cautiously selected four others.

The need for caution was paramount. In the hell-holes of the hulks, men would have betrayed their own mothers if it could gain them the slightest advantage; and if an informer brought an escape plot to the notice of the authorities, then he was rewarded generously, being allowed to go to one of the small towns where prisoners-of-war were given freedom of parole and supplied with subsistence and money for his needs. The temptation was one which most men found irresistible and many escape attempts were foiled by these means.

Up until this point all had gone well with Henri's plans. Tonight was the crucial time. A parcel containing weapons, charts, navigation instruments, and instructions as to a safe hiding-place where the escapers could lie low until the procurement of a boat, should even now be on its way from Sarah. The parcel would also contain the prime requisite of any escape ... Gold! Gold enough to purchase a deaf ear and blind eye from the sentries on the gallery—gold to buy the help of sufficient prisoners in the upper battery, so that any attempt to raise the alarm while the escape was in progress would mean a slit throat for the man who made that attempt. Gold to pay for the hiding-place and gold to pay for the boat. Henri lay rigid and sweating in his hammock and not for the first time that night prayed fervently to his God to let the parcel reach him safely.

When Molly reached the beer-ken, which was one of a dozen tumbledown hovels fronting the Camber anchorage separating Portsmouth from Spice Island, her arms were strained and her back ached from the weight of the parcel. Spice Island was unusually quiet, no fresh ships had entered the harbour for days and money was scarce. The cold night had driven the beggars and urchins from the streets to the kitchens of their doss-houses, or wherever else gave some shelter from the wind and rain. Only the patrols of the town provost marshal could be seen wandering, shivering and cursing their ill-luck at being selected for the task. And these were only seen infrequently, since the old soldiers and sailors who led them knew many discreet little drinking dens where tired men could have a pot of mulled ale to keep out the chill of the weather.

The beer-ken that Molly went to consisted of a single room. Low-roofed and dirty, its only furniture a few wooden kegs turned on end to serve as tables and seats. A greasy-topped narrow counter divided the customers from the barrels of ale and cider that lay on a low brick shelf, and hanging from the ceiling two oil-lamps gave light and enough heat to accentuate the musty smell of the room. There was only one customer in the place, leaning over the counter in quiet conversation with the pockmarked, filthy-aproned, unshaven tub of a landlord.

Molly glanced at the customer and was struck by his appearance. He was very tall and wore a long black military cloak which stretched to his Hessian boots. On his blond hair was a high-crowned beaver hat. As if sensing her regard, the tall man swung to look at her. Molly's bold hazel eyes met his pale grey stare and she felt a tremor of excitement course through her body.

He appraised her admiringly and despite the cruelty that she saw in his lean weathered face, and the hard lines of his thin lips, she thought him one of the most handsome men she had ever seen. He smiled at her, showing even white teeth and for all her wide experience of men, Molly became suddenly shy. Flustered, she looked away and placing her parcel on the counter asked the landlord to give her a glass of gin. For some minutes she sipped the yellow-clouded liquid and felt its heat spreading through her, calming her sudden nervousness and restoring her customary confident boldness. She studiously ignored the tall man, and was so intent on doing so that when a young sailor entered the beer-ken, she failed to notice him. For all his tarred pigtail, tarpaulin jacket, wide trousers and glazed round hat, the sailor was little more than a boy, and with the brashness of youth he went straight to her, asking loudly,

'Be you the gel from Mistress Sarah Jenkins?'

William Seymour was just lifting his own glass of gin to his lips when he heard the question. The words almost made him drop his glass, so unexpected were they. Fortunately for him, both Molly Bawn and the landlord had turned to look at the sailor and neither had noticed his shocked reaction. Covertly he watched and listened.

'That's right,' Molly Bawn answered. 'And keep your voice down a bit, can't you. I doon't want the whole o' bloody Pompey to hear my business ... And another thing, who might you be? I don't know you.'

The youth became exaggeratedly quiet. 'I'm Dick's messmate,' he whispered hoarsely. 'He warn't able to come tonight. He's bin took orf the shore boat crew, so 'e's sent me instead.' The sailor produced a sealed letter. ''Ere, he give me this to give for your mistress, and 'e says that you'm to gi' me the parcel to take back.'

For a few moments Molly bit her lip in indecision, then remembering Sarah's instructions she said rapidly, 'All right, Jack Tar, there's the package ... Now listen careful ...' She instructed him as to his coming back to tell her all was well.

He knuckled his forehead and grinned cheekily. 'Doon't you fret, my pretty. We'll be bringin' the boat back and forrards all night long by the look on it. I'se never known so much comin' and gooin' by the bloody orfficers, I'm buggered if I 'as ... I'll come back and let you know all's well, doon't fret.'

'Mind that you does,' she admonished severely.

He hefted the parcel and whistled through his teeth in surprise. 'Bugger me! But 'tis heavy. What's you got in 'ere? A bloody cannonball by the weight on it, I shouldn't wonder.' He grunted with effort as he hefted the parcel on to his shoulder and left swaggering jauntily. Molly watched him go, then ordered another gin. When she put a coin on the counter to pay for it, the landlord pushed it back to her.

'It's paid for,' he told her gruffly.

'I hope that you'll not take offence, mistress.' William Seymour swept his hat from his blond hair and bowed with courtly grace. Still bending, he smiled at her. 'It is only that I was so charmed by your appearance, I wished to make your acquaintance.'

Molly felt her heart start to thump. She could not remember ever having been so strongly attracted physically to a man.

Seymour straightened. 'May I join your company?' he asked politely.

Molly drew a deep breath to steady her heartbeat and returned his smile. 'If you wish, sir. For I have to remain here awhile, and company is always welcome.'

He came close and smiled down at her. 'Then I am a very fortunate man, mistress. To have met someone as beautiful as yourself, to whom company is welcome, is indeed a blessing for a man as lonely as I am . . .'

CHAPTER TWENTY-FOUR

It was during the second week in March that Captain Joseph Ward, officer commanding the Grenadier Company, sent for Jethro Stanton. Sergeant Turner marched the young private into the company office, but told him nothing of what was to happen. So it was with some apprehension that Jethro, standing rigidly to attention before the captain's desk, waited to hear what was to be said. Joseph Ward laid down the feathered quill he had been writing with in the ledger in front of him, and leant back in his chair.

'Ah yes, Private Stanton,' he began. 'I wish to ask you one or two questions.'

Jethro's hand flashed to the peak of his shako in salute and remained there.

'Put down your hand,' the captain told him.

Jethro stayed as he was.

Ward's lips twitched in a gratified smile. Some old soldier had obviously given the young man some tips. It was a custom brought back by veterans from India that in the presence of an officer, the soldier, to show his respect, remained at the salute until the officer manually pulled down the raised hand. Ward nodded his close-cropped brown hair and Sergeant Turner stepped up to Jethro and pulled his hand down.

'Your courteous respect does you credit, Stanton,' Ward said. 'Tell me, do you know aught of reading and writing?'

'Yes, sir.'

'Do you scribe a neat hand and read well?'

'Yes, sir.'

'Do you like the army?'

Jethro hesitated perceptibly before answering. 'I find it a very interesting experience, sir.'

The captain chuckled in amusement. 'A natural courtier this one, what say you, sergeant?'

The sergeant grinned in agreement. 'I should say yes, sir.'

Inside Jethro's mind his thoughts were racing. He feared that the captain had found out that he and Turpin were fugitives, and he was waiting for the man to begin questioning him about the fact. Jethro's temper started to rise as the captain chuckled once more, and he thought that Ward was baiting him deliberately. To his amazement he heard Ward say,

'I have had excellent reports on your ability and conduct, Stanton. Therefore I have decided to appoint you to a vacant corporalcy in the Grenadier Company.' He paused and waited for the private's grateful thanks. None came. Instead Jethro replied calmly,

'With all respect, sir ... I've no wish for it.'

'What?' the captain came bolt upright in his chair. 'No wish for the chevrons? And why not, pray?'

Jethro's confusion had left him, also his apprehension that the other man knew of his past. 'I wouldn't feel justified in accepting the promotion, sir,' he said quietly. 'After all, I have scarcely served above two months in the army.'

'That is neither here nor there, man,' the captain told him impatiently. 'Length of service is not so important as ability. Sergeant-Major Gresham and Sergeant Turner both feel you would make a good N.C.O. I can easily appoint N.C.O.s, Stanton, but it is not so often that I can appoint first-class ones. If you take this vacancy, then perhaps in a few months you could become a sergeant ... The rank of sergeant is not to be treated lightly, it is an honour!' Ward brought his flat hand sharply down upon the desk to emphasize the point.

Jethro felt the terrible urge to tell the captain his real reasons for not wanting to become a corporal. In the short time he had been in the army, he had seen other men flogged, apart from the artisan. A dozen, twenty-five, or thirty lashes were meted out frequently for the most trifling faults in men's drill or turnout. Soldiers were battered and banged about by officers and N.C.O.s, it seemed to Jethro for no apparent reason other than the whim of the castigators. Feeling as strongly and bitterly as he did against these methods of maintaining discipline, Jethro did not want to become one of those who enforced it.

Sergeant Turner, standing by the young man's side, was watching the play of emotions across his face. A shrewd and experienced man, he sensed what the young private felt. Jethro opened his mouth to speak, but before the angry words could come the sergeant intervened.

'Permission to speak privately with you, sir?' he requested. The captain nodded.

Marched outside, Jethro stood on the veranda and listened to the rumble of voices from the office. At first he seethed inwardly at being robbed of his opportunity of saying what he really thought about the army, but as the minutes passed and still the voices droned on the other side of the door, he began to realize how fortunate it had been that the sergeant had intervened.

'God save me,' the young man thought. 'I might have ended upon the triangle. They say Ward's a just man, but he's got a hot temper when crossed, that I know.'

The voices stopped, the door opened and Sergeant Turner marched out. He jerked his head at Jethro.

'Follow me,' he ordered, and led the way to the rear of the barrack blocks and behind the lines of drying washing and airing bedding swinging and flapping in the wind. Moving away from the curious soldiers, one from each barrackroom who were there to prevent their roommates' clothing and bedding from being stolen, the sergeant said in low-pitched tones,

'Now lissen hard, young Stanton. I'se saved your neck wi' Captain Ward and today you puts up the chevrons ...'

He clamped his hand across the younger man's mouth, cutting short the protest that erupted. 'Shurrup and lissen, you born fool! I knows what you thinks o' the floggin' and the beatin' and the bad treatment we gets. Does you think I'm a bloody wooden-yedded bugger who carn't see beyond me nose? If it's any consolation I feels the same way about it ... But you'll take the chevrons none the less. I'se bin in the army for a good many years, boy. I took the shillin' as a regular afore you was born, and I'm only wi' the militia now because me old regiment was disbanded back in '02 arter the Peace o' Amiens ... I knows all there is to know about this life, and I'll tell you now that iffen you doon't take this chance to transfer into the Bacon Bolters, then sure as theer's an 'ole in your arse, you'm agooin' to be kissing the Drummer's Daughter afore many weeks be out.'

Jethro felt surprise. 'But why, Sar'nt? I intend to continue to conduct myself well and attend to my duties.'

The sergeant's large brown teeth glistened in a savage grin. 'That's as may be,' he chuckled grimly. 'But you shouldn't

269

ha' rogered Bertha Morrison.'

The chuckle became a belly laugh as Jethro's face worked in dismayed incredulity.

'Nay lad,' he went on. 'Don't take it so hard. You'm not the first drunken Johnny Raw to be sucked in by that whore, nor wun't be the larst neither ... But you take it from me, she's got a hatred for you because you 'udden't goo on rogerin' her, and she's poisoned Bert Morrison's mind agen yer. He arn't so thick-skulled as he seems to be, that 'un arn't. He'll wait and wait for his chance, and then he'll put you right in the muck. He'd done it afore, lad, to many a good man ... And then there's that Irish barstard as well, Rourke ... You upset him when you went wi' Bertha. 'E was forever putting a tail on her until you come along, now she'll ha' nothing to do wi' him.'

'But he's always been friendly to me,' Jethro exclaimed.

'Ahr, I know he has. That's his way. But he's a sly barstard, is that 'un. He'll have his revenge sooner or later and get you on to the triangle if he can.'

'But if I become a corporal, what happens to Turpin Wright? I've no wish to part from the rogue,' Jethro said.

'Doon't you worry none about old Turpin,' the sergeant reassured him. 'For he's gooing to the Bacon Bolters as well ... And I've a bit more news for you. Captain Ward's agoing to take the Grenadiers and two other companies across to Fort Cumberland next week to reinforce the garrison theer, so you'll be well out of harm's way ... Now get on over to the tailor's shop and get your chevrons on ... Corporal Stanton.'

After a few seconds of silence, during which Jethro digested fully all that the other man had told him, he smiled and said, 'Thank you Sar'nt Turner, you're a good man ... I'll not forget this kindness.'

The sergeant patted him on the shoulder. 'Mind you doon't, young un, mind you doon't ...' he laughed.

The reason for the reinforcement of the Fort Cumberland garrison was that extra convict labour was being drafted to work on its outer ditches and fortifications, and that extra labour was to be found from the French prisoners-of-war, as well as the civilian convicts already being used. Since the middle of the previous century, there had been earthworks on the site to prevent any invader landing troops in Langstone

Harbour. Following the outbreak of the wars against revolutionary France, it had been decided by the authorities that the fort must become a major strongpoint. The mutinies of the fleets at Spithead and the Nore gave warning that England could no longer rely solely on her wooden walls, she must also have stone ones. Consequently, civilian convicts had been slowly rebuilding the fort for some years. Some hundreds of them were quartered on the hulks *Ceres* and *Fortune* in Langstone Harbour. The rest were in casemates in the fort itself.

It was the noise of shouting men coming from some of these casemates that David Warburton could faintly hear as he walked along the unmetalled road that skirted the shoreline from Portsmouth right up to the Land Gate of the fort. Behind him, the Wards' soldier servant grumblingly pushed a wheelbarrow on which the officer's trunk and other possessions were piled. The morning was springlike with soft-breezes and to his right the sea was green and sparkling. The young man's spirits were high, for the previous evening, following his return from his several days of absence in London, he and Jessica Ward had reached an understanding. She had promised to marry him when the war was over.

David followed the road as it ran almost on to the beach then swung back northwards to pass into the fort. He halted and surveyed his new quarters. In front, lay the half-dug unlined dry moat and outer earthworks, and beyond them reared the high greystone walls topped by a layer of red bricks. It was a star fort, with great four-sided bastions thrusting out from the long curtain walls to form the points of the star. From the embrasures of the bastions frowned the rounded cannon muzzles, sixteen guns to a bastion which, well-served, could throw sufficient weight of metal to smash and sink any vessel that was foolhardy enough to challenge their might.

On the tops of the battlements, David could see the blue uniforms of the Royal Artillerymen who manned the guns, but at the Land Gate stood the redcoats of the unit he was to join ... The Eighth Veteran Battalion. The young officer grimaced ... 'Veteran Battalion!' He felt almost ashamed. True, his right arm was stiff and without its full strength. But he didn't feel that he was so infirm as to be posted to a battalion of men who were either too shattered by war or too old and feeble to guard convicts working on the fort.

'Never mind,' he told himself. 'At least I'm near to Jessie

here, and will be able to see her at times.' A vision of her lovely face came before him and his heart swelled. 'God! I'm a lucky dog!'

'Be we moving on, sir?' The servant was standing beside him, a sullen look on his miserable hollow-cheeked face. He moved his shoulders to ease the cutting edges of the leather strap which passed across them to each handle to take the weight of the barrow. 'Only this bleedin' barrow's abreakin' me back ... sir,' he added aggrievedly.

David nodded, and passed under the arched tunnel of the entrance, returning the creaking Present Arms of the white-haired sentinels with a casual wave of his hand. The gravelled parade ground stretched before him, covering the entire inner area of the fort and nearly a quarter-mile in radius. On the near right, close to the broad platforms of the walls, were two terraces of brick-built officers' houses. Before them was the triple-gabled men's canteen and away over in the far left corner stood the cluster of tall-sided stable buildings. The troops' and convicts' barracks and all the storerooms and offices were in the rows of brick-fronted arched casemates that were set at ground level into every curtain wall of the fort's perimeter. It was from a row of casemates near to the stables that the noises David had heard originated. As he passed under the gate tunnel, it came loudly to his ears. He saw two long lines of scarlet-coated veterans drawn up in battle formation facing the casemates at the ready position. On the incline that led down from the platform of the nearest bastion, sweating artillerymen were manhandling two long-snouted cannon, guiding the garrison carriages with steel crowbars, and hauling on ropes lashed about the guns to prevent their near three tons in weight from breaking free to career out of control down the incline.

'Wait here,' David ordered the servant and went towards the lines of troops. As he neared them, he perceived a small group of officers on the flank nearest him, engaged in earnest discussion. He approached them and coming to a halt took off his shako and stood to attention.

'May I report my arrival, sir,' he said loudly enough to be heard despite the tumult of shouting from the casemates.

'Lieutenant Warburton, Twenty-Fourth Foot. Under orders to join the Eighth Veteran Battalion on temporary posting.'

The men turned to him, presenting a gruesome illustration of what battle could do to human flesh and blood. A fine-built, soldierly-looking major bowed briefly. He appeared slightly incongruous since instead of a shako, he wore pulled down low on his head a bright blue stocking cap with a large bobbin dangling from it. He spoke with a strong north country accent.

'That'rt welcome, Warburton. I command here, Oliver Caldwell, late of the Fifth ... Captain Flaherty there told us thee wast coming.'

David bowed to his erstwhile travelling companion in pleased recognition. The major performed the rest of the introductions.

'Captain Cresswell ... Thirty-sixth Foot.' He was a swarthy man who wore a black eye-patch over an empty socket, as a memento of the plains of Salamanca.

'Captain Picard of the Ninety-fifth.' A short stocky ex-rifleman who had left his lower left arm in the breach at Badajoz.

'Lieutenant Moorehead, Seventh Fusiliers.' A tall willowy person who could speak only in whispers and whose breath rasped painfully. The result of the four musket balls the French had lodged in his chest on the bloody slopes of Albuhera Ridge.

'Thee'st arrived at a bonny time, Warburton,' the major informed him.

The noise from the convicts inside the casemates had started to die down, but now redoubled its intensity as the artillerymen ran the two cannon, wheels crunching over the gravel, and brought them to a halt, their muzzles trained on the doors of two of the casemates.

'May I ask what is the matter here, sir?' David questioned.

'It's them damned jail-rats in theer. The bastards ha' barricaded theirsen inside and are refusing to perform their labour. They've heard that Froggie prisoners-o'-war are to be sent here from the Portsmouth hulks to help finish the work on the outer ditches. These buggers 'ull not wark wi' the French, so they say. The difficulty is, that so long as they only stops in their quarters and diven't make any attack on my men, or try to escape, then I darsn't open fire on 'um ... Them bloody reformers and mealy-mouthed Methodys up in London 'ud ha' me on trial for murder if I killed one o' these villains ... I'm going to try and bluff the buggers out on it wi' the cannon. But if they refuses to move, then I'll ha' to think agen.'

There came a lull in the convicts' howls. Immediately Caldwell left the group of officers and, going to the casemates, hammered on the door of one and shouted,

'If you scum diven't come out o' theer in less than a minnit, I'm going to let a cannonball do the wark o' getting thee out ... D'ye hear me plain?'

'Aye Caldwell. We hears yer,' a solitary voice shouted back, and in a crack in the door's thick planking could be seen a bloodshot eyeball staring out ... 'And I'll answer yer for all on us,' the voice continued. 'We might be scum in your eyes, but we'em still King George's loyal subjects and we'em not going to labour be the side of a load o' bleedin' Frogs.'

'Why not, blast ye?' The major's face showed his temper to be warming fast. 'Why dost thee object? The wark has to be completed, and what cannier way o' using the King's enemies than to have them toiling for him ... Tha'rt just using this as an excuse to stop warkin', ye idle dogs.'

'That's as may be.' The speaker's tone was surly. 'But them-bleedin' Frogs oughter stay wheer they be ... On the bleedin' hulks ... Why, iffen they comes here, what's to prevent 'um slittin' all our bleedin' froats one night, when old Boney comes to rescue 'um.'

'Oh that's it, is it?' The major grinned contemptuously. 'Tha'rt afraid, art thou ... Well theer's no call to be afraid. We're here to protect thee, as well as stand guard o'er thee.'

A wave of jeering laughter greeted his words.

'Protect us from old Boney?' The spokesman's voice cracked, so high in scoffing disbelief was it pitched. 'How could that load o' bleedin' walkin' death you got wi' you protect us? They'm only fit for the bleedin' knacker's yard, and well you knows it.'

The convicts howled their sneering agreement with the words. David felt a surge of rage. He looked at the resentful faces of the Veterans, men who had given blood, youth, strength and health fighting their country's battles, and he wanted to drag the convicts from their boltholes and force them to their knees in abject apology. If David's reaction was rage, Major Caldwell's was maniacal fury.

'Tha'rt an insolent barstard!' he roared, and tearing his stocking cap from his head, he threw it to the ground and stamped on it to vent his feelings. David drew in his breath as he saw why the major was in the Veterans. The top of the man's forehead had been caved in and his scalp ripped from

274

his skull, leaving a wide channel of grotesquely furrowed bone and livid skin behind his caved-in forehead. Abruptly the major's shouted oaths changed to a scream of pain. He staggered and fell against the door, both hands clapped to his wound.

'God damn their festering souls!' Captain Picard burst out. 'I feared this would bring on one of the major's attacks. He always gets an attack like this when he is baited into fury.'

The ex-rifle officer ran to the major and, supporting him with his one good arm about the waist, led the groaning man towards the officers' houses.

With the major gone, Captain Flaherty as senior officer was left in command. The situation was now at an impasse. The captain was also answerable to the Transport Office and to Parliament in London if he caused any convicts to be needlessly killed, so he in turn dared not open fire with the cannon. The windows of the casemates were small and high up in the brick fronts. They had closed-space grilles across them, which prevented the men outside from throwing in smoke bombs to force the convicts out ...

'Have you any ideas on what's to be done, gentlemen?' the Irishman asked the remaining officers.

'Cannot we break in the doors and drag them out by force?' David suggested.

Flaherty shook his head doubtfully. 'These poor lads are no match physically for the convicts,' he said, referring to the war-shattered veterans. 'And at this time there's only a few artillerymen here in the Fort. There's nigh on sixty prisoners in each casemate, and even one casemate full would outnumber all our able-bodied fellows ...'

'Well, what shall we do then?' Lieutenant Moorhead whispered. 'I don't relish standing here and allowing those hounds to mock us with impunity.'

The Irishman's twisted mouth grinned. 'I think that all we can do is to look up at Heaven and beg for a miracle.' As if God had heard his rueful joke, at that very moment Captain Joseph Ward came riding through the land gate arch and on to the parade ground at the head of his company of grenadiers. The reinforcement for the garrison of Fort Cumberland had arrived.

The situation was quickly explained to Ward by the veterans' officers. He had dismounted and was standing with their group on the flank of the battle-line.

'Well, gentlemen, I think that we must begin as we intend to continue. These rebellious dogs must be brought to heel and quickly. The other companies under my command are even now at the dockyard to collect and escort the first detachment of the French prisoners here. If those damned Frogs see fellows of this low calibre holding us at defiance, then I fear it will be impossible to control them. For at least they were soldiers of Napoleon Bonaparte once and undoubtedly retain some pride in that fact.' Ward spoke directly to Flaherty. 'Do I have your consent, sir, to deal with this matter?'

The Irishman's features were a study of conflicting emotions. At least the unwounded side of his face was, the disfigured part remained a motionless mask. He felt shame that the despised militia should have to be called upon to deal with something that he and his men, through no fault of their own, could not.

Once more the convicts started to heckle and taunt their guards.

'Why doon't you fire they big guns, cully? Ain't you got the bottom for it?'

'Come on in and meet us man to man, you crippled barstards!'

'Yerss, come in ... Iffen you con walk this far!'

'Come on, walkin' death!' one convict shouted, and the jeering cry was taken up by all of them.

'WALKIN' DEATH! WALKIN' DEATH! WALKIN' DEATH! WALKIN' DEATH!'

'God above, Flaherty! This is not to be borne!' David exclaimed angrily, and turned to Joseph Ward. 'Sir, by your leave. Give me the picking of a score of your strongest and most daring fellows, I beg you.'

Ward smiled fondly at his prospective son-in-law. 'I'm sorry, David, but it is not the custom of the Third to place our men under the command of officers from another regiment. Particularly when my own lieutenants and ensigns are straining at the leash to get at those rogues in there.'

'Sir, would you add to the shame of the Eighth Veterans by forbidding us?' Warburton asked quietly.

The older man studied the despondent faces surrounding him and conceded the point.

'Very well, David. You may select the men and lead them.'

'I must insist, sir, that we all share with Lieutenant Warburton the honour of leading your men. For we must strike at different points simultaneously,' Flaherty stated firmly, and his companions added their voices.

'I too.'

'And I ...'

Ward smiled and nodded agreement. 'So be it, gentlemen, so be it. I shall watch with great interest, for I'm sure that you will demonstrate to my men how real soldiers conduct themselves in the face of danger.'

'I doubt that there is much danger to be feared from scum such as these convicts,' Cresswell said scathingly.

'I own to the same feeling,' Lieutenant Moorehead whispered.

Ward and the veterans then walked back to where the Grenadier Company was drawn up. The grenadiers themselves were a fine-looking set of men. Not one was less than five feet ten inches in height and many topped six feet. Recruited for the most part from rural districts, their bodies were strong and muscular from years of hard outdoor work and their faces were ruddy with good health. The average age amongst them was around the middle and late twenties, with a leavening of older men.

Corporal Jethro Stanton stood on the right of his subdivision next to Turpin Wright, who now wore the solitary white chevron of a Chosen Man on his sleeve, and watched the group of officers come nearer. Up until now, Jethro had found nothing to admire in his officers and a lot to dislike and despise. To him the overwhelming impression he had received of officers was that of callous rigidity and stupid inefficiency. He found within himself a cynical feeling of anticipation as to how badly these regular officers would conduct themselves ... He was forced to admit, however, that from their appearances they were no strangers to desperate conflict.

Ward and his companions came to stand in front of the centre of the company, and Ward shouted,

'Grenadiers! I have a task for you ... In the casemates are rioting convicts who refuse to obey the lawful commands of those set above them ... In a moment I shall call for volunteers from among you to fetch the convicts out from their boltholes and restore order ... These gentlemen from the Eighth Veteran Battalion will lead you who volunteer. Mind that you bear yourselves so as to bring honour to your company and to your battalion ... Those men wishing to volunteer, THREE PACES TO THE FRONT ... MARCH!' Jethro had no intention of volunteering. His sympathy lay with the convicts.

'No doubt but that the poor devils have been bullied and badgered into rebellion,' he thought.

Other men did not share his opinions. From all along the ranks men came out to form a line three paces forward of the company.

'They are certainly eager to fight, Captain Ward,' Flaherty observed, and Ward smiled in gratification.

David let his gaze roam idly along the lines of those men who had not chosen to come forward. A smile of reminiscence quirked his lips. He had seen this sort of happening so many times, and had always been struck by the contradictions between men's outward appearance and their inner qualities. Some of the hardest-seeming and toughest-featured men always hung back from danger, while some soft-looking, timid-faced fellows hurried towards it. His gentle grey eyes suddenly locked upon the dark eyes of a tall well-built corporal in the front rank. His smile broadened.

'Now there is a classic illustration of my thinking,' he told himself. 'One would imagine by seeing that man's face that he would be a most daring and reckless fellow. While the older one next to him looks the very epitome of brutal courage. Yet they both stand and let others push forward to fight in their stead.'

Jethro returned the stare of the lieutenant. He saw the smile on the well-shaped lips broaden and realized with a sense of shocked surprise, 'Goddam me! That officer thinks me to be afraid to volunteer. He thinks I'm a coward!'

Reacting instinctively, Jethro marched smartly forward and stamped to a halt alongside the line of volunteers. A second later, and Turpin Wright joined him. The older man hissed from the corner of his mouth,

'Be you gone out o' your yed, cully? I'se told you a thousand times, ne'er offer yourself for nothin'.'

'Be silent in the ranks! Goddam your loose mouths!' Ward roared in quick anger. 'You are soldiers of the militia, not chattering women ... Try and behave as such, God rot you!' Jethro inwardly cursed himself for volunteering. 'You see you stupid fool! No matter what a man does, they still treat him worse than they would treat a dog ...'

It was decided to form two assault groups and attack the two centre casemates simultaneously. Two more groups would be held in reserve ready to come in when required. The remainder of the volunteers would then, if necessary, provide fresh groups to storm the rest of the casemates. David Warburton was to lead one of the initial assaults and Captain Cresswell the other. Picard and Moorehead would command the reserve groups and Flaherty would take overall charge. The one-armed rifleman, Picard, had come hurrying back from Major Caldwell's house in time for the planning.

'The major's being cared for by the surgeon's mate,' he told his friends in reply to their questions, then grumbled jokingly, 'Dammee, Flaherty. It's no use letting Cresswell lead a storm, he's not had the experience for it. You'd do better to let me take his place.'

'I don't know about that,' the swarthy, one-eyed captain chuckled. 'Judging by the looks o' you, Picard, your experience of storming parties ain't been very successful. God rot me! It ain't likely to give your men much confidence to know they're being led by a fellow who was fool enough to leave an arm in Badajoz breach.'

'At least I'm able to see the way to where I want to go,' the rifleman jeered good-naturedly. 'If one of those villains so much as spits in your good eye, it'll become a case of the blind leading the blind.'

Jethro listened to the rough badinage and felt a reluctant admiration. If these veterans felt any timidity, then no man could have known it from their manner. He himself felt the familiar flutterings in his stomach that always assailed him at the prospect of physical violence. But he knew that when the action began, his nervousness would leave him.

'Corporal, what's your name?'

Jethro realized with a start that the young lieutenant's question was for him.

'It's Stanton, sir,' he snapped to attention and replied.

'Very well, Corporal Stanton. Select twenty men, you and they will form my assault party,' David Warburton told him.

Quickly the preparations were made. The storm parties stripped off their tunics and accoutrements and armed themselves only with cudgels. Two long brass-headed, multi-handled battering rams were brought up from the stores.

Inside the casemates the convicts also made ready to fight. Some bunks were pushed up against the doors to strengthen the barricades. Other bunks were smashed up and the heavy billets of broken wood distributed for clubs. There were no more taunts and challenges hurled, only the grim silence of determination.

At a signal from Flaherty the storm parties picked up the battering rams. Joseph Ward and his officers looked on with avid interest, and along the facing parapets, the white plumes of the artillerymen's shakos and the red cockades of the veterans' wall sentries crowded to watch the drama.

'Make ready, men!' Flaherty shouted. 'Advance!'

'HURRAH!' The attackers gave a short barking cheer and the battering rams surged forward and smashed into the doors with a hollow crashing of metal against wood.

'And again!' David Warburton shouted. The ram pounded once more and the door cracked and sagged a little.

'And again!' Brass crashed on wood, and the door buckled inwards against the makeshift barriers inside. The convicts now began to scream their defiance and hatred but the attackers stayed silent except for the panting grunts of the ram-handlers' effort, as they drew back, then ran forward yet again. CRASH ... The door smashed in completely, but still the barrier of bunks remained. The top of the barrier had fallen and when David, waving his rattan cane and shouting for his men to follow, attempted to straddle the fallen bunks he was beaten back by the flailing clubs of the convicts.

Jethro shouted at the ram-crew who were still close to the doorway, 'Push that ram forward and keep a grip on it.'

They did as he ordered and the front part of the ram partly bridged the barricade of bunks ... Jethro jumped up on to the thick pole and, running along its length with catlike surefootedness, hurled himself over the barrier and into the mass of howling convicts. Billets and clubs flailed the air and for a brief moment Jethro was alone, pitting his strength and cudgel against a dozen assailants.

David Warburton had watched the corporal's daring attack with amazement, then swore aloud.

'Goddammit, he shall not shame me with his bravery.' He followed Jethro's path, running along the ram bridge to launch himself into the casemate. His example was repeated instantly by Turpin Wright and others and in only seconds the casemate became a jammed mass of swearing, shrieking, struggling men.

Jethro found himself face to face with a big, gap-toothed

convict who spat curses and saliva in a continual stream, and grabbed Jethro's throat in his spatulate hands. A sudden shift in the pattern of bodies trapped Jethro's arms at his sides and in spite of his frantic heavings he was unable to free them. The thick, black-grimed thumbs dug deep into his windpipe cutting off the air from his lungs. His sight darkened, he felt a red-hot pain knife across his chest and his tortured lungs seemed about to burst.

David Warburton was fighting two opponents, both of whom were battering wildly at his ever-shifting litheness in an animal lust to kill. As always in conflict, Warburton's mind was working with as much agility as his body. He used his rattan cane like a rapier deftly to parry the heavy blows, and then, seeing his opening, thrust the spiked metal tip of the cane neatly into one man's eye. The convict's eyeball burst like an overripe grape and the blood-streaked slime ran on to his cheek. The man dropped his cudgel and reeled vomiting in agony.

A surge of the fighting masses swung David away from the two assailants and battered him against Jethro Stanton. The young officer saw the blackening face of the corporal and the brutal hands crushing the life from him. Jethro's arms were still trapped and suddenly David felt his own hands pinned. In his concern for the corporal, Warburton became for an instant a raging savage. Ducking his head forward he sank his teeth into the convict's biceps, tearing and worrying the flesh as would a mad dog. The convict bellowed in shock and pain and let fall his grip from Jethro's throat. For a second or two Jethro felt no relief then his straining lungs dragged in a huge gulp of the dusty, stench-filled air and his senses cleared.

The big convict drove his fist into the lieutenant's face and the weight of the blow tore the clenched teeth from the bloody, ragged-edged wound they had made. The man drew back his fist to hammer the half-stunned officer into sense-lessness, but before he could let it fly, Jethro's ironshod boot smashed down upon his bare foot, breaking the delicate bones as if they were dry twigs. The convict shrieked and would have fallen, but the press of bodies was too tight to allow him to. Again and again, so rapidly as to seem almost one continuous impact, the boot smashed down on the foot, splintering the already broken bones into fragments. A sheet of crimson torment veiled the man's sight and he fainted. Once more the jammed crowd shifted and heaved and Jethro and

David came chest to chest as if in a lover's embrace. To Jethro's surprise the lieutenant grinned happily as though he were enjoying the nightmarish tumult they were trapped in.

'My thanks for your timely assistance, corporal,' Warburton gasped. 'By God, it's hot work, is it not!'

Jethro's own lips curved and parted in a grin and a wave of admiration for this slender, gentle-faced young man welled up in his mind.

Warburton shouted at him, 'It's time for the second part of the plan. Order the men out, corporal ... And order loud, for I fear they'll find it hard to hear us in this din.'

The pair of them started to bellow at the tops of their voices.

'All out! All out! All out! All out! All out!'

Those militiamen not locked in desperate conflict heard and obeyed, and pushed through the door dragging their injured and unconscious comrades with them. Left so suddenly in possession of the casemate, the convicts hardly had time to draw breath, let alone reorganize and clear their fallen from under foot, before the reserve assault group under the command of Captain Picard burst through the shattered doorway. The savage impact of these fresh and eager men was too much for the sorely tired and battered convicts, and in less than a minute the fight was over. The convicts threw down their weapons and cowered against the walls crying their surrender, until one by one they were driven under a rain of kicks and blows outside on to the parade ground.

Much the same thing occurred in the second casemate. The sudden withdrawal of the initial stormers, followed immediately by the onset of a second group, proved too much for the convicts to deal with and there also resistance collapsed. The remaining convicts seeing the bloody heads and broken bodies of their comrades, and the brutal completeness of their overthrow, gave in without a fight.

Joseph Ward hurried to the bloodstained officers who had led the attack.

'Well done, gentlemen, well done indeed!' he congratulated them heartily. 'Tell me, are you satisfied with the spirit of my men?'

David Warburton, tenderly exploring the fast-swelling bruises on his face, nodded and smiled. 'I think they may have some potential as fighting soldiers, sir,' he teased. 'What say you, Cresswell?'

The swarthy captain had just succeeded in staunching his bleeding nose. 'I would not object to leading them in battle,' he chuckled. Then cursed softly. 'Damn you for making me speak, Warburton. It's brought my nose on to bleed again.'

David looked about him and saw Jethro helping to tend his injured comrades. The lieutenant pointed out the corporal to Joseph Ward.

'That is a good man in a tight spot, sir.' He was forced to smile. 'And I mean that quite literally.'

Jethro, who with Turpin Wright was busily engaged in splinting a groaning man's broken arm, was not aware of his superiors' interest in him. His thoughts were mixed as he found himself revising some of his previous held opinions concerning officers.

'Goddam me! But I must admit there are some brave men among them ... That lieutenant who led our party, for instance,' he told himself with some reluctance. 'I begin to fear that perhaps my bias has made me blind to all but the faults of the bad ones ... Can it be possible that there are as many officers who are good at their profession and treat their men fairly, as there are those who are useless, stupid fools and petty tyrants?'

CHAPTER TWENTY-FIVE

The following morning, Jethro had cause to modify his opinion of his officers still further. The warning drum beat for the seven o'clock parade and from their casemate barrack-rooms, the Grenadier Company poured out to form up for the company officer's inspection, which took place half an hour before the main parade. The roll was called by a sergeant and when Jethro answered to his name, the only officer present, Ensign Spooner, stopped the sergeant from continuing.

'Corporal Stanton.' The ensign's boyish face was solemn. 'You will fall out of the ranks and report to the company office.'

Jethro did as he was ordered. Puzzled and a little anxious, he rapped on the door of the office.

'Enter, blast you!' a gruff shout came from within.

Inside the long arched casemate Joseph Ward and David Warburton stood, together with the stocking-capped Major Caldwell, by the smoking fire set into the centre of one side wall.

'Corporal Stanton, sir. Reporting as ordered,' Jethro presented himself.

The three men stared at him keenly, then Major Caldwell spoke. 'Stand at ease, lad. Thee'st not in any bother so diven't fret thysen. Thee con tell him, Ward. He's one of thine, after all.'

'Very well, sir,' Joseph Ward replied, and smiled kindly at the young corporal. 'Major Caldwell has been told of your conduct yesterday, Stanton. It is his wish, and also Lieutenant Warburton's, that you should receive some reward for your actions. They want to give you this ... Here.' He held out his hand, and a coin glinted in his fingers. 'Come on, man. Take it.'

Jethro took the golden guinea from the captain. 'My thanks,

sir,' he said quietly, his surprise at the reward showing in his face.

Major Caldwell waved Jethro's words away. 'Thee had best get on, lad, iffen thee's to ha' time to spend that this day.'

Ward saw the puzzlement deepen in the young man's eyes and explained, 'You are being allowed a two-day furlough, corporal.' He went to the desk at the far end of the room and returned with a leave pass. He handed it to Jethro and then took another guinea from his waistcoat pocket and gave the young man that also. 'You may spend the time in Portsmouth town, or remain here in the barracks, if you prefer. This other guinea is from the company funds. I feel that you have well earned it by bringing such credit to us yesterday.'

Jethro again thanked him.

'Go on wi' thee now, lad. Or thy furlough will be finished afore thee leaves this damned room.' Caldwell dismissed him, and Jethro went from the casemate.

'He's a mannerly, well-spoken fellow,' David observed. 'He could almost pass for a gentleman.'

Ward nodded. 'Yes, so he could. Yet he was 'listed from the town lock-up in Kidderminster, together with a man called Turpin Wright ... who is a double dyed-in-the-wool rogue, if I ever saw one.'

Major Caldwell laughed gruffly. ''Pon my soul, Ward! How many of our soldiers and sailors are recruited from the gaols. I wish I had a penny-piece for every man that comes to the colours wi' the gaol stink on him, I'll take me oath I do.'

'I have to agree with you, sir,' David smiled. 'A good half of my men in the Peninsula were old acquaintances of the turnkeys. But they made good fighting soldiers, for all that. Though it took a deal of flogging to keep them under control, especially when there was drink to be had.'

'I don't doubt the truth of your words, my boy,' Ward said seriously. 'But there are times when I wish the army's recruits could be found from a better class of men ... Then perhaps we could treat them a little more humanely than we do.'

'Amen to that, Ward,' Caldwell agreed fervently. 'For I grow sick o' spending so much o' my time on flogging parades. I could put that time to better use. But then, think of the scum we have to deal with. A good lashing's the only way to discipline the buggers ...'

'With respect, sir,' David said, 'I feel that there are other ways.'

'What ways would they be?' the major came back at him.

'We could try and give them back their self-respect,' the lieutenant said firmly. 'And begin by treating them humanely and justly. I know that there are many rogues who come to the army, and this is one thing I fail to see the sense in. Why permit the known bad lots to enlist to start with?'

The major threw back his head and roared with laughter.

'That's easy answered, young 'un,' he said, when he had recovered sufficiently to speak, 'there's no other buggers will come forward to do so ...'

To this statement David could find no short answer, so he let the subject drop.

Jethro, dressed in his full regimentals, but without accoutrements other than his bayonet, and wearing a porkpie forage cap, walked out of the Land Gate, his spirits lightening with every step. All around the ditches and outer earthworks of the fort, civilian convicts and squads of prisoners-of-war were forming up to begin their day's toil, under the watchful eyes of fully armed veterans and militiamen. To overawe the newly arrived and potentially rebellious foreign prisoners still further, cannons had been dragged to various points and placed so that the canisters of grape-shot they were loaded with could sweep the whole length of the ditches where the majority of prisoners would be working.

The morning was again unusually fine and the skies overhead held only a few scattered puffs of white cloud which emphasized the clear blue of their background. The sea was calm and still, not a single foam-fleck disturbing its pond-like green surface.

Jethro felt the jingle of the gold guineas in his trouser pocket as he marched smartly away from the fort and he revelled in his unexpected freedom. The road to Portsmouth was empty for much of the way, and Jethro met no one as he passed the odd isolated farmhouse or labourer's hovel, except for a solitary sea-booted fisherman, carrying over his shoulder a great black-grey bunch of writhing eels, threaded together by a ring of wire passing through their sinuous bodies. Even the turf-covered earth ramparts of the shore batteries at Eastney and Lumps Fort showed no signs of life, and their guns appeared to have been left deserted but for the swooping, wheeling, squawking gulls that abounded along the coastline.

The brisk walk made Jethro begin to sweat and under the immaculate finery of his uniform his skin felt stale and itched him uncomfortably. He grimaced at the memory of the vile body-odours of the barrackrooms, where one roller towel changed every Wednesday and Saturday had to serve for the needs of up to forty men, women, and children, and even those few individuals inclined to personal cleanliness found it increasingly irksome to wash any part of their bodies other than face and hands.

It was the sight of the bathing machines, of which there were several on the stretch of beach between Portsmouth and the derelict Southsea Castle, that put the notion of a swim into Jethro's mind. The bathing machines resembled large slope-roofed sheds raised on great broad-rimmed wheels. They were dragged by horses far enough into the sea for the water nearly to reach their floorboards. Then a temporary plank-walk was set up to enable the ladies, and also those invalids whose prescribed treatment was immersion in the sea, to walk dry-shod to the machines. From the side that faced out to sea an overhanging awning shielded the female bathers from the lustful oglings of the passers-by. Jethro smiled in amusement. One of the machines was in use, and he guessed that the users were females when he saw on the parapet of Southsea Castle the flashes of sunlight reflecting from the lenses of several telescopes. As always, the voyeurs' ingenuity was more than a match for the obstacles placed in the way of their pastime.

He went a little way past the castle, then stripped off his clothing, taking care to hide his money beneath the shingle, and ran naked into the waiting sea. Its coldness cut deep into his body but he welcomed it, feeling the stale sweat of weeks loosen and wash away. Taking a full breath, Jethro arrowed down through the clear water and swam along the hard-packed ridges of the sand bed, startling the feeding fishes and causing the tiny crabs to scuttle in sudden terror from his looming whiteness. He passed above a wide sea forest of waving dark fronds and let their soft feathers caress his body and wind their delicate traceries about his arms and legs.

Jethro surfaced and breathed vast draughts of salt-fresh air, cleansing the fetid stench of jail and barrackroom from his lungs and dived once more into the green limpidity. He went down and down, spiralling lazily like a creature of the deep until his fingers touched and sank beneath the ocean floor, and countless grains of sand swirled up to cloud his hands and arms, his head and shoulders. Again he rose to the light of the sun, exulting in the sheer joy of being alive. Using a fast crawl, he sent his hard body spearing through the water for hundreds of yards, then slowed and twisted to face upwards and float. Filling his sight with the blueness above him, so that all else was blotted from his senses but its soothing deeps. Time lost all meaning for Jethro, and it was as if he slept, so tranced was he by sea and air and cool colours.

Up on the parapet of Southsea Castle, William Seymour took his small spyglass from his eye and snapped it shut. Molly Bawn had told him the truth. Sarah Jenkins was in that bathing machine with Molly and another girl. Since he had met Molly Bawn, Seymour had done his utmost to make the girl infatuated with him, and had succeeded beyond all his expectations. For the first time in her life, a man had courted her and treated her like a gentlewoman. Practically every moment of her free time she had spent with her new admirer, who had constantly flattered her and shown her nothing but tender respect and kindness. Little by little, without arousing her suspicions, Seymour had extracted from the girl all that she could tell him of Sarah Jenkins' doings in Portsmouth. He knew about the partnership with Shimson Levi, and the success of The Golden Venture. The only wrong information that the girl had given him was that concerning the mysterious letters. Molly assumed that they went to Arthur Redmond and she had artlessly told Seymour, whom she knew as William Brady, the same.

Seymour had stored each nugget of information in his mind and felt that now he knew enough to confront Sarah herself. The problem he faced was how to get her alone, completely alone. With the patience of an old campaigner, he had begun to dog her movements, sure that sooner or later his opportunity would arise. His financial position was good, thanks to Molly Bawn. He had told the girl that he was waiting for funds to arrive from an almost completed business transaction, and she in the fullness of her new-found romance had insisted on loaning him money until the mythical funds should reach him.

There was a flurry of splashing water under the awning and the peals of the girls' laughter came clearly to his ears. He lifted his spyglass again and watched. In the water up to her massive hips was a mountainously fat woman, the proprietress of the machine, dressed in a black serge smock and a huge-peaked poke bonnet. She had hold of Molly Bawn and was making the girl lie flat on the water. Seymour stared appreciatively at the thrusting breasts and the lushly rounded belly, hips, and thighs that the flimsy, clinging, wet bathing gown only accentuated.

'My oath! But you're a toothsome baggage, little Molly,' he thought. 'I really think that it's time you and I bedded down for a few nights.' Up until now Seymour had made no pressing sexual advances towards the girl. Experienced in the ways of whores and camp-followers, he had sensed her overwhelming hunger to be treated with gallantry and courted romantically. To serve his own ends, he had willingly catered to this desire, although celibacy came hard to him. 'But enough is enough,' he murmured, as if to her. 'Once I've got Sarah Jenkins where I want her, then I'll have no more of this damned chivalrous nonsense. You'll give me what I need, and damn quick too.'

Time passed and the sun began to sink lower. The air grew cooler and a fresh breeze came whispering over the Spit Sands, driving the warm air back from the beaches and chilling the bathers. The women re-entered the machine and the several men who had been watching them grumbled their disappointment, put away their spyglasses and telescopes and wandered off in their different directions. Sarah and the girls dressed quickly, joking and laughing amongst themselves. Sarah felt light-hearted and gay. The parcel had reached Henri safely, and she considered her self-imposed obligation to him had been fulfilled. The rest was up to him and his comrades on the hulk. She could do no more.

'Here, Mother Spencer.' She took her purse from her reticule and paid the bathing woman, who grunted her thanks and waddled breathlessly across the plankwalk to disappear in the direction of the town, riding a tiny donkey that visibly sagged beneath her great bulk.

The three young women strolled in a leisurely fashion in the same direction. Molly particularly was in high spirits and kept playfully pinching the third girl, Susan, who would pretend indignation and chase after her friend threatening revenge. Sarah laughed to see them so happy.

'I'm sure Molly has got a secret lover,' she mused. 'And I'm contented for her because he must be a good man if he makes her as happy as she has been these last weeks.'

They were almost at the town's defence perimeter when Sarah realized that instead of putting her purse back into her reticule, she had left it lying in the machine.

'Oh damn it!' she exclaimed, then called to the girls who were a distance ahead, giggling as they chased each other, 'Go on without me, I'll be along presently.' They waved, and with a smile of farewell Sarah returned along the pathway towards the beach.

William Seymour had been trailing the women discreetly and when Sarah turned back, he concealed himself behind some convenient shrubs and watched to see where she would go. He let her pass him and then, keeping well behind followed, using for cover the clumps of shrubs and bushes dotted along the fringes of the bogs that composed large areas of Southsea Common. Sarah went over the plankwalk and disappeared into the bathing machine. Seymour looked around searchingly. He made sure that there was no one in sight, then broke from cover and ran swiftly towards the plankwalk.

The drop in temperature roused Jethro from his drifting reverie. He shivered and trod water while he took his bearings. The current had carried him a good distance out to sea, and the tower of the castle looked like a toy fort.

'It's as well it turned out cold when it did,' he smiled to himself. 'Otherwise I would have gone dreaming, clean across to France.'

He struck for the shore, his legs and arms moving in perfectly executed strokes that covered the water with surprising speed. On the beach his pile of clothing was a vivid spot of colour upon the pale grey shingle and he shivered in the sharp breeze as he dried his head and body with the coarse army shirt. Once booted and dressed, he retrieved his money from its hiding place and putting his forage cap at a jaunty angle on his head decided his next move.

'I'll go into Portsmouth, drink a few glasses, eat a good meal, and then let fancy take me.' Happier than he had been for a long time, he moved on.

* * *

Sarah found her purse lying on the narrow wall-bench and twitted herself for her carelessness. Humming a tune, she left the machine and started back across the plankwalk. Where it ended on the beach, a tall well-dressed man was leaning against the handrail, half-turned away from her and idly swinging a walking cane between his fingers. She hesitated momentarily, then took confidence from the obvious excellence of his clothes. The royal-blue swallow-tailed coat, the buff breeches, the highly-polished Hessian boots, and the lace at throat and cuffs were those of a gentleman, not some ruffianly footpad.

She went on, the pattens she wore to raise her satin-topped shoes from the damp beach tapping sharply on the weathered boards. She was almost up to the man when he swung to face her. He raised his glossy black beaver hat and bowed gallantly.

'Good afternoon, Mistress Sarah Jenkins. This is indeed a pleasure.'

For a moment she thought that he must be one of the bucks who frequented The Golden Venture. Then the blond hair and the pale grey eyes brought recollection flooding back. She halted abruptly.

'You're the captain of dragoons,' she exclaimed. 'I met you in Bishops Castle.'

His thin lips curved in a cruel smile. 'You are correct, my pretty.'

Sarah felt intuitively that this man's sudden appearance boded danger for her. She forced herself to smile pleasantly. 'I am happy to have met you again, Captain. But regretfully I have urgent business to attend to. I bid you good day, sir.' She went to walk on past him but he moved the cane to block her.

'Don't hurry so, my pretty. I would regard your leaving so sudden as most unmannerly.'

She felt a tremor of fear, but struggled to stay calm.

'Indeed, sir? Then you must feel free to regard it so. For I wish to go past.'

His smile widened, but did not reach his cold eyes.

'You shall go past, mistress. That you can be sure on. But there is a little matter to discuss between us.'

'It is not possible that we can have anything to discuss,' Sarah retorted angrily. 'Now let me pass!'

She struck the cane aside and again tried to move by him, but this time he used his body to crowd her against the handrail of the plankwalk and placed an arm on the rail each side of her to keep her there. Their faces were only inches apart and he noticed the tempting flawlessness of her skin and soft neck, and felt the gentle pressure of her full firm breasts where her tight coat bodice touched his chest. A hot spasm of excitement in his groin caused him to rest the full weight of his hips against her soft belly. His voice jerky with barely controlled desire, he said,

'The matter we must discuss concerns a certain grave back in Bishops Castle, and what was in that grave.'

A sudden rush of nausea made Sarah close her eyes. The vivid memories of a rotting skull and the vile smell of the tomb overwhelmed her and bile rose in her throat to fill her mouth with its bitterness. Seymour grinned in triumph at seeing her reaction to his words.

'I knew I'd guessed rightly,' he told himself. 'I knew it.'

The scented nearness of her desirable body coupled with his delight at his success combined to lift him to a pitch of heady excitement that heightened unbearably his lust to possess and degrade this woman, and caused him to take a wild gamble.

'Listen, my pretty,' he said urgently. 'There's no need for you to fear me, or the knowledge I have of you. We make a good pair. I'm no longer with the army and am fleeing from the authorities. Like you, I've left all my troubles far behind me and do not intend to let them catch up with me. We can trust each other, you and I. Because each of us could put the other into a convict-transport if we told what we knew to a magistrate. So let us join forces. We can make our fortunes together, and I'm man enough to keep you happy.'

His mouth clamped over her moist red lips and his hands moved greedily on her body. Sarah writhed and twisted in a frantic effort to get free. His mouth left hers and he bit the soft whiteness of her throat. She threw her head to one side and screamed with all the force of her lungs.

'Shut your noise, you hell-bitch!' he threatened, and whip-lashed his hand backwards and forwards across her face.

She screamed again as he dragged her from the plankwalk and threw her brutally to the shingle. Before she could recover, he was on her, forcing her arms above her head and ramming her hands painfully into the shingle. Then, clamping them in one strong hand, he tried to rip the clothing from her heaving body with the other.

Jethro heard the first terrified scream and halted in shock. The second scream rang out and suddenly he saw the flurrying petticoats of the woman as she strained upwards beneath the straddling of the man. He shouted aloud and began to run towards the pair, scattering the pebbles from under his heavy boots as he pounded across the shingle.

Seymour's loss of control had not deadened the instincts bred during years of combat. He heard the shout and the boots crunching the stones and his lust to rape was overlaid by the ingrained habits of survival. He came to his feet and dived for the elegant gold-handled walking cane that he had left propped against the handrail. Before Jethro reached him, his hands grabbed the cane and his fingers slipped a hidden catch in the intricate moulding of the handle.

Jethro, running at full tilt towards the woman's attacker barely managed to twist aside from the lunge of the deadly steel rapier that slid from the interior of the cane. Even as his body twisted, Jethro's own fingers reached for and found his hip-slung bayonet. Its triangular blade hissed from the greased metal scabbard and parried the next lightning-swift stroke of Seymour's swordstick. Recognition came to each man simultaneously, and the shocked curses they uttered at the sight of each other might have been issued on the same breath. Jethro didn't allow himself any further wonderment over this unexpected encounter. Instead, he read clearly the murderous intent in his opponent's eyes and realized that he must kill, or be killed.

For a few moments, the two men circled warily, then Seymour sprang into the attack, his swordstick flickering in and out in a blur of sun-flashed steel. The young corporal could only retreat along the beach, windmilling his bayonet to set up a clumsy defence each time the deadly skill of his enemy came frighteningly closer to killing him.

Sarah had not believed her eyes when she had seen Jethro come to her rescue. Many times she had thought of the handsome fugitive she had met at her father's smithy, and of the attraction she had felt towards him. Many times also, she had day-dreamed about him, imagining circumstances in which she might meet him again. But never in her most extravagant fancies had she imagined he would come to her rescue in such a way as had first occurred. Watching fearfully as the two men clashed, parted and clashed again, she realized that Jethro was in mortal danger. He was so obviously outclassed as a swordsman by Seymour. Desperately she started to look about her for something to use as a weapon so that she might go to Jethro's aid. Before she could find anything, another shout echoed in her ears and a slender young army officer came running from the direction of the castle.

David Warburton had been on his way to visit Jessica Ward when he had seen the civilian and the soldier fighting. Seymour had by now forced Jethro back to the next bathing machine. Both men were panting heavily and sweat ran down their faces.

'Hey there! What's happening here?' David shouted as he neared them.

'Help the soldier!' Sarah screamed. 'The other is a madman!' Warburton halted and drew his sabre, then went on running. Seymour lunged and Jethro leapt back to avoid it. His boots landed on a small ragged heap of rotting seaweed and he slipped and fell heavily.

Seymour grinned savagely. 'Now I'll pay you out!' he gasped, and drove his swordstick at the fallen man's body. The sweat stinging his eyes affected his aim. The rapier point hit the brass plate of Jethro's clossbelt. The slender blade bent sharply, shivered and snapped clean at the handle.

'God rot your eyes!' Seymour swore bitterly. He sprang back and glanced behind him. David Warburton was only yards away. The tiny nerve at the side of the murderous grey eyes throbbed erratically. 'You'll not escape me next time,' Seymour hissed, and threw the useless handle at Jethro's head.

David suddenly recognized his cousin. 'William?' he shouted incredulously. 'What are you doing?'

Seymour's face twisted in shock at the sound of the well-known voice. Without looking at the young officer, he jumped across Jethro's legs and ran. David gave chase, but the long strides of the older man rapidly lengthened the distance and he disappeared into the shrubland of the bogs. Warburton retraced his footsteps to where Sarah and Jethro were waiting. Seeing his cousin in such circumstances had shaken him badly and he snapped at Jethro.

'What happened, Corporal Stanton?'

Jethro told him what he could. That he had seen the civilian attacking the woman and had come to her aid. He did not tell of his previous encounters with the man.

Warburton turned to Sarah. 'She's a handsome piece,' he

thought, 'and has something of good breeding in her face and dress.'

'Is this true, ma'am?' he questioned. 'Did the civilian attack you?'

Sarah came from tough hardy stock. The terrifying ordeal she had undergone had not unnerved her and now she answered clearly and calmly, telling her questioner about the attempted rape. She claimed, however, that Seymour was a complete stranger to her.

David was, if anything, the most upset of the three. There was not in his heart any great love for his cousin but they had grown up together and he felt the responsibilities of kinship strongly.

'Is it true what my instinct tells me?' he asked himself silently. 'Can William have been the highwayman as well as the undoubted attacker of this woman? Is he mad, I wonder?' With an effort he gathered his wits, and said aloud, 'You have again done well, Corporal. I shall see that your officers hear of this.'

Jethro glanced at Sarah and saw in her green eyes an expression of fear. He sensed what caused it, and told Warburton,

'With all respect, sir, this has been a most painful occurrence for this lady. I'm sure that she would wish the whole matter to be kept solely between we three.'

David hesitated for some time before replying. He also had no wish for this event to be publicized. He wanted above all to find his cousin and talk with him, discover what was causing William to behave in this insane way.

Sarah agreed with Jethro. 'I think the corporal is right, sir,' she put in quietly. 'This would be most embarrassing for me if it became a subject of gossip. I would much prefer to forget the whole incident. The man is so obviously deranged that I imagine he will not long remain at liberty anyway.'

'Very well, ma'am,' Warburton seized his chance. 'I shall respect your wishes in this affair. It shall be a secret shared between us.'

Sarah regarded him keenly, then asked unexpectedly, 'Tell me, sir, did you think you knew the man?' She saw the flicker of apprehension in the young officer's soft grey eyes, and pressed a little harder. 'Only I thought that I heard you call to him by name.'

David shook his head. 'No, ma'am,' he said quickly. 'You

are mistaken, I'm afraid. Though such a mistake is understandable in a situation of danger and confusion. No! I did not recognize him as anyone I knew, I've never seen him before.' He stopped speaking, waiting for her reception of his denials.

She merely said aloud, 'I must indeed have been mistaken, sir.' Inwardly she thought that he protested too much. Jethro also thought that Warburton's words were suspiciously vehement, and felt doubt rising.

'And now, ma'am, I think that I had better escort you to your home and ensure your safe arrival,' the officer offered. She shook her head, and rearranged her bonnet which had been knocked askew in the struggle with Seymour. 'My thanks for your courtesy, sir, but there is no need for you to discommode yourself further ... The corporal can escort me. I have much that I wish to say to him.'

Wishing to be alone with his own thoughts, Warburton was happy to accede to her wishes without further discussion.

He bowed. 'My compliments, ma'am. I could not hope to leave you in better and safer hands.' He nodded in reply to Jethro's salute and walked on towards Portsmouth. Left alone, Sarah and Jethro looked at each other in a silence which was finally broken by Sarah saying, 'I feel that I must give my rescuer a token of my gratitude.'

She leant towards him and touched her soft lips to his. The kiss lengthened and deepened. They broke apart and she smiled brilliantly.

'I'm so very very happy to meet you again, Jethro. I've thought much about you ... There's so much I wish to tell you, and to have you tell me.'

Jethro returned her smile, feeling once more the certainty that he and this woman could mean a great deal to each other.

'Then let us waste no more time in doing so,' he said happily.

They settled themselves comfortably on the shingle and began to talk.

CHAPTER TWENTY-SIX

Molly Bawn's romantic dreams about William Seymour came brutally to an end on a narrow bed in the dirty, cheerless attic room above the sleazy beer-ken where she had first met him. It was more than a week since his abortive attempt to rape Sarah Jenkins and in that time Seymour's underlying instability of character had threatened to break all bonds of restraint and burst out into insanity. The hatred he felt for both Sarah and Jethro Stanton festered in his mind and it took all the self-discipline he possessed to stop himself taking his pistols and hunting them down openly to blow their heads off. For eight days and nights, Seymour had forced himself to stay in the attic. The beer-ken owner brought him food and drink, and an old crone came in sporadically to dispose of his slops. Seymour hardly touched the food. He seemed to be able to draw what susentance his body required from the flasks of fiery gin that he would reach for when he awoke and drain one after the other until the next collapse into sodden drunken sleep.

On the evening of the eighth day, Molly came to find her lover. Wheezing for breath the squat, pock-marked landlord led the way up the steep rickety staircase that led to the attic; frequently he stopped to cough rackingly and spit using his filthy apron to wipe his wet mouth, while the hand holding the lighted candle shook so that the hot liquefied tallow spattered on to his hairy arm, causing him to curse aloud and set off another paroxysm of coughing.

'I doon't know as if Brady 'ull be pleased to see yer,' he informed the girl.

'Why, is he ill?' she demanded.

The man's black-green stubs of teeth bared themselves in a grimace. 'I reckon in a manner o' speaking that he is, my wench. You'd do better to stay away from 'im, I reckon. He's actin' real strange lately, so he is.'

297

'I'll do no such thing,' Molly retorted spiritedly. 'It sounds to me as if Mr Brady's upset or ill, and I'm not surprised to hear it. Living in this midden 'ud make a pig sick.'

'All right, my wench, have it your own bleedin' way,' the landlord told her disgruntledly. 'But doon't you come abawlin' to me arterwards, that's all ... Doon't you come abawlin' to me.'

'There's no danger o' that, you fat bugger.' Molly's temper was well aroused by the man's veiled aspersions against her beloved, and she promised herself, 'If he opens his fat chops once more I'll kick him where it hurts, so I will.'

'Theer thee be.' The man held up the candle so that its dull glow flickered upon the half-rotted panels of the attic door.

Grunting and wheezing, he squeezed back past her, his stale-urine stink filling her nostrils, and descended heavily, the stairs creaking ominously beneath his weight. Molly, left alone in the darkness, felt with her hands for the door and pushed. It swung open, its rusty hinges groaning in protest. Lighted only by a small, broken-paned, rag-stuffed dormer window, the room was practically as dark as the stairway.

'William?' she called softly. 'William, are you here?'

She felt rather than saw a swift movement, and suddenly the hard round coldness of a pistol barrel rammed up under her chin to dig painfully into the soft skin. She shrieked faintly in fright and then felt a gust of hot gin-reeking breath on her face.

'Who is it comes like a thief in the night?' a man's voice growled in her ear, and so unlike was it to William's normal tone that for a moment she feared it was a stranger.

'It's Molly ... Molly Bawn!' she blurted out, in a rising surge of panic.

The man laughed softly. 'Ahh yes ... my sweet Molly. My own toothsome little bitch who's not let me touch so much as her tits.'

'Sweetheart, light a candle,' Molly begged. 'I knows you'm only teasin' me, but it makes me nervous, so it does ... Light a candle, honey.'

The pistol barrel fell from her throat and she sensed the man moving away. Steel and flint struck sparks and tinder glowed redly. The man's thin lips reflected in the red glow as they puffed gently to keep the spark alive. A small yellow flame leapt up from a greased spill and moved swiftly to set another larger flame burning in the oil lamp set on the crude-fashioned stool which, but for the narrow bed and wooden slop bucket, was the sole furnishing of the attic.

In the oil lamp's soft light, Seymour's lean face was wolfish and held a strangeness of expression that Molly had never seen before. He wore only a pair of pantaloons and his hard well-muscled body glistened with sweat in spite of the chillness of the room. He had not shaved for days and the stubble on his face and neck glinted gold, as did his tousled uncombed hair.

Molly's breath caught in her throat with the intensity of her loving anxiety. 'Are you ill, sweetheart?' she questioned. 'Are you ill?' And went to him, holding out her arms.

Seymour's pale eyes feasted on the inviting curves of her body and he pulled her to him, his hands grabbing and kneeding the firm roundness of her hips.

'I need you so much, Molly,' he said hoarsely. 'I need to have you under me on that bed, sweet Molly. Sweet little bitch!'

She ached to help him, to give him whatever he wanted.

'You shall, honey,' she told him, and pushed him away while she slipped out of her cloak and gown and shift. He threw his own clothing off and unable to restrain his hungry impatience pushed her roughly down on to the bed. For a few seconds he let his eyes and hands roam greedily over the lush warmth of her flesh. She gazed up at him, her face dreamily loving and reached upwards with her white arms for his lean torso.

'I love you, sweetheart ... I love you so much,' she told him. Then her eyes widened in shock. 'What is it? What's the matter?'

A guttural sound rumbled from deep in his chest and his teeth, glistening whitely in the lamplight, gave him the appearance of a ravening animal. His pale stare glazed and she saw the shadow of a tiny muscle start to twitch at the side of his eye. The guttural sound came again, and then, like some savage beast, he was on her.

The nightmare dragged on and on and on and, experienced as Molly was in the violent lusts of men, never before had she suffered such brutality of sexual congress. Again and again he took her, using and abusing every orifice of her body. Biting and mauling at her breasts and neck and thighs and belly until her flesh felt as if it were torn and bleeding. He stifled her cries of pain and protest with his cruel hands and crushed his mouth on hers as he degraded her, until she was near fainting with suffocation. At long last his perverted desires reached satiation and he calmed. Finally he lifted himself from her tormented body and as though nothing untoward had occurred began to dress in his street clothes. Molly huddled on to her side, her fingers hesitantly exploring the raw wounds he had given her.

'By God, but you've used me sorely,' she choked out.

'Be quiet, girl,' he ordered sharply. 'I have much to think about.'

Her hot temper flared. She came to a sitting position and lifted her full breasts with her hands so that the blue indentations of his teethmarks could clearly be seen in the lamplight.

'Look at that!' she expostulated angrily. 'You've served me like a tomcat serves a she, only a bloody sight crueller.'

He didn't look at her, but concentrated on the tying of his cravat. When he spoke, his words were cold and contemptuous. 'I've used you as any man has the right to use a whore,' he stated flatly.

To Molly it was as if he had struck her physically. She stared at him, not wanting to believe that she had heard him correctly.

'Why do you say that to me?' she questioned shrilly. He ignored her, put the finishing touches to his cravat, slipped on his brocaded waistcoat, then lifted his blue swallowtailed coat from the foot of the bed. She snatched at the fine cloth and tugged hard.

'I asked you summat!' she shrilled.

He bent forward and grasped her wrist in his strong fingers, twisting viciously until she cried out and released his coat. Seymour shrugged it on and straightened the set of it.

'Come, girl, get dressed,' he ordered harshly.

She shook her head. 'I want an answer,' she insisted stubbornly. 'I want to know why you said such a thing to me?'

He sighed impatiently, 'Very well ... I used you like a whore because that is what you are, and have always been ... A man may do as he pleases with purchased goods.'

Tears smarted, and blurred her sight, but she fought to hold them back. 'Yes, I was a whore,' she replied quietly. 'I've bin a whore for a good many years ... It was either that or starve to death. But I've not sold my body for many months now, and God willing, I'll never sell it again. I didn't roger wi' you as a whore rogers wi' a flat ... I came to you and gave myself to you in love ... Doon't treat me so cruel bad, William ... I love you truly, and with you I never acted the whore ... only as a woman who loves you. You've done things to me this night that I've never let any man do to me afore, no matter how wicked I might ha' bin. But if you loves me as I loves you, then I doon't care how much you hurts and degrades me in the bed. Some men am made that way, and if you are then I'll bear it, all on it, and make you a good wife ...'

He gave a short yelp of laughter. 'Wife?' he demanded. 'You? Be my wife?'

The tears fell freely from her eyes and wetted her cheeks so that they glistened brightly in the lamplight.

'Well then, if you doon't want me for wife, have me as your mistress and let me keep house for you,' she begged, her misery overwhelming her so that her voice choked with sobs.

Seymour shook his head and sneered. 'I need no whore to keep house for me. If and when I decide to set up house, then I'll have a gentlewoman to share my bed and board. A lady who will be fit to mix with society and bring credit to me. Now get dressed, if you don't want your head broken, for you must accompany me,' he finished threateningly.

It was Molly's fierce gutter-devil temper that stilled her sobs, not his threats. Dashing the tears from her eyes with the back of her hand she swallowed hard and began to dress. Sullenly she pulled on her shift and petticoats, her gown and long black cotton stockings. She felt the aches of her abused body and the torment of her sneered-at love and used both feelings to fuel the anger and desire for vengeance that was already beginning to burgeon in her mind. She considered that this man to whom she had offered her devotion had betrayed her. Hardship, hunger, abuse, kicks, and blows she would have accepted from him, for these were the age-old gifts that men gave to women. It was the contemptuous rejection of her as a person that angered Molly Bawn.

'Just you wait, my bucko,' she promised silently as she dressed. 'I'll get me own back on you, and then you'll see as how Molly Bawn is a woman worth having. You'll be glad to ask me to live with you then ...' her thoughts momentarily softened. 'And we'll be happy together, sweetheart, I know we will ... But first I've got to show you that I'm no soft silly cow, and humble you a bit as well.'

CHAPTER TWENTY-SEVEN

'I do declare, Henry, this is a most pleasant and improving way of spending one's day.' Nathan Caldicott gestured about him at the squads of yellow-orange-clad convicts who were toiling in the outer ditches of Fort Cumberland, swinging pickaxes and shovels, wheeling loaded barrows or staggering along under the weight of the great slabs of rock which were used to line the floors and sides of the ditch.

'I have to ask myself, who? Who else but the chivalrous Britishers would have gone to so much trouble and expense to bring us to this salubrious and delightful spot, and give us such an interesting pastime?'

For all the heaviness of his thoughts, Henri Chanteur could not help but smile at the drollness of the bald-headed cadaverous American, leaning now on the handle of his pick-axe as if he were a dandy at his ease.

'Hey, baldy! Keep that pick aswingin',' a militiaman standing on the upper slopes of the ditch shouted.

Nathan Caldicott waved to him languidly. 'I surely will, soldier boy. But at least allow me to draw a breath now and again ... For as the good book tells us, man does not live by bread alone ... he must also take in some oxygen.' The militiaman's heavy bovine face creased in suspicion.

'Be you amaking mock o' me, baldy?' he demanded.

The New Englander placed both hands flat on his bony chest. 'May the Good Lord tear this sinful heart of mine from my body if I am either denigrating or disparaging you in any way, Limey.'

Other prisoners noticed the exchange and ceased work to watch Caldicott bait the guard. Jethro Stanton, who was in charge of the guards on this section, saw the men stop work and hurried towards them.

As he neared the guard, he heard the man say, 'That be another thing I doon't loike, Yankee. Being called a Limey.'

The skeletal convict, who Jethro recognized as one of the newly transferred prisoners-of-war, raised his eyes to Heaven and assumed an expression of great piety.

'Did you hear that, God?' he said loudly. 'This gentleman does not enjoy being called Limey.' He looked directly at the guard. 'My good sir, I understand your fully justified resentment at being addressed by that title. I want to assure you that I fully sympathize. Naturally any man such as yourself, who possesses a large degree of pride and sensitivity must hate being called a Limey ... I know that I would. Why, I declare that I would sooner be called a hog, than called a Limey, and that's the truth, so help me God!'

His flow of words delivered in a respectful tone left the slow-witted militiaman gaping. Those prisoners who understood English began to laugh jeeringly, and explain to their friends what had been said.

Jethro felt angry at the guard for allowing himself to be drawn into such a position, but was careful to keep all expression from his voice.

'Private Butler, go and fill this for me.' He handed his round wooden water-canteen to the man. Nathan Caldicott bowed to Jethro, realizing why the corporal had intervened.

'Why good morning, Corporal. What a lovely day it is. It makes a man's heart just fill to the brim with joy and contentment, does it not?'

Jethro was conscious of the interested stares of the other convicts and realized that this was to be something of a test of him in their eyes. He grinned back at the New Englander.

'It is indeed a pleasant morning, Yankee Doodle,' he said lightly. 'And I'm most happy to see how much you appreciate our fine English weather. Now in return for our favouring you with such a pleasant day, I want you to favour me.'

Caldicott bared his toothless gums in a smile. 'But how can I do that, Corporal? Let me hasten to assure you that if I could favour you then I would ... But I'm hardly in a position to do so.'

'On the contrary, my friend,' Jethro told him solemnly. 'You're in the ideal position to favour me. All you have to do is to keep on using that pick. Your comrades will follow your example and within a very short space of time the ditch will be completed and England will be made safe from invasion.'

The American chuckled and asked. 'Why should I wish to make England safe from invasion, Corporal Limey?'

Before replying, Jethro let his eyes roam over the men standing around the New Englander. One in particular held his gaze. A tall, blond-haired Frenchman with flamboyant mustachios and dark brown eyes suddenly struck a chord in his memory ... 'I wonder if that is the one Sarah told me of,' Jethro thought, then said aloud,

'Because, Yankee Doodle, if England were invaded then the war would stretch on for many years and you would remain a prisoner, perhaps for the rest of your life. So it is to your advantage to keep this country inviolate. Then we English will win the war sooner and you will all be set free to return home.'

'Well, that's a mighty convincing argument, Corporal,' Caldicott grinned, and lifted his pick in readiness to strike. 'I only wish that someone had explained the situation so concisely to me before ... Then I would never have ceased from labour.'

The steel pick spike bit deep into the hard ground and the men recommenced their work.

Henri had caught the speculation in the corporal's eyes when he had stared at him, and he felt a sudden rush of hope. Perhaps the man had been approached by Sarah. The Frenchman's thoughts were bitter as they ranged back over the preceding weeks. The parcel had reached him safely and he had split the contents between his group of would-be escapers. Gaston de Chambray, as the elected leader of the party, had taken the charts and compass. The pistols, balls, and powder had been secreted in a hollow beam. The gold, all in half-sovereigns, had been divided equally and hidden in the securest place the men could find, their own bodies. The coins were put in slender hollow tubes fashioned from bone or wood and smoothed and polished. Each man then inserted his tube into his rectal passage. The discomfort of such a hiding place was considered a small price to pay in return for the absolute security of the money.

It had seemed to Henri that nothing could now prevent their escape. The gallery sentries had been delicately approached and had proved amenable when given gold, with the promise of more to come. All that the plotters had wanted was a stormy moonless night to shield the noise and movement of the breakout. Then, without any prior warning, an extra muster of the upper battery had been called two days before and from the ranks of *les officiers* and *messieurs ou bourgeois* men had been indiscriminately picked out, bundled immediately into lighters and taken ashore. Henri and Nathan had been the only members of the escape group chosen, and had not been able to exchange even a word with the others. Under the watchful eyes of militiamen, prisoners from every one of the hulks had been formed up into a long column and marched to Fort Cumberland. Henri's one hope now was that his comrades still on the *Crown* could get word to Sarah as to what had happened, so that she could re-establish the chain of communications between them and he. But up to this time no message had reached Sarah telling of Henri's transfer.

Satisfied that the prisoners were now working well, Jethro went a little distance along the ditch, then turned to study the blond Frenchman. He had spent long hours of quiet talk with Sarah and during those hours she had told him all that had befallen her, and why she had come to Portsmouth. It was her description of Henri Chanteur that had struck the chord in Jethro's memory; that and the fleeting glimpse he had had of the man in Bishops Castle. Now unable to cast it from his mind he went back and beckoned the man.

'What's your name?' he asked.

Henri was shovelling dirt into a wheelbarrow, one of a long line of barrows that formed a continuous procession along the floor of the ditch. The Frenchman gazed steadily at Jethro and saluted smartly.

'It is Chanteur, Corporal. Lieutenant Henri Chanteur of His Imperial Majesty's Third Chasseurs à Cheval.'

Jethro kept his face impassive, showing no reaction to the knowledge that this was Sarah's one-time lover before him. Instead, he turned and asked the American the same question.

'It's Captain Nathan Caldicott, of the brig *Susanna*.'

The skeletal body stiffened as he executed a grotesque parody of a military salute. 'That's a merchant mariner's salute, Corporal,' he grinned. 'Not so Goddam precise as you soldiers do it maybe, but adequate none the less.'

Jethro smiled at the man, feeling a liking for him. 'You'll not get me to rise to your baiting, Captain Caldicott,' he replied and moved on past them.

'I'll have to get word to Sarah,' he told himself. 'She has a right to know that her French friend is here, and not on the hulks ... Goddam me, if I don't feel jealous,' he suddenly thought. 'Like a bloody silly schoolboy.'

At noon a bugle was blown from the parapet of the fort and all the prisoners downed tools. They were formed into a column, three abreast, then after being counted, were marched back into the fort and halted on the parade ground. Orders were shouted and the front and rear ranks shuffled until a gap of a full five yards or more separated the lines of men.

The senior sergeant of the guards shouted, 'Parade SIT!' and the prisoners squatted or sat where they had stood.

A party of convicts came hurrying from the kitchens, some carrying between them great steaming iron cauldrons, and some with sacks of bread over their shoulders. All the prisoners produced battered metal pannikins from their waist-bags, and each man held his pannikin high above his head. The cauldron parties passed along the ranks of seated and squatting men, and as they passed, two convicts using long-handled ladles splashed a portion of the watery gruel into every pannikin. The sack carriers tossed cobs of bread on to the gravel before each prisoner. The men stayed as they were with the pannikins held high until the entire parade had been served. Only then, and not before, the senior sergeant bellowed,

'Parade EAT!'

Under the muzzles of aimed muskets and cannons turned from the embrasures to cover them, the prisoners took their dinner. Jethro and his squad of guards patrolled up and down the centre rank. He watched with pity the stinking, emaciated, stubble-jawed prisoners wolfing the foul-smelling grey gruel and sour bread, and he knew that he could no longer continue in this type of duty. He walked side by side with his friend Turpin Wright.

'It's no good Turpin,' Jethro told him. 'I can no longer remain here ... I intend to volunteer to the next Quotal.'

The one-time convict regarded the corporal with shrewd eyes. 'That doon't surprise me, cully,' he answered. 'I bin wondering how long you'd be able to stick this bloody work.'

'And you?' Jethro asked. 'Will you remain here?'

Turpin had his arms crossed over each other at his waist to carry his musket in the support position. Now he moved the gun smartly to the shoulder as an elegantly-uniformed officer came strolling along the ranks towards them. They both halted and turned to face the officer. Jethro saluted and turned his head as the man languidly passed so that his eyes were always fixed on him. It was Lieutenant the Hon. John Coventry. He ignored the corporal and Chosen Man, not bothering to return their salute, and kept his gaze fixed on some distant point as if the sight and smell of prisoners and soldiers alike, offended his sensibilities. Once the adjutant had passed the two friends walked on.

'Which regiment will you volunteer to?' Turpin wanted to know.

'Any ... So long as it's in the Peninsula,' Jethro told him. 'For I've a strong wish to see some real fighting men. I'm sick and tired of fireside heroes and blusterers like that fop who's just passed us.'

'Well, I suppose I might as well come wi' you.' Wright showed his brown stubs of teeth in a cheeky grin. 'These poxy barrack-women are not for a lover o' my tender years. I've a fancy for an armful o' black-eyed señoritas.'

Jethro chuckled at his friend's words.

'Caporal Stanton.' The voice sounded from the centre rank. 'Caporal Stanton ... May I request something?'

Jethro saw that it was Henri Chanteur. 'Yes, Lieutenant Chanteur,' he replied. 'You may certainly make your request ... Whether I can grant it remains to be seen.'

'It is a small thing, Caporal. I merely wish permission to go up on to the walls and pick a few sprigs of garlic in order to flavour this bread, so that I cannot taste how bad it is.'

Jethro smiled at the man. It was a common enough request he had made, for on the earth-topped fillings of the bastions and walls of the fort, the wild garlic planted by previous French prisoners flourished thickly.

'Come, Chanteur, I will go with you myself,' he told the Frenchman.

Together they mounted the inclined gunwalk and on to the bastion platform. Then, while Jethro leant against one of the long-snouted thirty-two-pounder guns, the Frenchman scrambled up on to the broad parapet itself and foraged about for the young tender shoots of garlic. Jethro watched the man for a little time, then impelled by an overpowering curiosity, he asked,

'Have you been a prisoner long, Lieutenant Chanteur?'

The Frenchman's white even teeth glistened. 'Over three years now, Caporal. I was wounded and taken at Talavera.'

'I expect you have come to hate England during those years,' Jethro stated.

Chanteur shook his handsome head vigorously. 'Pas du

tout! ... Not at all. On the contrary, England holds for me some of my happiest and most pleasing memories. You see, I was a parolee in the county of Shropshire until only a few weeks since. It was a very happy time for me ...' he smiled reminiscently and touched his fingers to his lips. 'Yes, very happy,' he breathed.

Jethro felt jealousy again twist his innards. Unable to stop himself, he was driven to go on, 'They say that the girls of Shropshire are very accommodating to the French ... Did you find them so?'

He waited the Frenchman's answer, tense and keyed up, not knowing how he would react if the man spoke boastingly of his love affair with Sarah. To his surprise the Frenchman's eyes were sad, as he shrugged silently and expressively. Jealousy was now a hot torment in Jethro's brain and he could not bear to leave the subject, but must prod and poke at it, as a child worries an open sore.

'Did you find the Shropshire women to be easy to conquer?' he persisted.

Henri Chanteur, when he finally answered, appeared to be talking to himself, as he toyed with the sprigs of wild garlic.

'Easy to conquer? Of that I can say nothing ... Perhaps there are some parolees who would regard an Englishwoman as an object to be conquered. I cannot feel this way. I know only that for me there is one Englishwoman for whom I have a deep and abiding love. If there can be a conqueror in the emotion of love, then it was she who conquered me ... My only regret is that she would not take me for husband.' He shrugged again and looked directly at Jethro. 'I wonder if you know what it is, Caporal Stanton, to be in love with a woman who wants you only for a friend.' He uttered the last words in tones of such sadness that Jethro's jealousy died within him.

'Goddam me! But the Frenchie really loved Sarah,' he thought, with something akin to pity in his heart. 'And he still feels her loss badly, by the look of him.'

Jethro experienced a sudden liking for the other man, and admiration for his gentlemanly honesty, knowing how many men would have hit back at a woman who had rejected them by telling lies to blacken her character.

'Come,' he said aloud. 'We must return or the dinner period will be gone and you'll not have time to eat your bread and garlic.'

'*Bon!*' Chanteur pushed the plants into his waist-bag and the pair returned to the parade ground.

The guards went a few at a time to their barrackrooms to eat their beef and bread and before Jethro had finished his, the prisoners had gone back to work. While he made his way along the ditch to rejoin his section, Jethro turned over in his mind what Sarah had told him of her attempts to ensure Henri's escape.

'What would I do if she were to ask me to help the Frenchie get away?' he asked himself. 'I don't really know,' was the answer he arrived at. 'After all the man, pleasant and likeable fellow though he may be, is still an enemy soldier. If he returned to France he would undoubtedly go back to the Eagles, and then might well end up in Spain, fighting against our troops there. If I helped him escape, it is not beyond the bounds of probability that he could even kill me in battle ... And yet it grieves me to know that someone whom Sarah holds dear should be rotting alive here.'

Later that same afternoon something occurred that would help when the time came to resolve his quandary. Jethro was standing opposite a party of prisoners who were sweating and straining to manhandle slabs of roughly dressed rock into position as a lining for the inner face of the ditch. Henri Chanteur was one of the party. A cart piled high with stone slabs and dragged by a pair of lather-streaked oxen came lurching and creaking along the top of the ditch. Directly above the spot where Jethro stood talking to the sentinel, the cartwheels skidded perilously close to the edge. The driver cursed loudly and stabbed viciously into the beasts' rumps with his goad. They jerked clumsily away from the edge and the cart yawed violently and swung. The sudden change in direction caused the pile of slabs to shift. Henri Chanteur glanced up and saw the danger that Jethro Stanton and the sentinel were in.

'Jump, Stanton! Jump!' the Frenchman shouted urgently, as the slabs on the cart above the corporal's head started to slide. Jethro heard the shout and reacted instinctively, pulling the sentry with him as he moved.

There came a loud scraping of rough stone and the top of the load toppled down into the ditch, crashing on to the spot where Jethro had been standing only a split-second before. The dust and chips of the rocks flew like shards of shrapnel and a small jagged piece tore the flesh below Henri's left eye causing blood to trickle.

Jethro went to the man. 'Are you hurt, Lieutenant Chanteur?'

'*Non, merci,*' the Frenchman answered quietly, '*C' est rien* ... It's nothing!'

Jethro looked into the brown eyes of the other for long moments, then said quietly, 'That is a life I owe you. I hope that someday I will be able to repay that debt.'

Later, when they had finished work and were sitting on the floor of their casemate prison, searching for the lice that abounded on their bodies and in the rags that covered them, Nathan Caldicott asked Henri,

'Tell me Henry, what in all the name of Heaven, made you warn them goddam Limeys?'

The Frenchman shrugged. 'The corporal is a man, is he not? And a good one, I think.'

The American chuckled grimly. 'In here there are no good or bad men, Henry. Only the quick and the dead ...'

CHAPTER TWENTY-EIGHT

All that day the stump of Major Harry King's missing arm had been tormenting him. The pain had started as a dull ache and steadily worsened as the hours passed until it became a constant pulsing throb of agony. To deaden that agony, the major had begun to drink neat rum early in the afternoon, and by the time the convicts of the *Fortune* and *Ceres* had completed their day's labour at Fort Cumberland and were being ferried back to the hulks on the broad-beamed, flat-bottomed lighters, the major was well drunk. He staggered up the ladder and on to the quarter-deck when the noise and bustle of the ship's garrison told him that the convicts were coming back aboard the *Fortune*. The major steadied himself by holding on to the taffrail with his single hand, and stared, bleary-eyed at the scene below him.

The hulk's garrison were all militiamen now, except for half a dozen invalided sailors from the Channel Fleet. The marines had been drafted to the American war, and to Harry King's bitter chagrin he had been left behind as hulk commander. The major did not have a very high regard for the militia, or any other type of soldier, come to that. The only men he considered to be worth their salt were his own beloved Corps of Royal Marines. Some sailors, he admitted, were brave enough dogs in battle. But in his opinion they lacked the loyalty and steadfast discipline of the marines. Therefore, when the militia sergeant came to report that there was some illness amongst the prisoners which the sergeant considered warranted the attentions of a surgeon, the major sneered at the man.

'Is that what you think, sergeant?' He belched loudly and swayed. 'Then pray tell me how can a Johnny Raw from some militia regiment of clod-hopping yokels know when a surgeon is required?'

'If you please, sir,' Sergeant Blenkinsop was not the

311

brightest of men, but he had a retentive memory, and as a parish constable some years before he had encountered this type of sickness. 'If you please, sir. There be four men took badly from Winchester gaol larst Monday.'

'So?' The major glared at the beefy-faced sergeant. The man plodded on doggedly. 'I rackon they'se got the gaol-fever on 'um, sir. And that being the case, then a surgeon's needed badly, or we'em all likely to catch it.'

'Jail-fever! God rot me, Sergeant! You sound like an old woman, frightened of shadows. It's probably something they ate that's upset them. Where are they?'

'I'se had 'um carried down to the upper battery, sir.'

Major King drew himself uncertainly erect. 'I'll come myself and look at them.'

In the fetid stench-filled gloom of the upper battery, the four sick men were lying side by side on the bare boards. King went to stand over them, swaying and hicupping.

The orange-yellow rags, the shaven heads and the filth-grimed skins gave the men a remarkable similarity of appearance so that they could have been facsimiles of each other.

King pointed at the nearest. 'What ails you, man?' he growled.

The skull-like head shifted on the greasy planking and the deep-sunk eyes were badly bloodshot, while his body heat was a tangible aura. 'If it please, yer honour ... I feel as if me 'ead's breaking and I'm burnin' up, and me guts is tearing at me summat chronic,' he croaked through cracked dry lips.

The man next to him groaned loudly and his legs jerked. He broke wind audibly and a stain of dark liquid oozed from under his hips. The vileness of the released smell overlaid even the thick foulness of the odours already present.

'God rot me! The dirty bugger's mucked himself!' the major cursed. 'It's the flux, these buggers ha' got, Sar'nt. Nothing more and nothing less. Give them a purge, man. That'll clear the badness from their systems. They've been eating rats again without a doubt, and naturally they've got a dose o' the flux ... Serve 'um right!'

He used his toe to prod the nearest man's verminous body. 'You'll be given a purge, my man ... And tomorrow you'll go to your work, or I'll know the reason why.' He bent to the convict and tore the rags from his bony chest. 'D'you hear me, man ... I'll know the reason why.' Then, swaying wildly,

312

he left the battery.

The militia sergeant also bent over the sick man, to look carefully at the flesh of stomach and chest. There was a rash of small red pustules covering both. He straightened and hurried after King.

'Please, sir.'

King swung to face him, a dull flush darkening neck and face and demanded angrily, 'What is it now, man?'

The sergeant hesitated, fearful of the major's choleric temper, then swallowed hard and said,

'The flux you say these men ha' got, sir ... Only one on 'um has it ... The others ha' got the gaol fever. I'se sin it afore, sir. Back home in Worcester ... I'se sin it at the lock-up there.'

The major's mouth gaped wide as he roared at the man. 'I've told you what the trouble is with those men ... Now if you pester me any further I'll ha' you triced up and flogged ... Understand?'

The sergeant blenched and saluted.

Harry King stared hard at the N.C.O., then waved him away. The stump of his arm still throbbed dreadfully and he returned to his cabin to drink more rum. It was an hour or two later when, lying fully clothed in his box hammock, he felt the first itch of insects on his groin.

He grumbled and scratched the spot through the thick white kersey of his breeches. 'Goddam these bloody convicts,' he muttered aloud. 'I've picked up a damn flea from one of the filthy buggers.'

He drifted into a drunken doze and some hours later woke to the sounds of the sentries clumping round and round the gallery catwalk, and the echoing shouts of 'All's well ... All's well ... All's well ...'

His groin itched intolerably in half a score of places.

'Goddammit, I've picked up an army of fleas,' he groaned miserably, fumbling with the laced codpiece of his breeches. Opening it he slipped his hand inside and rucked at his hairy groin with blunt, thick fingers. One stained fingernail trapped and crushed one of the tiny pale lice that had itched him. It was one of several that had found their way on to his uniform while he had been examining the sick men in the upper battery. The louse died instantly but the Rickettsia germs of typhus that it and its companions carried had already passed through the scratched skin and were beginning to multiply in

313

Jethro had decided not to burden Sarah with the knowledge that the man she had wished to help was still a prisoner. His present unease, as he now walked up and down the top of the ditch where the prisoners were labouring, was caused by his sense of being obligated to Henri Chanteur. The Frenchman had not himself referred to his saving of Jethro from the rock fall, and paradoxically it was this very failure to remind Jethro of it that heightened the young corporal's consciousness of the debt he owed Chanteur. But how to repay that debt was the problem.

'Corporal Stanton! Corporal Stanton!' one of the sentries farther along the ditch shouted and beckoned.

When Jethro reached him, the man pointed. 'Look there, corporal. There's another on 'um just fell down.'

A convict was lying on the ground, jerking spasmodically and groaning.

'Goddam it!' Jethro cursed softly and slid down the banked sandy incline to cross to the man. Nathan Caldicott was there before him and he looked up at Jethro.

'It's another o' them from the *Fortune* hulk, Corporal,' he said solemnly. 'I reckon that it's the fever they got ... Why there's been near a score o' the poor critters just up and fell down real sick in the last day or so.'

The young corporal knelt by the fallen convict, whose frightened eyes gazed beseechingly at him.

'Try and tell me where the pain is?' Jethro ordered gently. The man's body abruptly stiffened and the cords of tendons stood out from his thin unshaven throat. The spasm passed as abruptly as it had begun and the man gasped ...

'I'm boilin' hot, bleedin' boilin' and me head's burstin', Corporal ... It warn't too bad when I was roused this mornin', but now it's like some bleeder is astickin' knives all over me ... Aggghhh, God save me, it's bleedin' killin' me!' He clenched his fists, driving his long gnarled black fingernails deep into his leathery palms. Blood spurted from his lips where his teeth had bitten, as he writhed in agony once more.

Nathan Caldicott went on to his knees facing Jethro across the stricken man. He used both hands to lift the jacket away from the twisting body. 'Lookee here, Corporal.'

Jethro looked and saw under the grey mat of chest hair a

314

rash of angry crimson points.

'Goddam you, you little bastard!' the American swore and brushed away a minute pale speck from the back of one hand. 'Goddam lice!' he spat out. 'These men from the *Fortune* and *Ceres* both, are eaten alive with the blamed pests.'

Shaking his head, Jethro rose to his feet. 'It's the gaol fever right enough,' he murmured, and prayed silently ... 'God above, help us all.'

Major Harry King tossed and turned in his high-sided box hammock, the sweat of his body glimmering in the light of the oil lamp slung above him, and raved deliriously.

'Stand ready, blast you! Sergeant Ryder, cover that gun-port the Frogs will be jumpin' through the damned thing in a minute! Avast there, you lubberly swabs ... Hold hard, I say! Hold hard! Curse your thick wooden heads ... Uggghhhh? Uggghhhh! Aggghhh!'

His bare feet beat a bruising furious tattoo on the wooden hammock panels and his body arched upwards, as if to throw off the pain that was assaulting him so mercilessly, devouring even the hallucinated images of his mindless delirium.

Matthew Purpost, surgeon of the Third Worcestershire Militia, rested his hand on the burning skin of the sick man's forehead and pulled a long face.

'There's nothing to be done, I'm afraid.' He indicated the fiery rash on abdomen and chest. 'It's the gaol fever.'

'I feared as much when Blenkinsop reported to me,' Captain Joseph Ward murmured. He was standing by the surgeon's side, his head bent under the low deck-head.

'God blast the man!' the surgeon suddenly exploded. 'Why was I not informed of this before? Why did Blenkinsop only come to you today, Joseph?'

The captain placed his hand on his companion's shoulder.

'Because Major King, here, considered the sickness afflicting some of the prisoners to be a mild dose of the flux, or just self-induced illness to avoid working on the fort. Why, he threatened to have Blenkinsop flogged if he persisted in saying that it was not the flux, but the fever.'

The surgeon tossed his head in anger. 'Then dying though he may be, I can feel no pity for this block-headed fool,' he said grimly. 'For the fever will by now have been spread to God knows how many others, and all this incense,' he pointed to a small portable brazier whose burning coals had been smothered in herbs to give off pungent-smelling fumes, 'all that damned stinking smoke that we shall be producing on these hulks and in the casemate cells will not save a single one of the poor devils who have been infected.' His eyes were tragic as he stared at Joseph Ward. 'There are times, Joseph, when I could curse myself and my entire profession for our helplessness, and sheer bloody ignorance when we face this type of fever.'

'But what can anyone expect you to do, either to prevent these outbreaks or to cure them?' the captain said sympathetically. 'Men can do nothing against the invisible humours and miasmas in the atmosphere.'

Purpost clucked his tongue against his teeth. 'Tst! Tst! Humours? Miasmas? ... Cannot you see that these are only the excuses we medical men use to cover up our lack of knowledge,' he said forcefully. 'And because of that lack of knowledge, thousands die miserably, as this one here will die ...' Muttering to himself in disgust, Purpost took a scalpel from his box of instruments and lifted King's arm from the hammock. 'Sentry?' he bellowed.

'Sir.' A grizzled old militiaman stamped into the cabin.

'Come here and hold this bowl close up under the Major's arm for me, will you.' The surgeon touched with his toe a crock bowl on the floor beside his instrument box. Then he spoke to Joseph Ward. 'Here I go once more, Captain, undoubtedly doing the wrong thing by bleeding the poor devil.' He paused and pulled a wry grimace. 'But then, that's the only sovereign remedy I was ever taught, and all the most learned doctors swear to its efficacy, do they not?'

Without listening for any reply, he took a firm grip of the major's twitching forearm and cut a neat incision in one of the ropy veins. The black blood ran over the white skin and fell splashing into the shiny bowl beneath ...

Through the days and nights that followed, Matthew Purpost and his mates bled and purged, and blistered and cupped. They dosed with laudanum and mercury and syrup of angelica. Applied plasters of mustard, linseed meal and dried violets. Pungent fumes poured from a score of braziers on the 'tween decks of the *Fortune* and *Ceres* and such quantities of smoke billowed from the gunports that at times the hulks appeared to be ablaze from stem to stern, But still the epidemic took its toll. Convicts and their guards alike fell ill with headaches and high fevers. Their chests and stomachs developed the fiery red rashes and their bodies were racked with agonies. Delirium set in and they raved and cursed imagined foes, cowered from nightmarish hallucinations, and spoke tenderly to non-existent lovers. The delirium was superseded by a mental and physical torpor and then the tormented flesh chilled, and kindly death released them frcm their purgatories. Purpost worked as if he had the strength of ten men. Driving himself relentlessly on until his exhausted body failed him, he would slump down in a corner and sleep for brief hours, which on awaking he sorely grudged.

Major Caldwell and Captain Ward did everything they could to aid Purpost in his fight against the disease. They turned the *Fortune* and the *Ceres* into isolation hospitals and forbade any direct contact between them and the fort. Supplies would be placed on the spit of land that curled out into Langstone Harbour and left there for the boats to fetch. If any man, woman or child in the fort showed symptoms of illness, then they were immediately carried out on to the spit to await the hulks' boats. Armed sentries patrolled the beaches constantly by day and ensured that this *cordon sanitaire* was not breached. By night all traffic from hulks to shore was stopped. The only action left now was for men to pray.

CHAPTER TWENTY-NINE

It wanted an hour to tattoo on a bleak day at the end of March when the small son of one of the veterans came to the casemate barrackroom to tell Jethro that he was wanted at the Land Gate guardroom. The day's duties had only finished a few minutes previously and he had just changed into his white canvas fatigue rig to begin the interminable pipe-claying and black-balling of his accoutrements. The casemate was full of men busily engaged on the same task, some sitting on their beds, others at the tables that ran down the centre of the room. The low hum of conversation and laughter, the cheerful crackling of the driftwood fire in the grate, the profligate glow of many candles, for today had been the weekly ration issue, gave to the white-washed casemate a cosily domestic air.

Jethro rose from his corner bed which, now he was a corporal was his alone, and, putting on his forage cap, followed the boy. Turpin Wright looked up at him as he passed. He nudged his bedmate, a lanky lugubrious-faced Scotsman, and started to sing softly.

'On the banks o' the roses me love and I sat down ...
And I pulled out me German flute to play me love a
    tune ...'

He paused and grinned. 'I could guess what sort o' tune you'll be playing on your flute in a few minutes, Corporal Stanton.' And smacked his lips salaciously.

'Just get on with your cleaning, Chosen Man Wright, or you'll not have to guess what the inside of the Black Hole looks like,' Jethro threatened jokingly. His heavy boots crunched the gravel outside the casemate and he paused momentarily to clear his head of the barrack fug. His heart was light when he thought that the message might be from

Sarah.

'Goddam me! I've not felt this way about a woman since Abi.' His face clouded as the last name flashed through his mind. Lovely Abi ... Abigail Bartleet ... a woman of the gentry that he had loved and lost in Redditch town, it seemed centuries ago.

Dismissing the painful memory, he went on to the Land Gate. The veterans were providing the guard and their sergeant, a young one-armed ex-hussar asked, 'Be you Corporal Stanton?'

Jethro nodded. 'Yes Sar'nt.'

'Theer's a young 'ooman wants to see yer. Her's over theer in that coach.'

The coach was standing some twenty-five yards from the gate, a single-horsed, canvas-topped carriage, whose ancient driver was slumped dozing in his seat. Jethro thanked the veteran and ran across the intervening distance. Sarah was waiting for him inside its dark interior. They kissed long and hard. Then he gently held her away so that he might enjoy the sight of her glossy chestnut hair and green eyes set off to perfection by the white carriage costume and feathered poke bonnet she wore.

Ever since the day they had met each other again, they had seen each other at every opportunity. At the week-ends when Jethro received a few precious hours of liberty they had spent those hours together in a quiet country inn near Hilsea, and when she could, Sarah had slipped away from The Golden Venture to come here to Fort Cumberland on the chance of snatching a few minutes with Jethro.

'You should not come here at this time,' he told her with concern. 'There is fever on the hulks out there.'

She smiled lovingly at him. 'Is there fever in the fort?' she asked.

'No, but it's still ...' He began to speak and she stopped his words with a kiss.

'Then the risk is well worth the taking,' she whispered, as the kiss ended.

'Is there any news yet?' he asked expectantly.

Her face saddened. 'It's bad, Jethro. I've been to see your colonel. He listened most sympathetically to what I had to say ...'

'He would,' Jethro interjected forcefully. Lieutenant-Colonel the Viscount Deerhurst was always prepared to listen

319

sympathetically to a beautiful woman.

Sarah continued. 'But he said there was nothing to be done, and your discharge could not be purchased. You are in the militia and must stay in it until the Army of the Reserve is no longer needed and can be disbanded.'

His face was grim. He looked down at their clasped hands and went on, 'It's not the army I hate, Sarah. It's this damn business of guarding convicts and prisoners-of-war. I've no wish to be a turnkey. I detest having to drive men to labour and to stand over them as if they were only dumb beasts. That is not my idea of soldiering. I have been thinking of transferring to the regulars.'

'Can you do so?' she asked.

He nodded. 'Yes, there is something called a Quota Act which requires the militia to furnish replacements for the regular battalions.'

Sarah's hands freed themselves and stroked his hair nervously. 'Tell me truthfully, Jethro, do you intend to transfer?'

'It is in my mind to do so,' he told her seriously.

'But why do you wish to go to the wars?' she demanded uncomprehendingly. 'You could be killed! Or maimed like one of those poor fellows there.' She jerked her shapely chin in the direction of the veteran gate sentinels.

He smiled at her and touched his lips briefly to hers before replying. 'It's difficult to explain, Sarah. I'm not a man who believes that the King and his Ministers should be fought for or defended. We live in a cruel and corrupt country, where justice is something that only the rich and powerful can buy. To be truthful, I could find more reasons to fight against the throne of England and its adherents, than to fight for it. But still, I am an Englishman born and this, with all its dreadful faults, is still my nation. I've no wish to see a foreign Emperor ruling over us. The foreign king we have is bad enough,' he said vehemently. Then he drew a long breath and said reflectively, 'I think though that my main reason is that here in the militia we are only pretending to be soldiers. The opinion I hold of most of the officers and men in this battalion is a low one. Yet in the ranks of those veterans, there are officers and men for whom I hold a sincere respect. They laugh at we fellows when we strut about rattling our muskets and sabres in sham battles on our field days; and I do not resent their mocking us. Because they know what real soldiering is. Battle, death and suffering have been intimate companions to them. They have experienced events that I feel I must experience also.'

A sudden premonition that she might lose him made Sarah speak out angrily. 'It's your own foolish vanity that causes you to think that. You sound like some silly addle-pated boy, when you say such things.'

He smiled gently and shook his head. 'No, Sarah, in all honesty I do not think it to be my vanity that drives me in this matter ... Rather it is my self-respect.'

'And me?' she cried out. 'What of me, if you go to the wars? I thought that you had some tenderness of feeling for me, as I have for you.'

Jethro again kissed her mouth. 'It may be that I am growing to love you, Sarah ... But the sum total of a man is not to be found in his love for woman. He must firstly know and respect himself, and he can only achieve that by putting himself to the test in many different ways.' He looked searchingly at her and asked gently, 'If I should go away, will you wait for me to return?'

Her face set in stubborn lines and she would not meet his eyes or answer him. The hollow thump of a cannon shot sounded in the distance.

'Dammit! That's the evening gun. I'll have to go back into the fort,' Jethro told her, and touched her averted cheek. 'We'll talk of this again, love. Take care on your return journey.'

Still sulking, she would not reply. Jethro jumped from the carriage and headed back to the Land Gate. 'She'll recover her good humour in a couple of days,' he smiled to himself. 'How like a child she is at times ... But then, are not we all—'

Sarah entered The Golden Venture through her private entrance and went up the stairs to the first floor. She walked along the passageway that led to the salon. Her partner was standing behind the bead curtain that covered the narrow-arched doorway.

'So there you are, Sarah. I vas vondering when you might get around to doing some vork here.' Shimson Levi's protuberant dark eyes were as resentful as the tone in which he greeted her.

'Look!' He waved a bejewelled hand, pushing aside the strings of the bead curtain to point into the salon. The room was thronged with sunburned naval and marine officers, and prosperous-looking sharp-eyed civilians. 'The busiest night ve have had for veeks and you vere novhere to be found.'

Sarah, having only parted a short while before from Jethro, and with anxiety about his possible transfer gnawing at her, tried her best to appear apologetic.

'I'm sorry Shim. I didn't expect this trade. Where have they all sprung from?'

'The *Aurolia*,' the Hebrew told her. 'She's in from the West Indies with two American merchantmen she took as prizes. They held rich cargoes. That's vhy all these flash covers are down here, there's good profits to be made for those who can find the rhino to bid at the auction. The officers have got an advance on the prize money I shouldn't vonder. That's vhy they're all here to make their fortunes.'

Sarah nodded and let her gaze rove. The room was brilliantly lit by four great hanging chandeliers, each holding a mass of tall oil-lamps, burning yellow-flamed and giving off a pleasant smell from the scented oils they were filled with.

'Are there any of the high flyers here yet?' she asked.

Levi shook his head. 'It's a trifle early for them. But they'll come, never fear. The governor and his hangers-on vill surely be along to try and get a share of all this money.'

Sarah continued to stare at the crowd. A great oblong table six yards long and two and a half yards broad used for the game of Rouge-et-Noir dominated the centre of the room. Around it were scattered other smaller tables for dice, French hazard, whist and a dozen other games of chance. Each table was presided over by a dealer, either a priest or priestess. The priests dressed well and sombrely in black with white linen. The priestesses wore scarlet gowns, but cut low to display their powdered shoulders and breasts. The gamblers were seated around the green baize-covered table, the colours of the military and naval uniforms outshone by the brilliant hues of the Corinthians and their women, while the graceful effeminate gestures and languid glances of a bevy of painted and powdered, scented and patched young creatures, whose sex was uncertain, outdid the most delicate moues and coy simpers of the fan-waving beauties who hung on the arms of their beaux or flirted with the hungry-eyed men.

White-aproned waiters hurried from group to group, and table to table, holding trays of bottles, glasses, lobsters, crabs, oysters and every conceivable variety of sweetmeat high above their heads. The perspiration caused by the thick heated air showed in great spreading patches on the waiters' shirts and their cravats were sodden folds of cloth. At the end of the room an elegant screen of lacquered willowwork formed a separate section for the Roly-Poly table, or as the French termed the newly introduced game, La Roulette.

For all the numbers of people present the noise was curiously muted, only the occasional loud uttered oath at bad luck, or cry of pleasure at a winning hand breaking the low-pitched murmurous speech of the players and spectators.

'I see Molly Bawn is not here,' Sarah stated. 'It's becoming a matter of some concern to me ... She's not been seen for over two weeks now.'

'The disappearance of a bloody doxy is of no concern to me,' Shimson snapped gruffly. 'It's your frequent absences that are my concern.'

Sarah stopped trying to apologize. 'I can come and go as I please,' she said frostily. 'I'm equal partners with you in this club, Shimson. You have no right to dictate my mode of life.'

'I thought that when we opened the club, ve vould be more than just business partners,' he muttered sullenly. 'At least, that is vhat you led me to believe.'

Not for the first time in her life Sarah inwardly cursed the fact that a great many men desired her. 'You chose to believe what your fancies dictated,' her voice was adamant. 'I have never given you cause to think that I wanted to, or would share your bed.'

The Hebrew's tone became placatory. 'It could be an honourable bed, Sarah. I will marry you, if that is what you want.'

'Oh Shim!' She shook her head wearily. 'I do like you a great deal, but as a friend ... Not as a lover.' She placed her gloved hand on his arm. 'Let us not haggle any more. We seem to do naught else these days and now that your uncle and Portugal John have gone back to London, we need to work closely togeth ... Oh my God!' Her exclamation was given added intensity by the force with which her fingers suddenly dug deep into his arm.

'Vot is it, Sarah?'

'Over there,' she said faintly, and her face was pale. 'In the main doorway.'

His black eyes scanned the spot she indicated.

'Vell, vell ... the return of the Prodigal Daughter. She looks ill, don't she?'

Molly Bawn had come into the room. The weeks of absence could have been years, so greatly had she altered. She was dressed once more in the bedraggled body-displaying finery of a street prostitute. Her hair was piled high under a garish plumed turban and the heavily rouged and painted face beneath could have been that of a doll, so devoid was it of all the animated spirit and gaiety that had been her most noticeable attribute. By her side was William Seymour, clad in bottle-green coat and white pantaloons. Immaculately groomed and barbered, and in glaring contrast to the woman, his features glowed with health and vitality, while his whole being radiated an air of barely suppressed glee.

The couple were closely followed by another man. A very tall, very fat man dressed in the latest high-ton of fashionable pastel-coloured dress-coat and breeches with dainty satin dancing pumps on his incongruously tiny feet. His thick silver-bleached hair was trimmed in the Brutus mode, and he haughtily surveyed the room through gold-handled quizzing glasses. The great moon of a face under the frame of silver hair was rouged and powdered and even his pudgy hands had their palms tinted with vermilion and the backs whitened with enamel. His bizarre appearance was heightened by the unmistakable wasp waist effect of an Apollo corset.

Shimson Levi's brow furrowed and he beckoned to a passing waiter. 'Go to Andrew and ask him if he can put a name to the big cove who's just come in.'

The man hurried to the dice table where the London-imported head priest was presiding. The priest stared at the fat man while the waiter whispered in his ear then handed the dice to another croupier and sidled across to Shimson.

'I fear we've got trouble here, Master Shimson,' the man said urgently. 'That fat cove who's new come is Mother Bunch. He's one o' the flyest sharps in the whole o' London. He's probably brought a few pigeons wi' him. Yes, I thought so ...'

A party of young bucks, half-drunk and in high spirits came into the room to cluster about the man known as Mother Bunch.

'He'll not be here long enough to finish plucking his pigeons,' Levi growled, and moved forwards but halfway through the curtains the priest prevented him.

'Hold hard, Master Levi. I knows that fat cove of old. He'll no ha' come alone ... There 'ull be one or two bruisers wi' him to take care of any flat who might take objection to being fleeced by Mother Bunch.'

Levi hesitated and turned the problem in his agile brain. There were no strongarm men employed as bullies at the club. Levi himself was a handy man with his fists and was quite capable of dealing with any troublemaker or obstreperous drunk. But this was a lot more difficult to handle. A notorious sharp in company with a group of young bloods, who would regard the man as a dear friend and who would undoubtedly turn on anyone who challenged him, not to mention the possibility of a couple of professional bullies employed as bodyguards.

Sarah had drawn farther back behind the curtains at the sight of Molly Bawn and Seymour. Unable to take her eyes from them, she had only half-heard the conversation between the two men. Now she saw Seymour turn briefly and nod to the big fat man behind him.

The fat man returned the nod, and then in a fluting, lisping voice herded his pigeons across to the table where rouge-et-noir was being played.

'Come my chickth ... come my heartth delightth ... Your thaintly Mother Hen will thow you how to lothe all your ill-gotten gainth.'

'Shim!' Sarah tugged at the Hebrew's coat. 'What you were just talking about ... the bullies, I mean. I think that man with Molly is one of them.'

Levi gazed hard at Seymour and observed, 'There's a dangerous look about the cove, that's for sure ... Do you know him, Andrew?'

The priest shook his head.

'Very well.' Levi came to a decision. 'Sarah, you stay here and watch for anything else that might mean trouble. Andrew, you and me vill take the deals at rouge-et-noir. That way ve can be sure that if there's any cribbin', it'll not have come from us, and ve can act accordingly ...'

Some of the other club servants and dealers had by this time seen Molly and her companion, but they only winked and smiled knowingly at each other. If Molly had got herself a rich fancy-man, then good luck to the wench. Only two of the priestesses, wise in the ways of men with bought women, recognized the deadness in Molly's eyes for what it was. The hopelessness of utter misery and despair.

'More fool her,' the one girl muttered to her friend. 'You'd ha' thought she'd ha' learned by now what a load o' pigs men are.'

Her friend slipped her arm about the slim waist next to her in a fond caress.

William Seymour was deeply happy. He had spent his time first in London, where he had disposed of the stolen bank-notes and jewellery for a very good sum, then back here in Portsmouth, making careful and detailed plans with his old acquaintance, Mother Bunch. The fat man's demands had taken nearly all Seymour's new found wealth, but he thought it well worth the price. Molly had been an added inducement for Mother Bunch to join with Seymour. The fat man had very peculiar sexual requirements. Requirements of such a nature, that after one experience of them it was almost impossible for Mother Bunch to persuade any woman to meet them again. Seymour had needed Molly to cater to the fat man's needs. At first her gutter temper had caused her to rebel furiously, but Seymour knew only too well how to break the most turbulent spirit and, in only days in a filthy cellar in the Seven Dials, had reduced Molly Bawn to a cowed, subservient slave. Seymour glanced at the girl distastefully.

'I couldn't bear to touch her again, after what she and Mother Bunch have been doing together,' he thought, then smiled to himself. 'Thank God, that after tonight I'll not need her any more.'

The only thing that marred his pleasure at this moment was that he could not see Sarah Jenkins in the room. He wanted her to be there, so that at the end of the night she would know who had been responsible for her ruin. There came another flurry of movement, loud voices, and laughter at the doorway as the General the Earl of Harcourt made his robust and genial entrance.

Seymour's thin lips curved in a smile. 'Perfect!' he thought. 'That's another factor of the plan fulfilled. The rest will be easy.'

By this time, Shimson Levi and his head dealer Andrew, had taken the dealers' chairs facing each other across the great oblong rouge-et-noir table. Lord Harcourt lowered his plump hips into a seat to the left side of Shimson, while Mother Bunch, with a couple of his pigeons was almost opposite the earl. The table could accommodate a score of players and each seat was taken with spectators crowding at the chair backs, eager to fill any vacated place. There was an atmosphere of expectant excitement charging the air. Everyone knew that with the fresh prize money about, the stakes would run high and heavy. The game itself was basically simple, and Shimson thought it to be the most satisfactory possible from the club's point of view. The odds in the bank's favour were two and a half percent, even without the priests cheating the flats.

Shimson's mercenary heart gloried in it. With three six-pack deals taking place every hour and the game continuing for perhaps eight hours a night, the profits were of a comforting steadiness for the club.

Andrew took and shuffled the six new packs of cards and invited a further shuffle. The governor, mellow with good wine, accepted. The players backed their fancies and the game began.

Shimson toyed idly with the pile of gold and banknotes that both he and his head priest had in front of them and watched Mother Bunch closely. The fat man appeared unconscious of the attention he was getting from Levi. He laughed and joked in his lisping voice and placed smallish bets. Losing a little, winning a little. The long flexible fingers of Andrew riffled and shuffled and flicked the cards over on to the green cloth. An ace, an eight, a ten, a five, a queen, total thirty-four...

'Four!' Andrew called loudly, and dealt the second row. Knave, ten, queen, two, total thirty-two. 'Two, red wins!' His voice sounded out and in concert with Shimson, he used his wooden hoe-shaped rake to draw in the losers' stakes and push gold and banknotes to the winners. The green of the cloth, the clicking of the cards, the rustle of white banknotes, the heavy chink of golden guineas, the slithering of rakes, the minute scintillating flashes from jewelled rings on smooth hands ... the shimmering, blurring, ever-shifting blues, creams, scarlets, lavenders, yellows, purples, magentas, cerises and silver of buckles, buttons, braids, coats, jewels, gowns, fans ... the scents of perfumes, pomades, snuffs, tobaccos, wines, brandies, took soothing effect on Shimson's senses and calmed and lulled the shivers of dangers invoked by Mother Bunch's presence.

'One apres. Will you halve your stakes, gentlemen?' 'Six, red wins!' 'Three, red loses!' 'Two, red wins!' 'Eight, red wins!' 'Six, red loses!' 'Four, red wins!' 'Will any gentleman shuffle?' 'Eight ... nine, red loses!' 'Damn my luck!' 'That's the card, sir.' 'Blast it!' 'God rot me!' 'Oh, you little beauty you!' The muted murmurs and whispers of the players was a constant susurration over the table. 'Five ... two, red wins! Seven ... nine, red loses!'

The piles of banknotes and gold before the dealers began to increase perceptibly as the hours wore on. Gamblers lost their all and left the table ... Others took their places. Voices grew hushed and hoarse, and stakes grew bigger as those who won gained confidence in their luck. Then, for the first time Mother Bunch took the offered shuffle. Shimson's eyes gave bleak warning to the great rouged, decadent Roman Emperor's face, now overlaid with a sheen of sweat. Mother Bunch's tiny rosebud of purple-painted mouth moued at the Hebrew.

'Heaventh! What mutht you think of me, thir? Thtaring at me in thuch a thearching manner?'

The table tittered at the words and Shimson felt momentarily outfaced.

'Forgive me, sir,' he replied. 'I was sure for a moment that ve had met before ... In London, perhaps?'

'Heaventh! That think of iniquity ... That Thodom and Gomorrah!' The fat man rolled his kohled eyes in flirtatious roguishness. 'Let me athure you, thir, that if I had met thuch a handthome devil ath you, ethpethially in London, then athuredly you would remember me perfectly.'

The table exploded with laughter and Shimson forced himself to share in this joke at his expense. The forced smile died on his lips when in the next series of coups that comprised the full six-pack deal, Mother Bunch suddenly upped his stakes and ended by winning about five hundred guineas, an amount that equalled a week's good gross takings at the club. Shimson's thoughts raced. He had watched the shuffle closely and had not taken his eyes from the fat man while he played. Shimson was sure that the sharp had not switched any cards or been able to cheat in any other way. He glanced at Andrew who slightly narrowed his eyes to negate any idea that the fat man had cheated them. The deal finished and the cards were taken by Andrew.

Mother Bunch smiled archly. 'Yeth, itth your turn now, you thauthy fellow,' he simpered. 'Itth going to be a thuccethful night for me, I'm thure . . . Itth a pity that you're thuch a thad-looking dog. Or perhapth I might have been interethted in a thport with thome profit for yourthelf in it.'

Once more the table roared with laughter and the Governor's pot belly shook as he slapped his plump thighs and bellowed, ''Pon my soul, sir! But you're a droll, waggish fellow. I'll be damned, if you ain't!'

During Andrew's three deals, Mother Bunch accepted the shuffle four times. The crowd switched their play to follow the fat man's luck and twice Shimson was obliged to have more money brought to the table to pay the winning wagers. He found himself becoming worried, at this rate he could be a pauper by morning; and yet he could not catch the fat man cheating. It seemed to be one of those legendary, nightmarish runs of luck that the owners of gambling hells spoke of in hushed, mournful whispers. As Andrew reached the end of his deals and handed the cards to him, Shimson glanced at a man across the table to his right who had slipped into a vacated seat. His eyes met those of William Seymour. Shimson could not see Molly Bawn. As he went to look away, Seymour grinned wolfishly and nodded as if in triumphant dismissal. Shimson realized that he himself must now take some protective measures. He feigned a clumsiness in the shuffle and managed to tear the corners of two cards.

'Goddammit!' he exclaimed. 'I beg all of your pardons, gentlemen. I fear that I've damaged the cards. With your permission, I'll call for fresh decks.'

Before he could shout for a waiter, Andrew did a surprising thing.

'There's no need for the waiter, Master Shimson. I remember that I put those fresh decks you gave me in the table drawer.'

The drawer in question was some distance from the dealer and directly in front of Seymour's chair. Shimson was for an instant a little surprised. He had thought that the drawer was not normally used. He shrugged. It was of no importance. He rarely took the deal at this table and was uncertain about the normal usages.

The drawer was opened and was full of packs of cards. Six were taken out and passed along the players so that they might confirm that the seals on the packs were intact. The

packs were then passed to Shimson who broke them open.
His momentary worry had gone. Andrew knew well that
Shimson's action in tearing the other cards was to enable him
to introduce specially treated packs, and the man was surely
too experienced to have erred. Quite possibly Andrew had
put all the treated packs in that drawer purposely to avoid
incurring any suspicion amongst the gamblers, by letting
them pull out and select the packs themselves.

Shimson began to check through each deck to see that they
were complete. As he checked his sensitive fingers and his
educated eyes searched for the certain marks on each key
card which would enable him to control the game sufficiently
to gain an advantage. The cards riffled from his fingers in a
continuous fluttering stream and as the stack in front of him
rose, his stomach sank into a nauseous deep. These cards
were unmarked. The certainty mushroomed that something
was terribly wrong.

'Andrew!' a voice shouted deafeningly within his mind.
'That bastard Andrew has gammoned me ... Mother Bunch
is only the decoy!'

Sarah had remained in the passageway behind the bead
curtains, watching and waiting for her opportunity. It was a
long and tiresome time before it came, and if she had not
been patient she would have missed it.

Seymour and Molly Bawn wandered from table to table for
some hours. Throwing dice for a while, taking some hands of
French hazard, then passing into the Roly Poly room to cast
a few bets on the wheel. All the time Sarah noticed that
Seymour's gaze constantly flickered towards the rouge-et-
noir. Then, quite suddenly, Molly was alone. Sarah moved
instantly. She came to the side of Molly, took a firm grip on
the girl's elbow and pulled her into the passageway.

'No, Miss Sarah ... No!' Molly protested weakly, and
tried to break free of the restraining hand.

'Be quiet, you little fool!' Sarah scolded and made the girl
go with her to her private apartments above the club. Once
inside she locked the door and forced Molly to sit down on
one of the chaise-longues.

'Here.' She poured a large brandy and pushed it into the
girl's stiff fingers. 'Drink this ... it will steady you.' She placed
a chair directly in front of the chaise-longue and seated her-

self upon it.

'Now, Molly Bawn,' she said kindly. 'I ask you, as one who is your true friend, to tell me what has happened to you during these past weeks.'

For a few moments the girl sat staring blankly down at the tapestry carpet. Then she broke and wept bitterly. The tears streamed down her face and the sobs choked her throat, but still she held the glass of brandy before her. Sarah took the glass and moved to sit beside Molly, cradling the girl in her arms and rocking her as if she were a child.

'That's it,' Sarah crooned. 'Weep ... weep all the pain away. I'll take care of you, never fear. Weep child. Weep.'

As her sobs stilled, Molly began to tell her story. Of how she had met Seymour, and of his courtship. How she had come to love him deeply and think him a kind and good man. 'But he's served me cruel bad, Mistress ... He's bin like a devil, like Old Nick hisself to me. He took me to London and 'im and that fat barstard 'e's wi', they served me as if I was an animal ... Worse than that even.' The sobs tore from her once more, loud and harsh and heart-broken.

Sarah's anger came hot and strong. 'They'll not touch you again, Molly,' she promised fiercely. 'Nor any other poor wench either, I'll see to that. I swear on my mother's grave that I'll make them pay for what they've done to you.'

Molly straightened to look with frightened eyes at her friend, her paint and rouge a smeared mess from her tears.

She shook her head fearfully. 'No Mistress. Doon't you go near them. You doon't know that devil like I do. He told me that he was a merchant called Brady, but I found out that his name's Seymour, and that he's running from the army. He means to ruin you, Miss Sarah. I doon't know why, but he hates your very name, so he does. He'll kill you if he can, I'm sure of it. Just as he'll kill me, now I've told you all this.' Her face crumpled piteously and she started to weep in abject terror.

Sarah calmed the girl, murmuring gently to her and stroking the pale neck and shoulders where the livid fresh bruises and weals were barely hidden by the thick layers of powder and cosmetics.

'But why are Seymour and the fat man playing at the rouge-et-noir?' she questioned. 'It's not possible to cheat successfully there, if it is by cheating they intend our ruin.'

The girl sniffed and drew a gasp of breath. With a

331

tremendous effort she steadied herself long enough to say, 'The priest, the thin dark 'un. He's in it wi' 'um.'

'Andrew?' Sarah said incredulously.

'Yes, Mistress, that's his name ain't it ... Andrew.'

'Shim must know of this immediately,' Sarah told her. 'You'll stay here in this room, Molly.' She handed the girl a key. 'Unlock the door and let me through. Then lock it behind me and don't open it again until I come back. Don't open it for anyone or anything until I return myself, do you understand?'

Molly Bawn nodded and made a pathetic attempt to smile. 'Thank you for being so kind to me, Mistress Sarah.'

Sarah smiled back at her. 'There'll be time enough for gratitude later, Molly, and if it comes to that, then it is I who owe you thanks for bringing me this information ... Now I must go to Shim.'

Shimson fought for control and mastered himself so that only a very careful observer would have seen any indication that something was seriously amiss. He shuffled and offered the cards. Mother Bunch leaned forward so that the rolls of fat pushed up to his pouter chest by the corset threatened to burst his tight-stretched shirt and waistcoat.

'Yeth, thir, I'll take it ... my fingerth are itching for more of your gold.' His tiny eyes, almost buried in the vastness of his face twinkled happily as he finished the shuffle and handed the cards back. 'Well, I mutht confeth, I don't remember ever enjoying a game of cardth more than tonightth game. I mutht return here very thoon.' He winked archly at Lord Harcourt. 'What thay you, your grathe?'

The Governor's plump chins quivered as he laughed uproariously. ''Pon my soul! But you're a tonic, sir ... Dammee if you ain't.' He asked the table to confirm his words, 'A regular tonic, ain't he?'

'May we have your wagers, Gentlemen,' Shimson requested, and the gamblers waited to see which way the fat man would bet. With an air of doubtful reluctance he selected a single guinea from the money in front of him and placed it on the black. A collective sigh came from the absorbed spectators. Mother Bunch smiled and cocked his head as he peered around at the eager faces.

'I'm only teathing you, you thauthy fellowth,' he simpered

and used both of his pudgy hands to push his large pile of winnings forward on to the red patch. 'Thith ith the one to win, I fanthy.' There was a lash of viciousness in his voice.

The entire table followed suit and the money poured on to the red patch until its colour was almost hidden. Shimson felt the sweat burst from all the pores of his body. There was, he calculated, near to six thousand guineas wagered on the next coup.

'If I lose it's all up with me and the club,' he thought. 'But how in hell's name can they cheat on this? Is that fat pig merely taking a gamble?'

It took all his willpower to prevent his hands from trembling. He glanced at Andrew, who sat staring at the money, his mouth slightly open and his eyes mirroring his greed. Shimson's gaze switched to William Seymour. The lean cruel face wore an expression of gloating triumph and, even as Shimson looked, a tiny muscle started to throb erratically at the side of the pale grey eyes.

The Hebrew drew a long breath. 'Ah vell, gentlemen,' he said quietly. 'Here ve go ... All aboard the carousel.' The cards flicked over. King of spades ... three of spades ... king of diamonds. His beringed fingers toyed for a moment with the next card ... Any eight or above and he had a chance. He turned the stiff pasteboard and placed it neatly to the side of the others, then looked. It was the eight of hearts. Total, thirty-one. Shimson's held breath gusted out noisily and he felt weak with relief. A collective groan of disappointment dragged around the table.

His heart light, Shimson dealt the second row. Four of clubs, nine of diamonds, five of clubs, six of spades and another king of diamonds ... Total thirty-four.

'Four ... black wins,' Shimson called joyously and flashed a smile of victory at Mother Bunch. The smile faltered on his lips as the fat man shook his great head ponderously, then lifted both hands high to gain the crowd's attention and shouted.

'Your Grathe! I beg you to check thothe cardthe ... I fear we have been gulled, gentlemen. That deck ith packed.'

The Governor's genial face was thunderous. He snatched the cards and looked at them closely. Shimson's bewilderment only lasted for a split second. He glanced at Seymour, Andrew, and Mother Bunch in quick succession and knew with sickening certainty that they had tricked him utterly and completely.

Without a doubt, the cards would be marked, only in a code not known to Shimson and since he had not known what to look for, he had allowed himself to be fooled into thinking the cards were unmarked.

The Governor suddenly cursed aloud, and pointed to the backs of some court-cards, they all bore a similar minute irregularity in one part of their ornate back pattern. The other cards did not bear that irregularity. There was a hush, then came a babble of cursing, shouting, threatening voices.

It was at that precise instant that the old ropelock holding one of the vast, heavy chandeliers slipped a ratchet, caught, then slipped three more in a split second and broke. The chandelier tumbled in a whoosh of fire, and the lamps smashed across the dice table, chairs and carpet.

On the impact the flaming oil exploded in all directions. Women screamed in terror as the gouts of fire landed on their gowns to set the flimsy cloth ablaze. Men shouted in agony as more gouts of fire hit faces, hands, and powdered heads. The hangings and varnished, polished furnishings, tinder dry from the constant heat of the room, took fire like matchwood and in only seconds the salon was filled from end to end with flame and smoke. The crowd stampeded in panic, chairs and tables were sent crashing over, glasses and bottles smashed and crunched underfoot with the debris of sweet-meats and food. A woman tripped on her own gown to fall headfirst into a pool of flaming oil and shrieked hideously as her gown and turban became part of the flames. A man was sent flying by a roundhouse blow as he struggled to get through the main doorway, he staggered backwards and fell over a broken table; for a moment his body blocked the crowd as it struggled to escape, then he vanished beneath the trampling feet.

Some of the cooler heads paused before joining the stampede from the salon to snatch up some of the gold guineas and banknotes which had been sent spilling across the floors in the mad panic. William Seymour was one of them. Coolly and calmly he began to fill his pockets from the money abandoned at the rouge-et-noir table. Shimson Levi sat in his dealer's chair and watched him. The crowd was now splitting into two segments. One, the largest, was a screaming, bellowing, fighting, heaving mass at the main doorway. The other was a line of sheer terror running the gauntlet of the flaming private passageway. The area around the great table gave the curious illusion of an oasis of peace and tranquillity.

Seymour suddenly became aware of the Hebrew staring at him. He looked up and grinned savagely into Shimson's eyes.

'I knew my day would come, Jewboy,' he sneered. 'You should have remained with your old clothes ... When you next see that whore, Sarah Jenkins, be sure to tell her that it is William Seymour who has ruined her.'

A growl started rising from the innermost depths of Shimson Levi's being and crimson hate filled his sight. Using the chair as a springboard, he launched himself across the table at the other man. They grappled ferociously, hands locked in death-grips about each other's throats, and stumbled to fall and roll in their deadly embrace over and over and over through the pools of flame and smashed glass and smoking blazing furnishings.

Sarah heard the noise and smelt the smoke as she started to descend from the top floor. She went only far enough to see men and women hurling themselves down her private staircase with clothes and hair smoking and smouldering then she ran back upstairs. She knew only too well that the centuries-old, ramshackle house would burn as rapidly and fiercely as a pitch-soaked pine needle.

She hammered on the locked door. 'Molly! Molly, quick! The house is afire. Quick girl! Quick, or we'll both be dead.'

Molly was sitting on the chaise-longue, the bottle of brandy tilted to her lips. She took a long slow drink, ignoring the increasingly frantic hammering and shouting of Sarah. She was trying to decide whether she wanted to live or die. She feared that the Fat Man had infected her, but what was worse was the damage done to her whole being and spirit by William Seymour.

'Why keep on bleedin' living?' she asked herself.

The flames smothered the passageway and started to claw both up and down the staircase.

Sarah saw the fearsome glare and screamed out, 'Molly, would you be the cause of my death?'

The girl listened and heard the snapping of the fire and smelt the acrid smoke. Sarah screamed again.

'Molly, for the love of God, come now! Or we're both dead.'

'Bollocks to it!' Molly Bawn's fierce spirit resurrected itself. 'Life's no bleedin' good ... But frying is worse.'

335

She tossed the bottle from her and ran to unlock the door. The fierce heat and smoke assaulted her throat and flesh and she coughed violently.

'Come on Molly, run! Run!' Sarah gasped, and dragged the girl behind her, down through the choking heat and smoke and scorching flames and out amongst the milling crowds in the cold dampness of the street.

Once she could breathe, Sarah looked at The Golden Venture. It was blazing from top to bottom. She saw one of the priests and shouted, 'Where's Shimson Levi? Did he get out?'

The priest was shamefaced. 'I dunno for certain, missus ... I ran for it meself ... But they do say as how he's still in there. Fightin' wi' a tall cove wi' fair hair.'

'Yer, he was fighting wi' a fair-haired cove all right. I saw um,' a waiter put in. 'But I've not sin either on 'um come out ... And I ben watching all the time. I reckon they've croaked it.'

Sarah's heart started to thud as if it were trying to destroy itself. She knew instinctively without needing to ask further, or to go along the burnt and wailing rows of casualties of the fire, that Shimson Levi and William Seymour were inside that inferno, which was also their funeral pyre.

The alarm had been raised and from all over the town and dockyards men came rushing with grappling irons, axes, leather hoses, buckets and hand-driven pumps ... But all their efforts were to prevent the conflagration spreading to engulf the whole area. For already inside The Golden Venture the sounds of crashing beams and the thick billows of smoke and sparks gushing from the smashed windows showed that the club was doomed.

All through the remaining hours of darkness, Sarah Jenkins and Molly Bawn, their dresses torn and filthy, their hair and skin layered with fine ash, their eyes red with heat and smoke, stood side by side and watched their dreams slowly crumble to a heap of charred, smoking rubble.

CHAPTER THIRTY

'What will you do now, Molly?' Sarah Jenkins asked. In the cold grey light of the dawn, both women looked haggard and bone-weary. The young whore yawned and rubbed her sore eyes with both hands, leaving patches of grey-black ash powder mingled with the rouge on her cheekbones.

'Can't I goo wi' you, mistress?' she asked.

Sarah sighed heavily. 'You may come with me, if you want to, Molly, but I have nothing now ... Everything I owned in the world was in there.' She nodded at the smouldering heaps of fire-charred rubble and timbers. 'I'm going to Fort Cumberland to see if Jethro Stanton will take me in. I don't doubt that if you so wished, you could find a husband from amongst the soldiers there.'

The girl stared with surprise. 'But how about your Jack Tar ... the captin? I thought you were meeting with him these past months.'

Sarah smiled tiredly and shook her head. She was still wearing her white poke-bonnet and carriage dress, but so dirtied were they from the smoke and ash that their one-time elegance had gone, and they appeared to be a beggar-woman's rags.

'I was meeting the captain for very different reasons from those you assume, Molly ... The man I love is a soldier, a corporal in the militia. I pray God that he will feel sufficiently tender towards me to take me under his protection ... Will you come with me?'

Her friend appeared to consider the question. Then she laughed harshly.

'No, Miss Sarah, I think not ... I've no wish to go wi' any soldier, at least not for a while ... I've had my fill o' soldiers. No, Molly Bawn will go back to Spice Island, where she belongs. I was stupid to think that I'd ever be able to leave it.'

There was both bitterness and sadness underlying her words.

Abruptly she kissed Sarah's cheek. 'God go with you, Sarah Jenkins,' she whispered. 'You've bin a good friend to me ... The best I ever had. Molly Bawn won't ever forget you, and that's no lie.'

She gathered the scorched folds of her bedraggled finery about her and without another word ran down the street in the direction of the King James Gate. Sarah watched her go, and felt the tears sting her eyes. The ruins of The Golden Venture shifted and sparks rose as a timber finally smouldered through and collapsed. Sarah sighed once more.

'Good-bye, Shim,' she murmured, and turned to make her way to Fort Cumberland.

On Southsea beach, Sarah went to the sea's edge and untying the ribbons of her bonnet she threw it far out into the tiny rippling waves ... 'Soldiers' wives wear shawls, not fine bonnets,' she thought.

She stooped and, cupping her hands, bathed her face and neck in the cold salt water, feeling its clean bite lave away the weariness of the long night's vigil at the funeral pyre of Shimson Levi. Her thick chestnut hair tumbled down in long waves of rich rippling colour and suddenly all her cares disappeared and a feeling of light-headed gaiety overwhelmed her.

'I'm free once more,' she told herself exultantly. 'I'm free of sharps and flats and crows and pigeons and priests ... I'm free of profits and losses and nights of false smiles and falser promises ... I'm free to do what I choose to do ... I'm free!'

She looked down at her torn, smoke-blackened gown and grimaced ruefully. 'Free I might be, but before God! I make a poor spectacle considering I'm on my way to ask a man to take me as his woman,' she thought, and then laughed aloud. 'Never fret, girl ... It's what's beneath the clothes that men desire and I've no fears on that score.'

She continued her journey until she was only about five hundred yards from the fort, then settled herself behind one of the beach groynes and waited patiently for the day to pass, knowing that Jethro would be engaged with his duties until early evening. The day was gentle and the spot she lay in sheltered from the wind. Drowsiness crept upon her and, pillowing her head on her arms, Sarah slept.

Sarah felt a certain timidity as Jethro Stanton, wearing his full regimentals and white-plumed shako, came through the Land Gate, and walked to where she waited some yards beyond the outer ditch.

When he neared her, he exclaimed with surprise, 'Sarah! What's happened?'

'There was a fire,' she told him. 'I wasn't hurt, but The Golden Venture is destroyed.'

'So that's what it was,' he murmured, and then told her in explanation, 'I was up on the west gun-platform last night and saw the glow ... I wondered what was burning so fierce.'

They walked side by side in silence towards the beach groynes. The woman screwed up her courage and asked point-blank,

'Jethro, do you have any feeling for me? ... Of love perhaps?'

In Jethro's mind conflicting emotions battled with one another. He had already sensed why Sarah had come to him and knew what she hoped for. But he was reluctant to make her a barrack woman. While he struggled to come to a decision, she waited, uncertainty tormenting her. At last Jethro stopped and turned Sarah to face him.

'Have you lost everything, Sarah?' he asked gently.

She nodded tearfully and the whole story of the night's terrible happenings poured from her lips. He listened without interruption until she reached the end of her story and stood gazing at him with fearful, wide-eyed anxiety. He watched a single teardrop as it trickled down her smooth cheek and mentally shrugged. 'Here you go again, you damned fool!' he scoffed at himself silently. 'Will you never be able to resist a woman's weeping?'

Aloud he asked, 'Would you consider being a soldier's woman, Sarah?'

Relief coursed through her and she could only say, 'Oh yes, with all my heart. Do you really mean it, Jethro? Can I come to you?'

He smiled and nodded.

'But do you really want me?' she worried him for reassurance. 'Do you love me? ... Or is it only pity you feel?'

Jethro could not in all truthfulness have told her the doubts he was feeling at that moment. But he kept the smile on his lips and said with deep sincerity,

'I care for you very much, Sarah ... But have you stopped to think what being a soldier's woman means? I'm volunteering for the Quota. There's a party of recruiters due any day now. It means that you'll have to follow the drum across the Peninsula, and risk great suffering ... even death.'

She shook her head dismissively, happiness glowing from her handsome face. 'I care naught for those dangers, Jethro. All that I want is for us to be together. I'll be a faithful and a loving wife to you, I swear I will.'

'There still remains a problem.' His face became grave. 'I'll have to get permission to marry you from my officer; and I'm not sure that he'll give it. The battalion already has more than its official number of women on the strength.'

'What if we were already married?' she asked.

'Then I don't think he would refuse your entrance to the company.'

'Then tell him we are long since married.' Sarah was determined that nothing should stop her achieving what she wanted. 'The certificate of proof will present no difficulty. I know a parson across on Spice Island who marries sailors and their girls for a crown and a noggin of rum. If they've not got a crown to spend then he does it just for the rum. He'll give us a certificate stating we've been married for years.'

'But that wouldn't be legal, and you wouldn't really be married to me,' Jethro said doubtfully.

She laughed happily. 'Who gives a damn. I do not, that's for sure ... You know as well as I do, Jethro, that the bond that joins a man to a maid has nothing to do with banns being called and words mumbled in a church ... Another thing, how many of the women with the army are really married to their men by due legal process? Not one in ten, I'll wager.'

Jethro accepted the inevitable with good grace. 'Very well, Sarah ... Here, take this.' He handed her some coins. 'There's enough here for your needs and to spare. Go to that parson and get the necessary. I'll apply to my company commander tomorrow morning and I'll meet you here at noontime ...'

She nodded contentedly. He drew her close and lifted her chin with his fingers so that their eyes met. He looked searchingly at her and said, 'Listen carefully to me. Life in the barracks is a hard thing for a woman. You'll hear naught but rough talk and oaths; and see naught but brutality and wickedness ... There's not much kindness there, and a deal of kicks and harsh treatment ... Are you really sure that this is what you want?'

Sarah wrapped her arms about his neck and smiled into his

concerned features. She kissed him hungrily on the mouth, then whispered in his ear, 'We'll have the loving in our bed of nights, won't we, my handsome? That will do much to sweeten life for both of us, will it not? ... don't concern yourself about me. So long as I shall be with you, then I will be happy.'

Jethro's senses filled with her fragrance as he tasted the warm moistness of her lips. He felt the sensual promise of her firm breasts and belly and the full roundness of her hips and thighs pressing hard into his body, and could only admit that there was much truth in what she said of their lives being sweetened.

For once, everything went smoothly and without hindrance. The next morning Jethro made an application to Captain Joseph Ward. The captain heard him out and since he felt that the corporal was a fine soldier, granted him permission to have his suddenly-appeared wife placed on the ration strength. They met at the noontime as arranged, and later that afternoon Sarah Jenkins walked through the Land Gate and up to the casemate that was to be her first home with Jethro.

Martha Danks and Josie Collins were sat at opposite sides of the firegrate on low three-legged stools. They shared a companionable silence and also the short stubby clay pipe of black-shag tobacco, which they passed back and forth between them. Both women suckled rag-swaddled babies at their breasts and both leaned over at intervals to spit into the wood fire.

Brought up in the unremitting slavery of Bromsgrove nail-makers' cottage workshops, all they had known from infancy had been the thudding hammers and red-hot forges. And all the never-ending toil with these articles had given them were sweat, hunger and grinding poverty. The casemate at Fort Cumberland, now deserted but for them, was in many ways the most pleasant and peaceful room they had ever lived in.

When Sarah Jenkins nervously pushed open the door to stand framed in the entrance, the two young women turned hostile eyes to this intruder upon their quarters. Sarah had used the money Jethro had given her wisely. She was clad in a decent dark-brown gown and shawl, and her glossy hair was tucked neatly under a snowy-white mobcap. Her hands were empty, for she possessed nothing more than what she stood in. For a while she remained in the doorway, silently gazing at her new home, with the tremors of doubt engendered by the hostile glares of the women rapidly increasing. The general layout and furnishings of the room were of a similar style to Colewort Garden barracks, but, not knowing what to expect, Sarah was surprised at its spartan neatness and order.

Martha Danks, clouds of smoke wreathing her thin, small-pox-pitted face, took a final puff of the rank-smelling tobacco and handed the pipe to her friend. Then asked in unfriendly tones,

'What con us do for thee, my wench? The way you'm astarin', teks it you wants to buy summat ... Or 'as you come to save our souls?'

Sarah looked tensely at the slovenly pair. Both alike in their open-bodiced checked gingham dresses, with the strands of greasy, lank hair escaping from under their dirt-stained mob-caps.

'No, I've not come to buy, or to save souls,' she replied hesitantly. 'I've come to stay here for a time.'

Josie Collins, a fatter edition of her friend stared questioningly.

''Oo be you wife to?' she demanded to know.

'To Corporal Stanton ... Corporal Jethro Stanton,' Sarah answered.

Both women received this news in silence. Digesting it and ruminating on its implications. Then Josie hissed in annoyance and moved the swaddled baby from her plump hanging breast to turn it around. The puny little chest swelled and the thin high squalls of outrage went on until she silenced them by pushing the big dark nipple of the fresh breast into the greedily sucking mouth. Her lips twisted and she swore loudly.

'God rot yer, yer little barstard! You'll bite the bleedin' end off it afore you've done.' She grinned in a kindly way at Sarah, displaying half-decayed teeth. 'Come you in and shut the door then, my wench. It's letting áll the warm get out while it's open.' Reaching behind her, she pulled another stool into view and placed it in front of the fire. 'Sit yoursen down and be comfortable ... 'E's a nice sort o' cove, Jethro is. So I rackon his missus 'ull turn out to be the same.'

Sarah accepted the proffered kindness. She seated herself on the stool between the others and admired both their babies in turn.

Martha Danks held the pipe towards her. ''Ull you try a taste?'

Sarah nodded, sensing that she was being tested for pridefulness. She sucked hard at the pipe stem, causing the dottle to gurgle. The hot harsh smoke rasped her throat and threatened to choke her. She forced back the coughs until her eyes filled with tears, and tried to look as if the pipe was pleasurable.

Martha Danks watched the newcomer through narrowed eyes, then also grinned in a friendly way.

'We'em a bit rough and ready, 'ere, my wench,' she chuckled. 'But we'em good at 'eart, me and Josie 'ere ... I rackon you'll do for us, you seems the right sort anyway ... Don't worry about settlin' in. We'll keep an eye for you and show you the ropes. Wun't we, Jose?'

Her friend nodded grinning. 'Ahr, that we 'ull.'

Sarah experienced a sudden feeling of relief and warmed to the women. 'I'm sure you will, and thank you for it,' she answered, and smiled at them with a strange feeling of belonging ...

CHAPTER THIRTY-ONE

The epidemic of gaol fever burnt itself out as suddenly as it had begun. Fresh cases of the disease became fewer daily and then ceased entirely. Both prisoners and guards breathed easily again, and now spared thought for the dead. There were still many of the dead who remained unburied and their bodies were rotting in the Orlop decks of the *Fortune* and *Ceres*, creating further hazards to health.

Matthew Purpost sent word to the fort asking that a mass grave should be dug in the shingle on the curving spit of land. Jethro Stanton was detailed as second-in-command of the guard for the party of convicts and prisoners-of-war who were to carry out the surgeon's request.

The work began at dawn. Nathan Caldicott and Henri Chanteur were amongst the pick-swinging, shovelling men doing it. A trench three yards wide and twenty yards long was to be sunk. The foot-deep layer of shingle was easily cleared, as was the thin layer of sand directly beneath it. Then the picks' steel points hit the hard-packed rocks and gravel and the mauling toil began. Slowly the trench deepened and the sea seeped through to fill the holes created as each shovel of material was taken out. The water rose to the men's ankles, then to their knees and crept up towards their thighs. Nathan Caldicott's face was clammy white and his bald head shone with sweat. He coughed constantly, his chest bubbling painfully with inner congestion. Henri Chanteur kept glancing at his friend as he laboured by his side. Finally he asked,

'Nathan, are you ill?'

The American stopped working and leant upon his long-handled shovel, his breath rasping in his lungs.

'I must confess to feeling a mite shaky today, Henry my boy.' He tried to smile but another bout of coughing tore through his throat.

The noise caught the attention of one of the guards. The

man's nerves were ragged. He had, like all the others lived with the fear of the fever for weeks.

'Hey, you there? Are you badly?' he shouted.

Nathan opened his mouth to answer but could not, for yet another fit of coughing shook his bony shoulders.

Henri spoke out. 'He has a chill, nothing more.'

The guard's face plainly showed his suspicious fear. 'Sar'nt!' he shouted.

A heavy-shouldered, halbert-carrying sergeant came over to him. 'What is it?'

The guard pointed his musket barrel at Nathan. 'That cove's bin took badly,' he reported nervously.

The sergeant, normally a placid, easy-going man, was also nervous, and his nervousness was increased by the other convicts in the water trench who, muttering and afraid, had moved as far away as they could from Nathan and Henri. By this time, Jethro had also come up.

'What's the trouble, Sar'nt?' he questioned.

'I think that that baldy cove 'as took the fever. He'll ha' to goo out to the spit,' the senior N.C.O. told him, and shouted to Nathan, 'Come on out o' theer, cully, and goo to the spit ... The *Fortune*'s boat 'ull fetch you tonight.' Nathan stopped coughing in time to restrain Henri's angry protests. 'No Henry!' he panted raspingly. 'The man's right, it could be the fever I got.'

The American waded to the side and hauled himself from the trench. Then, with water pouring from his ragged trousers, he made his way, coughing and stumbling along the spit of land towards the end that jutted farthest into the harbour entrance.

The sergeant then ordered Henri, ''Ere, pull up your jacket and let me see your chest.'

The Frenchman obeyed and the guards, keeping their distance, squinted to see if he bore the tell-tale rash on his smooth skin. When they were satisfied that he did not, they shouted to all the prisoners to resume their work. Some of the convicts showed a marked reluctance to go by the Frenchman, but their objections were overcome by Jethro, who aimed his musket at one of the most vociferous grumblers and said quietly,

'If you don't obey the order in one second flat, then this ball is going to find a billet in your loud mouth, cully.'

The labour recommenced and Henri turned so that each time he straightened his back he could see the lonely figure of Nathan Caldicott sitting hunched over his knees at the end of the landspit. The grey sky and sea, and cold biting wind added to the sadness of the pathetic spectacle. Jethro found to his own surprise that he felt concern for the Frenchman who was so obviously distressed by what had happened to his friend.

'But what in God's name, can I do about it?' he thought helplessly.

Later that morning, when the dinner drum sounded in the fort, the rations of both guards and prisoners were brought out to them at the grave. Turpin Wright was one of the escort to the ration party. He came to talk to Jethro, who was standing at the edge of the digging, his tough leathery face eager with his news.

'They'se come, matey. The first recruiters for the Quota.'

Jethro's heart leapt at the news. 'From where, and what regiment?' he asked.

'From the Twenty-Fourth Foot in Portugal,' his friend told him. 'There's bin a bit o' fun down in Colewort this morning as well, from all accounts.'

'Oh yes ... What about?' Jethro was only mildly curious. His main interest was the arrival of the recruiting party. Turpin laughed in high glee. 'It's Rourke, he's agooin, to meet the Drummer's Daughter by the sound on it.'

Jethro's interest quickened. 'Why? What's the Irish bastard done?'

'He was one o' the guard on the *Crown* hulk larst night,' Turpin told him, nudging and winking. 'And a bunch o' bleeding Froggies got clean away from it ... the hulk's captin is ablaming Rourke, because he was corporal o' the gallery sentries and the Frogs broke out of a gunport on the gallery. The officers rackon that the Frogs give Rourke a pile o' gold to close his eyes while they scarpered.'

Jethro nodded slowly. 'Ah well, it's hard luck for Rourke, but I don't doubt but that he and the rest knew something of it ... Did they find gold on him?'

'Nooo!' Turpin spat on the ground to emphasize his next words. 'That Paddy is too bleedin' fly for that. He'd split the rhino wi' the other coves, but he stowed his own somewhere safe. The orfficers found the other coves' gold, but they never found Rourke's ... 'E's a bugger, arn't he!' he finished, shaking his head in admiration.

In the trench beneath them, Henri Chanteur's heart raced.

'De Chambray has escaped,' he thought, and hope flooded through him. 'If Gaston got away, then he must now be at the hideout, and he must already have arranged for a boat ... *Mon Dieu!* I have a chance, if I can get to him. I have a chance of going home ...'

Barely able to conceal his rush of emotion, he worked on silently, his mind desperately formulating plans. Finally he was decided.

'I'll have to take the risk,' he told himself. 'If I don't do it before evening, then it will be too late for Nathan.'

The Frenchman nerved himself and began to stare at Jethro, willing the corporal to look at him. When their eyes eventually met, Henri winked and nodded slightly towards the barrel of drinking water that was set on a heap of shingle some yards away.

Jethro realized that the man wished to speak privately with him. He returned an almost imperceptible nod of affirmation and Henri raised his arm.

'Can I get some water, caporal?' he asked loudly.

'Carry on,' Jethro told him, and walked casually to stand by the barrel.

Henri lifted the rusty drinking can that was chained to the wooden strakes and under cover of sipping from it whispered urgently,

'Will you help me, Caporal?'

Jethro kept his gaze fixed on the trench and spoke from the corner of his mouth. 'Is it to escape?'

The Frenchman did not attempt to prevaricate. 'Yes ... I want to get myself and Nathan Caldicott back to France ...' He paused and fought successfully against the urge to remind the other man of his debt of life.

Jethro stared at the solitary hunched figure of the American in the distance, and thought of how the Frenchman had risked the anger of his fellow prisoners to warn one of the hated English of danger. All his instincts pushed him inexorably in the same direction.

'What do you want me to do?' he asked.

Henri could have sagged to the ground, so intense was his relief. 'I shall pretend to be ill,' he whispered rapidly. 'Send me to the spit, then make sure that it is you who stays to guard Nathan and myself until the hulks' boat comes. Then Nathan and I will feign death and you will see to it that we are both thrown into the grave with the bodies that will come

347

from the hulks. Then just leave us there ... I will do the rest.'

'Very well, I'll help you,' Jethro whispered, then shouted aloud, 'Come on you lazy French hound, get back to your work. You've spent too much time already sipping water like a fancy doxy.'

Henri waited until the grave was finished and the prisoners were starting to form up for the return to the fort before he made his move. He staggered suddenly and dropped to his face on the shingle. The hard pebbles dug painfully into his flesh and aided him to groan realistically. It was Jethro who came to look at him. The corporal turned him flat on his back and lifted his jacket to examine beneath.

'Goddam it!' Jethro cursed aloud and shouted over his shoulder to the sergeant. 'This bugger's got the fever by the look of it.'

'I'm not surprised,' his superior answered. 'He was next to the baldy one all morning. Will you stay here and hand them both over to the *Fortune*'s boat, Corporal Stanton.'

Jethro feigned annoyance. 'Why me? I want to go back to my quarters as much as the rest of you.'

The sergeant tried to mollify him. 'There's only these three privates here apart from me and you, Corporal Stanton; and it must be a man that can be trusted that I leave here. A private man won't do, will he?'

'Arrggh!' Jethro made a gesture of dismissal with his hand. 'All right, I'll stay ... But I'll want this extra duty made up to me,' he demanded.

The sergeant, anxious to leave this cold bleak beach, nodded. 'You shall, I promise you.'

The working party, tools over their shoulders, shambled off into the murk, the white crossbelts of the escorts forming a shifting pattern on the fringes of the amorphous orange-yellow oblong of the prisoners. The darkness deepened and once Jethro knew that he could not be observed except with great difficulty from either the fort or hulks, he slapped Henri's chest.

'Go and get your friend,' he ordered. 'Then both of you come back here and lie face down behind that water barrel. I'll have to make certain that you'll be the last two put into the trench, or you'll drown in it.'

Henri wasted no words, but did as he was instructed. Nathan was shivering uncontrollably and constant spasms of coughs shook his meagre frame. Jethro regarded him doubtfully.

'You'll not be able to sham dead very successfully, Yankee Doodle.'

Caldicott bared his toothless gums with a trace of his old drollness.

'Never fear about a New Englander bein' able to sham dead, Corporal,' he gasped. 'That's the reason so few of us died on Bunker Hill. We just played possum and let the Limeys run straight over us and keep on chasing shadows.'

Jethro grinned, admiring the dauntless spirit of the man. The pair lay down behind the water barrel and the three waited for the hulks' boats to appear. Periodically the muffled, choking coughs of Nathan Caldicott sounded, but as time wore on the attacks became wider spaced and of shorter duration and eventually ceased.

It was fully dark when lights could be seen moving on the water and two heavily laden longboats, their oars splashing and rowlocks squealing, came slowly towards the shore and beached, crunching on the shingle. Jethro went to them. The oarsmen were all civilian convicts, who stayed on the hulks to help Matthew Purpost and his mates, on the promise of a pardon of their sentences if they should survive. Every man of them was drunk for it was only by swilling down enough rum that they could blot out the horror of the charnel-like decks of the hulks and the constant fear of death.

A surgeon's mate was in charge of the party and he too was drunk. Jethro shouldered his musket and saluted.

'The grave is prepared, sir.'

The surgeon's mate, a tiny wisp of a man wearing a soiled, red coat and blue pantaloons, with his black-feathered cocked hat crazily askew on his narrow head, returned the salute. Then he held his lantern high above his head to cast its beams into the boat behind him, and hiccupped, slurring the words,

'It don't matter a damn whether the grave's prepared or not, Corporal. These buggers ain't particular as to where they lie this night.'

The light shone on a tangle of heads, arms, sightless staring eyes, legs, feet, and slack gaping jaws. The corpses were still dressed in the orange-yellow rags they had lived in and now wore for shrouds.

The dead men were dragged across the shingle by staggering, swearing convicts and let drop into the trench. Jethro, watching from the side, now fully understood why this burial

349

was being carried out by night under the fitful light of dull lanterns. The corpses were an obscene parody of human beings, and the singing, cursing, stumbling men who toppled the poor dead flesh so callously into the splashing surging water were also obscene parodies of humankind.

Before the task was finished, the wind gusted ever stronger, and showers of rain spattered on the shingle.

'Goddam and blast this bloody inclement weather,' the surgeon's mate slurred.

'When you have finished the unloading, sir, there are two men who died today in the fort to add to the list,' Jethro said politely.

'Where are they?' the surgeon's mate peered owlishly about him.

'Over there, lying by the waterbutt, just beyond the trench.' Jethro pointed into the darkness. 'Their names are . . .'

'Don't bother to tell me, Corporal.' The tiny man shook his head hard, causing his hat to tip even more crazily and the long feathers to brush across Jethro's face. 'It don't matter a cuss to me, what names they bore . . . we only record the numbers who die. I'll add a two to the total and that will be sufficient.'

The rain came heavier, spitting on the hot opaque horn sides of the lanterns. The large drops multiplied and hammered in a hissing roar across the beach. The last bodies from the hulks had been tossed into the grave by now, and the surgeon's mate shouted in a reedy voice,

'Man your oars, we'll go back to the *Fortune* until this storm blows over, then return and cover these buggers up.' He blinked several times in rapid succession at the tall militiaman in front of him, trying to focus his wavering sight.

'Be a good fellow, Corporal and drop them two o' yours into the hole, will you?'

Jethro saluted. 'Very good, sir.'

'You are a good man, by God!' The tiny man spaced every word very precisely, then staggered to the waiting boats. The oars splashed and the boats pulled away into the blackness of the night.

Jethro ran to the water barrel. 'Lieutenant Chanteur! Captain Caldicott!' He shook them both by the shoulders. 'Quick, now's your chance.'

Henri was on his feet instantly.

'Nathan, come on!' He bent to urge his friend. The

350

American lay motionless. The young Frenchman felt a clutch of dread, and gently turned his friend's limp figure. Nathan could have been asleep, so peaceful was his face in death.

'Don't stop to grieve, Chanteur,' Jethro told him gently. 'Do your weeping for your friend when you arrive safely back in your homeland.'

Henri swallowed hard and replied quietly, 'My thanks to you, Caporal Stanton, for your help.'

Jethro shook his head. 'Don't thank me, Frenchman. Our nations are still at war and we must remain enemies who will try and kill each other if we meet in battle. If we should meet again when peace comes, then give me your thanks, and I will give you mine for saving my life as you did ... Go quickly now. I will attend to Caldicott.'

Henri took a final look at the peaceful face of Nathan Caldicott and bent to touch the cold lips with his fingers.

'God be with you, Nathan, wherever your soul has gone to,' he murmured.

Jethro watched the young Frenchman disappear into the dark veils of rain, then gently lifted the American's body to the edge of the grave. He let it slip down to join the others that awaited and muttered, 'May the place you have gone to show you more mercy than you found here on earth, Yankee Doodle.'

Jethro turned and squelched his sodden way back to the fort and to Sarah, and as his boots crunched over the shingle his spirits began to lighten.

'Tomorrow I'll volunteer to the Twenty-Fourth,' he thought happily. 'And then Turpin and I will be off to the Peninsula, and the sun there will make Sarah's cheeks bloom like young roses.'

The veteran sentry at the Land Gate stepped from his sentry box and came to the charge, his bayoneted musket glinting wetly in the lamplight from the archway.

'Who comes there?' his old voice quavered fiercely, and the pouring rain ran in streams from his oilskin-covered shako and caped watchcoat.

'Corporal Jethro Stanton, of the Grenadier Company.' Jethro answered, and then laughed aloud in sudden exultant joy at simply being alive. 'A man who's going to help chase the Frogs clean across the Pyrénées to Paris ... That's who comes here, my old bucko,' he joked and entered under the great stone arch, whistling the Rogues' March.

THE END